D1320140

Me Too

Books by Donald Jack

The Bandy Papers

Plays

Nonfiction

Me Too

The Bandy Papers

DONALD JACK

DOUBLEDAY CANADA LIMITED, TORONTO, ONTARIO
DOUBLEDAY & COMPANY INC., GARDEN CITY, NEW YORK
1983

Library of Congress Cataloging in Publication Data

Jack, Donald Lamont.
  Me too

  I. Title.
PR9199.3.J3M4 1983   813'.54
ISBN 0-385-18228-7
Library of Congress Catalog Card Number 82-45251

Contents

Having the First Word:
A Note from the Editor

Bartholomew Bandy usually tells his story in chronological order, but in this latest volume of *The Bandy Papers* he backtracks to Russia in 1919, before resuming the narrative roughly where he left off. In doing so he is obviously attempting to prove that he was not exaggerating when he remarked in *Me Bandy, You Cissie* that, directly or indirectly, his Russian experience ". . . was to affect everything that happened to me from then on."

Before we get to the backsliding, a brief summary of Bandy's career up to 1919 might be helpful to those who have denied themselves the inspiring experience of a previous acquaintanceship with one of Canada's greatest and most unjustly neglected heroes.

Bartholomew Wolfe Bandy was born in 1893, on July 14 (Bastille Day), in Beamington, Ontario, the son of Frederick Edward de Winter Bandy, B.A., and Martha Amiss, the daughter of an Ottawa embalmer. He evidenced unusually early signs of contumacy. Apart from a tendency to instigate civil disorder with his whining drawl, he inhabited a face that even at the age of six so infuriated the family physician, T. H. House, as to cause him to fling a rubber douche at the little beast; though, as usually happened when anyone took the offensive against Bandy, the result was not entirely satisfactory, the vulcanized shot merely upsetting a sample of yellowish fluid onto the good doctor's hacking jacket.

After a distinguished school career—distinguished, that is, for the record number of times his teacher, Mr. Swingler,* thrashed him for resembling a supercilious gelding—Bandy was admitted in 1912 to the University of Toronto as a straight Meds man, disdaining the superior premedical course in biological and physical sciences because he wasn't qualified for it. However, he abandoned the accelerated wartime course only a few months before graduation day.

Bandy explains this wasteful action in *Three Cheers for Me* by claiming that he ". . . failed the fourth year, after shooting the Professor of Surgery in the back during some C.O.T.C. maneuvers and then trying to pry out the bullet with a rusty penknife blade normally used for digging stones out of horses' hoofs."

This, of course, is another example of Bandy's tendency to place himself in the worst light and to hide his light under a bush; to denigrate himself, despite occasional bombast, by exaggeration and even by outright fibbing, a proclivity that may have arisen from a deep-seated sense of his own unworthiness, derived from the attitude of his parents. In this example, he did not fail his final year at all but voluntarily abandoned medical school because of a desire to get into the War to End All Wars before it ended all wars.

It was while he was in England that Bandy met and married Katherine Lewis, who, in dying of Spanish influenza, was as much a victim of the war as any front-line soldier. Here again Bandy slides away from the truth just as determinedly as he attempts to divert the reader's attention from his obviously exceptional abilities. The truth was that Katherine was the one true love of his life, which is possibly why the reader was as ill prepared for her death as was Bandy. He couldn't bear to dwell on it, so the account is shockingly abbreviated.

Bandy's military advancement was undoubtedly spectacular, though some academic historians (who, with their determination to stick to the facts, are notoriously unreliable) claim that his charge up the ladder of success was accomplished mainly through the impetus of others. For the most part, they claim, his

* J. H. Swingler, *Glowing Memories of a Rural Ontario Schoolmaster* (Hedgehog Press, 1928).

superiors were not so much rewarding him for services rendered as trying to stop him from rendering those services to *them*. They were promoting him to get rid of him.

Which explains, they say, why Bandy was an acting temporary major general by the time he took part in the Allied intervention in Russia.

It was while he was fighting on the Archangel front that he had the misfortune to be captured by the Bolsheviks on, of all days, November 11, 1918. At first imprisoned in the Peter and Paul Fortress in Petrograd, he was subsequently allowed the freedom of that city, and later Moscow, on the understanding that he would not attempt to leave Russia until all Allied forces had been withdrawn. This form of parole was extended to several Allied prisoners during the war, and in Bandy's case, at least, it had consequences that continued to pester, pother, and provoke him, as he would say himself, for years to come.

PART I

Petrified in Petrograd; Moody in Moscow

After being dragged out of jail and placed on parole by Comrade Trotsky, I was transferred that same day from the Evropeievskaya to the Astoria. And there they gave me the key to my very own hotel room.

Though there was not a guard in sight, and though I was told several times that I was free to go out whenever I wished, provided I didn't leave the city, I knew it was a trick. I was quite convinced that at any moment they would fling me back into the fortress with a cry of "April Foolsky."

Actually it was well into April, but everyone knew what a defective sense of time Russians had. They were quite capable of playing an April Fool halfway through the month. After all, hadn't they held their October Revolution in November?

However, after a couple of days when nothing ominous happened, my native boldness, optimism, and resolution reasserted themselves, and I emerged from the Victorian cupboard. After all, I told myself, they were hardly likely to produce this violent contrast in my living standards merely to unsettle me. They had placed me in the most comfortable hotel in Petrograd. Not only that, they had given me an advance of a thousand rubles, enough to purchase a diamond necklace or more than a pound of butter.

Furthermore, they had togged me out in splendidly warm clothes, real woolen trousers, a sheepskin shuba, and a caftan of the sort worn by Tolstoy while he was preaching that everyone should be a law unto himself, restrained solely by reason and moral suasion—the old fool.

So after another day spent pacing my hotel room (eight steps from the wax fruit to the chamber-pot commode), I started to take an interest in the world outside my window. The hotel was on St. Isaac's Square and had a splendid view of the massive gold dome of St. Isaac's Cathedral, the elaborate statue of Nicholas I—somewhat scarred by pot shots—and the imperial ballet building, through whose windows one could obtain occasional glimpses of the ballerinas as they undressed.

I sat at the window for hours, admiring the imperial ballet's architecture.

On the fourth day, encouraged by Trotsky's aide-de-camp, George Garanine, who was a really warmhearted and sympathetic fellow in spite of his good looks, I ventured forth into the city.

Though badly neglected after six years of war, Petrograd was still an extraordinarily beautiful place. George, who accompanied me on my first trip outside, told me all about it. It was, he said, a mineral testament to the willpower of Peter the Great. Peter had flogged a generation of cowed citizenry into embedding his new capital among the swampy islands at the mouth of the Neva River. After he had used up all the local serfs, he imported others from all parts of the Empire, until their extremities, too, dropped off from summer rot and winter frostbite.

By the time they were all dead, Peter had a capital of entrancing baroque and classical architecture, done in the purest colors ever splashed around a city: vivid facades of blue and white, yellow and white, and green and white, highlighted with gold; and for Peter personally a palace for each season, plus a spare for Ivan the Terrible bank holidays.

All the same, the city was too spacious and orderly to inspire much affection. Spacious? Even the architect had never seen all the rooms in the Winter Palace. And you needed a fortnight's vacation to cross one of the squares.

After a few days I grew tired of gawking at gilt and being scrutinized by statues, and put upon by pillars and dazzled by domes; and that was when I attempted to make friends with the fellow who was following me.

For I was feeling as lonely as if I were still in solitary confinement. Even a secret police agent—I assumed that was what he was—was better than nothing. So I waved to him a couple of times, and then one morning I hid in a doorway and as he was scuttling past I jumped out and cried jovially in my fluent and superbly pronounced Russian, "Why, hello, there! Fancy meeting you here!"

He started violently and backed away, mumbling. I grabbed for his right hand and shook it. "Well, well, and how are you today?" I cried. "My name is Bandyeh—but I suppose you know that. And what's your name, Comrade?"

He continued to retreat. I couldn't quite see how he was doing this, as I was still pumping his hand. Then I realized that I was shaking an empty mitt.

This turned out to be a good thing, however. Even in April the temperature was still well below zero, so he was forced to come back for his mitt before his fingers fell off.

"Listen," I said, gripping his shoulder, "I know you're following me, so why don't we just stroll around together? I promise not to seduce you with tales of the decadent West, with its freedom of speech, limitless opportunities for advancement, its gaiety, charm, vitality, plentiful butter, beautiful women for the asking, and so forth."

"*Pazhalsta.* My glove," he mumbled, looking around in fright.

"I'll give you your glove, Uncle, if you'll walk beside me, instead of shuffling along in the rear."

"Please, Comrade."

"You're a Cheka agent, I suppose?"

"Cheka, Cheka? What's that? Oh, please, they will see me."

"They could hardly fail to, Uncle, you're so conspicuous," I said heartily.

"Conspicuous?" he said, looking down at himself. He was attired in a black coat, black muffler, black bowler, and, judging by his air of seediness, black underwear.

"I'm surprised you're not carrying a hammer in one hand and a sickle in the other, Comrade, so there'd be no doubt."

"Please. My hand is freezing," he whimpered. Then, when I held his mitt archly behind my back: "Oh, go to the devil, then!"

he hissed furiously, and hurried off, mashing his hand under his armpit.

Next morning I went after him again, holding out his mitt as if to entice a nervous dog. When this failed to work, I cornered him in Rastrelli's grotto.

"I'm thinking of going to Peterhof today," I said. "Want to come?"

"This is not right, Comrade. We are not supposed to chat like this. It is against the rules."

"Oh, don't be such a fussbudget. Come on." And I took his arm and started to haul him along.

"I will be seen!" he squealed, wrenching his arm away, his eyes rolling like two blood alleys. "You don't understand. It is possible somebody is watching."

"You mean you're following me and somebody's following you?"

"Of course! Don't they do that in your country?"

"Where is he?" I asked, peering around. "Maybe we can all go to Peterhof together."

But once again Sergei Ossipov (for such was his name) ran off, and was half a mile away across the Sriboldova Canal before he remembered that he was supposed to be behind me. But that was all right: I was going his way anyway.

I caught him by surprise again next day as he alighted from a droshky.

"Look," I said, "this is silly. What's the sense in both of us taking droshkies? We could ride together. Think of the money we could save."

He stared hopelessly at his feet.

"You could pay for both of us," I said.

"Me? Why should I pay?"

"Well, you're on expenses, aren't you?"

The breakthrough came three days later when I caught him in the Volkhov cemetery. He saw me coming and dodged behind Turgenev's tomb. We had a lovely time playing round the monuments.

"Oh, God."

"Hello, what's all this about God?" quoth I. "I thought you chaps had done away with religion and all that."

"Will you leave me alone! What will they say at head-quarters!"

"Ah! So you admit you're with Cheka."

"Actually we are thinking of calling it the G.P.U.—Cheka sounds too friendly," he muttered; then stamped his foot. "Oh, very well! Yes, I work for Cheka. But you behave as if *you* did. Devil take it, Comrade, it is you who are supposed to feel hunted!"

His annoyance turned to anxiety again. "Please do not do this to me, Bartalamyeh Fyodorevitch. Things are difficult enough as it is."

"Oh, how's that, Sergei?"

"How can you be so heartless? You will get me into serious trouble."

"Gosh, I wouldn't want to do that, Sergei."

"Shut up, shut up! As if things are not bad enough, with all this walking. Look at my boots! It's all right for you, Comrade, they have given you fine new boots, but mine—you see that?" He stood, quivering, on one leg and, removing his left boot, thrust it in my face. "That is all I have to keep out the cold. You see the holes? I have to fill my boots with copies of *Izvestya!*"

"Hello," I said, drawing out the newspaper. "It says here that barley production is up eighty-six percent."

"If you won't think of my reputation," he cried, rolling his blood alleys, "at least think of my feet. Stop walking around and seeing so many sights!"

"Tell you what, Sergei. I'll stop if you'll come up to my room for a glass of vodka."

"No, no, no! Oh, God."

"There you go again, Sergei, being anti-Bolshevik."

"Shhh!"

"But don't you see, Sergei—we just can't go on meeting this way."

He turned and started to butt his head against a tombstone. "I am beginning to have dreams about you every night," he said brokenly. He had terrible bad breath. Fortunately his breath was visible as clouds of steam in the cold air, so I could see it coming in time and clap my nostrils shut. "Last night," he went on, "I dreamed I was in the path of a herd of galloping reindeer, and every one of them was wearing your face. They were all shouting at me in a loud voice to pull myself together or they would trample on my good conduct medal."

"As a matter of fact," I replied earnestly, "I have been thinking of complaining to Cheka that you're not cooperating. That you're being antisocial, as well as rude, irritable, foulmouthed, and religious."

"Please, please," he whimpered, almost on his knees.

"Come and have a drink with me, then. I want to hear all about Cheka and how it works."

Slowly he relaxed. The mottled effect left his face, leaving it wet and gray, like a typical North Russian sky.

"Oh, devil take it," he said hopelessly. "Why not? It's probably too late anyway. But I cannot go to your room. Astoria is full of spies. We'll go to my apartment. I, too, feel like getting drunk."

So we sneaked along to his apartment, which turned out to be a wine cellar. It was below a ruined mansion off an inner courtyard choked with rubble and refuse.

Lying on the rows and rows of wine racks were three lonely bottles of *starka*. He passed one of them across to me, and after a morose silence and several swigs, suddenly he began to explain what he'd meant when he said that things were difficult enough as it was.

"You see, before I was in Cheka, I was in the imperial secret police, the Okhrana," he said, shrugging hopelessly and kicking at the straw with his foot. Still without looking up, he added, "By the way, if you tell any of this, I have a friend who will see that you are returned to the fortress, you understand."

"You can trust me not to breathe a word, Sergei," I replied, sipping wisely. Whatever *starka* was, it was pretty powerful stuff, judging by its effect on Sergei. After drinking only a quarter of his bottle, he was decidedly unsteady on his feet. "So you were a former tsarist agent, were you?"

He nodded and began to tell a story so complicated that I was not at all sure I comprehended all its violent, devious, and treacherous nuances. Apparently, even before the 1905 Revolution, the tsarist secret police, the Okhrana, had infiltrated most of the revolutionary movements, not only in Russia but throughout

Europe, to such an extent that some of the movements contained more Okhrana agents than terrorists.

"You were one of these agents-provocateur, were you, Sergei?" I asked, leaning nonchalantly back in my armchair before remembering I was sitting on a barrel.

"I was, Bartalamyeh Fyodorevitch," he said, helping me up again and breathing all over me. "In fact it was I who assassinated the deputy head of Okhrana, Alexander Miroshnikov."

"You what?"

"Is true," he muttered, handing me the last bottle of *starka*. For some reason the bottle I'd been drinking from was empty. I must have spilled it when I fell off the barrel.

"You killed your own boss?"

"The head of Okhrana knew all about it."

"He did?"

"It was his idea. He wanted me to prove to revolutionaries that I was a dedicated terrorist, you see. So they would trust me all the more."

Apparently the Okhrana agents were expected to take an active part in terrorist affairs. It was not uncommon for the spies to demonstrate their sincerity and dedication to the cause by assassinating the very members of the imperial hierarchy that they were supposed to be safeguarding, with the full approval of everybody (except, presumably, the ones who were actually murdered).

"But, Sergei," I said, "after infiltrating the revolutionary groups, why didn't you just break them up?"

"Was not Okhrana policy. Besides, if we destroyed revolutionary movements, how would we know what they were up to?" he added, looking at me pityingly, as if I had no common sense whatsoever. He gestured at my bottle. "*Zdarovyeh.*"

"*Zdarovyeh,*" I said faintly. As I raised the bottle I lurched against the empty wine racks and had to cling to them for a moment. It suddenly occurred to me that, after six months of enforced temperance, I'd better not drink too much myself. I had to keep my wits about me. I didn't feel I could entirely trust Sergei Ossipov.

"So," I said, drawing myself up and looking dignified, "the

tsarist police were content merely to divide and corrupt the movements they had infiltrated?"

"*Par exemple*," Sergei said, receding approximately four hundred feet, "once, on behalf of revolutionaries, I wrote a seditious article for a Communist newspaper. The revolutionaries were very pleased and paid me handsomely. Then I took it to the Okhrana to have it approved. They were very pleased, too, and they paid me as well. But then, of course, naturally, they had it suppressed.

"Another time," he went on dreamily, "there was this woman in the revolutionary group . . . her name was Olga . . . she was so beautiful. But she slept with everybody except me. You see, I was not quite so prepossessing, then."

"*Tiens.*"

"Anyway, one day I had brilliant idea how to make her sufficiently grateful, that she would bestow her favors on me . . ."

"Yes? How did you manage that, Sergei?"

"Ehk? Oh . . . it was simple. I betrayed her to Okhrana. As a result, she was arrested."

"Ah. And then?"

"Surely it's obvious. I got the Okhrana to let me rescue her, of course.

"And of course, after that," he leered, "she was suitably grateful. You understand?"

Then came the Revolution, and in November 1917 the Bolsheviks seized the Okhrana files. These included the dossiers of thousands of tsarist spies in the Bolshevik movement, Sergei's among them.

"So why haven't you been liquidated?" I demanded.

"Because my friend Joseph got hold of several of the dossiers, including mine, and his own, of course, before the party saw them."

"Your friend Joseph was a tsarist spy as well?"

"Yes. And he is now high up in the party. That is why I do not feel entirely safe. He may get rid of me to make himself more secure. So you see, Bartalamyeh Fyodorevitch," Sergei said, "if you care anything at all for truth, justice, freedom, and all the other Russian ideals, you really must start behaving with proper respect for the situation and act like normal guilty person when I follow you. As we say in Russia, *A man who changes his socks only at Easter is not likely to be served first in a shoe store.*"

"I'll try and remember that, Sergei," I mumbled as we helped each other up the steps, back into the ruins.

"It is difficult not to worry," he said. We staggered over the rubble. "I don't trust him an inch, that swine, Stalin."

"Who?"

"My dear friend Joseph."

"Oh," I mumbled, losing interest in his affairs. After all, he and his friend were not likely to affect the destiny of nations or anything, whether they were exposed as former tsarist agents-provocateur or not. All I wanted was to get back to the hotel and sleep . . . making a mental note not to mention to my guardian, George Garanine, that I had been out on a binge with a secret police agent. . . . He might not have understood. I know *I* didn't.

Though it was now May, it was still hideously cold in Moscow, to which yellow ochre city I had seen transferred after that Bolshie ballet with Sergei the spy. In Red Square the snow was in six-foot drifts. Since the last snowfall, nobody had cleared so much as a bloody shovelful of the stuff. Presumably the Snow-Clearing Committee had not yet gotten around to that item on the agenda.

The weather was only one reason I was in such a thoroughly bad temper that morning, as I floundered home through the aftermath of the latest spring blizzard. God, I hated Moscow. The new capital was shapeless, neglected, and boorish, a muzhik's backyard pretending to be the Champs de Mars. No wonder Moscow was so rarely mentioned in Russian literature, except derogatorily. It had none of the mystery and poetry of Petrograd, née Petersburg. It wasn't surprising that the citizens were fleeing it by the thousands.

Though, to be reluctantly honest, the reason so many people were leaving the city was because there wasn't enough to eat, not because the place was all that horrible. George and I, for instance, were receiving the best food ration going, the workman's *payok;* but food was so scarce that even that priority allowance wasn't being fully honored.

Another reason for my irritable mood was the accommodation. George Garanine and I were living in a requisitioned house on a side street off the Petrovka Ulitsa, a short flounder from Sverdlova Place, where the Bolshoi was. All the houses in our street were made of wood. With their splintered sills, flaking whitewash, leaning walls, and tottering chimneys, the street looked like a backdrop for an Ostrovsky comedy.

Inside, however, it was pure Gogol. The place was positively littered with people, for a horde of George's relatives had joined us during the past three weeks.

What the hell were they all doing there, anyway? The government had requisitioned the house for me, not them. But they had swept down on us out of the steppes within days of our taking up residence in Firewood Manor. There were so many of them that I still wasn't sure I'd accounted for them all. And they were all women.

Worse than that, there wasn't a decent-looking frail among them. In fact, most of them were really ugly, especially Granny, Lisa, Natalie, Grusha, Clava, Irina, Olga, Eugenie, and Dounatchka.

Which, I think, only left Anna. She was the one over there at the side of the giant stove, cooking some filthy-looking bran mash out of sunflower seeds. She had a shy, gentle expression, but her teeth had been carved from walnut husks.

Even all that wasn't the principal reason I was in such a bad temper. It was because George was once again hogging the stove.

The stove was not the small, Franklin-type effort we were used to back home. In Russian peasant houses, one huge central stove supplied the heat for the entire house, with each room sharing a side of the stove. The living room contained the warmest part of all, the front of the stove above the main firebox. And, as usual, that was where George was reclining, when I staggered in that morning.

Among the monstrous regiment living with us and sharing our *payoks* were at least two old women. Not only was George denying them the traditional best bed in the house—he had hardly budged from it in days.

I should have been used to it by now. George Garanine's sloth, I knew, was in direct ratio to his good nature. And he was getting more good-natured every bloody day.

I'd been out in the snow all morning, and I was cold, wet, and hungry. I shot him a look of unadulterated hatred.

It didn't do a bit of good. He greeted me with as much affection as if I had just returned from a vacation in the salt mines. In a trice he had all the women scuttling about like Rhode Island reds, to labor in my service. "Annushka, my love, a glass of tea for dearest little Uncle! Come and warm yourself, my dear fellow, you look frightfully cold and damp. Olgakins, let Bartalamyeh have that second-best niche in the stove, will you, dearest?" he cried, looking joyfully around at all the ugly faces, which, at that moment, included mine. "Ah, what a wonderful life it is, to have such a family and such a friend as Bartalamyeh Fyodorevitch! As our Russian proverb has it, *The snow feels coldest to the peasant whose thatch is afire*. Granny, be a dear little Mamushka and comb the icicles out of Bartushka's beard, there's a love." And lots more of the same.

"Don't you have a job to go to?" I demanded.

"Yes. As well as seeing to your wants, Bartushka," George said, plumping up his pillow, "I'm in charge of the motorcar pool at *der Kreml*."

"Then why aren't you down at the Kremlin?"

"We haven't any motorcars, Bartushka."

"Bah!" I said, and in a fury kicked the dining-room table.

"Just what we needed," George cried, delighted. "Some more firewood. What a thoughtful fellow you are, Bartalamyeh. Put some of that wood on the stove, dearest little Uncle. It's getting quite cool up here."

"Do it yourself, you two-toed sloth," I shouted in English. Fortunately George knew enough of that language to understand a few insults. "No wonder Trotsky got rid of you—before he ended up as *your* aide-de-camp."

"Mercy upon us, but you are in a surly mood lately," George said with a smile so forgiving that I couldn't help picking up a table leg and advancing on him in a white-knuckled sort of way.

At the last moment I opened the firebox under him and flung in a couple of legs and a handful of screws, growling like a grizzly. I knew that if I didn't feed the stove one of the women would be forced to do so, and thus show me up—again.

"My, he is a bad-tempered one," Granny cackled, nodding and grinning at me delightedly. "He's a right Georgian, isn't he?"

"Well," I muttered, subsiding into a slot in the vast, tiled stove, and plucking slush out of my collar, and wondering for the twentieth time how to drive him from the best bed. It shouldn't have been difficult. He was in many ways a naive and impressionable fellow. But so far I had failed to come up with a single idea, short of hurling him out the window.

I glared around at his relatives, my face wreathed in scowls. As usual they were all slaving to keep George warm and well supplied with tea. In the corner, plump Eugenie was reknitting some old underwear into a muffler for his sensitive throat. And Anna was stirring the sunflower seed mash so that he'd have something to keep up his strength.

I growled again. It was their fault that George was like that. He was a handsome orphan who had been cuddled, mollycoddled, and handmaidened all his life. The result of all the petting and cosseting was that his self-reliance had diminished to the point where he would have had difficulty in competing with a one-legged flea. How ruthless, driving Trotsky had managed to put up with him for so long was one of the mysteries of the universe.

"Perhaps the trouble is, dear old Uncle, that you don't have enough to do," George said, reclining on the stove again with a happy sigh.

I looked at him, steaming with frustration.

"You were once a medical student," George continued, "and a brilliant one, I have not the slightest doubt. Maybe we could find a job for you in that line of work."

"Oh yes?" I snapped. "And what would you suggest?"

"You could queue up for my cough medicine."

Anna was just returning with another glass of tea for George. She recoiled at the sight of my face and offered placatingly to help me off with my boots.

Sulkily, I allowed her to do so. "Perhaps I do need some occupation," I muttered.

"Of course you do, dearest Bartalamyeh!"

"It's true I have always been a man of action," I continued, as Anna panted and struggled with my footgear. "Vigorous, positive, and determined, ever since the time that my father saw me playing in a puddle at the age of seven and thundered about the devil and idle hands, and immediately arranged for me to take piano lessons."

Several of the women turned and listened to me, wearing looks of intelligent concentration betokening a total lack of comprehension. The situation struck me as being so Chekhovian that I started to enjoy myself, in a vicious sort of way. I had always delighted in the passions and frustrations portrayed in Russian literature. I began to fancy myself as a character in an undiscovered play of Chekhov's—*The Three Cherry Sisters*, perhaps, or *Uncle Bandyeh*.

"Even when I joined the army, where, as you know, Granny, it is possible to do nothing while seeming to be the very personification of efficiency, I always managed to keep busy," I said, toying with my beard, which I had not yet amputated. "And the higher I rose in the hierarchy and the more able to force others to do all the work, the harder I tried, until by the time I had my own squadron I was busy for eighteen hours a day, as described in Volume Three of my memoirs, which, of course, I shall never finish, now that the cherry sisters are to be cut down."

For a bit of stage action I wrenched up a floorboard or two and fed them into the stove. "And now look at me," I went on. "I have done nothing for what seems like months."

GEORGE: But surely it *is* months, dear old Uncle.

BANDYEH: Ah, devil take it, I am so weary. I even do nothing wearily. In a minute or two, winter will be over, and nature will stir and send forth buds and stamens and shoots and things, and be revived. Only I shall not be revived. I am suffocated by the thought that my life has been wasted, like a pine needle floating in the dry bed of a river. I have no past, it has all been stupidly wasted on trifles and absurdities.

IRINA: Why do you never look at me, Bartalamyeh Fyodorevitch?

BANDYEH: It's all so unutterably boring, you see.

ANNA: I should go to the dentist. But I can't be bothered.

BANDYEH: Yes, boring. In a word, boresome, tiresome, tedious,
monotonous, wearisome, and drearisome. I have been cheated,
I see it now. Unutterably cheated.

DOUNATCHKA: How much did you lose?

BANDYEH: Just my life. I've become dull, drab, useless—and
hairy. Look at this beard. What a silly beard it is, spreading all
over my face like that orchard out there, as it spreads over the
garden, choking all meaning and significance from the weeds!

(*Eleven relatives enter on hands and knees. Lisa goes to the
window. Then she comes back again.*)

I'm bubbling over with sheer apathy, Lisa. It can't go on. I
shall shoot myself. Or better still, I shall shoot George. But of
course I would probably miss and hit a sea gull. Look at him,
reeking up there on that stove!

(*George has fallen asleep. Uncle Bandyeh throws a sewing basket and two daguerreotypes into the firebox and slams the door
noisily—twice.*)

Look at him! Each day he stirs from his bed of red-hot calories
only just long enough to allow his adoring relatives to brush,
comb, and dust him. Whereupon he goes back to bed and lies
there, musing on art, science, God, and the universe!

(*George snores loudly.*)

Just think about him! The son of a common archbishop, he has
risen through the ranks of the cavalry to become a handsome
captain, and has somehow managed to reach the age of thirty
without becoming sour, bitter, cynical, disillusioned, and vindictive. He has utterly failed to grow up and mature. Just consider! At the age of thirty he is cheerful, affectionate, and
loved by everybody! He has learned absolutely nothing from
life except cartography, military law, physics, calculus, history,
geography, geology, economics, and motor mechanics. In
thirty years he has achieved nothing except comfort, content-

ment, security, and respect! And yet what an opinion he has of himself! He is quite convinced that he is utterly unimportant and destined for obscurity, whereas in actual fact he has a great future in front of him! I can't stand it any longer!

(*Bandyeh draws out a catapult and shoots at George.*)

What? Missed? My life is ruined.

(*He shoots again.*)

Missed again? This is intolerable! My soul is smoldering, my brain is on fire, my head is aflame!

(*As Irina gently strums her Jew's harp, Anna comforts him.*)

ANNA: Never mind, Bartalamyeh Fyodorevitch, the sun has come out and is shining in the duck pond, and all our sufferings will be swept away in a great tide of peace and futility. Here, have some bran mush.

BANDYEH: Yes . . . And let us all rest . . . rest . . . rest . . .

(*The curtain falls so slowly that half the actors wander off to the greenroom for a round of bezique.*)

And it was then that I got the idea.

Some time later, as soon as the relatives were out of the way, I shook George's sleeping form and whispered in his ear, "George? George! Wake up! You're sick!"

His eyes flicked open.

"What?"

"You've been thrashing about, muttering and moaning in your sleep, you poor devil. Heaving about restlessly, and gibbering and calling out."

"I have?"

"As well as gasping and jerking and twitching and moaning. George—don't you see?"

"What is it, Bartalamyeh?"

"You're delirious."

"Course I'm not. Surely not?"

"If you could have heard yourself. I'm terribly concerned," I said, taking his pulse.

"I'm not delirious. I understand at least half of what you say."

"You see—only half."

"Because your Russian is so bad, Bartalamyeh."

"No, George. It's because your brain is in an uproar. George, haven't you realized it yet? You have an unspeakable fever."

"It's true that I am feeling rather hot . . ."

This was hardly surprising. As soon as the women were out of the room, I had stoked the stove with every remaining scrap of firewood.

"It's true . . . I'm sweating," he said, feeling his forehead and beginning to look worried.

"You have a fever. And your pulse is racing. Oh, if only I had some medicine in my little black bag—or even a little black bag. Oh dear, what are we going to do?" I said, and was busily wringing my hands when the relatives, attracted by George's moans, poured into the room to ask anxiously what the matter was.

"I'm not feeling very well," George said. "My heart is beating. It's obvious I have a fever."

"I'm afraid it's very grave," I said gravely.

"It's true, he's sweating," Grusha said, and put her hand on George's forehead. She had just come in from her daily shopping trip and her hand was ice cold. George jumped.

"Just as I feared," I said. "Convulsions."

I drew plump little Aunt Eugenie forward for a better view. She was the pessimistic one.

"It's terrible," she faltered. "Look at the steam."

"What's wrong with him, do you think, Bartalamyeh Fyodore-vitch?" Anna whispered.

I tried to smile encouragingly and started to pat George's shoulder—then hurriedly withdrew my hand and wiped it surreptitiously.

The gesture—and my expression of professional embarrassment at my own squeamishness—did not go entirely unnoticed. In fact everybody moved back several feet. This alarmed George even more.

"What can you do?" he whispered hoarsely, now drenched in sweat from the heat of the stove.

I bit my lip and looked away. George tried to struggle up, his eyes growing in size like inflated balloons. With an obvious effort, as if to make amends for my former display of unprofessional conduct, I pressed him back onto the stove. "You must keep cool," I said. "You see, I suspect that what is wrong with you is . . ." I hesitated.

"Yes, yes, what, Bartalamyeh?"

"Tell us what is wrong with him, Bartalamyeh Fyodorevitch," the others cried.

"I can't, of course, be certain without doing a lymph node biopsy," I murmured, "but I fear it's . . . laxus."

"Laxus!" the women cried.

"I knew it," Eugenie said, nodding proudly. "Vera Ourspenskaya had it. Don't you remember, Granny? Her ears started to flake, and she turned yellow. Laxus, that's what they said it was, I distinctly remember."

"The main thing is to keep cool," I said.

"How can I keep cool," George croaked, twitching, and sweating like a ham, "with my ears flaking off and the rest of me turning yellow?"

"I mean cool in the sense of not being hot," I said. "The first thing to do, of course, is to move into the coldest bedroom in the house."

Later that afternoon I had to report to the police on Lubyanka Street. When I got back I found that the stupid relatives had gone and carted him off to hospital.

When I got there myself, I found that they had not only admitted him but had put him in the warmest part of the ward—right next to the stove.

"He will need constant care and attention," the nurse said as she and her fellow sisters of mercy plumped up George's extra pillow and soothed his placid brow with adoring hands, and fed the swine with jelly.

"But what exactly is wrong with him?" I asked Dr. Glinkov.

"It is nothing serious of course," he said, fumbling out a pair of spectacles. One of the lenses was cracked and had been mended with a thin strip of passe-partout. It must have given him a curiously bifurcated view of life.

"You wouldn't understand, being a layman," he said loftily, breathing on the good lens. "There are certain symptoms that suggest a relatively obscure ailment . . ."

"He looks contented enough to me," I said bitterly.

"There is a certain elation present, to be sure," Glinkov said. "That is one of the symptoms, of course. It must be. The way things are in this country, it could hardly be anything else."

"Well, how long are you going to keep him? After all, he's my guardian—I have to keep an eye on him."

"Naturally, he must remain under observation. Then we shall see what develops."

"But you must have some idea what's wrong with him," I said, darting a hateful glance at George's brave, suffering face.

"You would not be any the wiser if I told you," Glinkov snapped back. Then: "Oh, very well. We believe it's a little-known disease, laxus."

"Laxus?"

"I told you you wouldn't understand," he said, turning away.

I certainly didn't. I had only invented it four hours ago.

Queen Street, Gallop

From the moment I fled from Russia in 1920, right up to the startling developments of 1923, I had only one ambition, and that was to design and build aircraft for the Canadian market. Unfortunately I kept being shoved off course by the magnetic repulsions of chance. First there was that disgraceful beano with Dasha, a Slav hellcat who had reclaimed me in New York as her husband on the ridiculous grounds that I had married her in Moscow. She thought that the wedding was entirely valid, though in fact I had only been cohabiting with her for something to do. Besides, the Bolsheviks had officially abolished marriage.

Next there was the involvement with the millionaire's daughter, Cissie, another ungrateful wretch. After I had spent two years teaching her to fly and encouraging her to think for herself and behave independently, she became so independent that she finally left me to join a flying circus. And then there were the filums. Between the success of my first two movies, *Plane Crazy*, and *Blenkinsop of the Mounted*, when I appeared to be plotting a course toward fame and fortune, and the subsequent mistake on the producer's part in featuring me in an ambitious six-reeler, the burden on one totally untrained for the acting profession had proved to be too great. Though I appeared subsequently in a pair of shorts—and looked very nice in them, I thought—my career never recovered from the disaster of that six-reeler. My treasury of expressions, ranging from smug complacency to blank incomprehension, which had served me reasonably well in my first

two films, was not sufficiently well stocked to see me through a
role that demanded genuine ability. My contract was rudely terminated. Of course, I had only gone into films to make money to
subsidize my aviation endeavors. Even so, it did tend to sap
one's self-esteem a bit to return to one's portable dressing room
after a day's work on a Western—being shot in Brooklyn—to find
that it had been taken over by my co-worker. One day I may expose that horse for what it was, the scheming swine.

It was January 1923 before I finally got home, or *to hum,* as
we say in the Ottawa Valley. Despite years of discouragement I
was still intent on establishing an aircraft manufacturing company, and in fact had a design more or less ready for the market.
This was the Gander, a high-wing amphibian which I had left,
for the time being, in its hangar on Long Island. Instead I came
home to Gallop just in time for the next deviation, which began
with the worst crisis to hit the town since the discovery that the
superintendent of the local jail had been allowing the prisoners
out every evening to burgle the surrounding countryside, and
then readmitting them in the morning, to provide them with air-
tight, or celltight, alibis.

Part of the explanation for the success of the superintendent's
unconventional though profitable penology—he had been getting
a cut of the proceeds—was the inaccessibility of the jail to the inspector of prisons in Ottawa. In 1923, too few Ontario towns had
a unity or focus that a village green or town square might have
provided. The province's towns and villages were usually littered
along the highway like debris, and the new, paved surfaces provided by the major road improvement program that had begun
just after the war seemed only to have emphasized the merciless
bifurcation. But Gallop had managed to avoid this fate. It had
practically no road to it at all.

According to the maps, access to the town was gained by a
route leading off the Ottawa–Prescott highway. Actually this was
a cleverly concealed dead-end trail. Even if foreigners managed
to find the camouflaged entrance from the highway, the route
into Gallop was so soggy in spring, corrugated in summer, dusty
in fall, and invisible in winter as to discourage all but the most
persistent traveler. The reason for this arterial neglect was the
proximity of Ottawa. The citizens of Gallop viewed the capital

with surly suspicion, not least because it contained so many inspectors. The vague trail was the town's chief defence against a
steadily growing band of federal nosy Parkers. Old Gallopians
still recounted with satisfaction the story of the tax inspector
who had, with mulish determination, attempted the drive to Gallop along the official route. He managed to find the concealed
entrance off the Ottawa–Prescott highway but that was only the
beginning of his tribulations. For the next two days he was continuously detoured across country by various helpful citizens,
through gullies, fields of six-foot cornstalks, garbage dumps, middens, marsh, and somebody's root cellar, where he was forced to
put up for the night, and in which he caught diarrhea, fleas, and
a wallop from the farmer's wife when she caught him relieving
himself on her rutabagas. He was still blubbering and laughing
in a crazed fashion when he finally regained the highway and returned to Ottawa, where he was promptly dusted with Dr.
Witcherley's Powdered Fleabane and docked half a week's pay.

The local citizens, of course, had no great difficulty finding
their way in and out of town. They used the proper route along
the Rideau River and past the Talbot Distillery.

Thus Gallop had managed to retain some semblance of indi-
viduality if not of character, of entity if not of personality. The
burg even had a center, the Rock Gardens, so named because of
the giant boulder that, resisting all efforts to remove it after its
excavation, completely blocked the entrance to the town hall.

The town hall was in the usual Victorian Gothic tradition of
narrow, pointed window and turret topped by sharp-tipped
wrought iron, the interior filled with cracked tiles.

Also on the town square was a museum, containing agricultural implements, two-headed calves, muskets, needlework, Indian artifacts, several enormous paintings of overweight Victorian highbinders, and a statue of a male nude in the entrance
hall, with a placard decently covering the marble loins (VISITING
HOURS: WEEKDAYS 10–4. CLOSED SEPT.–JUNE). A few private houses
and some shops also faced the square, including a handsome department store, Willoughby's, and a Presbyterian church which
was surrounded by a vicious railing broken by an eight-foot gate.
Whether this sequence of iron halberds was designed to keep

vandals out or the congregation in was a moot point—or at least old Dr. McKay, a right heathen, considered it a moot point.

Other notable buildings included the Queen's Hotel just off the Rock Gardens on the petrol-pump-populated main street, Queen Street; the Regal Mortgage and Loan Company, assets $ 0,000,000 (presumably some urchin had scraped off the initial gilt digit), and the Wildebeest Lodge, which, because it had no members, was available for any respectable gatherings such as Saturday night hops, church suppers, improving lectures, and lantern slide shows such as the Reverend Mr. Wattle's illustrations of Egyptian tombs.

As for the crisis that shook Gallop to its combinations in January a few days after my return, it concerned the town's most important industry, the Talbot Distillery.

Though prohibition had been established in Ontario in 1916, long before the Americans put through their Volstead Act, the province's distillers, unlike their American counterparts, had been allowed to continue the production of alcohol for export and for industrial and medicinal use at home. Talbot Distillers Limited was one; not the biggest in the country but certainly of vital consequence to Gallop. Sprawled on the eastern outskirts of town on the Rideau River, it employed about three hundred persons directly, but so many others indirectly that at least a third of the population depended on its operations. Local farmers, for instance, supplied it with most of its corn, and the Hipsey Glass Works with all of its bottles. Consequently when Mrs. Philippa Talbot announced in January that the entire operation would be closing down in eight or nine months, and moving to new premises in Montreal, it caused perturbation, consternation, agitation, and various other sorts of botheration throughout the town and countryside.

The crisis continued throughout the winter and into spring. The town council passed resolutions offering increasingly desperate tax concessions. Delegations of citizens importuned the distillery president, Mrs. Talbot, protest meetings were held in the Wildebeest Lodge, and petitions were sent to the national and provincial governments. As a last resort the townspeople even asked their federal representative to take a hand in the affair. This was a Conservative M.P. who for sixteen years had never uttered a word in Parliament until somebody slammed a desk lid on his fingers, his brief comment on that occasion earning him a reprimand from the Speaker. The M.P. had been urged to table a question on the Talbot move. It would very likely have been answered, too, had he not expired just in time.

The protests had not the slightest effect. Philippa Talbot continued to insist that the move was essential, in order to put her company in a viable economic position to exploit the overseas market—or, as Dr. McKay put it, to enable her to smuggle more booze across the U.S. border.

Actually Mrs. Talbot was suspect even before the move was announced. A forty-year-old American of unknown origin, it was said that she had married young Rupert Talbot solely in order to get her hands on the family-owned business. The acquisition had been formalized a couple of years previously when Rupert was drowned in a yachting accident on Long Island Sound.

Now that she had shown herself ready, willing, and able to betray the town to which the Talbots had remained loyal for a hundred years, the suspicion of her had turned to such dislike that one octogenarian pensioner had even been constrained to heave a rock at her chauffeur-driven Packard, and would likely have hit it had he not overbalanced while winding up for the pitch and fallen into the horse trough outside the Queen's Hotel.

Not knowing how vital a part the Talbot move would play in my future, I remained preoccupied with my own affairs—firstly to obtain orders for my new aircraft, and secondly to seek investment capital to establish an aircraft manufacturing plant on the site of the farm that I had purchased in 1920 with my demobilization loot.

However, I was careful to simulate a grave concern over the Talbot move. For business reasons I felt obliged to back the community to the hilt, even if the hilt was to stick out of Mrs. Talbot's back.

Actually I became even more involved in the community than I had intended when, within a week of my return, my old wartime friend, Captain Karley, invited me to join the local Liberal association.

He called round one snow-packed Saturday morning, which both flustered and impressed my parents. They hadn't realized until then that I was intimately acquainted with one of the town's most important citizens.

They were even more impressed when I invited Karley to stay for lunch and he actually agreed to grace our table with his nimble bulk.

Mother was quite flushed and flustered with pleasure. "I hope you like bean soup, Mr. Karley," she said as she dumped a cauldron in front of my father, the reverend.

"My favorite soup, Mrs. Bandy," Karley said as gallantly as his flat, phlegmatic voice would allow; though he looked pretty mystified when he received his bowlful, drove a spoon into the coagulum, and failed to find any beans in it whatsoever.

The soup's beanless condition was explained by the fact that Mother had inherited every Ontario superstition going, including the association of beans with death or ghosts. "God save your soul/ Beans and all," were the first words I ever remember her uttering. She also believed that if a visitor placed his chair against the wall he would never return. (The only visitor who ever did was never invited back.)

It was only recently that I had learned that superstition was the explanation for so many of her actions that had puzzled me in the past. Like the way she wore vinegar corks, failed to pick up her gloves when she dropped them, or refused to turn a mattress on a Friday. When I finally asked her what it was all about, I learned that the corks were a cure for cramp, and dropping gloves and turning mattresses on Fridays brought bad luck. Similarly it was a grave mistake to point at the moon, laugh before breakfast, or pay a doctor's bill in full. This last superstition caused old Dr. McKay much annoyance. "Suppose I refused to tap your chest because I considered it unlucky?" he demanded one day; a mistake on his part, for, taking this to be one that she had missed, Mother refused any further thoracic percussion.

As Karley prodded his way through the rest of the meal, a prodigious but rather flavorless repast of ham, chutney, and various sorts of sodden vegetables, Father kept apologizing for the dilapidated state of the farmhouse, aware of how unfavorably it compared with Karley's fine brick mansion in the fashionable part of town. "Look at that stained ceiling," Father pointed out. "Bartholomew sleeps up there." And a few minutes later: "And doubtless you've observed the state of the clapboard outside, with its peeling paint, and the twisted gutters. There are more vegetables growing out of the eavestroughing than in Mother's garden; but of course we can't rely on Bartholomew for any help around here. He seems determined to spend most of his time in the barn, among those infernal flying machines of his."

"It's certainly a spacious house, though," said plump, phlegmatic Karley, shifting and sweating in the kitchen swelter, and gazing longingly out the window at a portcullis of icicles. His discomfort was caused by the red-hot fireplace rather than by Father's criticisms of me. Karley's chins were quite damp with perspiration. Papa invariably kept the inside temperature at about ninety degrees, winter and summer, his blood being as thin as a poor excuse.

"And if Bartholomew's neglect of our domestic quarters were not bad enough," Papa continued, glowering at me, "he's now talking about building outhouses all over the rest of the property."

"He means my aircraft manufacturing plant," I explained. "I'll show you the blueprints after lunch, Karley. I hope to put up a hundred-foot hangar and erecting shop along the road there, with a concrete floor and a cantilevered roof supported by steel trusses. And along the back of the building will be the woodworking and machine shops, the drawing and general offices, the power plant room, and a fabric and dope shop. Perhaps you'd be interested in bidding for the job when I get going?"

"I sure would."

I sprang up and bounded enthusiastically to the dining-room window. "And yonder, in the far corner of that foreign field that is forever Gallop," I cried fancifully, "I hope to put up a wind tunnel, powered by a war-surplus eighty-horsepower Renault engine, to produce a useful wind velocity of a hundred feet per second. And over there—"

"Do sit down, Bartholomew," Mother said. "You're causing a draft." While Father snorted and said, "Nothing will come of it, of course. You wait and see."

"Perhaps you haven't seen yesterday's paper, Reverend," Karley said, plucking out a copy of the *Gallop & District Advertiser*. He unfolded it and held it out in front of him, ostensibly so that

Papa could read the front page but actually to use it as a screen so that he could remove a piece of gristle from his mouth and hide it under a heap of spinach.

Father's razor-slit mouth gaped several millimeters as he beheld the headline: AN AIR HARBOR FOR GALLOP. LOCAL MAN TO BUILD AIRCRAFT PLANT HERE. As he took the paper and read the story, half a dozen chagrined parasites seemed to be scurrying about under his papyrus skin and fighting for egress through his pinched nostrils. While he rarely heeded a word of mine, he believed everything he read in the papers, so even the local rag's rather inaccurate summary of my plans came as something of a shock.

However, he was not yet ready to dismount after a lifetime of roughshod riding, so he merely muttered, "Seems all very vague to me. They probably only put it in to distract people from all the bad news about that distillery."

Mother was also leaning over to read the paper. "It says here you won quite a high honor after the war," she said. "The C.B.E. That can't be right, can it?"

Karley had been listening to the disrespectful family comments throughout dinner with some surprise. Now, perhaps feeling that I needed moral support, he murmured, "It should make Bart quite an important man in Gallop, you know," he said as Father twitched his gaze away from my sudden smirk. "As a matter of fact, that's why I came trotting along this morning." He laid his fork aside thankfully and said, "As a matter of fact, Bart, we were wondering—what are your politics?"

"Politics? I don't have any."

"Conservative, eh? You wouldn't consider coming over to the Liberals, would you?"

After adjusting to the abrupt change of topic, I gave the proposal considerable thought for at least five seconds. I seemed to remember that it was the Liberals who were presently in power. Sucking up to them would certainly do me no harm. In fact it might be quite useful, being a Liberal supporter, when the time came to apply to the government for a contract to build the Gander; for it was a well-known fact that the Liberal Party always looked after its own people, however competent.

Besides, I would have joined a witches' coven if it had promised to fulfill my ambition to establish an aircraft company.

"I've already mentioned you to the riding association," Karley added.

"Oh, I don't think I'd have time for horses as well as politics, Karley," I said.

"No, no, the Liberal riding association, old man. They're quite keen on having you, matter of fact. I told them you already have some political experience."

"I have?"

"In England. At the Air Ministry?"

"Ah," I said, realizing that he was referring to that time when I was aide to the Secretary of State for Air. I had held onto that post for, oh, quite a few weeks in 1918, until the ministry realized that I would be of even more use to the war effort digging trenches on the Somme front.

Knowing that Karley was president of the local Liberal association, the folks listened with almost sycophantic respect as he went on to talk about local politics. He was particularly preoccupied with the upcoming by-election. The Liberal candidate, he informed us, was a justice of the peace and a former army colonel, but Karley was candid enough to admit that the colonel J.P. did not have much of a chance. "You know what he's like, Reverend," Karley said, inviting Father into the inner circle with a knowing smile.

Father nodded and smiled sardonically, as if he knew exactly what the colonel J.P. was like; though in fact he had never met him or even heard of him until a minute ago.

Far from sneering at the old man's pretensions, I was quite touched. Papa lived in isolation even from local society, let alone local politics; so his eagerness to contribute to the conversation was all the keener. Both he and Mother were quite plainly thrilled to be discussing such esoteric topics.

At the same time I thought it was kind of Karley to pretend that they were in the know. It quite revived my affection for my former company commander.

"Now if only we could create an issue out of this Talbot business," Karley was saying to Mother, "we might have a chance of wresting the seat from the Conservatives. Don't you agree, Mrs. Bandy?"

"Oh yes," Mother said, flushing, and glancing at Papa to see if she had given the right answer. Actually both of them thought that losing the distillery would be a good thing for Gallop, not least because a couple of agrarian louts who lived nearby and who had been scolded once too often by Papa had taken to depositing their empties in the Bandy mailbox every Friday night when they staggered home from the Queen's Hotel, pissed to the gills.

As for me, I was hardly listening to Karley at all. I was too busy trying to work out why he was being so respectful to me these days. I still associated Karley so strongly with the trenches that I expected him to go on treating me as he had done then, with annoyed affection leavened with contempt for my priggishness, piety, temperance, patriotism, and other defects.

Maybe he thought I had improved since those macabre days that had left their psychic welts on so many veterans, not least Karley himself. Nearly half a decade after his subterranean years, huddled in the trenches, he was still apprehensive whenever he found himself in the open, as if he expected to be picked off by a sniper at any moment.

Now thirty-five years old, he had not changed much in appearance. He still owned a little snub nose that almost disappeared into his fat face, and the same patch of scalp peekabooed through his wispy brown hair. At the front he had been a splendid leader, imperturbable in attack and cynically cheerful during the boring stretches. I had been delighted to encounter him again in Gallop, relieved that he had survived a war that seemed to have been expressly designed to kill off all the best people. I had even told him so. (He had failed to reciprocate, though; confiding in return that he had not been the least surprised to learn that I had survived.)

After the war, impelled to build rather than to destroy, he had established a small construction company. Now, four years later, he was one of Gallop's leading citizens, president of the Board of Trade as well as of the Liberal riding association, and owner of the most expensive house in town, which had not just one indoor bathroom but two.

Which made his present attitude toward me slightly surprising. He never used to treat me with deference. Contumely, yes. Annoyance, vein-expanding rage, eye-popping fury, perhaps, but not deference.

It was only after I'd joined the Liberal Party and had been made chairman of the fund-raising committee that I discovered his motive in converting me to Liberalism. He'd only wanted to corner me into making a hefty donation to the by-election funds—"To kick things off as it were, and set a good example as chairman of the committee," as he cheerfully put it.

It appeared that he was no more impressed with me than he had been in 1916. It was only my money he was after. Little did he know what he was getting himself into.

Up to No Good in the Gazebo

I suppose that because I owned a largish farm, a shiny Pierce-Arrow, three aircraft, and a showy sheaf of blueprints, Karley thought I was rich and would be able to contribute substantially to the coming by-election. Naturally I didn't let on. Over the next few weeks I continued to look healthy, wealthy, and wise, and above all respectable. Fortunately my impersonation of a decent citizen was made easier by the fact that the populace, including my parents, were only dimly aware of my shady past, especially as a movie actor. Nobody in Gallop had seen any of my pictures, not even *Plane Crazy*. This was partly because of the town's determined isolation from filthy foreign influences, including news of the outside world, and partly because Gallop's only cinema had collapsed three years previously while the adjoining site was being excavated for a new branch of the Boiler Inspection and Insurance Company.

On the other hand, the impersonation was rendered more difficult by the fact that I was far from wallowing in oof. The truth was that, while a few months ago I had been worth a fortune, it had nearly all gone into the Gander. By April I had only a few hundred dollars left in the kitty.

Still, optimistic to the last, I was confident of obtaining an order for my first venture in aircraft design. But to carry out the order I would need financial backing, and I knew that no investors or partners would put up the money if they thought I really needed it. Which was why I was making an effort to sustain an affluent front.

Consequently I was really pleased when, early in the spring, I received an invitation to a garden party at Mrs. Hipsey's. For rich old Mrs. Hipsey was the acknowledged leader of the local family compact. Her forebears had been setting an example to the community since it was no more than a huddle of log cabins around the Hipsey mill. Down the years she and her relatives had acquired sizable chunks of Gallopian commerce through purchase, intermarriage, and other devious means, until now they were the most influential family for several hundred yards in all directions—not counting the Talbots, who were now being cut genealogically as well as socially.

The Hipseys had also collared most of the influential posts in town, and most of the posts were there that afternoon: Mrs. Hipsey's husband, the magistrate, her daughter Rosalie, president of the Women's Temperance League, her grandson Henry, known locally as "Hen" or "Cluck" Hipsey, the town clerk, and another relative, Gallop's latest general practitioner, who, though he had only been doctoring for six months, was already treasurer of the hospital board and chairman of the war memorial committee.

As for massive, dignified Mrs. Hipsey, though seventy, she was still director of the museum, patroness of the Decrepit People's Home, and an honorary fire fighter.

The Hipsey mansion was located in the northwest part of town. In Ontario the best people always built their houses in the northwest. This was to ensure that the prevailing winds carried the various stinks and effluvia of the industry that gave them their livelihood away from their sector and into the poor part of town where the smells belonged.

The garden, laid out in the symmetrical English manner, was dominated by a bandstand-sized gazebo—or gazebo-sized bandstand: there were certainly enough Hipseys to form a brass band. Except that Mrs. Hipsey preferred to call the structure a belvedere, and even pronounced it in the Italian fashion. This was where tea was to be served that afternoon. I had also been warned that this was the traditional way into the Gallopian establishment. If they found you suitable for the gazebo—the first test being to see how quickly you adopted their name for it, *belvedairy*—next time they invited you into the house.

As it turned out, quite killing my hopes for a Hipsey investment, I hardly even made it past the hyacinth beds.

The garden, gaudy with spring flowers and floral frocks—
under woolly cardigans, for it was still early in April—was already thronged with citizens when I arrived in my new blazer
and flannels. Naturally I made straight for Mrs. Hipsey to pay
my respects and ask her if she had twenty G's to spare; but there
were so many guests and relatives around her that I couldn't get
within fawning distance. As it appeared to be beneath the old
lady's dignity to leap three feet into the air to catch my eye over
the heads of the other sycophants, I withdrew to one side,
though ready at a moment's notice to impress her with my diamond cuff links and a gold wristwatch the size of a fried egg.

Ten minutes later I was still waiting to present myself to Mrs.
Hipsey, but she was now conversing with the Conservative candidate, Malachi Peel, presently the senior partner in the law firm
of Peel, Pell, Peel, and Bell. He was the second Peel from the
left. As he was almost certain to defeat our man, the colonel J.P.,
in the July by-election, I had already lobbied him in hopes of
creating a spokesman for the aviation industry in Parliament, but
the response had not been overly encouraging. "My dear sir," he
had replied, "we are paying millions to keep the railways running, without pouring public money into noisy, smelly aerial machines as well."

While I was busy rehearsing a few flowery phrases with which
to deck our hostess, I became aware that one of the Talbot Distillery people, Anne somebody, was standing nearby, holding a
glass of lemonade and looking stiltedly lonely. As I couldn't
avoid catching her eye, I nodded; but apparently mistaking my
snootiness for uncertainty, she came closer and said, "Hello. I
don't suppose you remember me. I was at that speech you gave
last month."

"Ah," I said.

"Does that mean you do remember me or you don't?"

"M'o yes, I remember you, Miss, uh . . ."

"Mrs. Mackie. Anne Mackie," she said, looking relieved to
have somebody to talk to at last. Though invited to the garden
party by her friend Isobel Hipsey, her presence, as a Talbot employee, was not particularly welcome, judging by the way she

was being neglected even by Granddad Hipsey, who usually took advantage of an immunity from prosecution guaranteed by his venerable age by running his hand up the comeliest limbs within reach of his wheelchair.

Actually I remembered her very well. I had met her at the Wildebeest Lodge three or four weeks ago after I had made some sort of speech. Every month during the winter the Liberal association invited guest lecturers to give a talk on current affairs or on a subject of educational interest, and early in March Karley had prevailed on me to talk about progress in aviation. The occasion had not been terrifically successful. The executive had outnumbered the audience. One of the people on the platform, the Reverend Mr. Wattle, had begun to snore just as I was approaching the climax of my speech—on the appalling lack of public interest in aviation. And as a committee member he was supposed to have set an example. Actually he did. A member of the audience had immediately emitted an answering snore.

So that, when Mrs. Mackie remarked afterward that she had found the speech stimulating, I thought she was being sarcastic, and had decided to take an instinctive dislike to her.

As she appeared to be waiting for me to continue the conversation: "You're a typewriter, I suppose," I said, "at Talbot's?"

"I look like a stenographer, do I, Mr. Bandy?"

"Well, I can't quite see you stirring a vat of whisky, or whatever they do in a distillery."

She turned her face away, her beautifully formed lips broadening; though when she looked up again they had sprung back to their former shape. "No, I do their advertising," she said.

For a moment her blue eyes turned almost as frigid as the breeze that was trying to see up her plain brown frock. "I suppose you're wondering," she said, "how a mere woman manages to hold down a job as advertising manager."

"I wasn't wondering anything of the sort. I was thinking that, as we're not allowed to drink your whisky, advertising it seems kind of pointless."

"Oh. Well, there's all kinds of ways of bringing a product to the public attention other than through ads," she said. Then, looking into her lemonade: "Sorry if I sounded defensive. A woman in business gets used to being treated condescendingly."

She wiped away a dribble of condensation from her glass with a forefinger, which drew my attention to her hands. They looked far too capable for my taste, broad and with distinctly businesslike fingers covered in skin that was obviously innocent of the softening creams that ladies usually slathered on their paws.

As if feeling the need to explain her attitude further, she went on, "When I was a girl I wanted to be a journalist. I was working on my father's newspaper in Smith Falls when I was fourteen, but when he died Mother sold the paper, even though I could easily have run it myself. I was so mad at her, I ran off and married a Scotsman."

"That was a terrible revenge to take on your mother."

"Oh, that wasn't her only humiliation. Two years later Gordon —that was my husband—took off with all the money Dad had left me. So I had to get a job. Except there weren't any jobs for women in journalism. I don't know why I'm blethering to you like this. That was one of Gordon's favorite words, blethering.

"But even that wasn't the end of Mother's sufferings—I wasn't letting her off that easily. I finally managed to get a position in Montreal with an advertising agency. I was really happy about that. It seemed too good to be true. It was. They sacked me a few weeks later, because I wasn't friendly enough with the boss."

"He had designs on your honor?"

"Right."

"The dirty dog."

"Of course, the way he explained it, he said it was because as a woman I wouldn't be able to mix on terms of equality with all the editors, printers, and people."

"So now you work for Mrs. Talbot, eh?" I said heartily, regarding her more warily than ever. Though stocky and a bit aggressive, she was undoubtedly attractive, with that fair hair pushed carelessly back from a broad brow, and those wide, full lips that looked as if they had been carved by an infatuated sculptor. But there was obviously something wrong with her, otherwise why would her husband have abandoned her after only two years of marriage? I mean, if Gordon didn't want her, *I* certainly wasn't interested.

As we stood shivering occasionally in the sunlit chill, I became aware that a strange-looking East Indian-type lady was billowing about in the background. At first I thought she was a colored servant who had wandered from an attic sickbed in her nightie, until I realized that the yellow and black garment she was swathed in was her national costume. She was drifting about on the lawn from one cluster of guests to another, like a wasp butting at jam sandwiches.

"Who on earth is that?" I asked.

"Pardon me? Oh, that's Mrs. Enerjee," Mrs. Mackie said, blushing for some reason. "I think Isobel Hipsey invited her." As she turned to look, the Indian lady was just abandoning another clique, the members of which were all gawking after her as if she had just said something obscene or original.

Seeing our faces turned in her direction, Mrs. Enerjee veered toward us. As she smiled, rows of largish white teeth snapped through the ectoplasmic headdress that covered her shiny black hair.

I couldn't quite decide how old she was, but the closer she came the more certain I became. She was somewhere between thirty and sixty years old.

Somewhat vaguely, Anne Mackie introduced the lady as a member of some Anglo-Indian cultural mission or other, who was touring Canada for some reason. "Pleased to meet you," I said, essaying a courtly bow and feeling surprised by the darkness of her complexion. It was the color of Bourneville chocolate. "And welcome to Gallop, madam."

"Oh, indeed yes," she replied in a high singsong. "I am being most impressed with your ever so beautiful town, Mr. Bandee, with its noble Gothic buildings in the finest Manchester traditions, bounded on the west by the beautiful Rideau River, which is comparing most effectively with our own Ganges, you know, not to mention your beautiful broad main thoroughfare with its most symmetrical telegraph poles and petrol pumps, and the beautiful garden in the center of town with its rock. But I am wondering all the time why you are putting such a great big rock right outside the noble entrance to your town hall, thus making it as impossible as possible to be getting inside, you see."

"Ah," I said, and took a deep breath. "Well, you see—"

"And tell me, Mr. Bandee, I am most curious, why is it that nearly everybody in Gallop is talking about a Madam Talbot all

the time? She is a bigwig, is she, Mr. Bandee, a local philan-
thropist, perhaps?"

"Ah. Well, I haven't met her myself, Mrs. Enerjee, but—"

"Oh, please, call me Laks. It is an abbreviation, you see, of
Lakshmi. Or would it be Laky? I believe that is the custom here,
is it not, to use first names and then cut them short as possible to
save time. For instance your name, according to this lovely big
lady here, is Batolomew, so no doubt they are calling you Batty
all the time?"

"No, not really."

"But my goodness, I am digressing. You were talking about
this Mrs. Talbot who is upsetting everybody because she is moving her whiskies, or am I not understanding properly? And is it
true that people are talking of burning down her house?"

"Er, no, I haven't heard *that* particular rumor."

"And you are not hating her yourself?"

"I haven't had time, actually," I said, looking around distract-
edly. "Look, I'm terribly sorry, but I really must . . . You see I
haven't yet paid my respects to Mrs. Hipsey, and . . ."

"You have not yet said howdy to our hostess? Oh, goodness
me," she cried, flapping her sari. "That will never do. Off you go,
then, off you go," she cried, shooing me off as if I were a school-
boy on the point of dampening the classroom lino.

As much disoriented by her peculiar speech as by this abrupt
dismissal, I lurched off in search of Mrs. Hipsey. I didn't have far
to go. She was only six feet away, still surrounded by relatives
and guests.

Mrs. Hipsey was an elderly, dignified lady, bulging in soft,
ample parabolas out of a silvery sort of gown with strings of
pearls wandering o'er hill and dale. She was regarding me surreptitiously as I turned, and something in her attitude suggested
that she was annoyed. The impression was confirmed by the way
she now called out, "Yes, I was wondering when we would have
the pleasure of meeting you, Mr. Bandy." Though she did attempt to warm the reproof with a condescending but kindly
smile.

Explaining that I hadn't wanted to interrupt her conversation,
I started forward with placating hand outstretched, and only just
in time realized that an impeccable flower bed was flaunting it-

self between me and her family, and that I was on the point of floundering through it.

That would never do. She, or more likely her gardener, had obviously made the bed with loving care. For a moment I considered jumping across it; but quite apart from the danger of tripping over the tulips, she was standing too close to the freshly weeded soil on the other side. I'd probably come down on her instep at two thousand pounds per square inch. But the brilliant display seemed to stretch for several hundred yards in each direction. It would take me so long to get around it that they would all probably be having their tea in the gazebo by the time I had completed the horticultural circumnavigation. So I didn't see what else I could do but address her across the quince, mock orange, tulips, etc.

I might just as well have leaped or floundered. The all too familiar effect of an unconventional countenance with its horselike proportions was already occurring, the inevitable reaction to my face, as if it were an instant threat to law and order. And her attitude did not mellow in the least when, coloring her censoriousness with arch tones, she remarked, "We have not seen you at church since your return to Gallop, Mr. Bandy," and my second attempt at an obsequious reply proved to be as unsatisfactory as the first. Having plainly adopted a wait-and-see attitude the moment she caught sight of me, she had now found that she hadn't had long to wait. She was regarding me with a Cyclopean eye—two Cyclopean eyes, in fact—as if I were some geometric deviation from the straight moral lines she ruled through the community. It was all too evident that I was not her idea of a dignified, God-fearing, upstanding citizen.

The rest of the mob, taking their cue from Mrs. Hipsey's manifest disapproval, proceeded to ignore me for the rest of the afternoon, except for Cluck Hipsey, who, catching a glimpse of my cuff links, waited until everybody could hear him before remarking with a sneer, "Gee whillikers, Bandy. Diamonds? With a *blazer?*"

However, I soon got my own back. I went over and sneered at their house. It had bricks sticking out all over the walls, the builders having done this deliberately, it seemed, under the impression that it enhanced the aesthetic appeal.

All in all, I was beginning to wonder if I was entirely succeeding in my role as respectable citizen. Apart from Anne Mackie, who as a Talbot employee was herself somewhat beyond the pale, the only ones who were willing to be seen with me that afternoon were Karley and his wife Kitty.

They came over while I was busily studying the gazebo, which stood highfalutingly slap dab in the middle of the garden. The size and shape of a bandstand, it was decorated with gingerbread woodwork and was surmounted by an exquisitely shaped weathercock, obediently pointing southeast. On the planks within, numerous tables were being set for tea. Two sullen-looking local girls dressed up as maids were putting out enough sandwiches and cakes to supply a factory of Stakhanovites.

"Just like an English garden party, eh, what?" said Karley as he approached with his wife on his arm. Kitty, a pretty but discontented girl, was wearing a cardigan over her spring frock, her hands bright orange with cold.

"Oh, hello, Karley, Mrs. Karley. Didn't think they'd invite you to this shindig."

"Why shouldn't they?"

"The Hipseys are Conservative supporters, aren't they?"

"Oh, they don't mind a token Liberal or two, provided we speak only when spoken to," Karley muttered, huddling close to the gazebo in case a sniper had a bead on him. "Talking about behaving ourselves, I hear you didn't hit it off too well with our hostess."

"Gets around fast, doesn't it? I'd have slunk off if I hadn't been so hungry," I said with an air of indifference; though in fact I was a bit annoyed at being treated like a coyote at a thoroughbred dog show. After all, damn it, I was a man of means. Or . . . no, I wasn't, was I? But they thought I was. "As for this being like an English garden party," I whispered meanly, looking around to make sure that Mrs. Hipsey was not in slandershot, "Mrs. Lewis would have laughed herself sick."

"Now, now, don't be snobby, old man, just because your mother-in-law was an earl's daughter or somebody."

"Well, I mean. We don't need to ape English customs; we have our own traditions in Canada."

"We do? What are they?"

"Well . . . quilting bees and barn raising, things like that."

Kitty, hugging her goose-bumped arms to her, looked at me curiously for a moment before turning back to examine the other women's frocks.

"You know what I mean. Why, I bet she's even serving cucumber sandwiches," I said sullenly and, reaching under a damp-cloth-covered plate on a nearby trolley, lifted a corner of one of the sandwiches. "See?"

I started guiltily as Mrs. Hipsey's voice megaphoned through the shrubbery.

"Come along, come along," she called out, leading a large pack of kith and kin toward us. The steps of the gazebo boomed as they trampled into the interior.

Having chivied half the guests into the gazebo, Mrs. Hipsey suddenly went all vague and frowned around at the second-best chinaware that was holding down the fluttering tablecloths. "Let me see, now, where does everyone sit?" she puffed, rattling her beads like a medicine woman. "I was going to put that new person at my table but . . . Let me see. George." This was her husband, the magistrate, a morose chap with a purple face and rounded shoulders, who looked as if he would have preferred to be in court, sentencing people. Like me, he was attired in a navy-blue blazer, though he had gone one better: he had a coat of arms on the breast pocket. "George, you sit here with Rosalie and Trevor. Or, no—perhaps with Harold and . . . No, wait a minute—Captain Karley, if you'd come over here for a moment. No, wait. I know. You two sit here . . ."

Everybody milled around, jerking up and down like rocker arms, as Mrs. Hipsey sent them first in one direction, then another. Wooden chair legs juddered and rasped over the planks as they were alternately pushed and pulled, the confusion worsened by the lack of space. The tables took up almost every square inch of the floor area. I think Mrs. Hipsey was trying to order the guests according to their estimated salaries, with the most expensive guests close to her table and the least important in the far corner, but she had not rehearsed the precedence in her own mind.

Not one to neglect his duties as a guest, I started to snake about, giving Mrs. Hipsey a hand—though out of modesty I did so as inconspicuously as possible. "Kitty, you go back there," I murmured briskly. "Miss Timmins, here you are, here's your place. And you two fellows here, come on, sit down, that's right. Mrs. Willing, you're over here. Look, let me help you. Henry, over here, please. Now let me see . . ."

"No, I know," Mrs. Hipsey shouted from behind a seething mass of people as one of the guests fell backward down the steps. "Trevor, Rosalie, you're at this table with Mr. Raymond, and—"

"But, Mother, he's sitting over there."

"And Mr. Hipsey, sir, if you wouldn't mind coming over here," I said quietly but firmly. "Now you two. Come on, come on, sit down, to make room for everybody else. That's fine. That's right, there. Perfect."

Mrs. Hipsey appeared and found her husband sitting at the table with the two maids.

"What's the meaning of this? What are you two doing there?" she bellowed as Anne Mackie caught my eye, then looked away quickly, her face scarlet.

"Ma'am, this gentleman made us—"

"Get up, get up, what d'you think you're doing? Who said you could sit down, you stupid girls?"

The maids got up, looking more mutinous than ever. Later one of them pushed an acorn into the trifle when nobody was looking.

"And who moved all the chairs away from that table?" Mrs. Hipsey blew exasperatedly. "I just don't understand what's . . . Rosalie, do get out of the way. George, you're not being the least helpful. Look, it's perfectly simple . . ."

Finally everybody was seated. I found myself in the far corner with Jake Judson, the farm equipment dealer, and his wife; Mrs. Enerjee, and Miss Rawsthorne, a lantern-jawed lady of fifty who was wearing a hat like a kindergarten raffia project, and a most unsuitable pink organdy frock that exposed the lengths of her sinewy arms. Her brachioradial muscles were the only ones present that weren't vibrating with cold.

"There, now, that's everybody settled," Mrs. Hipsey said, panting, just as the Reverend Mr. Wattle, down in the garden, tapped timidly on the gazebo and peered apologetically through the gingerbread.

"I'm awfully sorry, but I don't seem . . ." he said. So once again there was an uproar of rasping chairs as he tiptoed up the steps and slithered through the throng, to take his place on the only remaining seat, at the head of our table.

After a while things settled down and the level of conversation rose, amplified by the curved oaken ceiling of the gazebo. Mr. Judson, usually a sociable sort, seemed to sense that our end of the table was not in much favor. He was leaning the other way, as if one of us was manufacturing and distributing excessive quantities of gas bacilli. So I had only Wattle, the Indian lady, and Miss Rawsthorne to converse with.

Mr. Wattle was as tall as I was; or would have been had he not tended to hunch, as if he feared that his height might be construed as pretentiousness. Halfway through tea he began talking to me without so much as a whiffet of warning.

"Strangely enough, I had been in the Church for a number of years before I received the Call," he said. He had a peculiar habit of resuming conversations that had been initiated days previously. I realized that this was what was happening now—we had blethered together at the Wildebeest. "I was originally ordained mainly because that was what my father wanted," he murmured, "and it wasn't until one winter's day, when I was riding in a local train somewhere in the depths of Manitoba that I suddenly felt a warm hand on my shoulder and heard a voice saying to me as plain as plain could be, 'Go and visit Elfreda Ticker at once.'"

"Good heavens," I said, leaning over to hear him better. Mr. Wattle tended to mumble, as if mostly communicating with himself—and not getting through too well.

"I was most surprised," Wattle continued, "as I had not heard from Elfreda for many years. I looked at the seats behind me in the coach just in case it wasn't God, but they were entirely unoccupied; and I must admit that as I handed over my ticket to the waiting attendant I was inclined to dismiss the phenomenon, not least because Elfreda lived over a thousand miles away, in Toronto. Nevertheless in due course I journeyed thence, and do you know—I learned that *at the precise moment that I had heard*

those words on the train Elfreda was being struck on the head
by a portrait of the Right Reverend Porteus Clayburne, M.A.,
D.D., of Moral Insanity fame. Of course, by the time I reached
her," Wattle murmured, "she had long since—"

"Kicked the bucket?" I supplied sympathetically.

"—recovered. But the point is, of course, that she was employed as a cook at the Divine Healing Mission in Toronto,
which, you see, had been desperately seeking a new warden; and
there was I, turning up at precisely the right moment with the
appropriate qualifications—mainly a willingness to subsist on a
salary of two hundred a year. So I was taken on.

"Thus eleven years ago I was led by supernatural forces into
my life's work, which is to restore the fundamental purpose of
the primitive Church, not merely to preach but to heal by the
communication of divine peace and the laying on of hands."

"Heal physical afflictions, you mean? Can you do that, sir?"

"Not yet, but one has hopes," Wattle said, lapsing into a dis-
consolate silence.

Meanwhile Miss Rawsthorne was busy chatting to the Indian
lady. Like Wattle, Miss Rawsthorne was an executive member of
the Liberal constituency association. She was a tall, stringy spin-
ster who wrote poetry and had it privately printed on the presses
of the *Advertiser*. On our very first meeting she had bullied me
into purchasing six copies of her latest work, *Still Life With
Dreams*. However, that had made me a friend for life. She also
approved of me because I had fought the Bolsheviks. She
strongly disapproved of the Bolsheviks, feeling that they had
treated their royal family inconsiderately by shooting them and
dumping them down a well.

"Mind you, these tea parties of Mrs. Hipsey's are too much
like a church supper for the needy, for my taste," she was saying
—far too loudly—to Mrs. Enerjee. "I'm surprised she didn't orga-
nize you, Reverend," she went on, snatching up a salmon sand-
wich and looking at it scornfully before popping it into her muscular maw, "to give one of those long, dull sermons of yours, to
make us suitably grateful for her wet food and weak tea."

"Prepare yourself, dear lady," Wattle murmured. "She's asked
me to do so afterward."

Just as I was picking up my teacup, Miss Rawsthorne gave me

a nudge that almost sent it flying. "Talking about dull speeches, what are you doing these days, Bartholomew?"

"Oh, busily learning there's no civilian market for new aircraft these days," I grumbled. "Too much war surplus equipment available. That leaves only the military, and they keep saying they've no money."

"Take my advice. Manufacture donkey engines. There'll always be a demand for donkey engines."

Mrs. Enerjee stirred under her layers of silk and cotton. "My goodness, yes, I am understanding that you are a high flier, Mr. Bandee," she exclaimed, shifting in her seat. And she started to ask the usual silly questions about aviation.

At least she was showing an interest in the subject, which was more than could be said for anybody else. Or so I thought. Until, while I was expatiating on the advanced features of the Gander, the amphibian that I had been constructing on Long Island and would be collecting in a few days—as I was busy exaggerating its capabilities in the hope that Mrs. Enerjee was a rich investor in disguise—she placed her stockinged foot on my knee under the table.

Her expression of rapt interest—as much of it as could be discerned under the chocolate coating and the filmy headdress—stayed in place even if her foot did not. It was slowly sliding sideways and flattening itself along the inside of my thigh.

Though the sensation was thrilling enough, and was raising my cardiac revs to a spectacular rate, I was pretty shocked at this bold behavior. At a tea party, too. I had always thought of Eastern ladies as being decorous, judging by the one I had met in Paris in 1918. This was a Bahreinian lady encountered at Madame de Hautcloque's salon, who was so modest that not once during the entire evening did she lower her yashmak . . . though, come to think of it, while determinedly concealing her face she had not been the least disconcerted when a garden breeze caused her gown to billow to the waist, exposing a pair of bare café au lait limbs and an unclad behind. . . . Gad, that was a sight . . . if only I hadn't been under the influence of cocaine at the time . . .

However, it was Mrs. Enerjee I was talking about. Being an imperturbable sort of person, except in an emergency or other untoward circumstance, I managed to keep on talking about the Goose—Gander—as I had no wish to draw any further attention to myself that afternoon.

"Well, I must say it is all sounding wonderfully exciting," Mrs. Enerjee said, wearing an expression that I now recognized as one of mischievous challenge rather than of unbridled lust. Not that that deterred her from further exploration, for she was now running her silken foot slowly up the inside straight. And not only that but she was wiggling her toes at the same time.

Even Mr. Wattle was beginning to notice something. He was glancing at me curiously, possibly wondering why I was talking faster and faster on a rising octave. In desperation I attempted to move my chair back a few inches, but it was already jammed against the latticework of the gazebo.

Mrs. Enerjee's stockinged foot had now advanced so far that one toenail, presumably that of the big toe, was transmitting vibrations through the flannel material of my trousers and up a certain vertical row of buttons. Though the sensation was pleasurable enough—quite excruciatingly so—I had enough to worry about without getting involved with strange women—and Mrs. Enerjee was certainly strange enough. Besides, it was producing an uncomfortable textile binding effect . . .

"We all know what's going on, you know," Miss Rawsthorne said suddenly.

I got such a fright I actually ceased gibbering; until with overwhelming relief I realized that she was replying to something Wattle had said. They were discussing the Talbot affair, that subject having inevitably spread from the rest of the gathering to our table.

Happily the subject provided instant relief, for the moment it was broached Mrs. Enerjee ceased her metacarpal reconnaissance and her sly, slow eyes went all sharp, as if an operation for cataract had just been performed.

"My goodness, you are talking again about Mrs. Talbot?" she asked.

"I fear so, dear lady," Wattle said, touching her saried arm. "The Talbot move, you see, is such a grave blow to our local temperance movement."

"Goodness me, I am not quite understanding," Mrs. Enerjee

said in her singsong voice, as she finally withdrew her foot. "How can moving her whiskies out of your beautiful town be a grave blow to people who are not believing in whiskies?"

"Well, you see, dear lady, it took the temperance movement half a century to reconcile itself to the presence of a large distillery in its midst. There would, of course, have been no problem if Talbots had been a minor enterprise. Had it been a small company the temperancers would probably have succeeded in closing it down. Like knowledge, a little whisky is a dangerous thing. But Talbots produced so much *spiritus fermenti* that they could be neither suppressed nor ignored. So we placated our consciences with the thought that the distillery was essential for the economic well-being of the community. But now Mrs. Talbot is affronting the temperancers all over again by abrogating her company's hard-won respectability."

"I've been trying to get up a petition to have her hanged," Miss Rawsthorne said with a sharp nod of her raw cranium.

"My dear Miss Rawsthorne, that's going a little far, don't you think? We should surely not consider anything as extreme as placing her *in extremis*," Wattle chunnered, dabbing up a few crumbs from the salmon plate with a moistened forefinger. "I understand that the face of a hanged criminal is a trifle repellent to genteel sensibilities—the tongue blackened and engorged, the eyes bulging onto the cheeks, the limbs twitching for minutes on end, not to mention the abrupt release of waste matter, both fluid and—"

"Yes, yes, all right, forget hanging her," Miss Rawsthorne said hurriedly, just as one of the maids plonked a bowlful of runny trifle in front of her.

As Miss Rawsthorne averted her eyes from the mess and her mind from the conversation, I sat there slowly subsiding, and wishing now that I had seized Mrs. Enerjee's foot while I had the chance; for instance, while she was drinking her tea. I could have hauled on her foot, slowly and inexorably, causing her to slide down and disappear from sight, inch by inch. It would have supplied an admirable illustration of Mr. Wattle's thesis, as she appeared to drink herself under the table.

I was also wishing for a thoroughly uncomfortable April afternoon to end so that I could go home and mumble accusingly at

myself for not sticking to my original plans. For this was the day
I had intended traveling down to Long Island to collect my new
airplane and fly it back to Gallop.

I had put off the trip, of course, purely in order to cultivate
the Hipseys. What a waste of time it had all been, I thought, as I
sat goose-bumped in the gazebo—too late even to call it a belvedairy, now—not knowing that at least one encounter that afternoon would prove to be exceedingly useful—a future benefit
nicely balanced by the harm I would do myself by postponing
the trip for a week and picking the very weekend that the leader
of my political party would also select for a quick trip to Long
Island.

You Can't Quite See Us in the Fog

Mackenzie King was not the most courageous man in the western hemisphere, but I suppose his reaction to the sudden appearance out of a sinister mist of two unnatural figures, one yellow and mauve, and the other green, could be considered excusable, especially as one of the creatures was dripping what appeared to be viridescent blood.

This incident, which took place at Montauk, Long Island, on Easter Sunday that year, has never been mentioned in any of the accounts of Mackenzie King's life, but I can vouch for its authenticity, for I was there; and as everyone knows who has followed my inspiring exploits so far, I am not the least prone to exaggeration.

The fact that the Prime Minister took great pains to keep that Easter vacation on Long Island a close secret may explain why the anecdote has not been recorded elsewhere. Presumably the reason for this discretion was that his lady friend, Joan Patteson, was with him. Though their friendship was undoubtedly platonic —the concept of Mackenzie King and sex simply refuses to conjoin even in the wildest imagination—he was still as concerned for his reputation as if he had been towing a trainload of henna-haired doxies. In fact, paying a premium on his policy of utter respectability, he had also brought along the lady's husband, Godfroy; though whether the premium also covered Godfroy's sense of respectability is not known.

The other unnatural figure involved in the incident was Jim Boyce, a wartime acquaintance, former Department of External

Affairs official, and sex maniac. I had met Boyce in the American
Flying Club on East Thirty-eighth Street where I was staying for
a couple of days while readying the Gander for the flight home.
He had come down to New York to apply for a job in advertising. Unsuccessfully as it turned out, as they hadn't considered
Boyce to be quite the sort of person they were looking for. He
had turned up for the interview with a thoroughly bruised face,
the result of a thumping he had received from some young
woman's fiancé. The Madison Avenue types had preferred three-
color layouts in their ads rather than in the faces of their executives.

Learning that I was flying home the next morning, he had
asked for a lift, and as there was plenty of room in the monoplane with its enclosed cabin and its open flying cockpit
squinched between the cabin and the engine, I was agreeable
enough. Boyce was not quite so keen, though, when he arrived
at the American Standard Studio lot on Long Island at six in the
morning and saw the yellow amphibian standing there in the
wet, gray dawn.

"What in God's name is it?" he asked.

"It's a Gander, of course, you miserable old failure," I said
heartily, as if a Gander were a well-known make. Being invariably considerate of the feelings of others, I didn't think he would
wish to know that it was an experimental machine built by a
pure amateur.

"But it's only got one wing. Who ever heard of an airplane
with only one wing? Are you sure it'll fly?"

"Course. I've flown it for, oh, I don't know how many hours," I
replied; truthfully. I wasn't sure whether it was four hours or
four and a quarter.

"Good God, it's got wheels *and* floats. What kind of a beast is
this?"

"It was constructed in the Glenn Martin works," I replied. But
he looked only slightly reassured, so I refrained from explaining
that the Martin company had merely constructed it to my
specifications—after they had stated that they would not be held
responsible.

"I don't know," Boyce said, shivering in the brine-scented

gloom. A thin sea mist was wisping over the deserted studio lot. "I think maybe I'll take the train after all."

"Thought you said you were stony broke," I grunted as I walked around the amphibian to make sure that nobody had backed a truck into it during the night.

He mumbled something, following me closely as I did the line check, as if he were afraid to be alone with the Gander.

I could guess how he was feeling. With its high wing and unique substructure, the machine was pretty unconventional. I had gone for a single-wing configuration even though the vast majority of manufacturers were still sticking to the tried and tested biplane. But it had flown well enough, after I replaced the first engine, which had proved so underpowered that the top speed and the stalling speed practically coincided. I was immensely proud of the Gander, an aircraft specially designed for Canadian conditions, i.e., appallingly long distances, lack of hard, flat places to land on, ghastly winter weather, and the high cost of getting to all those appalling, lumpy, or freezing places. I'd spent part of '21 and much of '22 designing and building it, starting with the outline sketches and the weight estimates, wing area and layout work (my ideas mostly pinched from other designers, especially Glenn Martin, whom I had met while flying out of Cleveland for the U.S. airmail service), then passing the drawings to a qualified engineer for the stress calculations, to make sure that the thing would hold together in the air. Then the drafting stage, to produce the drawings of the various parts, so that they could be fabricated in a workshop.

The result, rolled out at Cleveland late the previous year, was the object that was now dripping with condensation on a deserted film studio lot on Long Island: a handsome monoplane, smoothly faired and tapered from engine cowling to tail root. I had seen no reason why an airplane should not be comely as well as functional, a design philosophy borrowed from the French, who traditionally turned out the cleanest-looking machines in the skies. So if there had been no need for landing gear it would have looked very graceful indeed.

However, it could hardly remain in the air all the time, so to enable it to plonk down on both land and water, long floats had been added, and also a pair of wheels that could be cranked up

and down by a clever piece of linkage geometry operated by a
wooden wheel outside the flying cockpit. Which made the Gander probably the world's first airplane to have a sort of re-
tractable undercarriage.

Otherwise the structure was conventional enough, with lami-
nated longerons joined by spruce struts and rectangular trans-
verse formers in the fuselage, and some tubular steel in the center section to take the strain of the high wing.

I was eager to explain to Boyce how everything worked, and
to boast about its unique features, but I couldn't do so without
revealing the frightful truth: that it was my own invention. He
was looking apprehensive enough as it was, as he stood on the
starboard float, ready to turn the starter handle.

Anyway, if *I* felt confident enough about flying the Gander the
three hundred fifty miles to Gallop, there was no reason for him
to be looking all knotted.

So I just called out, "Switch on, petrol on, throttle advanced,"
and waited for him to crank up. A minute later the engine was
bellowing and he was clambering reluctantly into the right-hand
seat of the cockpit.

Unfortunately we ran into trouble only a few minutes after
taking off. We had barely strained up to two thousand feet into
the dawn when the engine began to act up. Even before the
spluttering started, Boyce had been clutching the side of the
cockpit with carved ivory knuckles. Quite apart from his uneas-
iness at flying in an unfamiliar aircraft, as a former aviator he
disliked being piloted by anybody else, even when the going was
as smooth as celluloid. Now, with a tubercular engine hacking
away a few feet in front of him, he looked as if he were wondering how he would fare in heaven.

I wasn't worried, of course. After all, the engine was a tried
and tested piece of equipment. An Armstrong Siddeley Puma, I
had obtained it for fifteen dollars from a wrecker's yard.

"Don't worry," I sang out, "it'll settle down after a bit." But as
we faltered up Long Island, the coughing fits of the Puma began
to make even me a trifle uneasy, especially as the visibility below
was fast deteriorating. As for Jim Boyce, he was staring in a distinctly petrified way at the altimeter, which was unwinding at an

enthusiastic pace. Now he was gaping over the side, at the curly banks of mist that were rolling inland from the Atlantic.

"Don't just sit there, do something," he screamed, not the least ashamed of his hackneyed phrase.

"It's all right, it's probably just moisture in the carburetor," I hollered back, averting my eyes squeamishly from his colorful face. With all those fading bruises, it looked like one of those maps that show areas of scarce rainfall, lowland, mountainous terrain, and so forth, all yellow ocher with mauve patches, and the tributary of a split lip. With pallid panic added, the map was now illustrating the arctic wastes as well.

"We'll have moisture in *our* carburetors if you don't do something," he yelled.

As the seashore, dimly discerned through drifting banks of mist, was now hurtling up to meet us, I gave up tinkering with the engine controls and shut off all the spluttering and banging noises, and stuck a leather arm down the left side of the cockpit and hurriedly unwound the landing gear, even though I had only just finished winding it up.

I had barely time to lock the wheels in place when the sand started rushing about three feet below. A quick jerk on the stick and a second later we'd thumped down on a stretch of corrugated beach near Montauk at the eastern end of the island.

It took only a few minutes to locate and rectify the trouble—muck in the jet—but by then fresh quantities of fog had rolled in from the sea, reducing visibility to the distance between Boyce's two black eyes. Being thus unable to take off again, we decided to mooch inland in search of some early morning eatery. By the time we'd finished a second breakfast the fog would probably have cleared.

Montauk was only a few hundred yards away, but we must have veered in the wrong direction, for after twenty minutes none of its scattered dwellings had appeared. We thought of returning to the aircraft only to discover that we could no longer hear the slurping of the ocean to guide us back to the shore. We were enveloped in fog and silence. To make matters worse, as we felt our way through the clammy billows, conversing in whispers—the eerie hush was having that effect—I tripped over a tuft of grass and sprawled in a stagnant pool, covering my white shirt, hands, and face in slime.

But after a momentary annoyance at ruining my shirt and some yeching as I plucked away slippery strands of weed, even that further contretemps could not ruin the euphoria through which I was still gliding. Confident of ultimate success as an aircraft designer and constructor, I felt as happy as a squirrel in spring, and every prospect pleased, even if the present prospect was obscured by rolling banks of mist. The only jarring note being Jim Boyce's voice as he trudged up a bank of long yellow grass, saying peevishly, "There's a railway track just over here— it won't lead anywhere, of course."

I squelched up the bank and together we considered the rusty rails, trying to decide which way to follow them. Boyce solved the problem by shrugging irritably and turning to the right. So I followed, not the least put off by his surly manner. In fact I felt quite sorry for him, in a smug sort of way. He was far worse off than I was; no money, few prospects, and considerably more unemployed. He was so hard up he would have been stranded in New York had I not offered him the lift home.

Mind you, being unemployed was entirely his own fault. After the war he had joined the Department of External Affairs in some minor capacity but had been forced to resign earlier this year, on account of losing one of his socks. Though quite nondescript in appearance, with lumpy, Prussian-blue jowls and large, cowlike eyes, he was irresistible to women. A few magic passes and they went down like skittles. His secret was that he genuinely adored women and let them know it by enveloping them in such warmth, sympathy, and affection that few seemed able to resist him. I knew; I'd seen him operate, watching him with a jealousy cleverly disguised as moral indignation, as he went to work, wooing and mooing.

Unhappily for him, one of his conquests had been the wife of his department chief. His boss had come home unexpectedly one evening to find Boyce chatting nonchalantly to the wife with one of his socks missing and fresh teeth marks in his neck.

So now, as Boyce grumbled his way along the track, I gave him a pat on the back and said, "Never mind, Boyce, things could be worse. I'm sure you'll get a job sooner or later. Security

guard on a sewage farm, perhaps? Or you could apprentice yourself to a slush jollier."

"What the hell's that?"

"I don't know—I saw it in a list of occupations somewhere. It
sounded just right for you."

I gathered from the way he looked at me that I hadn't entirely
succeeded in raising his morale. He confirmed this a moment
later when he muttered, "'S all right for you, you're rich, after
making an ass of yourself in those ghastly movies of yours."

"Don't tell anyone in Gallop but actually I haven't much left."

"Down to your last few grand, are you? My heart bleeds for
you. You should be in my position, friendless, penniless, and
pointless—and now lost in a fog after only just surviving another
of your controlled crashes. Personally I hope we never manage
to find that bloody aircraft again, there's something funny about
the way it rears up like a horse—or like its master."

"There, there, Boyce," I said, giving him another pat. "You'll
feel better after you've had a cup of coffee."

"Eh, shaddup."

At which point, just as I was about to cheer him up still further, we both stopped dead at the unexpected sight before us.

"Say, will you look at that," I whispered.

Looming out of the mist, just twenty feet away, was a railway
car. It was standing alone on the rusty track, sheltered between
two banks of dune grass.

We stood and looked at it in considerable surprise. It was obviously no ordinary carriage. There were no railway company
markings on it, for one thing. It was faultlessly painted in royal
blue and had been lovingly polished. Even in the wet mist it
gleamed as if it had just come from the manufacturer. The
bogies and all the other ironmongery were totally free of rust.
The couplings at each end shone like conjurers' puzzles. There
was not a strain, a smear, or a streak of grease anywhere. I had
never seen such perfect coachwork.

We stared at it in wonder, then simultaneously looked around
for the rest of the train; but there was nothing else in sight, not
even an engine. The weedy track it stood on curved mysteriously
into nothingness.

"Must be one of those private cars," Boyce whispered. "Owned by the president of the railroad or somebody."

Fancy blinds were drawn on several of the windows. No lights were visible anywhere.

"Look, they've even put down fresh gravel for it," Boyce pointed out. It was true. Brand-new gravel had been scattered along the track on both sides of the car, though the clean white stones ended only a few feet beyond the ends of the coach.

I crunched over the gravel to the only door on our side, stepped up and tried the handle, but it was locked.

"You're not aiming to go in there, are you?"

"Eh? Why not? They'll be able to tell us where we are."

"You can't rouse them at this time in the morning," Boyce whispered anxiously. "I doubt they'll appreciate the dawn's early light."

"I don't see why not. *I'm* up, so I don't see why *they* should be allowed to sleep in," I said, and knocked on the door.

As Boyce retreated a couple of steps to draw on a thicker over-coat of mist, I tried again, but there was no response. So I walked around the car, followed somewhat uneasily by Boyce who, for a former naval man, was remarkably timid. Presumably working for a government department had crushed his sense of enterprise.

On the far side there was a large wooden box by the side of the track, half filled with sand. The train window directly above it was uncurtained, so I clambered onto the box to see inside.

As there was a three-foot gap between the box and the side of the car, I had to bridge the gap by overbalancing and slapping my hands onto the glass for support. This accomplished, I peered inside. And exclaimed faintly.

"What, what?" Boyce whispered from below.

"Pretty luxurious inside. Come and look."

"Anybody in there?"

"No," I said, adding as he climbed up beside me, "not that I can see, anyway."

Only there was, for just as Boyce also overbalanced in order to plant his palms on the window and peer inside, there was a movement from within, and a moment later a counterpane was thrust back and a roundish, saggy sort of face appeared on the pillow.

The eyes opened, looked at the window, then closed again. Then flicked wide open.

Instantly the middle-aged man in the bunk sprang up as if the mattress had caught fire. But instead of leaping out of bed he shoved himself rearward with a convulsive movement and cracked against the partition behind him, his legs drawn up and his arms outspread. He looked as if he were trying to force himself backward through the handsomely paneled woodwork, or to re-enact the Crucifixion.

His eyes and mouth gaped, and his hair, what there was of it, actually stood on end—unless it had gone all spiky like that because of the dishevelment of sleep.

I immediately divined that the double apparition at the window was causing a certain amount of perturbation in the occupant's nightshirted breast. Awakening from a dream and being confronted by two figures, each apparently ten feet tall, one with a yellow-ocher and mauve face and the other with a face green as putrefaction, and both looming out of a supernatural mist, was perhaps not the most satisfying way to greet the dawn. Still, I expected him to get over his surprise quickly enough, and to hasten the process I smiled in at him.

Instead of reassuring the occupant, this seemed to increase his terror. In fact he was now trying to climb the partition, scrabbling frantically at the fancy woodwork. At the same time he started to scream.

Boyce uttered an expletive and tried to push himself off from the window. But he was in too much of a hurry and overbalanced again, so that his hands once again slapped wetly onto the glass. And when he tried again he bumped into me, the collision not only forcing him to resume contact with the window but causing me to run my palms over the window as well in a desperate attempt to regain my own balance.

These distinctly unnatural movements upset the occupant of the stateroom more than ever. His cries of terror could be heard quite clearly through the stout sides of the private car. As Boyce and I alternately pushed away from the window and overbalanced back onto it, smearing the glass with Haitian slime, I sup-

pose that to the chap inside it must have seemed as if we were
trying, in a ghastly zombie sort of fashion, to get in at him.

It was presumably this dread mime that finally uncemented
him from the partition. Still shrieking and gibbering, he flung
himself off the bunk and over to the stateroom door. There he
proceeded to wrench at the handle, though even from where I
stood I could see that the door opened outward, not inward.
When he failed to claw it open, he screamed even more intem-
perately. That he was attempting to get out without turning his
back on the window made his frenzied efforts less effective than
ever.

I must say, I couldn't help feeling a certain disdain at the un-
manly conduct of the vaguely familiar figure within, though I
did try to calm him down by calling out of the mist in a hollow
voice, "Don't panic, don't panic. It's only us," at the same time
plastering my weed-green phiz closer to the glass, until it occurred to me that this effect—my lips spread over the surface like
crimson maggots and my green nose flattened sideways—was upsetting him more than ever, judging by the way he was now
beating at the door with his fists and sobbing in helpless funk.

Finally he discovered that a simple turn of the handle and a
push was all that was needed to save him from the living dead.
He was through the door in microseconds, now clawing his way
through the anxious-looking people who had gathered outside in
the corridor—and who had probably been yanking at the door on
their side while the occupant was hauling on it from the other.
One of the figures out there was a shocked-looking woman in a
dressing gown, later assumed to be Mrs. Patteson.

At the same time lights were beginning to appear at all the
other windows of the private car, and it was positively rocking
with panic-stricken movement and reverberating with anxious
cries. Which galvanized Boyce into one final effort to restore
himself to the vertical.

Managing to do so, he reached over and seized my collar and
wrenched me upright as well.

"Let's get out of here," quoth he in a shaky voice. "You know
who that was, don't you? King."

"The King! I *thought* he looked familiar."

"No, no, King, King—Mackenzie bleeding King—the Prime Minister!"

"Oh," I said; then, after a moment's thought: "In that case perhaps you're right, Boyce. Perhaps this isn't the right time of day for a social call."

But Boyce was already in midair, having taken a flying leap off the box, his feet already pedaling in anticipation of contact with the yellow grass ten feet away.

Likewise I abandoned the railway box, and seconds later we were both hurtling back across the dunes and through the mist, which was now starting to clear. We were giggling rather childishly by the time we got back to the seaside and saw the amphibian resting on the hard, corrugated sand a mile farther east, our spirits quite restored by the adventure. Fifteen minutes later we were aloft, the chill wind reaming our earholes as we sat in the open cockpit between the engine and the cabin, the shared experience having transformed a wary acquaintanceship into a lasting friendship; though, as I was soon to discover, it had also created an equally lasting enmity.

The Distillery

Two days after returning home with the Gander, I was surprised to receive a note from Mrs. Talbot on company stationery inviting me to call on her as soon as possible.

Naturally curious to find out what she wanted, I took her at her word and drove to the distillery that same day. However, I parked some distance from the main entrance at the end of the river road and approached it on foot, in case any of the townspeople were spying on me. Not that I cared a fig about public opinion, but it seemed to me, as I dodged from tree to tree along the riverbank, that there was no sense in *ostentatiously* fraternizing with the enemy.

The Talbot Distillery sprawled along the Rideau River at the eastern edge of town. It comprised an assortment of wooden buildings and several grimy brick warehouses, some of them as high as nine stories. This made them by far the tallest structures in Gallop. The most distinctive feature of the complex, though, was the round pump house. It was located on the banks of the river from which the distillery sucked its clean water, and into which it discharged its mash, slurry, fusel oil, muck, mire, old bottle caps, etc. I had seen the brown stain many times from the air as it swirled sluggishly downriver toward the town waterworks.

There were only two entrances through the high fence that surrounded the complex. Naturally I used the main gate at the end of the river road, as the other entrance, past a guard hut on the south side, was for freight trains. I had not made an appointment, so I was held up for ten minutes by the uniformed guards before somebody arrived to escort me to the office.

The escort turned out to be Mrs. Mackie, looking businesslike but elegant enough in a calf-length gray dress with a white lace collar. As we walked across the open square around which the distillery was untidily arranged, I asked her if all the heavy security meant that they were expecting an attack from a band of enraged Gallopians.

"Oh no. Naturally a distillery is always well protected," she said coolly, striding over the dirt with her strong legs. "If there's an attack, it's more likely to come from a band of thirst-maddened rather than enraged citizens."

As we approached one of the tall brick buildings, signboarded as *Excise Bonded Warehouse J,* I slowed down to peer through the open entrance; whereupon Mrs. Mackie asked, "Would you care for a tour of the distillery, Mr. Bandy?"

"No, thanks—I've given up drinking."

She regarded me uncertainly for a moment before glancing at her watch. "As a matter of fact," she said, "we have a few minutes to spare. Mrs. Talbot is"—for some reason she colored slightly before completing the sentence—"is conferring with the chief excise officer."

"M'o yes? I suppose he's the one who makes sure the government gets its cut before the liquor is shipped out."

"That's what he's paid for, yes," she replied.

Noting a certain stiffness in her tone, I glanced at her curiously, but she was careful to avoid my eye.

"This is where the various liquors are kept, to mature," she went on, gesturing at the rows and rows of barrels inside the huge warehouse. "There's over twenty thousand white oak barrels in this one warehouse alone."

"Mercy me."

"Some of the whisky has been here for twelve years."

"Can't get rid of it, eh?"

"Course we can, if we wish. It's supposed to stay here that long. It's used for blending with the new spirits," she said. And mechanically, as if she had said it all a hundred times, she proceeded to give a lengthy lecture on the distilling process for rye whisky, which was apparently made not from rye but from corn.

"First the corn is mechanically chopped into small pieces, then heated in pressure cookers," she explained. "Later the yeast is added. That's the fermentation stage, which takes from three to five days. The result is what we call distiller's beer—perhaps we'll have time to show you the copper vats. Next the distillation process, which produces a pure grain spirit. After that the blending takes place, using the material in these barrels to give color to the clear liquid and produce a fine, mellow— You're not the least interested in all this, are you?"

I went on nodding intelligently for several seconds before her concluding words fluttered into my belfry. We looked at each other; and grinned simultaneously.

I don't know what my smile did for me, but hers quite transformed her. For a moment she looked like the girl she must have been before undergoing such rough handling by her vamoosing Scotsman. I found that I no longer disliked her in the least.

Twenty minutes later we arrived at the administration building where, in a large but underpopulated outer office, I was passed over to Mrs. Talbot's private secretary. "See you later," Anne said with a nonchalant wave and just the faintest note of interrogation in her voice, as if she would not be averse to seeing me later.

The private secretary was not quite so friendly. A thin-faced, angry-looking girl, she was one of those who would soon be losing her job and was apparently determined to take out her resentment on others, even such an expensively tailored chap as myself. She had me shifting about in front of her desk for over a minute before looking up and asking sharply, "Is she expecting you?"

I explained that, no, but I had received a note from Mrs. Talbot, asking me to call round at my earliest convenience.

"But you don't have an appointment?"

"No."

She started to snap dismissively; but then suddenly stopped and glanced quickly around the office. There was only one other clerk in sight, a gray-tonsured Tiresias, whose sleeves, tourniqueted with rubber bands, were buried in crackling bills and manifests.

"In that case," she said, a mean smile pinching her features, and gesturing at the scarred and battered door behind her, "go right in."

When I barged in in my usual Whippet tank fashion, I received four surprises in an arithmetical progression of intensity. The first was the contrast between the dark, stuffy outer office and Mrs. Talbot's room. It was flooded to the moldy moldings in blinding sunlight from the uncurtained windows. The second was that Philippa Talbot was an auburn-haired knockout. The third was that she was still conferring with the chief excise officer, Mr. Jewell, though not at all in a conventional business posture. Mr. Jewell was naked from clavicle to patella, lying face down on the leather sofa against the far wall with his trousers down, while the president of Talbot Distillers Limited was busily massaging his shiny white buttocks with palm-oiled palms.

The chief excise officer even had a cushion under his stomach, to afford his excitement greater ground clearance. Or, no, it wasn't a cushion, it was the rest of his clothes, bunched up to form a cushion.

"Oh. I see you're busy," I said. "Um . . ." I thought for a minute. "I could come back later if that was more convenient," I said.

"No, no, I was just seeing him off," Mrs. Talbot said breathlessly.

Of the two, Mr. Jewell was perhaps the more flustered. A blue-veined fellow wearing an emergency life belt of fat around his waist, his reaction was as drastic as it must have been painful. In an attempt to conceal the evidence of his passive gratification, he rolled off the couch and smacked noisily to the floor, still face down, with results that would certainly be painful when the neurons in a particular peninsula of his nervous system recovered from the shock; from which location he attempted to haul up his underwear and trousers—not an easy task, partly because of the prone position, but mostly because his underwear had knotted below his pudgy quarters.

"I was just making sure the goods were in bond," he gasped obscurely, temporarily abandoning his drawers and struggling upright with his shiny back to us.

"He has a bad back," Mrs. Talbot explained, her face matching her hair, as I stood there, shamelessly scanning the customs man's rippling, oleaginous dorsal surface.

His front was not in much better condition either. As he hopped around, wrestling with his underwear, it looked decidedly the worse for wear, despite the physiotherapy. His stomach, which had also been oiled, had dabbed up a layer of dust from the office carpet, and his nose was bleeding. He had apparently rapped it during his precipitate descent; unless, of course, it tended to hemorrhage during moments of crisis.

When she saw the blood, Mrs. Talbot's reaction was distinctly peculiar. Her embarrassment, which was not particularly acute to start with, as if it were quite normal for her to smooth her business transactions in this fashion, vanished completely, to be replaced by a look not of concern but of utter revulsion.

"Oooh, look at the blood," she whispered, turning as white as a cyclamen. For a moment I thought she was going to thump the deck as well. And when Mr. Jewell continued to bleed shamelessly, she actually fled from the office.

She returned only after Mr. Jewell had made his sanguinary but far from sanguine departure. By then she was looking reasonably composed, if still a trifle pale; though her actions remained odd. When she reentered, she turned and locked the door.

I looked at her in alarm and clutched defensively at my breeks. But apparently she was merely testing the lock, for she then proceeded to yank on the knob—the doorknob, that is. And when the door opened with very little resistance, she studied the mechanism in a decidedly thin-lipped manner, before unlocking it again.

It was only then that I recollected the snapping sound it had made as I marched in.

However, she made no reference to the faulty lock but instead said with an apologetic laugh, "I just can't stand other people's blood, you see."

"Oh."

"I never have been able to. It makes me sick. I don't mind my own blood so much—in fact, periodically, I greet it with relief—but other people's . . . red matter, it revolts me, especially when they practically flaunt it, like when I was a li'ul girl"—she had a

New York accent—"and my daddy's best friend cut himself in
the bathroom one afternoon, and I walked in and slipped in a
great big pool of the stuff, and Mama came running in in her
pajama top and found me chewing the shower curtain, and soon
after that, Daddy went away, and I never saw him again.
Heavens," she said with a laugh, retreating behind her fat oak
desk and almost disappearing into the dazzling sunlight from the
window behind her, "I often think there might be something in
my past, like that guy Froude says, to explain why I turn against
people who've hurt themselves." She took a deep breath to slow
herself down, perhaps realizing that she had been babbling from
the moment I arrived. "Anyway, that's enough about that. Usually I can't even bear to pronounce the word."

"What word?"

With rather a sharp movement she placed a chair in front of
her desk and indicated that I was to sit. "Well, this is very nice,"
she said, snatching a cigarette from a gold case. "I'm *so* pleased
you were able to call on me so promptly."

"Yes, I thought I'd come right away."

"I noticed," she said, jamming the cigarette into an ivory cigarette holder as if damming a leak in the Zuider Zee. "You see,
I felt I just had to meet you again."

Again? The woman was still disoriented. We had never met
before. I'd have remembered *her,* all right.

She studied me thoughtfully for a moment, clicking the holder
against her teeth, then sat down rather heavily in her own chair;
whereupon, as she unblocked the light, I was hit full in the face
by the sun.

I wasn't sure whether she had maneuvered me into this position because she felt I deserved to be in a solar spotlight or because she wanted to blind me. In any event, though she could
see me in all my sunlit glory, all I could now see of her was that
she was wearing a halo.

"Whatever you've heard about me," I said warily, and blinking away like a stupefied lizard, "it's greatly exaggerated, I assure you."

By then her voice was beginning to recover some of its
warmth. "I'm sure it's not," her voice said from somewhere in
the middle of a sea of red corpuscles and slithering silver fila-

ments. "My Mrs. Mackie is very thorough about things like that. To begin with, I know that you have the reputation in aviation circles of being the most skilled, experienced, and daring pilot on the continent."

"Of course, people don't *always* exaggerate," I mused.

"In fact I'm really amazed at the range of your accomplishments, Mr. Bandy, right from the time when you were one of the most brilliant students at the University of Toronto, until forced by the circumstances of the war to volunteer, first for the infantry, then the air corps, where you quickly became a legend."

"Fortunately a living legend."

"As for your being stalwart, fearless, quick-witted, and blessed with a no'able power of personality, I don't need any reports on that, now that I can see for myself."

"M'm," I riposted quick-wittedly; but then, unable to think of anything else to say, lowered my eyelids and massaged away a riot of colors.

"However," said the insinuating voice behind the glare, "I know you're too modest to want me to go on with this recital of your virtues and characteristics—"

"No, it's all right, carry on."

"—in case you thought I was trying to flatter you," Mrs. Talbot concluded; and a moment later a chair scraped and a pair of plump, dimpled knees hove into view. Apparently wishing to appear less formal, she had come round the desk and drawn up a chair so close to mine that our knees were practically smooching.

Tremendously impressed by her honesty and sincerity, I twisted sideways out of the radiation for a better view and, as the abstract painting on my eyelids faded, saw her clearly for the first time.

She did not in the least resemble the picture I'd composed after listening to all the gossip and slander. Somehow I'd visualized her as being a red-nosed harridan with raw knuckles and a voice suitable to a livestock auction. Instead, only her hair was red; so flamingly so in the sunlight that I felt like rushing off for a fire extinguisher; while the voice she was now using could have been used for brushing the cat.

As for her face, it was as pleasant, direct, and honest as her assessment of me had been—as I perceived the moment I wrenched my gaze from her chock-full blouse, which was tucked rather carelessly into her black skirt. Even so, the curves above and below the narrow waist would have triumphed over any dishevelment short of an ensemble of barley sacks.

All in all, despite her forty years, she would have won a leading role in my untrammeled fantasies had Mr. Jewell's gleaming rump not kept pressing upon the memory.

The most dominant feature of her face now proved to be a pair of dark, bold eyes that made me feel as if I were being stripped of clothes and pretensions, right down to the skin, bone, and bank account; this last impression arising from her next words, which indicated that she had completed her course in flattery. "We've also found out," she said silkily, "that you're not quite as well off as you pretend, Mr. Bandy."

I blinked, wondering how she'd found me out.

"Please don't be offended," she added, laying a placating hand on my knee. "I only mention it because it gives me the courage to ask if you'd care to do a small job for us."

"Oh ar?"

"As you know, we'll be moving to Montreal round about October," she went on, "and the preparations have kind of interrupted our export trade. We need to find a way to ship emergency supplies to a certain destination, to keep the market going until the Montreal plant is in operation." She paused, arching her eyebrows archly.

I thought about it for a moment, then: "I suppose you're talking about the U.S. market."

She patted my knee approvingly and nodded. "Of course. And to come to the point, Bart—may I call you Bart?—a short time ago when I saw you flying around in that huge airplane of yours —the Vimy, that is, not the new one—I had this really spiffing idea I thought you might be interested in. Everything I've learned about you suggests that you might be just the man for it. I hope I'm not being too obscure?"

"You're talking about rumrunning to the U.S. by air."

"Of course," she said, as casually as if she were asking me to drop a letter in the mailbox if I happened to be passing one.

"In other words, breaking a few American laws."

"Good heavens, nobody here thinks of it as breaking the law," tittered she. "Your government regards the export trade to the States as a perfectly legitimate activity."

Which was true enough. The government was well aware that rivers of booze were flowing south, washing away great chunks of the Volstead Act. Naturally the Americans had protested about the trade, but Ottawa had blandly replied that none of its laws were being broken and saw no reason why it should help the Americans to enforce theirs. Besides, Ottawa believed that the trade was contributing to the balance of payments.

Actually the distilleries were also supplying the home market with plenty of alcohol, despite domestic prohibition. Regiments of homegrown bootleggers seemed able to obtain unlimited quantities of the stuff. And if there were no friendly neighborhood bootleggers available, you could always go to the medical profession. Patients seemed to have little difficulty in persuading the family doctor that their nerves or digestion required a periodic six-ounce injection of C_2H_5OH. Most of Dr. McKay's income, for instance, came from this source. Or if your doctor was sick or your bootlegger was temporarily strapped, you could always fall back on wine. In Ontario the wine lobby had ensured that the populace could continue to guzzle any amount of the stuff, which had become steadily more potent over the years, until now it was little more than pure alcohol in which a few grapeskins had been rinsed.

"Only a few deliveries would be necessary," Mrs. Talbot said with a persuasive smile, "until we could resume supplies from Montreal. And as I said, Bart, it would pay very well indeed. After all, you're not having much luck so far, are you, establishing your aircraft business?"

"Oh, I don't know. A government contract looks very promising," I lied.

"We're not talking promises, Bart, we're talking firm. And it's not as if there's any risk, you know. Just a matter of loading a few boxes—we'd truck them to your farm, of course—and then all you'd have to do would be to fly a few miles and land in a field. Nothing too difficult about that, is there?"

Seeing that I was about to refuse, she added quickly, "Anyways, you don't have to decide right now. But you'll think about it, will you?" Then, bringing her face so close that I could see beads of perspiration in the hair at her temples: "It might be worth your while in more ways than one," she said huskily, putting a hand on my thigh and running it slowly upward. "I'm sure we'd get on really well."

A moment later I received, belatedly, the fourth of the aforementioned surprises, when she suddenly whipped the handkerchief out of my breast pocket and held it over her face, until only her dark eyes were visible; and in Mrs. Enerjee's voice, said through it, "My goodness gracious yes, Batty—I am thinking we are going to be getting on very well together, indeed, my goodness, yes."

Me, Skulking

The principal reason I had bought the Machin farm—as it was still called in the neighborhood—was that it included a barn large enough to be used as a temporary hangar and workshop, and an exceptionally spacious field, easily long enough to accommodate the three aircraft I owned: the huge, twin-engined Vimy bomber that I had purchased from the American gangster, Tony Batt, a war surplus Avro 504K trainer, and the Gander wheel-and-float craft, which I now proceeded to evaluate over the next few weeks.

Unfortunately the test flights exposed several other problems in addition to those already encountered over Long Island. For instance, I discovered I had allowed too little clearance between the wheels and the floats. On my very first takeoff from the farm, watched by a crowd of assorted Gallopians, I hauled the stick back too roughly, with the result that the rear of the floats gouged into the grass, dragging the monoplane to an ignominious halt. I looked pretty silly, sitting up there in the open cockpit with a self-consciously preoccupied expression, then hurtling down the field with my best profile turned to the gaping locals, including my parents, looking as resolute as anything as I thundered over the grass with leather helmet cuddling noble pate and silk scarf fluttering like a knightly banner, presenting the very picture of the intrepid birdman taking to the blue, then at the climactic moment of takeoff crunching into the ground and grinding to a complete stop, with engine still bellowing.

Of course I had an excuse handy. "Just testing the brakes," I said, forgetting that I'd already mentioned that the Gander didn't have brakes.

No sooner was that problem licked than another arose in consequence. The lengthening of the undercarriage legs affected the retracting mechanism, which unlocked the next time I was taking off, again dragging the machine to a jolting halt on the floats, which were beginning to turn green from all the grassy friction. I didn't mind the color in itself, except that it clashed biliously with the yellow paint scheme.

I spent an entire week tinkering with the locking mechanism, which gave me plenty of time to consider the worst problem of all, the rearing effect. Whenever the throttle was slammed forward too enthusiastically, the nose reared in the air—a decidedly dangerous phenomenon at low speeds. The first time it happened I had to force the stick forward to prevent a power stall and hold it forward with both hands. I thought at first that some idiot had connected the throttle linkage to the elevator cable. And the substitution of a larger trim tab on the elevator helped only a little.

All in all, I was confirming that designing and building an airplane was much more difficult than it had first seemed. The worst of it was that, even if the new airplane had flown perfectly, it would not have made the marketing of it any easier, as I discovered when I tried to interest the Department of National Defence. In 1923 the Canadian government was putting as little money as possible into aviation. The public was hostile to military expenditure of any kind, even the little that would have benefited aviation in general. Well aware of the national attitude, the government had been looking for ways to reduce the aviation budget still further, and had achieved this a year or so previously by merging civil and military flying into a single organization under the Department of National Defence. This enabled the government to slash about forty percent off the total sum promised to aviation by the preceding Parliament. The result was that by this year the Canadian Air Force, the market I needed to make the Gander commercially feasible, had been reduced to an establishment of 171 men, with a share of the national budget so minute that there was not even enough in the kitty to train mechanics.

Nevertheless, I continued to pester the Department, trying to

convince them that it would be in the national interest to award
me a few coins from the public purse, but I must confess that
after two years of frustration and unresponsiveness I was beginning to lose heart by the time I reached the deputy director of
supply and research. This was a former engineering officer in the
Royal Air Force by the name of Ernest Mainbrace, who was no
more hopeful than anyone else had been, though he was friendly
enough, especially after learning that I was also a former air
force man.

"Good Lord—you're not *the* Bandy, are you?"

I smirked warily, thinking that I had met somebody who had
seen one of my movies.

"The parachute man!"

"Eh?"

"You're the one who drove everyone in the air force into a
frenzy over your campaign to equip air crew with parachutes."

"Oh, that. Yes, I suppose that was me."

"Well, I'm dashed," said the deputy director, regarding me
with something like pleasure—an extremely rare reaction in
someone meeting me for the first time. "I say, this is an occasion.
Wait till I tell the chaps I met the one and only Major Bandy. Or
—Colonel, was it?"

I had learned to keep quiet about the rank I had ended up
with, mainly because nobody would believe it, even after I explained that it was the result of peculiar political circumstances
in Russia; so, trying to find the crease in my pinstripe trousers, I
mumbled, "Something like that."

The deputy director—damn, I'd forgotten his name—stared at
me for a moment, then suddenly went all tactful, thinking that I
was being evasive because of my past record of being rather fre-
quently demoted. He probably thought I was turning shifty because I'd ended up as a corporal.

"Yes, well, that's all over and done with now, isn't it?" he said,
looking away and fiddling with the specifications I'd given him.
"Nobody wants to hear any more about the war."

"That's very true, Mr.—" I said. What the hell was that name
again? I fell back on my infallible association-of-ideas method.
Something nautical—splice the mainbrace. That was it. "That's
very true, Mr. Splice," I said.

"Uh, yes," he said. For a moment he looked as if about to explain something, but instead turned politely to the Gander specs and got down to business. He was really quite impressed, he said, by the Gander's original features—would it really fly?—but unfortunately an amphibian was not quite the sort of aircraft they needed just at the moment. "You don't have a trainer in the works, do you?" he asked. "We might just possibly have a requirement for a trainer, by about 1930."

"No, I'm afraid not, Mr. Splice."

"The trouble is, you see," he went on, hiding for a moment behind a blueprint, "that most of our budget is going into research. Problems of aero engine detonation, new prop designs, development of seat-pack parachutes, things like that. That's how I remembered you so readily, you see, because we've been working on parachutes. But, as I said, I'm afraid we have very little in the way of funds for new aircraft designs." He regarded me hopefully. "You wouldn't still be interested in parachutes, I don't suppose?"

"No."

"Or antifreeze? We have a requirement for antifreeze."

"I am quite determined to make a success of the Gander, Mr. Splice," I said hopelessly, "however hard the way or prolonged the toil."

"Splendid," the other said encouragingly. Then: "Look, tell you what, why don't you come back in about three years? I'm sure the budget will have increased by then."

"Just what is the budget for new aircraft, by the way?"

"I'm almost embarrassed to mention it," the deputy director said with a light laugh. "Actually all we have left is fourteen dollars."

However, he was good enough to put me onto the director of the C.A.F., who was second only to the C.G.S., who was under the D.M.D.N.D., and I guess I must have impressed them with my determination or exhausted them with my persistence—for I had never yet given up any endeavor (apart from medicine, the infantry, parachutes, marriage, movies, and the Russian Revolution) and I certainly wasn't going to start now, and finally I managed to get a commitment from the Department that they would

send a man along to Gallop on the second or third of June to test
the new airplane, and if the report was favorable they would see
what they could do about allocating special funds for the purchase of a few machines.

Which gave me very little time to prepare the Gander for the
official test flight. Accordingly I slaved over it for twelve hours a
day for the next two weeks, assisted by a local bruiser named
Whistler McMulligan. McMulligan was a mechanic who had
been working for Vickers in Montreal until he was laid off during last year's recession. Burly, surly, and thirty, he was a reasonably skilled mechanic but a difficult man to get along with,
partly because he had a temper like a detonator and partly because he drank. You could always tell what day of the week it
was by the contents of his tool chest. On the Monday after
payday it contained two bottles of the best local whisky, Talbot's
Gold Bullion. On Tuesday, one bottle of same. On Wednesday,
one bottle of the next best, Gold Vault. On Thursday, one bottle
of Superb Extra Special de luxe (the cheapest brand), and on
Friday, a half bottle of the Superb, or occasionally a Talbot rum
or gin.

God knows what he did at the weekend until the visit to his
bootlegger on Sunday. He probably went around bending the
galvanized iron plumbing. He had a terrible temper, which rose
in inverse ratio to the supply of booze. On one Friday he clob-
bered my filing cabinet with his fist so hard that one of the
drawers would never open again. Fortunately it was the drawer
that contained my copies of *La Vie parisienne*, which I didn't
particularly need for business purposes. Still, the cabinet never
looked quite the same afterward, with a six-inch dent in it—the
width of McMulligan's knuckles.

Frankly, I was scared stiff of him and often wondered how
Vickers had summoned up the nerve to dismiss him. Thank God
I had made it clear from the beginning that his job with me was
temporary. Otherwise he was well worth fifty cents an hour.

But though competent enough, he could not help me with my
main problem, the upward pitching effect on the Gander, which
was obviously an aerodynamic fault. The difficulty, I suspected,
was caused by a sudden increase in the air flow over the high
wing which was affecting the elevator ten feet or so farther back.

The difficulty didn't occur when the throttle was eased forward. I could manage to counteract the rearing motion by turning the trim tab wheel forward and holding the stick back against the increased pressure, but that was not a terribly practical solution. In a sudden emergency when full power was needed, I could hardly expect a pilot to perform four functions simultaneously: turn the trim wheel, hold the stick back, put on throttle, then jam the stick forward. With an imminent stall or crash in the offing he was not likely to remember the sequence too clearly.

"When he hears about it, I shouldn't think the guffmint test pilot will want to take the plane up," McMulligan observed one morning as we wheeled the machine back to the barn after another unsatisfactory trial.

"In that case I won't tell him," I said airily.

McMulligan looked at me out of his little eyes, the only small features in his otherwise extensively orthognathous countenance. "You can't not tell him, boss," he said, picking up a wrench and closing the jaws with his blackened thumb. "He might get himself killed, like."

"*I* can handle the airplane," I said, "so I don't see why he can't."

"But you know what to expect."

"I didn't know what to expect when it first happened, did I?"

When he continued to stare at me out of his mean little eyes: "You just don't understand how important this test flight is," I said loudly. "I'm finished if I don't get a contract soon from the government." I stared back at him, playing cunningly on his need for a steady job. "But when I get it, it'll mean a good job for you, McMulligan," I lied, "as my chief mechanic."

"Well, it's up to you, course," he said, fiddling with his tool. "Hell, I don't care if he kills himself. But you wouldn't feel too good about it, would you, if you lost your plane, like?"

I glared at him—hurriedly reaiming my eyes at a tail skid when he glared back—and continued to argue, pointing out that in the air force we had tested many aircraft that were known to be flawed but which had later developed into exceptional machines. But of course I knew that my blasted mechanic was right. I would have to warn the Ministry pilot.

As the time for the trial approached, I felt more concerned

than ever about the future. If the supply and research pilot turned in an unfavorable report, I'd be faced with structural alterations that would gobble up what little money I had left. Then what would I do? I had been searching for venture capital for two years and knew now that it was no use looking further. In 1923 nobody was interested in investing in aviation. The business was in a worldwide slump. I wondered what on earth I would do if the Gander was finally turned down. I might have to go to extremes and get an honest job.

Not the least of my difficulties at this time was the continued domestic devaluation. I just couldn't get it into my parents' heads that I was a great man. Though I was now at least twenty-nine, possibly even older, they still treated me as if I had accomplished nothing except to develop this ridiculous hobby of flying airplanes, which they placed on about the same level as playing with Meccano sets. If I had come to my senses and become a balding civil servant or something, they would have been better satisfied; but all I did was tinker with engines and tighten a few wires and fly around in circles. I kept telling myself that I didn't give a cuss what they thought of me, but I could never quite convince myself. Their low opinion had been rankling for years. I couldn't even prove that for a while I had done quite well in the moving pictures—I'd lost that fan letter. And they couldn't see for themselves, for naturally they'd never been to any of my movies.

I suppose the parental inability to comprehend that I had achieved a modicum of success in the industry was due partly to their conviction that an involvement in show business was about as honorable and lucrative as a tour with a burlesque road company—and they knew about *that* aspect of show business all right. Not far from the slummy, Parliament Hill area of Ottawa, where they had lived at one time, stood a theatrical boardinghouse, and they had been only too aware of the social standing of its denizens: fancy hussies in feather boas and faces painted in bordello shades, and loud, cheeky, ale-swilling fellows in mustard checks whose fair round bellies were as full as their purses were empty. Consequently my parents were convinced that after a year or so in the business I would return in a similarly gaudy and penurious condition.

The worst of it was that they were right. Though I had earned whacking sums of money in the movies, I couldn't prove that I was a cut or two above those dreadful artistes, for nearly all the profits had gone into the development of the Gander.

Finally, though still concerned for business reasons to keep the rest of the populace in blissful ignorance of my immediate past and my faltering financial position, I felt I just had to convince the folks once and for all that I amounted to a row of beans, otherwise I'd *never* get any respect around the flaking farmhouse. And at last, toward the end of May, came the great breakthrough in our relationship.

One day, when Father picked up the Ottawa newspaper—there was my name in an advertisement for the Majestic Cinema on Bank Street.

Admittedly it wasn't in terribly imposing letters; in fact Father had to get out his magnifying glass to see it; but the name was there all right, just below the title of the film: *Blenkinsop of the Mounted.* Playing for three nights and one Wednesday matinee.

And the very next day Father suddenly said over the breakfast table, "Perhaps we should see one of these cinematographic efforts of yours, Bartholomew, if only to enable us to refute your overwrought hyperbole."

I was thrilled to bits, but of course I skillfully hid my eagerness behind an expression of the utmost indifference. "You really mean it?" I asked, smoothing down my thinning hair. "Well, as you saw, one of my movies happens to be playing in Ottawa right now, as a matter of fact, and it just so happens that I have an appointment at the Department of National Defence on Wednesday, and I could give you a lift into town to see the movie if you liked. You could catch the matinee performance; it starts at two-thirty, and it would only cost fifteen cents each. Of course, I'd pay, and also take you all the way there in my expensive Pierce-Arrow motorcar. But of course," I concluded with an apathetic shrug, "only if you really wanted to see it. Uh, and I'd be glad to buy you an ice cream, too."

They looked at each other uncertainly. "Do you think we should?" Mother faltered.

By Jove, it would be a memorable day for them, I thought as we set off on the following Wednesday. It would not only be

their first visit to the cinema but also the first time they had rid-
den in my spanking new roadster with the wire wheels and the
shiny yellow body and black fenders. You could tell how
impressed they were by the way they clung to the sides of the
vehicle with really transfixed expressions as I bowled into town
along the baked mud streets, turned onto Bank Street in a cloud
of dust, darted into a parking space near the Majestic, right in
front of a stump-hauling wagon ("Speed demon," the driver
shouted), helped the old folks out, and guided them up to the
box office where, as I had promised, I paid for their admission.

As they disappeared apprehensively inside, clutching each
other's hands as if entering a bourne from which no traveler,
etc., I went about my business, which consisted in pacing up
and down the concrete sidewalk outside the cinema; for of
course I didn't have an appointment at all. I'd just made that excuse to get them to the theater.

I jittered up and down Bank Street for nearly half an hour before summoning up the courage to enter the cinema myself. I
hoped I wouldn't have too much difficulty in locating the folks in
the huge auditorium. I wanted to study their reactions to the
second most successful of my films.

As it turned out, they were quite easy to spot, for the place
was almost empty, as I saw the moment my eyes had adjusted to
the flickering gloom. There were only about half a dozen patrons
in the entire damp- and disinfectant-smelling theater. They included two boys, noisily sucking horehound drops, a well-
dressed couple dead center—the gentleman's right kneecap was
wearing a top hat—and a woman on the far side, wearing a tall
cornucopia of artificial fruit that would have drawn mutinous
murmurs had there been anybody behind her.

As for the aged parents, they had settled themselves right in
the middle of the front row. No doubt they thought that this was
the best position for viewing the screen. In fact they were so far
forward they were almost ahead of the pianist, an elderly lady
with a long black ribbon trailing from her spectacles, who was
accompanying the action on the screen with a version of the
"Marche Militaire."

I wished I'd thought of telling them to get a seat at least halfway back. The square picture flickering up there would be not

only grainy but distorted by the angle from which they were viewing it. As I sneaked, cursing, into a seat off to one side, I feared that they were seeing the comedy under the worst possible conditions, not only from a distorting angle but in an almost empty theater. There would be little communal laughter to let them know when the funny bits were occurring.

I felt so despondent that I actually started watching the movie myself, before averting my gaze as if from a pair of coupling hounds. My face had always seemed to me to be a splendidly aristocratic one, admittedly much longer and larger than normal, but otherwise well-enough proportioned; dignified, moreover, and splendidly distinctive; until the day I actually saw it on the screen. I had been utterly mortified. It had looked extraordinarily like that of a horse that had somehow learned to convey dismay, bewilderment, complacency, or alarm without the slightest discernible rearrangement of the features. I had refused to see any of my films since.

So if I glanced at the screen now and then, it was only to see where they were up to in the story of Constable Blenkinsop of the Royal Canadian Mounted Police, so that I would know what was coming next and would therefore be able to anticipate my parents' laughter.

The film, of course, was the one in which I play a Mountie who has been trying to get his man for ten years and has never quite managed it. This is mainly because his quarry, a dashing but villainous French-Canadian named Pierre (you could tell he was French-Canadian because he wore a tuque), has in the meantime joined the force himself and has been promoted to sergeant, and, from his vantage point at headquarters, keeps posting Percy Blenkinsop farther and farther away from Ottawa.

This situation established, we fade in on Percy taking breakfast in an igloo on Baffin Island. We see him fastidiously eating cold baked beans—one at a time—then tossing the can through the igloo entrance. Outside we see a pile of rusty cans thirty feet high.

Meanwhile Percy's dog team starts yapping and howling when they notice that the ice they are squatting on is splitting apart. From inside the igloo Percy calls on the dogs to shut their yaps. By the time he emerges from the igloo he is separated from his dog team by twenty feet of arctic H_2O and is drifting away on an ice pan.

That was as far as I wished to watch. Averting my eyes from Percy's expression as his predicament slowly dawns on him, I looked eagerly toward my parents, expecting them to react in the usual way. But they were just sitting there, blinking up at the screen, their pallid profiles quite unresponsive.

Even when Percy attempts to regain the mainland by frantically paddling the ice pan with a snowshoe, they failed to react but continued to gaze fixedly at the screen as if attending a lecture that would be followed by an exam paper.

Admittedly my last feature film, *The Butler,* had not been all that successful. In fact, at its sneak preview in California it had inspired some of the rudest remarks ever recorded on preview cards. But *Blenkinsop* was generally acknowledged to be director Wagnerian Jones's best farce and had been universally praised for its inventiveness and for the simplicity and economy with which its principal performer had achieved his effects (mainly because the director had ordered me never, ever to change my normal expression). Consequently I was really disturbed when, as the picture progressed from climax to comic climax, my parents failed not merely to laugh but even to smile at the antics that had convulsed audiences from Waco to Bangor.

It might have helped if others had been laughing, but not a sound modulated the antiseptic air in the huge auditorium. It was just my filthy luck that Mother and Father had picked a miserably attended matinee for the proof that for a time I had been almost as well known and successful as Buster Keaton in the art of conveying expressionless disorientation. I'd hoped that at long last I could present them with the celluloid proof that my life had not been entirely a waste. Now I began to see that the situation was hopeless. Father's mind simply could not encompass my bizarre experience. He didn't even understand aeronautics; it was as foreign to him as one of Mr. H. G. Wells's Martian machines would be to me if I met one in a cornfield.

Worse, none of the other members of the audience appeared to be finding the film amusing either. In fact the elderly gentleman seated a few rows behind my parents was not only unamused but was becoming positively hostile, judging by his growls. He appeared to be particularly upset about the way the film was making fun of the Mounted Police and its stiff, British-style traditions. I remembered reading a review in a Vancouver newspaper, whose critic had taken umbrage at the rather unrealistic picture of Canada that the film had presented: hordes of Eskimos who looked like Mexicans, Indians who looked like Cubans, and Ottawa citizens who looked like characters out of a novel by Anthony Trollope, not to mention Dawson City with glimpses of cactus, and French-Canadians who resembled refugees from a Viennese operetta.

The gentleman with the angry pate seemed particularly upset by the musical ride scene, the part where Percy Blenkinsop loses his horse and is forced to perform the musical ride mounted on a moose. Like my parents, the old gent utterly failed to chortle even at what was said to be the best scene in the film, when Blenkinsop, helplessly cavorting around on the moose, repeatedly and narrowly escapes being speared by the lances of the other Mounties.

In fact the musical ride scene caused such an outburst of rage from the gentleman with the top hat on his knee that he started to choke, and his wife had to call for one of the ushers to help support him from the cinema. And when I shuffled out myself a few minutes later, I found him lying on his back on the sidewalk under the awning of a haberdashery, surrounded by bonneted and bowlered citizens. He was still looking a trifle livid, I thought. Actually he was dead.

To complete a disastrous occasion, my parents spoke nary a word all the way home, even though I drove quite circumspectly.

Finally, after neither of them had uttered a word by the time dinner was ready, I could stand it no longer. I just had to get it over with.

"So," I prompted, tapping the barometer and straightening an embroidered sampler, "what did you think?"

"Presumably you are inquiring as to how impressed or otherwise we were after seeing your moving picture show," Father said.

Now that the moment was upon me, I suddenly wished I hadn't asked for the postmortem, especially after witnessing the

death throes. What the hell did I care that they had obviously
hated every minute of it? All the same, oh, God, if only the cinema had been crowded. The usual reaction would surely have
influenced them, even against their will. But the awful silence
from around them had killed any possibility of shared enjoy-
ment.

I started for the door, muttering that I had to go to the barn to
see how McMulligan was getting on. He'd promised to work
late, to prepare the machine for the test flight next day.

"Don't you want to hear what we thought?" Father asked
sharply.

"Ah. Yes. Sure."

"I must say, Bartholomew," Father said heavily, "that I found
it a remarkable experience. Quite remarkable."

"Well, it's not my fault," I muttered. "That's the kind of thing
people enjoy in the movies. I—what?"

"It was wonderful, Bartholomew," Mother said flatly. "We
had no idea it was going to be like that. People actually moving
about and riding horses and everything. Even if you couldn't see
them all sometimes, the way they were cut off, so you couldn't
see their legs, sometimes. And the strange way people kept disappearing off to one side."

"Indeed, it was sometimes quite mystifying," Father put in.
"And of course it could hardly be described as uplifting."

"I hardly recognized Ottawa," Mother said, "with all those
palm trees."

"And we certainly couldn't understand what *you* were supposed to be doing, Bartholomew," Father said severely. "It
seemed to me that, even for you, you were being unusually ob-
tuse. How could you possibly expect to paddle along on that
block of ice, for instance, using a snowshoe? Surely you could
see that the water was swishing right through it. And that's just
one example out of hundreds.

"But on the whole," he concluded, "it was quite an interesting
spectacle. Hardly on the same level as say, *Antigone*, of course,
but . . . Nevertheless, I must say, I found it a profoundly interesting experience."

"Do you think," Mother said, "we might just possibly go and
see it again sometime?"

Shortly after a most enjoyable dinner, McMulligan called in at the house on his way home. I was feeling so jaunty that several minutes elapsed before I realized that he had something on his mind. Reeking of Talbot's Gold Vault—for it was a Wednesday— he kept shuffling about on the veranda and glancing at me uneasily.

Finally he said, "The test pilot from the guffmint was here this afternoon."

"What?" I stared at him, my joy fading a touch. Then: "Damn. I wanted to be here when he came. Blast. Did he go up?"

"Yes."

"Blast. They said he was coming on the second or third of June, they'd let me know. Typical." It was now my turn to pace up and down the rotting veranda planks.

As a thought struck me I whirled. "What? You say he went up? And it was all right? He had no problems?"

"No. He got down no trouble at all."

I rose onto my toes, then sank back again, expelling an exhilarated sigh. "Thank goodness. That's tremendous, McMulligan. Did he say what he thought or anything? Make any comment or anything?"

McMulligan was pressing one of the spongy boards with his foot. "No, he didn't give no opinion. He just said we'd hear from the guffmint in due course."

"Ah."

"Except that, like I said, Mr. Bandy, there was a mix-up. He took the Avro."

"Took the Avro where?"

"Up."

"Up?" I asked bewilderedly. "How d'you mean, up?"

"He flew the wrong plane," McMulligan muttered to his feet.

"He what?"

"Flew the Avro by mistake," McMulligan said. Then, angrily: "Well, it wasn't my fault. The Avro was in the way, so when he asked me to swing the prop, I just thought he was going to move it out the way, park it beside the barn or somewhere, so he could get the Gander out. So while he was doing that I went into the barn to get the machine ready, like, and when I come out he was taxiing the Avro at the far end of the field. And then he took off."

"He flight-tested the Avro instead of the Gander. I see. M'm. I see. M'm."

"He flew it around for about twenty minutes or so. Pretty cautious like, I thought."

"M'm. And what did he say when you told him he'd taken up the wrong plane?"

"I didn't tell him."

"You didn't tell him."

"Well, he was in such a hurry. He wasn't in a good mood to start with. He kept saying how late it was, and it had taken him all day to find Gallop, and he'd be late getting home, if he ever managed to get home, he said. He just said he'd make his report to the Department and we'd hear in due course. Then he went off in his car, and . . . Well, what could I say?" McMulligan shouted aggressively. "In the mood he was in, after taking all day to get to Gallop. I just didn't think it was the right time."

"I see. M'm. M'm."

In due course the report came back from the government, informing me that they were turning down the Gander Experimental Mark I, as the test pilot had reported that it did not handle satisfactorily, nor was its performance up to the high standards set by the Department of National Defence. They deeply regretted the decision but it was final. I had to understand that with their limited funds they had to be very careful to choose the right kind of equipment for the C.A.F. And so forth.

The Avro 504, of course, was an aircraft that had been flying for about eight years and would still be providing flawless service to most of the world's air forces for many years to come.

In the Walled Garden

When a final meeting at the Ministry confirmed the suspicion that the government would not have given me a contract even if they had tested the right aircraft and found it acceptable, and when I finally faced up to it that there was no civil market for the Gander either, I felt so despondent that I stopped flying even for the fun of it, gave up pottering about in the barn, returned McMulligan to the unemployment queue, and started to rise later and later every day. After three years of effort and sacrifice, my aerial ambition had finally conked out and spun into the ground.

My parents, of course, thought I was merely malingering. Fearful that I was turning into another Cousin Eddie, who at thirty-eight was still living with his mother, however much she encouraged him to go out into the world, with thumps on the earhole, Mother began to look around for an eligible young woman who was skillful enough to disguise her social ambitions before marriage and use them to stand for no nonsense afterward, while Father urged me to visit the town's senior medical practitioner, to see if he had any pills or potions potent enough to prevent the iron in my system from rusting away completely.

But Dr. McKay couldn't do anything with me either, as he informed me quite plainly after a showdown in his surgery. A slow, economical Scots-Canadian with a contemptuous expression and a prodigious amount of hair curling from his nose and ears, he had plenty of time to upbraid me as there was nobody else in the waiting room. His patients had deserted him in droves the moment another G.P., Dr. Hipsey, had established a practice in Gallop. About the only patients he had left were the cronies he played poker with at the Queen's Hotel and a few old masochists who felt it was only right that he should abuse the likes of them.

Everybody else had grown tired of McKay's assertions that there was nothing wrong with them that lots of exercise and a good dose of cascara wouldn't cure. (He failed to explain to at least one patient the order in which these remedies should be followed, with the result that the unfortunate chap was caught short in the middle of a field during a horse-drawing contest.)

"After obtaining your medical history, and after a thorough physical examination," McKay said (two minutes after I walked into his surgery), "based on the lavishly dispensed time, sympathy, and understanding called for by the principles and practice of medicine, I have built up a comprehensive clinical picture of you, Bandy—not neglecting certain contributing emotional factors—and I have come to the conclusion that there is nothing wrong with you but bone idleness."

"It's all right, Doctor," I said. "You can tell me the worst. I can take it."

"I have told you the worst. I invariably tell my patients the worst."

"What, all four of them?"

McKay sneezed—he had a shocking cold—and regarded me blearily through the hanging gardens of his eyebrows. "You are an impertinent fellow, Bartholomew Bandy," he snuffled softly in his pease brose and Hudson's Bay Company accent, "with no respect even for a brilliant diagnostician like myself." He leaned down to pick up his tomcat, which had just sidled into the surgery. It had almost as much hair as its master.

"As for my diminishing practice," he went on, polishing the pussy, "it is not my fault if the townspeople wish to subject themselves to the naive flummery of this newcomer, Hipsey. Why, the fellow is so inexperienced that he even rushes out to medical emergencies in the middle of the night."

"The fool. By the way, Doc, the contributing emotional factors —which ones are those?"

"Eh?"

"You said that certain emotional factors were contributing to my idleness. What were you referring to?"

"Why, your prison record, of course."

"Oh. I thought you were referring to Dad. Incidentally, Doctor," I continued, with some dignity—not a lot, but enough to make him titter, "I hardly think my incarceration as a prisoner of war puts me in the 'prison record' category."

"You were in prison in Russia, were you not?"

"Yes."

"And they keep records there, presumably?"

"Well, yes. But—"

"So, you have a prison record."

"Well, if you put it that way . . ."

McKay continued to study me through the hirsute undergrowth for a solid minute. "I must admit, Bandy," he said at length, "that your presence does not entirely agree with the picture that was presented to me. I was led to expect a drab and spiritless oaf."

"Who could possibly have characterized me in such slanderous terms?" I asked listlessly, and perched my feet on his armchair.

"You are aware, I suppose," he said sharply, "that your parents are concerned about you?"

"M'm. They're afraid I'm going to go on living with them forever."

"And are you?"

"Only for a few years, Doctor, until I find my feet."

McKay glared at the feet in question. "I should not have thought that was so difficult," he snapped, suppressing a sneeze. "They are certainly obtrusive enough."

"Actually I'm seriously thinking of running away from home," I said. "Only trouble is, I never seem to have time for it. You see, Doctor," I said, removing my feet and leaning forward earnestly, "my problem is that by the time I've folded my jammies and made my toilet and had my pancakes it's almost time for my afternoon nap. And there aren't any trains out of Gallop in the evening."

He straightened his lips with an effort. "You could walk out," he said curtly. "Exercise is good for you."

"Before or after a good dose of cascara?"

He rose to his feet and laid the cat gently in a bin of sterile dressings.

"You will oblige me by getting out of my office this instant," he ordered. "After paying me my two dollars. Go on, out with you, you cheeky man."

As I was making my way through the waiting room—empty, of course—he followed me out. "You will agree to be one of the nominees for the Liberal candidacy, I trust?" he asked casually, before sneezing again and blowing his nose into a handkerchief that looked as if it hadn't been washed since the 1911 floods.

I stopped dead. "Eh?" I asked. "Whajamean, a nominee? We already have a candidate—the colonel J.P."

"You were not at the meeting last night."

"No, I was having a bath."

"I should not have examined you so intimately had you not. Anyway, you were one of five persons nominated, to replace Colonel whatsisname."

"Replace the Liberal candidate? Why, what's he done?"

"He has not done anything—except to meet his maker."

"Mackenzie King?"

"*God*, you great, blank-faced galoot." The handkerchief crackled as he stuffed it back into his pocket. "Had you not heard? You really have been burying yourself away. The colonel expired in Ottawa just the other day."

"Good Lord."

"Whilst attending a cinema show, I understand."

I started. After a moment, feigning no particular interest, I asked, "The colonel J.P. . . . never met him myself, actually. He, um, wasn't in the habit of wearing a top hat on his knee, by any chance?"

"A top hat was one of his pretensions. Why?"

"Oh, nothing," I said, looking preoccupied.

"Anyway, his death means they will have to postpone the by-election until October, while we look for a new candidate."

"And I've been nominated?"

"Aye. Not that you have any chance of being selected, mind you—especially now that *I* have joined the executive. Still, it will help to keep your mind occupied for a few days, until we decide in favor of a respectable representative."

Though I had been a member of the riding organization for only a few months, I was aware that the politics didn't just start with the hustings harangues and the by-election blather but commenced from the moment the chief electoral officer issued the writ of election. That was when the local executive got busy. Usually they already had a candidate in mind and had agreed among themselves to secure his nomination. However, in order to maintain the usual democratic pretense, the decision had to appear to come from the constituency organization as a whole. So there had to be several nominees to pick from. But, to ensure that their favorite candidate was selected, the executive would pad the list with people who had not the slightest intention of running; obliging fellows who would be quite happy to be eliminated during the final voting, leaving the field clear for the candidate whom the executive really wanted.

At the final stage of the selection process, it was usually contrived that two nominees were left, the sincere chap and the sake-of-appearances candidate. Whereupon, when the latter inevitably received the fewer number of votes, he would move that the nomination be made unanimous, thus pleasing everybody, except perhaps some fool who had nursed genuine ambitions to serve his country.

Naturally I was on the list to help make it look good to the constituency organization—part of the padding that enabled Karley and his pals to simulate the process of a democratic selection. The man they really wanted was an Ottawa lawyer named Gavin Sharp. Which was perfectly all right with me. I had no interest other than in aviation—and precious little in that, either, at the moment.

Then on the afternoon before the final nomination meeting, while I was lying stinking in bed—I'd caught Dr. McKay's vile cold—I received an urgent invitation to dinner at Karley's place.

When I arrived at six-thirty, attired in a tux and forty spare handkerchiefs, I was just in time to see a member of the executive, Arthur Wood, the hardware merchant, hurrying off in his Hupmobile. As he spluttered by he treated me to a shifty look—but I didn't need it, I already had one.

In the Karley drawing room, all mahogany and British Army watercolors of Canadian waterfalls, the air was powder blue, the ashtrays overflowing, the glasses smudged with sweaty prints. It looked as if there had been some sort of meeting—unless Kitty had not yet cleaned up after the last poker game.

For some reason, Karley seemed reluctant to explain either the afternoon's emergency meeting or the reason he had dragged me out of my deathbed. I didn't care. I was feeling too mumpish with blighted hopes and catarrh. Even by the time we sat down to dinner at eight he was still chunnering on about this and that and the good old days in the front line among the rats and lice.

Meanwhile Kitty kept edging farther and farther away from my side of the table, as I snuffled over the Limoges, coughed into the victuals, and blew out the candles with my sneezes.

It wasn't until the dessert plates had been cleared away—by the maid, not my explosive suspirations—and Kitty had fled from the bronchial uproar, that Karley started talking about our candidate, Gavin Sharp.

I had met Sharp only once and had found him a trifle irritating; affably condescending to us yokels; but Karley considered him to be a clever chap and a fluent speaker, who had quite a good chance of winning the seat from the Tories, if given half an issue and the whole support of the local association. Sharp, he said, was a legal adviser to the Prime Minister and had been promised the first by-election that came along. The death of our original candidate had provided an unexpected opportunity.

At the mention of the colonel J.P., who had died of cinematography, I felt worse than ever. Fortunately I was already so unwell that Karley couldn't tell the difference.

"Naturally," he said, leaning back in his dining chair and studying the wet, tattered end of his cigar, "we must all be one hundred percent behind Sharp all the way."

"Ye-HUH," I sneezed.

"That's a bad cold," Karley observed reproachfully as I blew over a vase of flowers. "You ought to be in bed."

"Dab it all, I would have bede, if you hadn't insisted on dragging me out of it." I coughed. Then: "Oh, God, I hope I'm dying."

"Well, just so long as you don't die until after the final nomination meeting tomorrow, old man," Karley said, laughing to show that he didn't mean it, not really. "I take it, by the way, that you're fully in favor of Sharp's nomination?"

"Yes, yes," I croaked sullenly. "He'll do as little for the country as anyone else."

"The important thing is that we all pull together, Bart," Karley murmured as he righted the vase and mopped up the water with Kitty's Chinese shawl—she had dropped it in her precipitate flight. "I know you agree that the good of the party always comes first."

I gazed at him through gummed, bleary eyes. "What are you getting at?" I rasped. "You surely didn't drag me into the cold night air, cough-cough, merely to tell me that, I hope."

Mine host abruptly snatched up his favorite hat, a deerstalker decorated with dry flies, and, heaving himself up, said, "We need a spot of air, old man. It's a fine evening, let's go for a stroll in the garden, shall we?"

Though Karley's house, Kitty Corners, was situated in open country, he had surrounded the back garden with high brick walls. He claimed that this was to keep groundhogs, raccoons, skunks, and children away from his fruit trees. The real reason, though, was that, after living for three years underground in deep dugouts and parapeted trenches, the wide-open spaces made him so uneasy that the slightest sound, even the snapping of a twig, might cause him to fling himself to the dirt, in case it was the spring arm of an enemy grenade. He could not even pass a fairly adequate obstruction, like a cedar hedge, without doubling over and proceeding alongside it in simian fashion with his arms dangling. So he had protected his back garden with brick walls that, in places, stood six feet high, to provide a safe haven for his evening stroll.

It was on the second circuit of the garden that he flung a grenade of his own. Just as we were passing the rose garden for the second time he informed me that a confidential poll among the local rank and file had exposed a marked division of opinion about the Prime Minister's personal choice.

The trouble was that Sharp was not a local resident—"and you know how suspicious people are here, of Ottawa." Worse, when

Sharp had finally condescended to meet the local executive, he had not made a good impression.

"That damned woman, Miss Rawsthorne, told him to his face that he was an arrogant earpiece. I suppose she meant mouthpiece," Karley said. "And now she's going around saying that he's been foisted on us by the Ottawa hierarchy. And people are beginning to listen to her."

As the finals of the nomination contest were to take place the following evening, and as I was the only other person who had not been eliminated, this news greatly disturbed me. In fact I was so alarmed I ran into a trellis.

"Oh, but the rank and file won't go against the wishes of the national executive," I croaked, shaking my head at him, as if attempting to set up a similar oscillation in his noodle. But the gesture merely cascaded snot over the roses.

"We're not at all sure of that," Karley said, puffing faster than usual at his cigar. "Miss Rawsthorne intends to speak out against Sharp—and she may not be the only one. And if the vote goes the wrong way—"

"You'd be stuck with me."

"Exactly."

"Well, that's completely out, I assure you," I wheezed, clutching my sore throat. The warm June air was making me feel absolutely terrible. I could feel sweat beading under my eyes, and there was nothing I hated more than beads under my eyes.

"I know. We all agree."

"I tell you that's completely out of the question."

"Goldarn right, Bart. It would be most unfortunate."

"It was understood right from the beginning—I was just supposed to plump out your list."

"That's right."

"It's the only reason I let my name stand. It's quite out of the question. I'm sorry. And I don't care what you say."

"Right. The result would be too horrible to contemplate. Utterly disastrous, a calamity."

At that, I couldn't help looking at him a bit offendedly.

"I was just agreeing with you, that's all," Karley said hurriedly. "Anyway, I'm pretty darned relieved you feel that way, Bart, because that's what I wanted to talk to you about. About withdrawing from the list at the start of the meeting tomorrow night."

"Okay."

"Would you do that, old man?" he asked anxiously.

"Yes, yes."

"Perhaps pleading pressure of work, or something like that—your airplane manufacturing business? Will you do that?"

"I said I would, didn't I?" I said with an exasperated rasp—my voice had descended a full octave since my arrival. Though I must say I felt just a shade annoyed at the panic he was exhibiting at the prospect of having me as the official Liberal candidate; which turned into outright resentment when he heaved a sigh of pure, unadulterated relief. "Oh, thank God," he said. "The thought of—

"Anyway," he added, stopping himself just in time, "that's settled. My God, you don't know how much of a relief that is to me, Bart."

But it wasn't settled. For on the following evening when I got up to make what the large audience thought was to be a speech appealing for their votes, and what the executive knew was to be the announcement of my withdrawal from the contest and an appeal for a unanimous decision in favor of Gavin Sharp, I found that laryngitis had me by the throat and I couldn't utter a word.

Which aroused so much sympathy in the audience that they applauded as enthusiastically as if I had actually delivered the speech—possibly even more enthusiastically at having escaped it; and despite all of Karley's frantic efforts to get me to mime my withdrawal, the constituency association failed to understand the situation and proceeded to vote for both nominees, defeating Mr. Sharp, despite a desperate search for an escape clause in the by-laws, by three votes, thus making me the official Liberal candidate for William and Mary Counties.

Well, it was all Karley's fault, as I informed him the very next day. If he hadn't dragged me out of my deathbed I would not have developed laryngitis and completely lost my voice. But he just looked at me hatefully and shouted, "I notice there's nothing wrong with your voice today, though," before stamping off in the most appalling fury, almost as if he thought I had failed to har-

monize not because I couldn't sing but because I had ignored
the score.

Well, damn it all, I had been feeling really unwell that evening, really down in the dumps. I mean, was it my fault if, grub-
bing among the ruins, I happened to come across destiny's splintered signpost, and was it not natural for me to reerect it to see
which way it pointed?

Besides, he should never have mentioned the airplane manufacturing business. It had reminded me that that avenue had
been thoroughly blocked, ditched, cratered, flooded, and mined,
and even closed off; by the very party, funnily enough, to which
I was now committed.

PART II

When Jim Boyce heard that I had been nominated as Liberal candidate for Parliament, he guffawed, confidently expecting me to join in; though his face rebounded fast enough when he saw me looking quite thoughtful.

"You don't seriously expect anybody to vote for you, do you?" he asked incredulously.

Boyce, still unemployed, was staying with us at the farm for a while, to get away, as he put it, from the hurly-burly of city life, i.e., for a few weeks of free food and lodgings.

"Why should they not vote for him, James?" Father asked naively. To my surprise, Father and Mother had taken a shine to the cow-eyed lecher from his first day in residence. "Admittedly, Bartholomew is not exactly your typical parliamentarian, but—"

"Exactly, sir. It's like entering a Clydesdale in the Derby. I don't wish to malign your son, Reverend—"

"Oh, that's all right."

"But it's hard to decide which is more bizarre, his equine countenance or his whining parlance, which, when raised in protest, can be heard, I understand, across the Hellespont."

"Surely a penetrating voice would stand him in good stead in politics?"

"Not *that* penetrating."

The folks, who had been struggling to convince themselves that I had finally entered a respectable profession, looked downcast. But, as for me, I didn't care what Boyce thought. I was already beginning to convince myself that I might have something worthwhile to contribute to politics. I wasn't sure what it was, but I knew I would have something to say, after I'd finished making my election speeches.

Bartholomew Bandy, M.P.—it looked quite impressive, scrawled there on the slate of my imagination. The more I thought about it the more appropriate it seemed, and the more impressed I became with the intelligence of the people who had nominated me. Who would have thought that Miss Rawsthorne, Mr. Giddy, our token farmer, the Reverend Mr. Wattle, and Dr. McKay would manifest such remarkable insight, acumen, and sheer downright common sense? By gad, there were a few perceptive people left in the world. Karley and the remaining members of the executive might have one or two doubts, poor misguided souls, but a few discerning people obviously recognized a man of promise when they saw one. Several promises, in fact. So, though initially as surprised by developments as everybody else, I was quickly converted by the sheer inevitability of it all.

Accordingly I hurled myself into the fray with renewed vigor, drive, and enthusiasm, even going so far as to have a telephone installed in my room at the farm so that I could speak to my staff without having to get out of bed. Though actually it was not all that useful, for it was a party line, and the more people who picked up the receiver to listen in on my conversations, the fainter grew the voice at the other end, until finally all I could hear was a distant bellowing and asthmatic breathing. But that was all right—I hated telephoning. Anyway, such was the enthusiasm for the cause that within days, my campaign team had soared to a total of two: Miss Rawsthorne, who agreed to manage the election office whenever it was established, and Jim Boyce, who, seeing I was quite serious about it, volunteered to be my campaign manager. He claimed to have had plenty of experience as an organizer in the Department of External Affairs— putting notepads and pencils round conference tables and so forth—and would therefore be an invaluable aide.

"Two hundred a week should take care of my immediate needs," he told me.

"Two hundred a week?"

"All right, fifty, then. Plus expenses, of course."

This was the first time that the question of financing the campaign had come up. Naturally I had no intention of forking out any of my own moola for the cause, especially as I didn't have any. So I went to see a member of the executive, Mr. Craikey, a retired woodwork teacher who acted as the party treasurer. A little man with a half-closed left eye and a mouth like the entrance to a piggy bank, he was one of the people who had voted against me, partly, I think, because of Miss Rawsthorne. Before introducing him back in February, she had told me that his name should be pronounced Crikey, so naturally that was how I addressed him. But when he discovered that I wasn't a Cockney and that my mispronunciation was deliberate, he had become distinctly snotty.

Miss Rawsthorne was always doing things like that, sewing dissension in order to liven up our meetings; like the time when, under "other business," she remarked that the chairman's fly was undone, and just as Karley was clutching embarrassedly at his crotch, she referred him to one of the fisherman's flies in his deerstalker, pointing out that it was unraveling.

"Well now, Mr. Craikey," I said, sprawling expansively in the best armchair in his little home, "you remember that, as chairman of the fund-raising committee, I was responsible for collecting a goodly sum for the party?"

"Seven hundred and four dollars and thirty cents, and a French coin with a hole in it."

"Exactly. Well, I want it all back, so I can become an M.P."

"Can't have it," Craikey snapped.

"Whajamean, I can't have it?"

"It's for administration, not just any odd operational expenditure."

"*Odd expenditure?*" I exclaimed, sitting up so abruptly that a loose spring in the armchair went *doyoyng.* "My dear Mr. Craikey, we're talking here about the *raison d'être* of the association, not a request for a luncheon voucher. We're talking about my election."

"Sorry."

"But it's my money," I whined. "I contributed most of it from my own bank account."

"Can't help that. It's not supposed to go for things like election campaigns," Mr. Craikey said, as if I were persisting in a frivolous request on a level with Miss Rawsthorne's latest suggestion to the executive, that they should subsidize the publication of her new book of poems on the grounds that the sentiments expressed in them were distinctly liberal.

Despite further protest, Craikey stuck to his peashooter, though in the end he rather grudgingly conceded that the constituency organization might be persuaded to pay my two-hundred-dollar deposit; but as for the rest of the money, I would have to follow the usual procedure, which was for the candidate to apply for funds to Liberal Party headquarters.

Accordingly, on the following morning I entrained for Montreal, taxied up to the Liberal headquarters on St. James Street, and was promptly shown up to the office of a M. Patinaude. He received me affably and respectfully and confirmed that financial support would be forthcoming. As they were between general elections, he said, the party coffers were filling up nicely. Why, only that week they had received a splendid donation from a company that was bidding on a government contract to build a new road to Senator Asselin's riding stables. So there would be no difficulty about a contribution to an official campaign of between four and five thousand dollars, which was considered ample to take care of salaries, office expenses, little gifts for wavering supporters, and so forth.

"Excellent," quoth I, greatly relieved. "So what do I have to do to get it, fill out a form or something?"

"Oh no, Mr.—what is the name, again?"

"Bandy."

"You just give us the name of your bank, Mr. Bandy, and we make a deposit in your . . ."

At which point he dribbled to a halt. "Bandy, did you say? There was a telephone call from Ottawa. . . . And the constituency is . . . ?"

"Gallop. William and Mary Counties, officially."

"Gallop, yes, that was the place." And a moment later he made some excuse and left the office. He was absent for quite a while. When he returned he was looking distinctly embarrassed. He started fiddling with his drawers, opening and closing them, and making ink blots on his pad, and after a desultory volley of evasions he finally informed me that there had been a change of policy. He was terribly sorry, it had quite slipped his memory, but he remembered now; it had been decided just the other hour that for the next few months there would be a moratorium on contributions to by-election expenses. The national office could not for the time being see its way to delve into its limited funds in support of candidates.

As soon as I got back to Gallop I went looking for Karley. I found him in the main street, huddled against the hoarding that surrounded his latest construction project, the new post office. I promptly confronted him and asked him what was going on. Was it he who had scuppered me with Liberal H.Q.?

"Course not," he said shortly, watching his crane as it hoisted up a block of granite. "First I've heard about it." Then, wrenching his gaze from the boom: "You mean you went to Montreal for election money?"

"Sure. Why not?"

"You've got a nerve."

"How?"

"Did you think for one minute the party would actually *reward* you for upsetting their plans that way?"

"Winning out over Gavin Sharp, you mean? I don't see what that has to do with it," I said, squinting at him through the sunlit dust. "Crikey said that as official candidate I was entitled to a share of the party funds."

"But, good God, man, you defeated the Prime Minister's personal choice."

"Oh, I'm sure he'll be a good sport about it."

Karley stared at me for a moment before muttering, "You've got a lot to learn about politics, then."

Seeing Karley standing there in the high street beside his latest construction project, it suddenly came to me, the reason he was behaving in such an unfriendly fashion these days. That was a federal building he was working on—a reward for his contributions to the party. He was worried that similar projects might not be forthcoming, now that he had failed to get the right man nominated.

"You don't think the party is going to fork out, then?" I asked, trying to sound as if it didn't matter a fig.

"I doubt if you'll even get a mention in the Liberal press from now on, after double-crossing them that way."

I started to protest. Karley interrupted. "That's how they'll see it, anyway," he said, his manner suggesting that he did not entirely disagree with his own opinion. "Only good thing you can say about this whole mess," he went on, brushing dust off his baggy blue suit, "is that you've nothing to worry about financially."

"Huh?"

"All that money you brought back from the States. A plute like you, some people would say you shouldn't have expected the party to help with your expenses even if they'd been willing."

I opened my gob to put him straight forthwith; then slowly snapped it shut again. For business reasons I had spent months confirming the impression, or at least not denying it, that I was practically a duplicate J. Pierpont Morgan. If I confessed that I was almost broke, and that the association had been saddled with a pecuniary impostor, my reputation would be damaged beyond repair.

"I don't see why they shouldn't help a fellow, just because he has a bit of money put by," I mumbled, digging up the sidewalk with my toe. "Anyway, it's standard procedure in Canada to subsidize those who don't need it. Well, we'll just see about that. I'll go to Ottawa—so there."

Actually Mr. Patinaude had already arranged for me to meet the national chairman in Ottawa. Accordingly I drove there a couple of days later, parked on Wellington Street, and strolled up Parliament Hill in the tranquilizing sunlight through the tourists in their straw boaters and country bonnets, and past the scarlet-coated Mounties at the main entrance below the Peace Tower.

It was the first time I had been inside the center part of the three-block parliamentary complex since it was rebuilt after the fire of 1916. I was to meet the national chairman, Mr. Beaucheney, in Confederation Hall. As I had a few minutes to spare, I tagged onto a school tour of the building and managed to view the splendid Commons chamber, a committee room, the Senate, and the magnificent library, before hasting back to the main entrance. By the time I got there I was completely converted to the political life. From the moment I gaped round at the carved Gothic arches, and all that black and blue and gold marble, and at the expensively groined ceilings, I had decided that this was where I belonged. I could already see myself pacing along sculpted corridors, pausing here to enlighten the world's press and there to issue an order or two to some parliamentary minion, before striding into the chamber to deliver an impassioned speech on . . . on some vital issue or other. I loved the Gothic style anyway, even if it did resolutely face the good old medieval days with faith and confidence. The amazing wealth of stone sculpture, woodcarving, wrought ironwork, and the magnificence of the ceiling friezes and complexity of stained glass made me feel thoroughly at home. The hell with fabric and dope shops, I thought; this would suit me far better. It was a much more suitable setting for somebody like me.

I was particularly intrigued with the stonework, with its age-old fossils locked in Tyndall limestone. "Just look at that old fossil," I said to one of the schoolboys on the tour—just as a stuffy-looking chap in a morning coat and white mustache was crossing Confederation Hall.

He stopped and glared, before taking a reluctant step forward. "Mr. Bandy?"

"Mr. Beaucheney?"

Adopting a long-suffering expression, he asked again, "Mr. Bandy?"

"Mr. Beaucheney?"

A muscle vibrated like mad in his stern cheek. "I'll ask you once more," he said in a suppressed way. "Is it Mr. Bandy?"

"Mr. Beaucheney, is it?"

When his eyes began to water, I wondered what was wrong with the fellow. Was he not familiar with the time-honored social convention whereby one confirmed one's identity through presumption: "Mr. Stanley? Dr. Livingstone?" sort of thing?

"Are you," he asked slowly, "or are you not Bandy?"

"Gosh, that's good, the way you can speak so clearly through your teeth," I said admiringly.

However, when his rigid old face began to suffuse with ancient humors, I thought perhaps I had better clarify the situation for him. "Yes, I'm Bandy. Mr. Beaucheney, I presume? How d'you do?"

"My name is Chegwin. Mr. Beaucheney requested me to escort you. Come with me."

Without further explanation he led the way along the corridor in the direction of the Commons chamber, up the stairs, and along toward the west front corner of the building where the Prime Minister had an office adjoining the Liberal caucus room.

As we passed Mackenzie King's closed door, Chegwin gestured at it and said, "When he gets here, Mr. Beaucheney will be seeing the Prime Minister first, so you'll have a few minutes to wait." He glanced into the adjoining office, then ushered me in. "You might as well wait in here," he said curtly, and promptly abandoned me in the otherwise unoccupied room without even inviting me to take a seat.

I stood there for a while, gazing around interestedly, though there was nothing particularly interesting to see. Just a desk and chair, and another chair piled with official reports with blue covers, and a few calf-bound volumes in a glass case. And a door in the far corner which, judging by its size, opened onto a cupboard.

There wasn't even anything of much interest on the private secretary's desk, just an appointment book, a pen and ink stand, and a paperweight. After circumnavigating the desk a couple of times I took a quick peek at the book to see if the P.M. had an appointment with any notable figures, ambassadors or heads of state, or the like. Then I opened the lid of the inkwell, to see if it needed filling. Next I picked up the paperweight and examined it. It was a rock with a vein of fool's gold running through it. Then I put it down again.

As the minutes lounged by, my eyes kept straying to the door in the far corner. It faintly intrigued me. It was set in the wall that separated this office from the Prime Minister's den, but it didn't look like an ordinary connecting door. It was narrow, for one thing, and about the same height as a coffin standing on end. If it did give onto the P.M.'s office, why had they made it so small and mingy? A satirical statement by the architect? But if it didn't lead to the P.M., where did it lead? If it wasn't a cupboard, that is.

However, I was not a nosy sort of person, so I looked away

and wandered around the room again, whistling a tune or two, and jingling the coin in my pocket, and stopping to read the titles in the glass case. Bound copies of Hansard, Law Society reports, a copy of Mr. King's book, *Industry and Humanity*. But somehow my gaze kept returning to the little door in the corner.

It was bound to be a cupboard, darn it. It didn't look like any connecting door I'd ever seen before. But naturally I made no attempt to investigate. I had long since learned my lesson, never to let curiosity overcome circumspection. If it really was a connecting door and I opened it, I would almost certainly be caught doing so by Mr. King and Mr. Beaucheney. They would look up from their affairs of state or game of ticktacktoe and see me peeking in, and it would be no good my pretending that I was a member of the cleaning staff or anything, and peeking in might trigger Mr. King's memory.

But perhaps there was nobody in there. Come to think of it, Mr. Beaucheney could not have arrived yet—I would have heard him outside in the corridor. Moreover, there would surely have been a murmur of voices from the office next door. Maybe Mr. King wasn't in there either. That fellow Chegwin hadn't actually said he was in occupancy.

Anyway, the door was probably locked. Merely to confirm this I tried the doorknob, twisting it a millimeter at a time and pulling it gently toward me. The door inched open. It wasn't locked. Utterly satisfied, I released the knob and stepped back, and looked out the window. Through the trees in their summer fuzz I could see a stretch of the Ottawa River, the sun sparkling on the rich brown water, the color of cough medicine.

Well, it was their fault that I finally glanced through the doorway. They shouldn't have kept me waiting for so long. Besides, the door was already half an inch ajar, and it was a pure accident that my left brogue just happened to catch at the bottom of the door and swing it open. And before I could rectify this accidental occurrence, I had seen inside and confirmed that it was, in fact, a connecting door, with another little door on the Prime Minister's side, but that between the doors was an unlit space of about thirty inches, a two-and-a-half-foot passageway occupied by a small wooden chair, with a wide, shapeless chap sitting on it.

Thoroughly satisfied, I pushed the door to and turned away.

So I was more or less right. Though it connected the offices, it was perhaps more of a cupboard than a passage, equally available to the occupants of both sides, rather than a formal . . .

A wide, shapeless chap sitting on a chair? In a cupboard—or passageway? In the dark?

I stared fixedly at the wall. It had looked like Mr. King. Sitting, quite oblivious to my presence, in the darkness, with his hands on his knees, leaning forward slightly, eyes glazed with thought or memory. Ensconced in the wall.

But that was absurd. People didn't wall themselves up in the dark, holding—what was it he had been clutching in one hand?— a dried flower, with yellow petals. Especially not the leader of the country. I must have been seeing things. The strain of command, and all that. So I looked again into the tiny passageway, feeling like Alice at the white rabbit's doorway. But of course there was nobody there, though the little wooden chair was still in place.

After that I felt I just had to sit down. And I had barely settled myself at the private secretary's desk when I heard somebody, presumably Mr. Beaucheney, approaching along the corridor outside. So I stood up, but he went into Mr. King's office. So I sat down again.

A few minutes later, while I was busily massaging my eyes, another set of feet approached, and a moment later a tall, skinny individual in a dark suit and a bright school tie looked in through the doorway from the corridor.

"Any chance of seeing the old man in the next couple of days?" he whispered.

"I should hope so," I said. "I wouldn't want to wait here that long myself."

Nervously fingering his blue and yellow tie, the newcomer took a couple of timid steps into the room. About thirty years old, his most distinctive features were his deep-set eyes and long, narrow hands, which tended to flap like flippers.

"Cyril Hawkspat," he said as he came over to the desk. "I'm a Member, just in case you don't know."

"B. W. Bandy. How d'you do?"

"You're new here, aren't you?"

"I hope to be."

He regarded me uncertainly, tapping his thin chin with a long, waxy forefinger. "Yes, I see. . . . So would it be possible to make an appointment, do you think?"

As the appointment diary was open on the desk in front of me I consulted it, then: "I see there's a blank space here. How about ten-fifteen tomorrow morning?"

"Splendid. That will suit me fine."

So I wrote in the appointment, laboriously copying the handwriting in the book, with my tongue peeking from the corner of my lips.

I suppose it was rather a mischievous thing to do, especially as Hawkspat looked a decent sort of chap for an M.P., but I had now been hanging around for well over half an hour and was beginning to feel awkward.

In fact a further twenty minutes elapsed before I heard voices at the P.M.'s doorway out there, and a murmured comment about "sorting this fellow out," and a moment later Beaucheney, a large, handsome man of fifty in a morning coat and black trousers, glided into the room.

"My dear fellow, I do apologize if I've kept you waiting," he said, shaking my hand warmly in both of his. "But you know how it is." And he proceeded to explain how it was at apologetic length, before ushering me out of the office.

For a moment I thought the interview was already over with, until I concluded that he was leading me out because of the unsatisfactory seating arrangement in the private secretary's office.

Unless he was emphasizing the temporary nature of our acquaintanceship; for, once in the corridor, there we remained, seated on a bench below a large portrait of a chap in muttonchops.

We continued to exchange pleasantries for a couple of minutes before getting down to business.

"Well, Mr. Bandy," Beaucheney said with a charming smile, "you realize, of course, that your nomination has presented us with rather an awkward situation."

"Gavin Sharp thought he'd be a shoo-in, eh?" I said.

"Er . . . just so. But you see, the P.M. thought so too. In fact he assured Sharp that he was to secure the nomination. I'm afraid it has caused Mr. King a certain embarrassment."

He was being so pleasant, tactful, considerate, and charming that I felt it only right that I should be nice and gentlemanly too. "I certainly wouldn't want to cause that," I said.

"However," Beaucheney said, touching my arm, "I'm sure we can come to a satisfactory arrangement, Mr. Bandy. All will be well, I am sure, as soon as you announce your intention to stand down for the good of the party."

"Actually," I began.

"Perhaps a simple statement that your health does not permit you to continue?" he suggested, gazing down the corridor in a preoccupied way. "It would seem only appropriate, as I understand that it was your poor state of health that secured you the nomination in the first place."

"Yes, you're quite right, Mr. Beaucheney," I agreed.

"I'm glad you understand," he said briskly, taking out a pocket watch and giving it so commanding a look that the lid snapped to attention. "Of course," he went on, "you would not have had a chance anyway, without the backing of the party. So this way we're really doing you a favor. Saving you the embarrassment of being soundly thrashed on polling day."

Until then, despite a rush of patriotism engendered by the grandeur of Confederation Hall, my new ambition had not really taken root. In fact, so overweeningly confident was Mr. Beaucheney's manner, so certain his attitude, that my ambition had even started to wither away completely.

It was the words "soundly thrashed" that caused my plumule and radicle to sprout rather more determinedly. I was not too pleased at being treated like a new boy at a private school who had neglected to polish the prefect's boots.

"Oh, I don't know," I began, just as the Prime Minister emerged from his lair.

At first the shapeless little man with the pudgy face seemed disinclined to stop and chat. He continued along the corridor with only a hunched, darting glance in our direction. But then he stopped dead, as if he had run into a solid motion of no confidence; and whirled, to stare at me almost as if he had seen me before somewhere.

I was staring at him too. There was a dried yellow petal clinging to his jacket.

Thank God. I hadn't been seeing things after all.

It was much later that I learned that he was in the habit of sitting in that dark space between the offices, communing with his mother.

"Ah, Prime Minister," Mr. Beaucheney said, recovering quickly from his surprise at this unexpected honor; and, with a fatherly hand on my arm, proceeded to introduce me to the leader of the party.

Mr. King's handshake was decidedly reluctant. "Haven't we met before somewhere?" he asked suspiciously.

"No, sir," I said quickly. "Definitely not had the pleasure of being introduced to you before, sir, at any time, sir, anywhere."

King glanced at the national chairman. Beaucheney said smoothly, "I was just about to discuss with Bandy what we might do to compensate him for his trouble."

King nodded, still regarding me warily out of the corner of his eye.

"Mr. Bandy agrees that the whole situation was obviously the result of an unfortunate misunderstanding," Beaucheney continued. "But there you are, these things do happen, and can be quickly rectified with goodwill on both sides. Isn't that so, Bandy?"

"Indubitably, Mr. Beaucheney."

"I think it quite possible that we might be able to find a position that would enable us to make use of Mr. Bandy's undoubted talents, wouldn't you agree, Prime Minister?"

As he looked to the boss for confirmation, I wondered what position Beaucheney had in mind. Prone?

Now looking uncertainly at the Prime Minister, as if he were not getting the support he had expected, Beaucheney faltered, "Something in Indian Affairs, perhaps . . . ?" Then, to me, with another of his smooth smiles: "I think I could assure you that it would pay somewhat more than you would receive as a Member, Mr. Bandy. And I'm sure that, with your abilities, promotion would not be long in forthcoming."

"Promotion, eh? That sounds good," I said with a little laugh. "After all, I wouldn't want to remain an ordinary M.P. all my life."

The Prime Minister looked at Beaucheney. Beaucheney looked

back at the Prime Minister. There was quite a long pause before
Mr. King turned sharply, as if dislodging a turkey buzzard from
his shoulder, and walked off, without a word of good-bye, or
even au revoir.

When Beaucheney turned back to me his expression was as
gentlemanly and considerate as ever. "Do I understand," he
asked politely, "that you intend to contest the election, regardless of the circumstances?"

"Course," quoth I with a smile and a placating bob. "I
couldn't possibly let the party down, sir. I only came along to get
five thousand dollars from the Liberal coffers. To, you know,
defray expenses, and all that."

"I see," Beaucheney said. After a moment he nodded. "Very
well, Mr. Bandy. If that's your final decision, we must, of course,
respect it."

He was being so nice I felt quite guilty for a moment, almost
as if it were I who was behaving unreasonably.

As he rose to his feet: "About the expenses," I said quickly.
"Um, I might just possibly manage with only four thousand."

Mr. Beaucheney smiled and shook my hand. "No doubt you'll
be hearing from us in due course," he said in a kindly, sympathetic sort of way, as if he had just learned that I had only a few
months to live.

"Three thousand?" I asked.

He turned away. "Two thousand? One?" Then, softly to his retreating back: "A nickel for a cup of coffee?"

So that was that. His reaction was to become thoroughly familiar in time; the cool, smiling dismissal of the Liberal bigwig
who had failed to persuade a chap to see sense, and who would
thenceforth have nothing more to do with the poor misguided
clod.

By the time I was halfway home in the Pierce-Arrow, I was
sorely regretting my stubborn behavior that afternoon. I had settled myself squarely on the horns of a dilemma—and the tusks
were now up as far as my liver. It was all very well asserting that
I intended to contest the election, but I couldn't do so without
financial backing. At the same time I didn't dare confess to the
Liberal association that I was practically penniless. So I would
have to sustain the pretense of affluence.

But how could I? I could hardly conduct a campaign with a treasury of only three hundred plunks. So I couldn't go on. On the other hand I couldn't go back. They had already been forced to cancel the by-election once, while a new candidate was selected. If I caused another postponement they would never forgive me—even without knowing that I was indirectly responsible for the first postponement as well.

I would have to leave town. Leave town? I would have to leave the whole country. I'd have to change my name. Fortunately I had one ready: Gaylord Allardyce. I'd always fancied that name, Gaylord Allardyce. Though I might just keep my middle name, Wolfe. Gaylord W. Allardyce. Junior? The Second? And grow a beard.

Damn, damn, damn. Why had I let my name go forward as a nominee in the first place? I'd only joined the party in order to ingratiate myself with the community for business reasons. Why, oh, why had I not made greater efforts to withdraw when I had the chance? It seemed that once again I was being blown onto the rocks by the zephyr of circumstance. Who was it who had claimed that he was the master of his destiny? Some poet or other who had probably set out to be a rich banker.

By the time I reached the river road at Gallop I had finally confirmed the suspicion that had been growing steadily for twenty-nine years: that I wasn't so much the captain of my ship as its elderly midshipman or stoker's mate. And one or other of them had opened the sea cocks. The situation was worse than ever. I would have to carry on regardless, and somehow finance the campaign out of my own resources, knowing that it was a wasted effort. Gavin Sharp was thought to have had a reasonable chance against the Conservatives because the party had been prepared to throw its full weight behind him, with a bombardment of dollars and work projects—the new post office was one of several government projects being realized or promised—and a creeping barrage of politicians to aid him on the hustings. The Prime Minister himself would probably have made at least one personal appearance in support of his protégé. But, as for me, I wasn't likely to be allocated even the most ill-favored backbencher. And without the big guns and the Liberal largesse the result was a foregone conclusion.

Had there been an issue on which to fight the Tory candidate

I might have had a chance, but there was nothing available to rouse the pastoral torpor. So now I would have to dispose of my assets in a hopeless cause. I'd have to hock my diamond cuff links, sell the Pierce-Arrow, and, oh, God, the aircraft as well. But even that would not be enough, for if it really did cost four to five thousand to sustain a campaign, the farm would have to be mortgaged as well.

Perhaps I could manage on three hundred, plus a small loan from the bank? Maybe I could hold hilltop meetings like the evangelists. I could tell the electorate it was for their own good; all that fresh air, wind, rain, and sleet, would be far better for their health than huddling in some stuffy meeting hall. And I could type my own pamphlets and handbills and deliver them myself, and make inexpensive speeches. After all, if I was going to lose, there was no point in going deeply into debt. . . .

No, that wasn't the answer either. Conducting a mean campaign would be almost as bad as quitting. Besides, I had an obligation to the people who had nominated me—the bloody pests.

I was in such a whirl by then over the injustice of it all—carefully averting a vicious gaze from the truth, that it was all my own fault—that I failed to hear the train until it had reached the crossing, though it was hissing almost as loudly as I was. I braked, and stopped just short of the tracks as the shunting engine loomed overhead and ground across the east end of Queen Street at five miles an hour, snorting steam and pawing the ground.

The engineer in his pink stripes shouted at me from his grimy cab, no doubt something highly uncomplimentary; but I merely waved wanly, to give the impression that I was perfectly aware that he had been about to grind me into mincemeat, and that I wouldn't have minded in the least.

The locomotive was towing about twenty sealed and padlocked cars, which clashed together noisily as they rolled slowly across the street. It took three or four minutes for the train to cross the street, giving me ample opportunity to see where it was going—through the freight yard on the far side of the street, with its cinder tracks and rusty rails, and onward to Brockville and points west.

It also gave me the opportunity to see where it had come

from: from the guarded gate in the high metal fence that surrounded a complex of high brick buildings and a chimney on which the words TALBOT DISTILLERY had been painted vertically in fading letters.

This time Mrs. Talbot was not quite so ingratiating, as she sat squarely behind the desk in her blinding office. "It'll take about a week to set up," she said briskly. "I'll let you know when you're to deliver the first consignment a few hours before it's time to leave. But I can tell you now that for that kind of money you're going to have to fly much farther than just across the border. Maybe as far as Albany. All right?"

"All right."

"You'll be paid only after you've completed a trip and handed me the proper receipt. You'll look after all your own expenses, including the services of this mechanic you say you'll need. And make damn sure you can trust him to keep his mouth shut, okay?"

"All right."

Seeing she was having it all her own way, she softened somewhat. "Even so," she said, "if you can squeeze in enough cases you should still make several hundred dollars a trip, so you'll have nothing to complain about," She nodded dismissively. "Okay. Well, I'll contact you when I'm ready." She got up from the desk and stretched, so that her skirt rose above her plump, dimpled knees. The gesture also exposed damp patches under her bloused arms. "Oh, and just one more thing, Bartholomew," she said, smoothing her skirt with her heavy, nail-bitten hands. "Each consignment will be worth one hell of a lot of money, so don't try anything, all right? You may get away with it at this end, but at the New York end they play rough." Her face darkened. "I know, believe me."

Looking at her solidly curved figure and at her soft, smooth face crowned by that glorious auburn hair, I sincerely doubted whether I would get away with it at this end either. I made a mental note to be as honest as the day was long, as soon as I went smuggling.

With Fred Toombs

When, with squared shoulders and truculent phiz I thrust open the swinging doors of the tavern of the Queen's Hotel, there was a dramatic hush.

The tavern, containing a score or so of tables, was decorated in various tasteful shades of brown. Even the atmosphere was brown. It wasn't until the smoke had cleared that I understood that the main reason for the instant hush was that there was nobody there. They had all rushed out to watch a fistfight in the backyard.

By the time the regulars had all trooped back inside, shouting excitedly, I was ensconced at a corner table, trying to persuade the waiter to bring me a drink. After negotiating with Mrs. Talbot in her hot, bright office for two hours, I was so demoralized that for once I was prepared to overlook the fact that I had given up drinking.

Besides, I had to see McMulligan, and he was usually to be found at the Queen's of an evening.

"There is such a thing as prohibition, you know," the waiter was saying loftily as he jingled the coins in his grubby white jacket. "You can have wine, of course," he added, wiping the table with a cloth that looked as if it had recently been blocking a drain. "Wine don't come under prohibition."

"It doesn't come under anything," I snapped. "I tell you I want a large whisky."

"Well, if it isn't Mr. Bandy," said an equally loud voice. A moment later Fred Toombs, Gallop's principal bootlegger, came

barging through the furniture, which was being rapidly reoc-
cupied by a throng of noisy, excited farm and factory workers.

As he shook hands with me: "What's the trouble, Al? The man
wants a drink, get him a drink."

"Thought he was that feller from the Machin farm."

"You don't want to worry about that," Toombs said. "Mr.
Bandy isn't one of your bon-ton crowd." He gave the waiter a
shove. "Go on, get him a drink. In fact, bring a bottle. On me,
Mr. Bandy, on me.

"And make sure it's the good stuff," he shouted after the
waiter. "Not that distillation of boiled diapers you usually
serve."

Within seconds a glass of undiluted rye stood brimming before
me. As about half the agrarian and industrial population of Gallop seemed to be watching, I felt compelled to hurl the lot at my
tonsils in one go.

I had barely ceased writhing before Toombs poured another
from the freshly opened bottle of Gold Bullion that Al had left
on the table.

When that one had finished straightening the convolutions of
my stomach, Toombs leaned back in his chair and looked me
over coolly with his hard blue eyes before saying, "Well, this is
an honor, Mr. Bandy. Come here to show us you're one of the
boys, eh? Started the election already, have you?"

"Fug the election," I snarled. "I came in to find McMulligan
and get drunk, not necessarily in that order."

As a couple of Toombs's cronies slid shyly into the other two
seats at the table, he said, "Feel like getting drunk, eh? You
must have been to see Phil Talbot."

I blinked at him, wondering how he knew. I'd only left her
twenty minutes ago.

"I think McMulligan's around somewhere," Toombs said
indifferently. "When they were having the barney out back, I
think I saw him kicking the one who was down." He took a sip
from his drink. "You want to watch out for that one, Mr.
Bandy."

"I can handle McMulligan—if there's a whip and a chair
handy."

"McMulligan?" Toombs said contemptuously. "He's nothing. I was referring to Mrs. Talbot."

"Oh." Then, trying to sound casual: "You know her, do you?"

"Naturally," Toombs said, but did not elaborate.

Two drinks later he was telling me how he himself had gotten into the rumrunning business. A red-haired bloke with shoulders like a Pamplona bull and a savage face that was at war with his breezy manner, Toombs was a former infantry major who had won two M.C.s. "I even had my own battalion for a few weeks," he confided, "until I caught clap."

Before the war he had been a bank teller. After it he had seriously considered becoming a bank robber. He had returned from the war naively believing the civvies when they asserted that nothing would be too good for our boys when they returned from the war. "When I reported back to the bank," he said, wrapping his fist with ease round the bottom of the now half-empty bottle of whisky, "they said the best they could offer was a clerkship at twenty-two fifty a week, under this weedy little skunk who had stayed behind to spray his way up to assistant manager. That's how I got into the business. I looked around and saw these turds in the Ontario government telling everybody they couldn't have a drink unless they were willing to crawl to some pimply third-year medical student for a six-ounce prescription. And I thought to myself, *right*."

Trying to look respectful, one of the men who had gathered around the table to listen said to me, "You was in France too, eh, Mr. Bandy?"

"In France too?" Toombs repeated with a loud laugh. "I'll say he was. This is one of the great ones, Jack. Until he stirred things up, and the frocks and the brass got together and shipped him off to Russia." He leaned on his arms and looked at me, his eyes like tungsten. "You won't get anywhere in this country, you know, Bandy. They'll just smile and then cut off your balls with the sharp end of the law. Of course they'll tell you it's for your own good. The smug, churchgoing lawyers who run this province always know what's best. No, you don't know what's happening in this neck of the woods. You've been away too long. As for making it as an M.P., that's a wheeze. You don't know anything about politics. You'd be a disaster in Parliament." There was an uncomfortable pause. "You have my vote for a start," Toombs said.

"Course, he'll never win," said a glassblower when the cheers had died away. I could tell he was a glassblower because his cheeks sagged. Unless he was a tuba player.

"Oh, I don't know," I said. "With such a recommendation from Mr. Toombs, how can I lose?" Then, grandly: "Ho, there, good tavernkeeper, another round of drinks for these fine fellows. Drinks all round, my good man."

Instead, the grubby waiter started to place teacups and teapots on the tables.

"What's all this?" I bellowed, gesturing authoritatively and knocking over an empty bottle. "Whisky, you fool, not tea."

"The police have had another complaint from the Hipseys," Toombs explained, glancing at the brown clock on the brown wall. "They're scheduled to raid the joint at nine pip emma."

"Howja know that, Fred, old bean?" I asked, successfully focusing on him even though he was receding as if being drawn backward through a sewer pipe.

"The cops told me, of course. We don't want to upset them, you know. They'd be darned annoyed if they busted in here and failed to find us sitting around sipping tea," Toombs said. Then shouted through the smoke: "Everybody got their pinkies ready?"

Everybody picked up a teacup and obediently raised a forest of pinkies.

By and by I needed to go to the bathroom. It was so long since I had partaken of ardent spirits that I was proceeding a trifle erratically by the time I reached the sordid facilities.

There was just one other man at the urinals. He was wearing a seedy suit and was busy shaking himself. He smiled across ingratiatingly. When I had finished he was still at the urinal, standing there with both hands up to smooth down his crinkly hair. For some reason he had lowered his trousers and underwear to his knees, so that his member was in full view. In fact he had shaken it so thoroughly that it had grown fat.

"Put that away at once," I said sternly. "Supposing somebody sees it?"

When I sashayed back to the table through the crush, noise,

and smoke, everybody was watching me, grinning away expectantly and nudging each other. "Meet anybody interesting in there, General?" one of them shouted.

"Just some shop assistant or other," I drawled. "In hardware, presumably."

"We've all decided to vote for you," said the whiskery old farmer at my table, as soon as the uproar had subsided. "Though I still think you don't stand a chance against them lawyers and people."

"Oh, I don't know," I said, beaming around at all the ugly faces. Which now included the ugliest of them all, Whistler McMulligan. He was arguing with the waiter, who was looking scared but determined enough. Apparently McMulligan had no money to pay for his drinks.

Just as I plumped back into my seat, McMulligan stood up and made a grab for the waiter. Toombs got between them and managed to quiet the mechanic.

"Hello, McMulligan," I said gaily. "Just the man I came in to see."

"What about?" he asked rudely.

"Lemmee see now, what was it about . . . ?"

I waited until the others had vanished into the smoke before scraping my chair closer to the brute for a confidential chat. But not too close. He looked thoroughly annoyed at being cut off in his prime. And I informed him that I had just concluded a deal with Talbots to deliver certain merchandise by air to a certain destination in a certain foreign country and would require his services as a flight mechanic, if he were prepared to volunteer.

His mean little eyes drilled into my nice big brown ones. "You mean you're going into the smuggling racket?" he asked, looking as surprised as his cemented features would allow.

"Please. The export rack—er, trade," I said with dignity, while dipping a forefinger into a puddle of Gold Bullion and drawing a pattern on the table top.

McMulligan sat staring at me in a calculating way. "It could be dangerous," he observed.

"Not according to what I've been told."

"With the risk of being nabbed and sent to Sing Sing."

He carried on like this for some time, obviously exaggerating the dangers in order to get the best deal. Finally I got tired of fencing and asked, "How much?"

"A hundred a trip," he answered promptly, licking his dry lips.

"A *hundred?*" I exclaimed, trying to sound indignant; though that figure was precisely what I'd calculated the job was worth.

"Oh, very well," I said. "But that must include your full-time services as a mechanic."

"Sure," McMulligan said. "It's a deal. With twenty bucks in advance."

"You mean, right now?"

"Yeah, right now."

Which, after some further grumbling, I paid him.

This turned out to be a mistake, for he immediately purchased two bottles of Gold Vault and started drinking up the down payment. Worse, he insisted on my keeping pace with him. As I was already somewhat squiffy, it was not easy to convince him that I had given up drinking. Besides, he was the sort of person who took umbrage if you declined his hospitality. He wasn't good enough for me, was that it? It was all right to employ him as a lowly mechanic but not to seal the agreement over one lousy little drink, was that it? So I had perforce to keep him alcoholic company.

But the real trouble started when the only man in Gallop who would confess to having seen any of my movies came over and began talking to me. "Sure I've seen one of your movies," he said. "Me and the wife saw it, couple of years ago. What was it about again? Oh yeah, where this big guy is beatin' you over the head with a wreckin' bar, and you're just standin' there against the wall, takin' it. Then it turns out you're standin' just under this spike, see, in the wall. So it's only the spike what he's hittin', eh?"

"That was Harold Lloyd," I said.

"Or, wait a minute, was it where your partner keeps walkin' into the cement or some'n'?"

"That was Laurel and Hardy."

"Jeez, they're funny."

Some time later I was still sitting there amidst the smoke and fumes and the tan, snuff, philamot, and burnt siena decor, cuddling a receptacle that had suddenly and mysteriously transformed itself from a glass to a nice cup of cold tea, while

McMulligan was growing steadily more irritated with the movie-goer's endless plot summaries, until finally, when my fan started on the plot of *Quo Vadis,* the mechanic suddenly seized him by the throat and was busy strangling him when the police, led by their chief, Mr. Lough, who was plainly anticipating a scene of domestic bliss, tranquillity, and tannin, arrived to find them-selves embroiled in a battle with a maddened McMulligan. Whereupon the rest of the clientele, forgetting that they were in a tea shop, and overjoyed at the opportunity to reestablish the pioneer tradition of the tavern brawl, joined in, until every stick of furniture in the place was shattered, including the large brown clock on the wall, which ended up in the street, having been thrown through the glass panel of the front door just sec-onds after I had lurched, giggling, through it—through the front door, that is, I having decided that, however enjoyable a tavern brawl might be, I had, as official Liberal candidate for the dis-trict, a certain dignity to maintain. So I ricocheted out practi-cally unscathed except for a set of skinned knuckles.

McMulligan, though, was not so lucky. It took four of the gen-darmes to subdue him and drag him up the street to the lockup, and worse, two days later, Magistrate Hipsey gave him a thorough wigging and thirty days in the cooler.

Oooh, I was annoyed at him for running amuckmulligan in that fashion. I really needed a mechanic for all sorts of chores, particularly engine starts. Now I would have to fly the huge Vimy bomber unaided until I could locate another mechanic who was both competent and disreputable enough to risk his freedom and reputation in the export business.

That it was I who had made McMulligan's sojourn in the hoosegow possible by enabling him to drink to his heart's con-tent did not in the least ameliorate my ire.

Peering Nervously from the Vimy

"I often think it's comical," I sang, fifteen hundred feet above the outskirts of Montreal,

> "How nature always does contrive
> That every boy and every gal
> That's born into the world alive
> Is either a little Liberal
> Or else a little Conserva-tive."

Some people liked to sing in the shower; I liked to sing in an airplane.

Today, though, the joys of Gilbert, Sullivan, and flight were not entirely unalloyed. I was flying a five-place bomber single-handedly, and beneath my warblings was a distinctly uneasy bass line. Not that a solitary pilot could not cope easily enough even with this huge biplane—in the air. The apprehension was caused by the prospect of having to handle it on the ground—inside enemy territory.

The momentary jollity evaporated completely as McMulligan bullied his way again into my thoughts. Damn the fellow. The only qualified man within a hundred miles, and he had to get himself jailed. I would have to find a replacement somehow. I really needed a mechanic, not just to monitor the engines in flight and maintain them on the ground, but for a number of other chores, especially cranking up. Unlike most aerial power plants, which were fired by twirling the propeller by hand, the Vimy's Rolls-Royce Eagles were started with built-in crank han-

dles, as in an automobile before the self-starter came along. You
had to stand, first on the starboard, then the port lower wing,
and wind the handles faster and faster until the generator summoned up enough energy to turn the crankshaft. A pilot could
manage it by himself in an emergency, but it was not a recom-
mended procedure, not least because it required an undignified
scramble from wing to wing, with the risk that the airplane
might start taxiing in circles by itself, or run into a bog, a building, a spectator, or a cliff if there was one handy.

Until I found another mechanic, I would just have to keep my
fingers crossed that nothing serious would go wrong with the engines during the number of trips required to accumulate
sufficient funds to see me through the fall election campaign.

Fortunately only eight or so trips would be necessary, for I
would be making a net profit of at least five hundred dollars a
trip. Mrs. Talbot was paying me two dollars fifty a bottle; and I
had managed to cram twenty-nine cases of the stuff into the
spare cockpits and into the reinforced fuselage of the Vimy.

The Talbot lorry had delivered the consignment to the farm
just three hours previously, every case secured with a red seal, to
indicate that the contents were for export and were therefore
duty-free. To make sure that the whisky was not going straight
to the domestic market, the chief excise officer had accompanied
the lorry. He had warned me that if he did not get back a properly receipted delivery note from the consignees I would end up
in jail on a charge of defrauding the customs.

Plump, middle-aged Mr. Jewell had been most officious about
the grave consequences if I ever reimported any bonded liquor;
but I wasn't offended. "It's all right, Mr. Jewell," I'd said in an
understanding sort of way. "I know why you're bullying me, but
you go right ahead if it makes you feel any better. It's psycho-
logical, you see. It stems from your childhood sixty or seventy
years ago—or possibly from the month before last—that shameful
incident in Mrs. Talbot's office? Come on now, 'fess up, old man,
that's the real reason you're being so shirty, isn't it?" And when
he said nothing but just keened a bit, clenching and unclenching
his fists, I added, in case he had forgotten, "*You* remember?
When I caught you with your trousers tangled in your sus-
penders? With you all covered in oil like a sardine?"

"You better watch what you're saying," he managed at length, sounding as if he were being massaged all over again all over. "Let me remind you I'm an officer of the Crown—I don't have to take this from a—a cheap smuggler."

"That's right," I'd said, giving him a sympathetic pat. "You get it out of your system, Mr. Jewell—just like last time when you were exposing your oleaginous quarters to all and sundry. I suppose you were doing that because you wanted to feel needed—or should that be kneaded—with a *k?*"

But Freud must have been wrong, for my profound psychoanalysis didn't appear to comfort him in the least, judging by the way he had lurched off, looking all knotted and blotchy, and started shouting at the lorry driver who was helping to load the Vimy. His kink may have been more deep-seated than I'd thought.

As the aging bomber droned toward the center of the city, I took a moment off work to squint over the side and admire the view. At least I was being treated to fine weather on this first mission into the unknown. The sky was cloudless, and even at fifteen hundred feet the air was caressingly warm. The gray waters of the St. Lawrence were sparkling in the sun. I could see a good thirty miles of the river, streaked here and there by the wakes of motorboats, barges, and cargo vessels.

Gazing across at the city, it suddenly occurred to me that this was an excellent opportunity to recce the new distillery. There was plenty of time, as my appointment was not until three o'clock, and I was curious to see how the new premises compared with the sprawling complex that was being abandoned in Gallop. Besides, one never knew—I might have to divert here in an emergency.

Mrs. Talbot had mentioned that there was plenty of room to land an airplane. So instead of turning south according to my flight plan, I banked over to line up with the long, straight slash of the Lachine Canal and continued downriver for a few miles.

Mount Royal, with its great cross sharp in the sunlight, drifted past on the left. Then the docks spoked below, crowded with shipping. A Cunard liner was being nudged and butted by tugs into its ocean terminal, the rails lined with waving passengers.

The new distillery was supposed to be about four miles be-

yond the Jacques Cartier Bridge, but I had to circle twice before
I managed to identify it by its circular pump house. It took up
much less acreage than the one in Gallop, but the buildings, five
of them, were obviously more capacious. Two of the warehouses
appeared to be still under construction. However, it was the
wide-open spaces I was interested in; they were not nearly as
wide open as Mrs. Talbot had indicated. What on earth did she
think I was driving, a dragonfly? The grassy area, partly enclosed by buildings, was barely two hundred yards long. There
wasn't even an adequate approach—there were tall trees along
the riverbank at one end, not to mention the building at the far
end, which had a high, narrow archway in the middle. I'd never
get down there without mashing the aircraft.

As I turned away and started to climb, I made a mental note
not to indulge in an emergency anywhere near these premises.

Less than an hour later I was at the far end of Lake Champlain at five thousand feet, still bellowing the occasional ditty in
the brilliant sunlight. It wasn't until I had started the descent toward Lake George that I realized that I was even less carefree
than I had suspected. As I pulled back the power levers I experienced a sinking sensation that had nothing to do with the physical descent. Until now this had been an innocent, two-hour trip
along the Ottawa River and over Montreal, and then down Lake
Champlain, with no laws broken. I could still be a cowardy custard and turn back. But the moment I nudged the wheel forward
and started down, I was committed to an enterprise that was as
uncertain as it was illegal; for there was no guarantee that the
reception committee would actually be at the rendezvous east of
Lake George. I might instead be met by a passel of excisemen
bearing invitations to a federal hoosegow.

But it's amazing how easy it is to convince yourself of the
rightness of a naughty cause when there's something in it for
you. Only a couple of weeks ago, despite an intimate knowledge
of the hardships of prohibition—for I had been a dedicated deni-
zen of the New York speakeasies myself at one time—I would not
have dreamed of contravening the regulations of our good neighbor to the south. I had nothing but friendly feelings for the
United States. That country had provided me with many friends
and a good living until the movie industry had been forced by

circumstances beyond their control to release me. Now here I was, defying its very government, which, with undoubtedly altruistic motives, had decreed that a hundred years of excessive alcoholic consumption and the resulting degredation, misery, hangovers, and would have to stop. How could I be so mean to the most open and generous society on earth, a nation almost without vices . . . except for its addiction to violent solutions, intolerance, and bombast? . . . No, it was sheer ingratitude on my part. The U.S. had been good to me. Well, fairly good. It had to be admitted, for instance, that the film industry had gotten rid of me fast enough the moment my utter lack of talent became too evident. That would never have happened in good old Canada where a lack of talent was no bar to advancement, provided one was skilled enough at self-promotion. As for my employment by the U.S. airmail service, it had been terminated quite rudely, now I came to think of it, through the intervention of one of the most dedicated of my American enemies, of whom I had many. More enemies than friends, when one really thought about it. No, but honestly, I didn't have all that much of an obligation to the States. Moreover, I had given the country at least as much as I had received. For example, I had contributed substantially to its hotel industry by staying in their best hostelries whenever possible. And what had the Americans ever done for me? Sacked me, neglected me, spurned me, that's what. Driven me out of the country, the country that I had fought and bled and died for—keeping it safe for three whole years, from 1914 to 1917, while I had single-handedly held back the German hordes, not to mention the Russian hordes, the Irish hordes, etc. No, but really, what did I *really* owe the United States? I'd only lived there in the first place because, while collecting surplus aircraft from Texas—all of them faulty, of course—I kept crashing on my way home, until finally I reached Long Island and ran out of aircraft. At one point the American government had even attempted to deport me. I'd only been saved because I had fought so hard to stay, showing the immigration people my medals, my alien resident visa, the tears in my eyes, and so forth. God, yes, how I had suffered down there, friendless, penniless, neglected, and despised. And look at that scurrilous campaign against me in Chaffington's New York newspaper, merely because I had blown

him up in his hotel suite, seduced his daughter, ruined his epic
movie, and exposed his moral turpitude. I mean, what bloody
right had the Yanks to impose prohibition anyway, merely because the work force were usually too hung over to go to work
on Monday mornings? Good Lord, I was doing them a favor, really, in bringing succor to their downtrodden masses who were
yearning to be free of enforced sobriety, using up my last reserves of adrenaline in order to replace their bathtub gins and
whoop-up bug juices and other blinding concoctions with the
finest alcohol obtainable, Philippa Talbot's top whiskies, which
had been aged for hours and hours in genuine sherry casks—God
damn it, I was doing the American people a tremendous favor.
What bloody right had they to criticize me for trying to make
their desiccated world a better place to live in, the ungrateful
swine?

By the time I realized that I was one of the great benefactors
of mankind, the Vimy was well past Fort Henry and droning
over beautiful Lake George. The airplane and I were still drifting downward at half throttle.

This was the point where I had to turn due east. Somewhat
anxiously I scanned the terrain below for signs of life—woods-
men, boatmen, bathers, hermits, anybody who was likely to
snitch to the authorities that there was a large foreign aircraft in
the neighborhood; but there was nobody in sight. Even in this
undeveloped part of the country, that seemed remarkable. Mrs.
Talbot's contacts appeared to have chosen the area well—assuming, of course, that they knew enough about airplanes not to
have selected some small, lumpy meadow as an airdrome, with
hundred-foot trees at one end and hydro pylons at the other.

Mrs. Talbot's assurances that there was plenty of room to land
in Montreal had sapped my confidence a bit in her planning
ability.

Well, we would see in a few minutes. And after all, if my
airdrome turned out to be volcanic terrain or something, I could
always turn back and blame her. So, darting a glance at the Pitot
and adding a touch of power, I revolved the Vimy's large steering wheel and trod daintily on the left elevator pedal. The great
sixty-eight-foot wings canted, then leveled again. The bright
waters of the lovely, tree-packaged lake, patched here and there

with shadows—high cloud was now forming overhead—disappeared under the flat snout of the airplane. Then a green carpet of untidy woodland unrolled. Six hundred feet indicated, three-quarter throttle, sixty-five miles an hour, heart thumping.

At which point some disaster had to occur. All four magnetos conking out simultaneously. A wing falling off. Three hundred and forty-eight bottles of Gold Bullion tearing through the reinforced floor of the fuselage and sterilizing the landscape with alcohol. A failure to find the landing ground or, more likely, the discovery that the reception committee had panicked and departed at high speed in their bulletproof Hupmobiles.

Instead, making me more uneasy than ever, nothing appeared to be awry. The field was exactly as Mrs. Talbot had described it: a long, unobstructed field alongside a straight stretch of railway track—or railroad track, as this was New York State—unless it was Vermont.

They had even complied with my request that they set out three lanterns, green at the threshold, white in the middle of the landing run, and red at the far end.

Slipping down to three hundred feet, I banked the big machine to the north, parallel to the railroad track, gazing suspiciously over the side as I flew past, expecting to find at least a few tussocks and humps carefully sited so as to tear off the double landing gear of the Vimy as efficiently as possible; but the ground seemed to be flat enough under the longish, wispy yellow grass. The only difficulty, and a minor one at that, was that the field was less than a hundred yards wide, with the railroad line—apparently a little used siding, for the lines were rusty—on one side, and the forest on the other. Otherwise there seemed to be no problems whatsoever. Even the reception committee was in place. As I flew over the red lantern, three men appeared from beneath a stand of scrub oak and saluted. Or perhaps they were merely shielding their eyes from the sun.

The only thing that puzzled me, as I flew round to survey the field a second time, was that there were no roads or even trails into the area. How were they going to get the consignment out again? However, that was their problem. Mine was to get down safely with eight thousand dollars' worth of booze.

So, completing the second circuit, I banked onto final a few hundred feet short of the field. A small reedy lake glimmered past, then a swamp, then dry bushland. I lowered the wing slightly, to allow for a crosswind from the left, the usual northwest wind. The wires hissed between the four sets of interplane struts, the engines merely murmuring. At fifty feet, now sheltered from the wind, I straightened the wings. The grass ceased to blur and came into focus. Steadily back on the wheel as the great biplane sank, hesitated, then bumped tidily onto all four wheels. Wait for it—some pothole, crevice, or granite step to crack the undercart and slew the machine onto one wing. No. It sped along with no more than the usual stately bump-bump, before coming to a stop hardly more than a hundred yards from where it had touched down.

Two members of the reception committee came trotting up a minute later, looking a trifle out of place in this kind of country. They were both attired in white shirts and sober ties, and the suspendered trousers of business suits. They were carrying the jackets over their arms—their only concession to the heat.

One of them was even wearing a homburg, though it was pushed back from a sallow, sweat-streaming brow, the tilted brim revealing a pair of tiny, unblinking eyes stolen from a Massasauga rattler.

"Hey," he shouted rudely over the splutter of the engines, pointing toward the track. "Drive this thing over there, will you? We ain't humpin' the stuff that far."

"Lead and we shall follow," I called out, feeling jaunty now that I was safely down.

After a blank stare, he turned and walked ahead, glancing back every few seconds as the huge aircraft blatted along a few feet behind his fancy two-tone shoes. His companion, an ox of a man with muscles bulging pinkly through his sweat-wrung shirt, merely stood and gaped at the Vimy's long gray fuselage and vermilion engines. He looked mentally defective and had a harelip.

It was only when we got there that I saw how they intended getting the merchandise out of this neck of the woods. I hadn't noticed it from the air. Sitting on the rusty tracks was one of those little railroad trolleys, the kind that were operated by

pumping a lever back and forth. Hooked up to it was another
wagon with a long wooden body with high sides, easily large
enough to take twenty-nine cases of whisky.

"Quite ingenious," quoth I as I climbed down from the cockpit and stretched luxuriously in the sunlight. "Though I don't
envy you the task of pumping your little freight train along the
track in this heat."

"Yeah. Let's go, let's go," said the one with the speaking part.
The third member of the reception committee was still some distance away. He was collecting the three lanterns that had delin-
eated the landing run. I looked toward him, shielding my eyes
from the sun. He seemed vaguely familiar. . . .

"Hey, you. Pierre. We ain't got all day, you know," said Snake
Eyes. His real name, I learned later, was Clutch Revalli. "We're
not here to get a suntan."

So I got down to the job of opening the hatch, formerly the
rear gunner's downward-firing aperture, and hauling out the
freight along the fuselage rollers. I was quite enjoying myself
now, in the heat and silence, after more than two hours of bellowing engine and trepidation. There was obviously going to be
no trouble from the authorities in this isolated spot. Even if they
managed to force a way through the tangled woods, we would
hear them coming from a mile away. It was a cleverly selected
landing site, all right, presumably the safest spot within reasonable distance of Albany.

As I heaved out box after box, Revalli inspected each one suspiciously before heaving it up to his thick chum, who was standing in the little railway truck. Presumably Revalli was making
sure that I hadn't been throwing any wild parties en route.

By the time we had finished maneuvering the last of the boxes
from the fuselage we were all sweating like bathroom tiles. As
we turned to the merchandise in the cockpits, I paused to stare
at the fellow in the distance, wondering why he didn't hurry
things up by coming forward to give us a hand. Judging by
Revalli's vicious glances, he was wondering the same thing.

"Who's he, the foreman?" I asked.

"Yeah, sure. Come on, get goan, will ya?"

Finally, as the last of the boxes were being stowed in the
titchy train, the third man started to amble toward us. The closer

he approached the more familiar he looked: a stalwart, elegant
figure in a cheap but spotlessly clean cotton shirt. He was holding a tweed jacket over his shoulder by one forefinger. It looked
just like . . . But no, it couldn't be.

"My dear friend, how overjoyed I am to see you again," the
fellow exclaimed, looking not the least surprised to encounter me
in the wilds of New York, or Vermont, or wherever it was.

As I gaped at him, my jaw hanging like that of a faultily wired
skeleton, he flung aside his jacket and placed his hands on my
upper arms, holding me at arm's length. "And you are just the
same," he said, his voice running amuck with emotion. "Perhaps,
yes, perhaps just a little less hair; though what a noble forehead
that reveals, to be sure. Other than that, the same old delightful
companion, the same, charming, loving fellow of old."

"What in flaming hell are you doing here, you indolent, good-
for-nothing, stove-hogging fop?" I asked faintly. But George
Garanine wasn't even listening. Quite indifferent to Harelip's
dull-witted gapes and Revalli's sneering gaze, he was hugging
me to his cheap cotton shirt, and then kissing me on the cheeks
as if he were a general and I had just won the bleeding Médaille
des Folies Bergères, with oak leaves.

Prisoner and Jailer, August '23

As there was nowhere else for George Garanine to go, his rumrunning associates apparently being eager to abandon him in the woods like Hansel and Gretel, there was nothing else for it but to take him home with me to Gallop. Thus once again I found myself sharing a dilapidated abode with Trotsky's right-hand man manqué.

"But don't think you're staying on the farm forever," I shouted. "You can live here until you find your feet, and that's all. I'll want you out of the house by eleven o'clock at the latest."

The slavering Slav just gave me another affectionate embrace and said, "Of course, Bartalamyeh. Oh, is it not vonderful that we are together again, after all these months? I am so happy it makes me vant to veep."

It made me vant to veep too. I'd hoped that I had seen the last of him, after thoroughly betraying him and abandoning him to his fate in Moscow.

However, the situation at the Machin farm proved to be rather more bearable than in that Muscovite shambles. He appeared to have hooked himself up to a battery charger since leaving Mother Russia. Perhaps the bustling North American atmosphere had invigorated him. At any rate he was soon making himself quite useful round the barn-board hangar, cheerfully helping even with chores that demanded much application and patience, like the tensionometer work on the rigging of the Vimy and the straining of the gasoline through the chamois filters.

He even volunteered to be my official mechanic. At first I

dismissed the idea as absurd. He had never worked on anything but motorcar engines. He had never even seen an aero engine until a pair of them flew him to Gallop. But he transferred what was obviously a considerable mechanical expertise to aircraft power plants with an ease that surprised me. He had an instinctive understanding of machinery. I looked on aero engines with awe and uncertainty, but, "Auto engine, airplane engine, is all the same," he said; and proved it when I gave him the old Renault engine to play with. He had it disassembled and put together again in one weekend. It even worked afterward.

After that I let him loose on the Puma, and finally, with trepidation, on the Vimy's Eagles. When nothing disastrous happened, one day I took a deep breath and asked if he was willing to accompany me on the next smuggling trip. When he accepted readily enough, I knew that, however apprehensive I might feel, he himself was confident enough of his maintenance work, otherwise he would surely never have accepted.

In other respects he was the same old George Garanine, blindly affectionate, tolerant to an intolerable degree, but still behaving as if the greatest satisfaction that others could experience in life was to serve him. I believe that even his former master, Trotsky, had once, without thinking, draped a rug over George's knees while George was driving him to the nearest Soviet snafu. If a hard case like Trotsky could be affected, even momentarily, by the vibrations of innocent expectancy that radiated from Garanine, the citizens of Gallop had no chance whatsoever. Within a fortnight of his arrival in town he had earned the devotion of about half the citizens. Young girls went all limp and lump-throated at the sight of his moist, smiling mouth accented by that perfectly symmetrical pencil mustache and those bright blue eyes canopied by long dark eyelashes. He looked more like a movie idol than a penniless refugee. Even the male population was conquered. Young store clerks adopted his sauntering walk, schoolboys followed him around, and the most oafish of street-corner loafers, who invariably nickered, neighed, or whinnied whenever I passed, fell silent at his approach, regarding him in a surreptitious, surly way as if moved to despise his elegant appearance but affected in spite of themselves by his open expression of childlike interest in everything around him.

Of course, it may have been the equally obvious power of his broad shoulders that restrained the idlers, but I didn't think so.

As for Miss Rawsthorne, who treated everybody from distillery worker to ministerial favorite with forthright disrespect, she practically simpered when he kissed her hand. And Karley offered him a job, and Mr. Wattle spoke of him as a perfect specimen of manhood, and Mr. Peel, the Conservative candidate, volunteered to legalize—free of charge—George's status with Immigration and Colonization, and Jim Boyce gave him half a dozen shirts, hardly worn, and Mrs. Hipsey had him to tea—*in the house.* And Mrs. Talbot had him to bed.

Plainly entranced by the extraordinarily handsome newcomer from the moment I first introduced them, Philippa had promptly invited him to dinner for a tit-à-tit—as she pronounced it—and he had not returned home until five the following morning.

"What a woman," he whispered when he arose the next afternoon. "What freedom from bourgeoise shame, what inwentiveness in boudoir. Truly she is the mother of inwention."

Even my parents had fallen instantly in love with my erstwhile jailer. From the moment she first carried his luggage up to his room, Mother was as enslaved as any of his gruesome relatives in Russia. As for Father, I was amazed. I had never seen him so entranced by another human being. He watched and listened to the mustachioed lodger the way a disciple might have looked at Jesus, for God's sake, after a particularly telling miracle. Even when George trotted out his Russian proverbs, Father continued to listen intently, like the time when they were discussing Homer's Odyssey—like Papa, George had studied Greek at school—and George decorated his remarks with, *"A cabbage may grow in rich soil, have crinkly leaves, and be very tasty, but it is still a cabbage."* Father continued to nod gravely and appreciatively, with only the slightest furrow of the brow, as if he suspected that the saying might have suffered slightly in translation. It was quite a contrast to his reception of *my* Russian proverbs. I remember quoting a very similar saying soon after my return from Russia, to wit: *"A hat does not sit well on the head of a lettuce."* Papa had rounded on me to ask if I was ever going to stop talking arrant nonsense, and when I replied, "Of course; for as we say in Russia, *Even an intellectual can fall into a hole in the road in pitch-darkness,"* he actually hit me with his *Church Times.*

All in all, through George, I was learning more about my parents that summer than during the whole of the previous twenty-nine. With the exception of Anne Mackie, who, in losing her husband, was considered to have been morally negligent, my parents liked and responded positively to all my friends. Age seemed to be releasing them from emotional atrophy. But their attitude to George Garanine went far beyond liking. I was quite flummoxed by their adoration. It wasn't as if he did anything for them; bought them presents, or agreed with their opinions, or was particularly attentive—it was Mother who drew out a chair for *him* at the dining table—and he talked too much, went through the larder like a grizzly in a garbage dump, and even slept late, formerly an indictable crime in the Bandy household. But Mother just said, "The poor boy needs his sleep, after the terrible times he's been through in Godless Russia. Why, he still has dark smudges under his eyes."

I nearly informed her that it was Mrs. Talbot who was responsible for that. Instead I muttered that if George had smudges it certainly wasn't because of the Bolshies.

"No," Mother retorted. "It's because you work him too hard, Bartalamyeh."

See?

Had my parents not been treating me with a little more respect lately because of the nomination, I should have felt quite mortified by their preference, which seemed to suggest that it was George who was the beloved son, while I was merely a lodger who was years behind with the rent.

Apart from me, only Anne Mackie refused to join the Slavonic dance. She took an instant scunner to George, a dislike in which jealousy, as I realized at the end, played no small part. But what she said was, "For any man to be so beautiful, charming, and sympathetic, as well as masculine, is unnatural. Darn it, it's a man's duty to live up to women's attitude toward him as being useful enough but rather brutish. George is a double agent in the battle of the sexes."

Otherwise I was the only person within magnetizing range who seemed able to resist George's personality. I wondered uneasily if my strong feelings about him were not the result of guilt. In 1919 as a prisoner of war I had been given the freedom of Moscow on the understanding that I would make no attempt to leave the city until the war ended. But I had gone back on my word—which, regardless of the circumstances, rather confirmed, I fear, the suspicion that I was not really a gentleman. A real gentleman would have stuck to his word of honor, like the second in command in my first battalion, Major Marmalade, who had been captured during the Boer War and had promised the Boers that he would not attempt to escape from his tent, and had kept his word of honor even after the Boer camp was overrun by Lancashire Fusiliers; though admittedly he had looked a bit silly, sitting there in his tent for days on end, while various Fusiliers, civilian officials, minor diplomats, his batman, and his old mother had tried to tempt him outside with offers of fresh fruit, promotion, a membership in the Reform Club, and so forth.

Major Marmalade would undoubtedly have considered me an utter cad, not least because, by my default, I had put George in grave danger. For allowing me to escape he could very easily have been convicted of counterrevolutionary formalism or something equally meaningless and deadly, and sent to Siberia. . . . Though actually he did end up in Siberia, as that was the route he took to eventual freedom.

Still, his escape from the vengeful Bolshies had not lessened my feelings of dissatisfaction at having perforce betrayed his trust. So it was a great relief to find somebody else who shared my feelings about him . . . whatever those feelings really were.

Otherwise he was a godsend. By the time he and I had flown half a dozen rescue missions in aid of our parched cousins to the south, he had proved himself to be a faultless mechanic. The engines could not have sounded sweeter even under the care of a Rolls-Royce technician. And I was well on the way to a net profit of three thousand simoleons. Which was not bad for a total of twenty-four hours' work—few citizens of Gallop earned that much in an entire year.

By the beginning of August I was convinced that, gosh, smuggling was *easy*. Apart from maintenance and navigational preparations, all we had to do was to receive a lorryload of hooch in a discreet corner of the farm, fly to the Lake George area, and offload into the two-car bootleg special. It was all so safe and uneventful that my morale twittered upward like a skylark, especially as the preparations for the fall election campaign were also going quite smoothly: the advertising and publicity arrangements, finances, rentals, and all the other ways and means of dazzling, seducing, or bribing the electorate.

Anne Mackie was one of my part-time volunteers, and this led to a situation which indicated that I had not entirely overcome a tendency to disorderliness in my affairs. As a potential political inspiration to the nation, this worried me. Canadians were mentally disheveled enough—as witness the dichotomy of the national disposition to revolt against authority and the wish to be dominated by it—without my setting them any further bad examples.

As a voluntary field agent, Anne was increasingly involved in our planning meetings, and until our headquarters, a shop on Queen Street, was ready for business, these usually took place in the front parlor of the Machin farm. One hot Friday evening in August she arrived on her bicycle to find that nobody else had turned up for the meeting. Miss Rawsthorne was in Toronto, attempting, unsuccessfully as it turned out, to bully a bona fide publisher into issuing her latest volume of verse, while Jim Boyce had gone to Ottawa to try and persuade the party to cancel the appointment of a Tory returning officer—also unsuccessfully. And as my parents were away on their annual round of the relatives, and as George was busily satiating Mrs. Talbot in her ritzy roost in the northwest part of town, Anne and I found that we had the entire house to ourselves.

This made Anne nervous for some reason, and for the first half hour she spoke in rather a formal fashion, as we discussed the returning-officer situation. Returning officers were then appointed only for the election to which the writ referred. Usually the appointment was made from among the supporters of the government of the day, but it was a mark of the indifference, if not outright hostility, of the Liberal bigwigs toward my candidature that this time they had agreed to the appointment of a Conservative; to whit, Magistrate Hipsey. As a returning officer could exert considerable influence on behalf of his own party, and often did, this was yet another blow to my already depreciated chances in Gallop.

"And this smuggling operation of yours could be dangerous," Anne said stiltedly, smoothing down her neat, pleated skirt. "I'm really concerned about that."

"No need to worry," I said with a terrifically brave smile. "I'm used to danger, you know."

"Oh, I'm not the least worried about *you*."

"No, of course not."

"It's the danger of the news getting out about you working for Mrs. Talbot, that's what worries us. Normally people wouldn't mind in the least. Rumrunners are quite the heroes these days. But if it gets out, it could cause resentment. It will make it look as if you were on Mrs. Talbot's side."

"Well, of course I'm not. George is the only one on her side— and on her back and front too."

"Don't be vulgar, please. Anyway, that's how it will look to others."

I got up and snaked through the overstuffed furniture to the window. "Well, in that case, I'll just have to be more discreet than ever, won't I?" I said, peering morosely through the glass at the setting sun. "It would certainly be ironic if the way I was being forced to finance the campaign reduced its chances still further."

When she answered, her voice sounded much more placating. "Yes, it would," she said. "Because I really want you to win, Bart."

"Do you really, Anne?"

"Yes. I need you to get my divorce bill through Parliament."

We laughed, and a moment later our eyes locked by accident, and for some reason neither of us seemed able to break the connection. Simultaneously we became aware of the silence. The house was hushed enough as it was. For a whole minute the only sound was a reverberation of squirrels along the twisted tin eavestroughing three floors up.

"You look really nice this evening," I said impulsively.

It was true. She looked different, somehow. My eyes started roller-coastering over the contours of her white silk blouse that not even the fashionably stern restraint of the underwear in that region could subdue, and down to her long tibias, outlined under a pleated gray skirt. Then I realized why she looked different.

"You've bobbed your hair," I said.

I thought that was courageous of her. Not even the sauciest of the local girls had yet begun to bob their hair. Anne's was now so short as to brazenly expose her entire ears. She would have looked quite like one of the svelte flappers in the *Saturday Evening Post* had her broad, calm face with its superbly molded lips exhibited a little less strength of character.

"Do you like it? I wasn't sure at first, but . . . Mrs. Talbot likes it too. It's hot in here."

"Yes."

"Do you have anything to drink?"

"Good idea," I said heartily. "Let's see if there's any lemonade in the icebox."

We had reached the kitchen before she said, "I was thinking of something stronger."

"Ah. Ah," I said, concealing my surprise by looking up at the fly-dotted light bowl in the ceiling, as if that was where we kept the liquor. "I fear," I said at length, "that alcohol is banned in this abode."

As I turned I bumped against her. She drew in a breath of outrage, as if I had clawed at her pleats. Though maybe it wasn't outrage. Her staring eyes seemed filled rather with suspense, and her breathing was unsteady.

Suddenly I needed a drink myself. "Wait—I think Jim Boyce keeps a bottle in his room," I said huskily. "Let's go and see."

I managed to locate a bottle of Talbot's Gold Bullion in the cupboard behind the water cistern in Boyce's room. "There's only a quarter left, though," I said doubtfully.

"That should be enough," she said.

"I'll get the glasses."

As I clumped down the back stairs—enough for what? I wondered. Though I thought I knew the answer. The suspicion was confirmed when she failed to follow me downstairs.

Gad, it was amazing how opportunities like this invariably arose unexpectedly, without the slightest lascivious hint of warning. Not that I expected women to announce it ahead of time: "I shall feel like making love at four-fifteen this afternoon," or nine pip emma, or whatever. Still, such decisions on their part always seemed to be impulsive—like a snap test in school.

Well, that was all right—I knew the lesson backward. So I

snatched out a couple of tumblers and shot up the back stairs again, feet thundering eagerly on the bare oak treads. When I regained the landing she was just glancing into my parents' bedroom at the front of the house. George had the second-best bedroom adjoining. Boyce and I slept in the back rooms.

"Having a look round? That's good," I panted. "Here, I'll show you the rest of the house." And as she had already seen Boyce's room, I showed her mine. "Mine's bigger than his," I said proudly.

"How do you know?"

"Eh? Well, see for yourself," I said, gesturing around at the tastefully wallpapered walls, with their design of purple grapes and hemlock, and at the oak bed, the mahogany cupboard, the bed, bedside table, faded red rug, and the wooden bed.

Which both of us busied ourselves not looking at. The bed was not really worth looking at anyway, especially as it was only thirty inches wide.

"I've fallen out more than once," I remarked.

"Who with?"

"The bed. I've fallen out of it more than once, it's so narrow."

I suddenly remembered that there was an old brass bedstead in the attic.

"And then there's the attic," I said, clearing my throat. "Nobody ever goes up there." So we went up there.

In the attic the horizontal sun was flaring through the Dutch dormer. It was stiflingly hot under the exposed rafters.

When I smacked open the window, hoping for a few gusts of fresh air, a spider scuttled over the sill. It was so big it left footprints in the dust.

I jumped back with an involuntary gasp. Frankly I was a bit scared of arachnids.

"What?" Anne whispered, clutching my arm, thinking I'd seen a posse of Puritan vigilantes through the window.

"Nothing. Just an insect," I said shakily.

"It's pretty dusty up here," she whispered, moving closer.

The touch of silk blouse and cotton thigh instantly had me even more hot and bothered. Before I knew what was happening, I was giving her a squelchy kiss and a quick fumble.

"It's silly to be so nervous," she whispered. "After all, we're both free . . . You're quite sure nobody will turn up?"

"Just me," I husked, looking at the bare, dusty mattress on the brass bedstead and wondering whether I dared break the spell by clumping downstairs again for clean sheets from the airing cupboard.

"You do like me, don't you, Bart?"

"Me too—I mean, yes."

"I didn't think you did, at first. But I did, right from the start. I thought you were . . ." She hesitated, apparently uncertain of the word to describe me. She solved the problem by using no word at all. "You're the kind of person people turn and look at more than once."

"Probably can't believe their eyes, first time."

She stared down at a nail that was sticking up from one of the floorboards. "You do want to, don't you?"

"You bet."

"*Quant à moi* . . . sorry, bit of pretentiousness—I tend to use French phrases when I'm nervous—as for me, it's no good my saying that I'm not one of those girls. I suppose every woman is one of those girls."

"Jolly good."

"It's been four years. Though I never really got much out of it. Gordon was not very sensitive. . . . Anyway, you're it. If you really want," she said, and laughed shakily, and waited, as the attic glowed rosy in the sunset.

Fifty-five asterisks later, as we lay talking softly in the gloaming, she murmured, "That wasn't too bad, really."

"M'kew."

"Mind you, I've only Gordon to compare you with, and he was no Halley's comet."

"M'm."

There was a longish but comfortable enough silence before she added, "Still, now I've been reminded, I'm no longer so keen on moving to Montreal with the firm." And after another long but slightly less comfortable pause: "Though of course there's nothing really to keep me here, is there?"

I stared guardedly through the twilit dust that still hung in the air after the beating the mattress had taken. At one critical point, half an hour ago, the dust had brought on quite a fit of coughing . . . though actually the pneumatic effect of the expirations had enhanced the proceedings.

"I suspect my wife Katherine used up most of the available love, Anne."

There was a rather empty silence from the other half of the bare mattress. When she spoke again it was over a laugh. "Sorry," she said. "I despise that sort of thing. Trying to get some kind of commitment. Just because we've . . ." She gestured down at our gleaming forms. "Sorry about the female lapse."

"'S all right—I like female laps."

"Anyway, I've had enough of that kind of maneuver. And the truth is I like working for Philippa. She treats me better than any man ever did."

A few minutes later she said, "By the way, is it true that when you were in New York you were mixed up with gangsters and people?"

It was such a casual inquiry that I immediately suspected that it wasn't. I wondered if she had just reported for duty. She was, after all, very close to Mrs. Talbot.

Which brought the corollary and slightly disappointing thought that we were now getting to the real reason she had taken to the mattress: to pump me in an entirely different sense.

"I wouldn't say that," I murmured. "I met a few bootleggers and such socially, that's all. Why?"

"Well, naturally I'm intrigued. It's not everyone who's hobnobbed with the underworld. You bought the Vimy from one of them, didn't you? What was his name again?"

"Tony Batt. That was just a straightforward business deal."

"Did you know that it's Tony Batt you're delivering the whisky to?"

I started so markedly that another cloud of dust arose.

"Tony? Are you sure?"

"Of course. Didn't you know?"

"No . . . I'll be darned," I said faintly.

Though I shouldn't have been all that surprised. I had known Tony Batt quite well, first in Archangel where he had dealt on the black market in vast quantities of merchandise, most of it appropriated from the U.S. Army, and later in New York, where he was now involved in numerous rackets from rumrunning to movie production.

"So that's who Mrs. Talbot has been supplying, is it?"

She leaned up on one elbow, her sturdy form gleaming phosphorescent in the moonlight, and poked curiously at my left tit. "She's been dealing with him for a couple of years or so. . . . Phew, it's hot up here."

"Well, I hope she knows what she's doing. He could be a dangerous man to get involved with."

"He sounds nice over the telephone."

"Oh, he's likable enough," I agreed, and told her a little about Tony and his charm and his generosity, especially toward Russian émigrés, and his depredations, including the liberation from the port of Archangel of a five-thousand-ton ship. "He seems civilized," I said, over a cavernous yawn, "until you look at some of the people who work for him."

And so we continued to chat softly in the dusty moonlight, shifting occasionally to separate, with a rasping sound, contiguous patches of sweaty skin.

Unfortunately that wasn't the only sound that hot night. Just as we were getting interested again in exploring the various woods, gullies, hills, and saplings of the dermatological landscape, there came the unmistakable whack of the screen door three floors below.

For five frozen-lunged seconds we lay there, praying that it was a freak gust of wind or some cheeky raccoon. But then came the faint rumble of voices in the front hall.

At which we shot up into a sitting position, two pairs of terrified eyes gleaming through the suspended dust particles.

"Oh, my God," I said. "Don't tell me they're back."

Anne flung herself off the bed and thrashed about frantically, clawing around for her clothes.

"Wait—we mustn't panic," I whispered, tearing my shirt over my head. "Panic only leads to utter confusion." But this experienced advice went unheeded, not least because my voice was muffled by the peculiar haberdashery. I was having trouble finding the hole for my head. When I finally managed to force my way through I found I'd drawn the trousers over my head. I could tell because there was a row of fly buttons at my throat.

By then I could hear Papa at the foot of the ground-floor stairs, muttering, "He isn't usually in bed this early." I heard him grunting, then, loudly: "Are you asleep, Bartholomew?"

"Yes, yes, here I am, I'll be right down, don't bother coming up," I called back in a jolly voice; and, like a stage villain emerging from a secret passage, snatched up the rest of my clothing and tiptoed to the attic door and down the stairs. "I'll be right down," I shouted, to dissuade them from ascending.

And right down I was, only a few seconds later, in my dressing gown. "Well, well," I cried as I floundered onto the bottom step, tying a fourth or fifth knot in the dressing-gown cord. "So you're back already. My, my, this is a surprise, you being home early like this. You should have telephoned and I could have collected you from the railway station even though Gallop doesn't have a railway station, you have to go to Manotick Station as you probably know, having no doubt just come from there, but I wouldn't have minded driving over there, even though I was sound asleep, and, gosh, this is nice, but really I could have come for you, still, you're here now, and that's what counts, eh?"

They were both staring at me. I looked down quickly to make sure my hems were in order, but the dressing gown was decently fastened. In fact, with all those knots sticking out like a fresh umbilical cord, it looked as if it would never open again. "So, how did it go, eh? You must tell me all about it."

"Where on earth have you been?" Mother asked.

"Been? Been?"

"You're all dusty."

"Dusty? Dusty?"

"You're covered in dust."

"Ah. Ah. That's strange," quoth I, looking exceedingly puzzled as I inspected my bare feet and hands, and then turned to the hall mirror to study my face. It was true. The exposed areas were, indeed, covered in dust. My eyes were staring back at me like two cracked eggs in an abandoned nest.

"I sincerely hope you didn't go to bed in that condition," Mother said.

"No, no, I was just mucking about, that's all, upstairs, searching for . . . But tell me," I continued, cleverly changing the subject, "how come you're home so early?"

After a final, hopeless inspection of my powdery countenance, Papa turned away, massaging his eyes as if resigned to yet another example of the bewildering range of his son's activities. Or perhaps he was merely feeling dispirited after the unrewarding vacation with one of his sisters in Blethering, Ontario. Apparently that was why he had returned a couple of days early. The town being temporarily without a minister, he had been asked to officiate at a number of funerals. Normally he enjoyed the intellectual challenge of finding something good to say about the departed, while observing the custom of obscuring the fact that anybody had died at all. During this vacation, however, there were so many obsequies, he had the impression that the town's oldest inhabitants had all been waiting for him to appear so that they could expire in large numbers. He had spent most of his holiday making lame excuses over coffins. Worse, the vices of several of the deceased had been particularly difficult to slough over, especially one farmer whose hobby had been molesting sheep, and who had died of rubbing alcohol.

It was one-thirty on Saturday morning before I had a chance to sneak back to the attic. There I found Anne sitting on the bed in the moonlight, fully dressed, hands composed in pleated lap.

However, she was not quite as tranquil as she looked, for when I appeared she started up, her eyes staring and brilliant.

"I'm afraid you'll have to spend the night here," I whispered. "They've left their bedroom door open down there, as usual, and they're restless—as usual."

"God, I feel awful. I'm itching all over."

"Oh, that's just the dust," I explained.

"Dust?"

"Didn't you know? You're covered in dust."

"I am?"

"Yes. I was too, but it's all right now. I've had a good bath."

She stared at me speechlessly.

"But don't worry, Anne," I added. "We'll get you out of here in a few hours."

"Covered in dust."

"M'm."

"Oh, God. I knew I'd have to pay for it," she said tonelessly. To comfort her, I reached for her hand; but then, seeing how grimy it was, patted her on the back instead—gently, to avoid another cloud of dust. "You're being wonderfully calm about all this, Anne," I whispered disapprovingly.

"Oh well. I mean, I'm used to being trapped in people's attics, in imminent danger of being discovered by a houseful of morally righteous zealots."

"You surely wouldn't classify Jim Boyce as such?" I queried, to keep up the conversation.

"I would die if I met either him or George. As for your parents . . ." She shuddered. "If they saw me covered in dust like you were, they'd add one and one together and come up with one and one together— No, please don't touch me, Bartholomew. I wouldn't want you to get all dusty again."

We spent the rest of that night more or less in silence, sitting side by side on the bed, waiting for the dawn when even Papa was likely to be asleep. As I told Anne, my father often slept so badly that when, by the middle of the night, he could no longer stand his own restless tossings and grumblings, he would arise and prowl, or read improving texts in his study downstairs. When I was a boy he also used to listen at my bedroom door, to make sure I wasn't going blind.

However, at four-fifty in the morning, Father's raucous insomnia ceased, to be replaced by a whistling snore. Accordingly, Anne and I started to steal down from the attic. It took us five minutes to creep across the landing to the front stairs. We couldn't use the back stairs leading to the kitchen, as the treads had at least two loud creaks built into them.

We had almost reached the bottom of the main staircase when the screen door opened and George Garanine's guardsman's figure shadowed the beveled glass. We had barely scuttled to the top of the stairs again when he entered.

He then proceeded to sneak upstairs surreptitiously, as if burlesquing our progress of a few seconds before.

Thus we found ourselves back in the attic, and after one further attempt to escape had proved abortive, we were still up there at seven in the morning, when the folks arose.

It was only when we heard them shuffling down to the kitchen that Anne suddenly remembered her bicycle.

"Oh, my God, my bicycle," she whistled into my earhole. "It's outside. They'll see it."

"Where is it?"

"Leaning against the house. Oh, how could I have been so *stupid?*"

"Don't worry," I whispered back, reluctantly releasing her starboard marquisette bust cup. "I'll take care of it." And promptly tiptoed down to my room, where I dressed at a rate of knots, then continued casually down the front staircase.

Just as it occurred to me that I had forgotten to establish the exact location of the bicycle, Father came trudging along the passageway from the kitchen.

"Ah, Bartholomew," he said, fastening his celluloid collar with his thin, nervous fingers. "You're up. You can help me carry the drum of disinfectant to the alfresco facilities."

This was Father's name for the outside bog. He preferred to use the exterior privy in summer. He kept his favorite reading material out there, my old *Manual of Jurisprudence and Toxicology.*

"It's okay, I'll see to it myself," I said quickly; but he followed me out the front door nevertheless; and worse, while I was jittering about, trying to guess where the bicycle might be, on the east or west side of the house, he strode past, heading east.

"Come along, don't dawdle," he grunted.

I didn't. Surprising him by my eagerness to carry a hundred-pound container of Muller's Toilaseptic, I raced past him to the corner and skidded round it out of sight.

It was the right direction, all right. Just beyond the corner was Anne's bicycle. It was leaning against the clapboard. It was only two feet away. Papa would see it in less than five seconds. And recognize it, too, for it sported Anne's distinctive tartan saddlebag—the MacHinery Clan, I believe.

There was only one thing to do. I hurled myself aboard and pedaled frantically to the next corner, and rounded it a split second before Papa appeared.

The only problem was that I was now compelled to continue along the back of the house past the kitchen where Mother was working. Her kitchen window, six feet above ground level, overlooked the north side of the house.

Hoping that she was not standing at the window at this particular moment, I pedaled at top speed toward yet another corner, ducking low over the handlebars as I hurtled past the window.

Mother, however, must have caught a puzzling glimpse of something as it flashed past, for a few seconds later I heard the back door opening. Which meant that I was now committed to cycling round to the front of the house again, in case she peered round the northeast corner to make sure that she had not been seeing things when she caught that glimpse of a scarlet face whipping past, seven feet from the ground.

So, praying that Father wouldn't retrace his steps, I banked around the fourth and final corner, and found myself at the front door again. There was nobody in sight. But there was still no safe direction in which to veer, as it was all open ground between the facade of the house and the concession road. So I took the only course possible: I dismounted and wheeled the bicycle into the house.

Thirty seconds later I was back in the attic with the bicycle under my arm.

For some reason, Anne kept staring at me, as if she thought I were behaving irrationally in bringing the bike into the house. But it was obviously the only thing I could do, in the circumstances.

It was after eleven in the morning before I was able to return to the attic. I found Anne twisting about, with her silk-clad knees locked together and her lower lip clenched between her teeth.

"George is still asleep and the others are out in the vegetable garden," I said, slinging the bike over my shoulder. "Come on."

"I have to go to the bathroom," she replied, squeezing out the words like icing onto a cake.

"Darn it, there's no time for a wash and brush-up."

"Oh yes, there is," she replied, going more knock-kneed than ever, the redness of her face combining with the gray dust to form a distinctly unpleasant shade of burnt carmine. "I'm not disgracing myself any more than I have already."

Thus it was her fault that this escape attempt, too, was foiled; for by the time she had emerged from the bathroom, looking pale but clean and somewhat less knotted, the folks were back in the house with armfuls of carrots. So we had to retreat back into the attic once more, Anne, me, the bicycle, and a chamber pot decorated with dandelions.

"I could have gotten clean away if you hadn't wasted so much time in the bathroom," I grumbled.

"I didn't waste time, I assure you."

"Now I'm stuck. It could be hours now before I have another chance to get clear," I said peevishly, kicking the nail that was sticking up from the floorboards.

"What d'you mean, *you* get clear?" Anne whispered. "*I'm* the one who's trying to get clear."

"Uh . . . Oh yes."

"You live here—don't you remember?"

"I know."

"Are you sure you've got it straight now?" she whispered, wearing a thoroughly mean expression. "*I'm* the one who is trying to escape, not you. Got it?"

"Yes, yes, you don't have to go on about it."

"I don't know about that. Tell me, is this confusion of yours the result of having to escape from other bedrooms in similar circumstances?"

"Certainly not," I snapped, then winced at the loudness—and untruthfulness—of my response.

"Anyway, you've got it straight now, have you?" Anne asked. "We're trying to get *me* out of the house before my reputation is ruined, not you. Right?"

I just glared at her, but it didn't do a bit of good. She continued to regard me in a disillusioned way, as if the commanding figure she had once known and respected was proving to be something of a counterfeit.

Well, she wasn't the only one to be disillusioned. I didn't think that she was behaving at all like a woman. Why wasn't she clinging to me for support, and having a good weep at the terrible situation she was in, instead of acting as if it were she who was in control and I was the one who was going to pieces? I don't know. It seemed to me that women had been getting above themselves ever since the war, when they discovered that they could build tanks and pour concrete as well as any man.

"Look, I have to make an appearance below, for the sake of—

of appearances," I whispered curtly. "But I tell you what I'll do. I'll bring up a dustpan and brush, so you'll have something to occupy yourself with. And maybe a few books—you know, to give you something to improve your mind."

"Don't bother," she answered just as curtly. "I'll just ride around the attic on my bicycle."

"Suit yourself. I was only trying to help," I said, attempting to exit with the last word.

But she beat me to it. "I'm beginning to think," she said, "that if I get any more help from you I could end up on the roof."

It was the middle of the afternoon before she had another chance to escape. Father had retired for his afternoon nap—he slept soundly in the afternoon—and Mother had gone shopping—probably for some gastronomic treat for George. This time Anne, the bicycle, and I reached the front door before we saw Jim Boyce coming up the driveway in my car. He had borrowed it to beard the Liberals in Ottawa. So once again we were forced to retreat.

To complicate matters, as we were halfway up the staircase, George Garanine emerged from his room and started across the landing, humming pleasantly to himself between satiated yawns. Luckily, instead of coming downstairs and trapping us between lodgers, he crossed to the bathroom. A moment later we heard him widdling furiously—with the door half open, as usual, the bloody hydraulic exhibitionist.

As the door to the attic was almost opposite the bathroom, he would likely see us if we continued to ascend. So there was no alternative but to detour into my room at the back of the house. Where I proceeded to dismantle the bicycle.

Luckily, Anne had a set of tools handy, in a little leather hold-all in her tartan bag; though she looked a bit stunned as I detached the wheels and wrapped the chain round the frame. But it was obvious that I had to do something with the bike, as I could hardly leave it as it was, leaning casually against my dresser for Mother to find. And it wouldn't fit into my clothes cupboard otherwise.

Another hour went by before I managed to sneak Anne back into the attic, and it was nearly dinnertime before I could take her up a snack of bread and cheese and a thermos of water. Oh yes, and a plum.

By then I was beginning to feel quite concerned at her predicament. Though she was still controlling herself remarkably well, there were distinct signs that her nerves were going. For instance when I emptied her chamber pot out the Dutch dormer and, to lighten the atmosphere, which was becoming a bit tense, called out softly as I upended it, "Gardyloo." You know, the medieval warning? But instead of joining me in a conspiratorial simper, she started to unscrew a brass ball from the bedstead, with the quite obvious intention of hurling it at me.

Fortunately I managed to get out of the room in time, with the hurried explanation, "Well, I better get down to dinner—we're having roast beef and Yorkshire pudding," before she had finished detaching it.

I was still worrying about her all through dinner, thinking about her up there in the fastness of the attic—when I heard Papa say, "Well?"

Glancing up, I saw that he was addressing me.

"Parn me?"

"I was remarking," he said patiently, "on your somewhat bemused, not to say agitated demeanor this weekend, Bartholomew. What on earth is the matter with you, boy? You've been jumping up and down like a flea ever since we got back."

"You don't have a tapeworm, do you?" Mother asked anxiously.

"A tapeworm would certainly account for the way he has been jumping up and down," Papa said. "But it wouldn't account for the noises."

"Noises?"

"I'm sure I heard a bicycle wheel clicking."

"A bicycle?" I laughed. "We don't own a bicycle, Father."

"I'm well aware of that," he replied tartly as he sawed away at a stubborn slice of roast. "I am merely reporting just one of a number of inexplicable sounds."

"Funnily enough, I heard some creaking and hissing noises," Jim Boyce said. "But I thought it was just the house settling."

There was an expectant pause while they all looked at me for a better explanation. I was really relieved when George changed the subject, albeit rather crudely.

"By the way, how is the election coming?" he asked.

"I haven't started it yet."

"Is it not wonderful," he exclaimed, looking around with his bright blue eyes, "to think that Bartalamyeh will one day be great statesman?"

"Wonderful? It will be a miracle," Papa grunted, pausing, slack-jawed, before renewing his orthodontal onslaught on the roast beef.

"Ah, my dear Mr. Bandyeh—may I call you Papa?—you do not know your son at all. Perhaps is because you know him too well. But as for me, I am convinced that he will win this election. For, as we say in Russia, *A bear is not necessarily a plutocrat, merely because it wears a fur coat.* Why, Trotsky himself said about Bartalamyeh that he would bear watching. Those were his very words—in Russian, of course," he added, looking so lovably naive that a lump came to Father's throat. However, he soon forced it down with a laryngeal effort and pushed aside his plate.

"You see the best in everybody, George," he said, looking at the glorious Russian so affectionately as almost to smooth out the creases that life's saber had slashed from the corners of his mouth.

"He's such a Christian," said Mother, all choked up, as Jim Boyce caught my eye and raised his to heaven.

"But is true about Bartalamyeh," George went on with a sweetly innocent smile. "He is great man, despite all his efforts. For as we also say in Russia . . ." He hesitated, then: "Perhaps you will translate for me, Bartalamyeh?" And he said something rapidly in Russian, his face as serious as a math exam.

I stared at him so fixedly that Boyce started to look at me curiously.

"Well?" Father asked. "What did he say?"

"Let me see—it might be translated as, *The winter feels especially cold to a muzhik with his feet in a bucket of slush.* Or, or, perhaps it might better be translated as, *A balalaika that has been run over by a droshky is not worth a pood of rotten apples.*"

Father regarded me suspiciously. "How the devil can it mean both?" he demanded.

Actually it meant neither; for what George had really said was, "I heard you up in the attic, Uncle. Got a woman up there, have you? Annushka, is it?"

It was nine that night before I had a chance to sneak back to the attic. The reason for the delay in returning to comfort Anne once more was the crystal set that Jim Boyce had brought back with him from Ottawa. It was the first one that my parents had ever heard, and they were so fascinated that they invited a neighboring family to drop in and listen in. And I could hardly abandon the party without seeming to be churlish or inhospitable. So I had to stay for a couple of hours or so, while Jim probed around the crystal with the cat's whisker. He actually managed to pick up a broadcast from station CFCF in Montreal. So it wasn't until Father, Mother, George, three neighbors and their children, Lonny, Donny, and Bonny, or some such names, crowded around, quarreling over the headphones, and listened obliviously to the warblings of a soprano, marveling that the sound was coming from an astounding hundred thirty miles away, that I managed to back out without being noticed, and tiptoed up to the attic; where I found Anne pacing up and down, seething with fury.

Her first words, though, were mild enough. "I've been thinking," she said, coming to a halt at the grimy window and staring out at her second—or was it her third?—attic sunset. "I've decided to take up permanent residence here."

"Eh?"

"Well, after all, my landlady won't take me back now, after my staying out all weekend, practically."

"Don't be silly, Anne," I whispered, touching her arm.

She shook it off. "Sure, why don't I just go down and offer to rent this place? After all, if they'll take you in, they'll take in anybody."

"Don't worry," I said placatingly. "I'm sure I'll be able to get you out of here sooner or later—Monday at the latest."

"Will you?" She turned and looked at me, her eyebrows almost fused together. "I'm not so sure of that. Do you know, Bartholomew, somehow I'm beginning to lose confidence in you."

"You are?"

"First you trap me in the attic, then your bedroom, then the stairs, then back in the attic, and in the meantime you dismantle my bike so I can't ride off into the sunset—" She was beginning to breathe faster and to clench and unclench her fists. "I'm sorry, I still can't quite grasp the reason for that. God knows I've tried, but . . ." She was positively panting by now, as if once again we had been pounding up various flights of stairs. "But tell me, where are you planning on leading me next? Up the chimney? Into the cellar? Down the drain?"

"Not the drain," I said. "The only way to do that would be to take you down to the bathroom and flush you away."

She suddenly went all still, staring at me. Then she started to spruce herself up in a disquietingly determined sort of way—straightening her silk stockings and her hair, tucking a now decidedly grimy blouse into her skirt, and so forth.

I regarded her uneasily and asked what she intended doing.

"I'm marching straight out of here," she said, abandoning a strained whisper for the first time since last Friday. "And I don't care whether anybody sees me or not."

Which is precisely what she did. And though the downstairs was now positively thronged with people, including three noisy children who had tired of listening to the crystal set and were running about in the passages between the kitchen, dining room, living room, and front parlor, she actually managed to march, looking neither to right nor left, straight down two flights of stairs and out the front door without being seen by a single soul. Except for me, of course, who was chasing after her, whispering urgently. But she had reached the road in front of the house before I could catch up with her and hand it over.

"You forgot your bicycle," I panted.

And I handed her the two wheels, the handlebar, and the frame—then the chain and the little tartan bag.

Whereupon she proved at last that she was all woman; for she took a deep breath and uttered a shrill scream—without even drawing back her lips, which really intrigued me; until she also drew back her fist and hit me on the nose.

I mean, really. I could understand her screaming like that, as a sort of relief from the weekend's tension and all that, but to biff me on the beezer like that seemed very uncalled for, especially as I had taken the trouble to collect all the pieces of her bicycle and carry them all the way down from my bedroom cupboard.

Campaigning Again

Until Jim Boyce went into action as my campaign manager I had never really understood how he had managed to do so well in the Royal Naval Air Service without being shot by somebody's husband or shipped to Scapa Flow by some disillusioned commodore. As far as I could make out, most of his energies went into seduction. At the age of twenty-eight he seemed to be going nowhere, except to bed. After losing his position with External Affairs on account of his internal affairs, he had done nothing but drift from one job interview to another, supported mainly by an impatient allowance from his father, who was a former attorney general of Nova Scotia.

But since that shared moment of danger, guilt, and hilarity on Long Island we had become good friends, and though he claimed to be quite pleased to be unoccupied, as it gave him more time to pursue the frails, I knew him well enough to discern that he was ashamed of being unemployed. The flame of the work ethic quite plainly burned in those gravy-brown eyes of his that basted women with such affection. He was intensely relieved to be given the responsibility for the campaign even for such an unlikely candidate as I. When he got down to it I soon understood how he had managed to attain the rank of lieutenant commander at the age of twenty-two. And when the final disastrous polling day came around on October 8, at least nobody would be able to blame him for the fiasco.

Throughout the six-week campaign, Boyce was out there every day, organizing, cajoling, scheming, and seducing the electorate, especially if they were pretty. His promotion was imaginative enough to bring newspaper reporters to Gallop from quite distant points—those who could find the town, that is. One Toronto journalist never made it past Smiths Falls, where he wrote a very interesting piece on a horse-drawing contest and contracted trichinosis.

It was Jim Boyce's use of aircraft that intrigued the outside journalists; for a few days, anyway. Among his aerial promotions were leaflet raids—the scattering of flimsy pamphlets from the cockpit of the Avro 504K, and joyriding trips, ten-minute flights around the town at a thousand feet. As the rides were free, quite a few citizens turned up at the farm on Saturdays, to be subjected to a ten-minute spiel by their host before being carried aloft, five at a time, in the three cockpits of the creaking Vimy.

The great advantage of this original promotion was that the crowds were not in the mood for heckling, or even asking awkward questions. The funfair atmosphere that Boyce created inhibited even the most good-natured raillery, what with the brass band of the Ottawa Valley Volunteer Firefighters and Stumphaulers Association oompahing away merrily, and the colorful tents dispensing free snacks, soft drinks, and election literature, and, rather more discreetly, free prescriptions of alcohol behind the barn.

But it was the flying circus that most delighted the crowds. No barnstorming troupe had ever visited Gallop, so though our display was limited to a few low-level stunts in the Avro and the aforementioned joyrides, the throngs of citizens were as happy as if we had laid on a full-scale show of parachute jumping, wing walking, and mock dogfights. And their euphoria ensured that they would listen quite uncritically when I delivered my pep talks.

These, too, had been cleverly designed by Jim Boyce. Ostensibly lectures on how to behave as joyriders—keeping seat belts fastened, not being sick over the side, and so forth—they also included a few subtle reminders that I was their Liberal candidate and that in return for the rides and the free fodder and sarsaparilla, and the booze behind the barn, the passengers were expected to vote for me come polling day.

The newspaper and pictorial magazine publicity was also

helpful, I suppose, though the locals were not likely to be influenced by what was said by foreigners from Ottawa, Peterborough, and Kingston. The most memorable interview was the one by the only Toronto reporter who managed to get through to Gallop. He interviewed me in conditions guaranteed to arouse widespread interest: the world's first aerial interview.

This was the original idea of a twenty-three-year-old rooster of a chap named Gordon Sinclair, who, despite a prim, moral sort of mouth, looked as if he belonged at a cockfight—in the arena. Interviewing me in flight would give him a new angle, he said. Accordingly I took him up to seven thousand feet in the Avro.

After asking a few questions about my life and ignoring the replies, he suddenly bawled from the front seat of the Avro, "Your opponents have described you as a nouveau riche, politically illiterate, obsequious troublemaker and fraud, with no talent except for disturbing the peace. What d'you say to that, Mr. Bandy?"

"Obsequious? I take exception to that," I shouted back. "I'll sue those darn Tories."

"It was the Liberals who said it."

"Oh."

"So, considering that, what makes you think you ought to be in Parliament?"

"It's the people who nominated me who think I ought to be in Parliament," I shot back, after smiling winningly and complimenting him on his probing but thoroughly fair questions.

"They also say you believe in privilege, class distinction, and the God-given right of people in power to decide what's best for the ignorant masses."

"What's wrong with that?"

"Okay. Let's get down to the important stuff. That farm we just took off from—is it yours?"

"Yes."

"How much money do you earn a year?"

"I'm not earning anything at the moment."

At that he made his first entry in his notepad: *Unemployed agricultural worker.*

"Ever been convicted of a criminal offense?"

"Certainly not."

Never been convicted, he wrote. "You were married once to some upper-class dame named Lewis, right?"

"Yes."

"Any kids?"

"No."

Unable to have children. "What d'you intend to do if you get into Parliament?"

"Well, to begin with," I bellowed modestly, "until I am thoroughly conversant with custom and procedure, I intend merely to sit and listen carefully and dutifully; in a word, to 'read, learn, and inwardly digest.'"

Says will do nothing in Parliament except sit and eat. "Okay, that should do it," Sinclair said. "You can take me down now."

"Certainly, Mr. Sinclair," I said with an oily smile—the rotary engine of the Avro sprayed castor oil quite lavishly—and, hoping he had forgotten to fasten his seat belt, did a slow roll.

The effectiveness of Boyce's promotion could be measured by the reaction of our opponents. At first the Conservative candidate, Malachi Peel, had a swell time drawing attention to the vulgar atmosphere of my campaign and equating it with a third-rate traveling medicine show. But his staff grew alarmed when they observed the crowds that were turning up at the farm every Saturday. It was that, I think, and the initially extensive news coverage that determined them to put their contingency plan into action in mid-September: the recruiting of a gang of hooligans to break up our election meetings. Until then, confident that the seat would remain Conservative, they had not considered it worthwhile to reestablish that time-honored electoral tradition.

But I wasn't worried. "By gad, Karley, we'll show them, eh?" I chortled one evening at one of our regular conferences at election headquarters, the shop on Queen Street next to Thompson's Funeral Parlor & Used Clothing Emporium. "You know, I'm beginning to think we have quite a good chance in this election."

Actually I was well beyond that optimistic boundary. I was already anticipating a spectacular career in politics. I felt certain I would make a big impression in the House of Commons. After all, I had been a marked man in my every other endeavor so far.

"I wouldn't get carried away by the success of a few joyrides,

old man," Karley said in his phlegmatic voice. "Quite apart from
having no real issue to lever the Tories out of the seat, we're
being pretty thoroughly sabotaged, in case you haven't noticed."

Returning from reveries of political glory . . . Prime Minister
the Right Honorable Batholomew Wolfe Bandy, C.B.E.—it
sounded right, you know—I gazed vaguely around the conference table, at Boyce's blue chin, then into Wattle's dim, introspective eyes, then along at Miss Rawsthorne's sinewy fore-
arms, and sideways at Anne's strong, capable hands, and finally,
when I realized that it was he who had spoken, at Captain
Karley.

Studying his plump, discontented features, I suspected that he
was still not entirely reconciled to my candidature; mostly, I suppose, because, regardless of the outcome, he was deep in the old
excreta. If I won, he would earn the displeasure of the national
executive; if I lost, his reputation as chairman and organizer of
the local association would suffer.

Actually I think he was secretly hoping that I would crash.
Nothing serious, of course, perhaps just a few broken legs, to im-
mobilize me until he could postpone the election for a third
time.

"What sabotage?" I asked.

"What sabotage? Our posters are being systematically torn
down, those Tory hooligans are intimidating our voters, the *Ga-
zette* is sneering at your speeches—when they report them at all.
Incidentally, why the hell did you have to insult the editor that
way?"

"I didn't do it on purpose. I merely complimented him on how
amazingly vigorous his mother was, considering. How was I to
know it was his wife?"

"Anyway, now we not only have the Tory-dominated town
council, the police, the lodges, and the entire Hipsey clan against
us, but the local paper as well."

"Talking about paper," Boyce said, "we need a decision on
the new leaflets."

It was now my turn to frown discontentedly. At first I had
been delighted with Boyce's leaflet raids—the scattering of election pamphlets from the air over Gallop and the surrounding
district. I was especially pleased because it had given me the op-

portunity to litter Mrs. Hipsey's garden from a safe five hundred feet. But after a while I had begun to wonder if leaflets were quite as efficacious as I'd thought, when one day I found a stack of them in our outdoor privy. It occurred to me that, if Father preferred them over the usual shiny tissues, then the rest of the population might also be using them for similar purposes. And indeed, an official survey of local outhouses had revealed such to be the case.

I was so annoyed that I now proposed that the next batch be printed on sandpaper. However, we finally compromised by selecting a less competent printer, whose ink tended to transfer to the fingers—or to whatever area of skin it came in contact with —so that if the leaflets were again used in such a disrespectful way my message might be perpetuated, at least until bath night.

By then we had been gassing for over two hours and, as often happened when I was in the chair, the discussion started to turn frivolous; though it was Anne, who had finally forgiven me for storing her in the attic that weekend, who started it off this time.

"Of course, the message would be a bit difficult to read back there," she remarked, "unless the voter had a rear-view mirror."

"Surely the message would also be printed backward," Wattle put in. Like many a churchman, he quite delighted in the occasional touch of low humor. "When transferred to the skin in that region, your immortal words, Bartholomew, would surely appear back to front, as it were."

"The message would not only be back to front at the back," Miss Rawsthorne said, "but upside down. Thus the only way for the voter to read the message would be for him to look backward through his legs with a mirror to handle an inverted image."

"An inverted image of the voter, you mean?" I asked.

"No, the message would be inverted. Though you're quite right," she added thoughtfully, "the voter would also present an inverted image."

"And a distinctly unprepossessing image, if I may say so," Wattle murmured.

"Yes, it's quite a thought," mused Boyce. "Trouserless voters all over the country busily reading Bartholomew's upside-down, back-to-front, rear-end election material—"

We started to giggle, until Karley said heavily, "I think you're all feeling tired. It's obviously time we went home—"

"For a good read," Boyce said, standing up and looking backward through his legs; which produced another outburst of merriment.

However, the Opposition ultimately solved the leaflet problem for us. The Hipseys prosecuted us for littering, and Magistrate Hipsey fined us twenty bucks.

Actually that was not the returning officer's only skulduggery. We were now discovering the full disadvantage of having a hostile returning officer, for among Hipsey's unseemly tactics was his surreptitious removal from the voting register of a number of known Liberals. By the time we found out what was happening, it was too late to reinstate them.

From then on, the campaign became increasingly unprincipled, at a time when even the conduct of a well-regulated contest was hardly exemplary, given the general acceptance of wholesale bribery. For instance, on the weekend before polling day, our opponents would openly hand out envelopes containing five-dollar bills to any voter who professed not to have made up his mind. It was absolutely outrageous, and forced us to dispense our own five-dollar bills prematurely.

But the worst blow was the discovery that the Tories had booked for their exclusive use throughout the campaign the town's only suitable meeting halls, the Wildebeest Lodge and the Temperance Hall. That left only the armory, a distinctly unsuitable place, for its vast drill hall was impossible to fill unless we shared it simultaneously with the William and Mary High School Marching Band, a convention of the Imperial Order of the Daughters of the Empire, and at least two battalions of the Victorian Light Infantry, complete with ration wagons. Besides, the hall harbored bats.

Worst of all, the Opposition also recruited a band of bully boys to intimidate those who were exhibiting our publicity material or cooperating with us in any way. As the leader of the thugs was the notorious McMulligan, few citizens felt sufficiently dedicated to our cause to put up much resistance.

Nor could I blame them. I'd had difficulty in resisting McMulligan myself, when, shortly after he got out of jail in July, he had marched up to the farm, confidently expecting to get his job back. He had looked really unpleasant when I informed him that I had taken on another mechanic, George Garanine. "But of course, Mr. McMulligan, if he doesn't work out, you'll be the very first to be considered," I'd said, showing my teeth and hunching, as if about to drive off the thirteenth tee with a bent putter. But he had not been the least placated by this obsequious posture and had departed issuing threats so graphic that I very nearly ran after him to say that I'd just remembered—I'd sacked George that very morning, and McMulligan could come back and start bludgeoning my filing cabinet again any time he wished.

For a while he and his boys refrained from confronting me personally and contented themselves with indirect intimidation; but they were bound to turn up at one of our election gatherings sooner or later, to create the usual riot and terrorize the audience.

Not that our meetings weren't disorderly enough as it was. One of the most disastrous was the giant rally—for thirty people —held in the Rock Gardens one damp Friday afternoon. It could hardly be described as a festive occasion even before I started speaking. It was September's first chilly day, it was drizzling, and the municipal authorities had refused to let us put up a decent hustings platform in the square, so that I was forced to make do with Boyce's homemade contraption. This was a small platform with a banner overhead reading BANDY TO WIN ☒. As Boyce had also added wheels and a couple of handles to make it easier to move, it looked rather like a tinker's handcart. In fact, on the way to the Rock Gardens, people kept coming up to me with offerings of rags and bones and demanding bars of yellow soap in exchange. Somehow this did not add much to the dignity of the occasion; but at least the hustings' mobility would enable me to make a quick getaway in case McMulligan turned up.

An ominous note was struck from the start, for about half the crowd seemed to be members of the Hipsey clan; who were now more hostile than ever, after I had flown low over Mrs. Hipsey's property one morning in the Avro and plastered her roof, garden, and gazebo with leaflets. Which was probably why Mrs. Hipsey herself had turned out for the meeting as well. She sat on a shooting stick right in the front row, wearing a black coat and a black helmet of a hat, her jaw outthrust like the blade of a bulldozer.

Throughout my speech I kept glancing at her apprehensively, guessing that she had come to plague me with precisely the sort of questions I had been making such efforts to avoid. Sure enough, the moment I dribbled to a halt, she heaved herself to her buckled feet. That was when the meeting really deteriorated. Thrusting out her jaw as if plowing into a pile of manure, she called out, "Mr. Bandy. You've been giving us all kinds of assurances about what you're going to do for Gallop if you're elected; but what I want to know, once and for all, is what you propose doing about the loss to Gallop of its major industry?"

There were just two reporters present that day. Until this moment they hadn't even bothered to take out their notepads. Now, however, they poised the pencils over their pads pointedly, as if Mrs. Hipsey had just warned me that anything I said might be taken down and used as evidence.

"Ah. I was coming to that," I said, shuddering as a gust of chill wind dislodged a shower of rain from the maple tree canopy overhead onto my thinning pate. Whereupon I paused, hoping that she would interrupt rudely before I had a chance to come to it. But the blasted woman just stood there, waiting.

"Ah. Well," I said. "Liberal policy, as you know, is concerned above all with people, their hopes and fears, their trials and tribulations, their welfare, their—their hopes and fears, and their expectations," I said, and paused again—hopefully. I had got that bit of Liberal policy from Miss Rawsthorne. "Liberals believe in people," she explained one day, "while Conservatives believe in banks." Though Miss Rawsthorne's interpretation of Conservative attitudes may have been a bit prejudiced—her Tory bank manager had refused her a loan to buy a racing car—a Bugatti, I believe.

"Or, to put it another way," I continued, borrowing that phrase from Wattle, "Liberals believe in people, while Conservatives . . ." I faltered a bit, as rows of hostile Tory eyes gazed back at me. "Er . . . naturally, we Liberals are deeply concerned about this impending Talbot move, and I can assure you . . ." and I proceeded to assure them of nothing whatsoever, carefully following Karley's advice to practice the political art of saying as little as possible in a fervent manner.

But Mrs. Hipsey was obviously determined to drive me into the open where the snipers could pick me off. She kept repeating the question in one form or another over and over, with patient zeal, until finally when the others started to shout, "Answer the question," I was forced to stick my napper at least a few inches above the parapet.

"Ah, well, you see," I said, plucking a sodden maple leaf off the back of my neck, "over the past nine months there have been something like fifty attempts to dissuade Mrs. Talbot from closing down the distillery. I myself have tried at least twice, but she is quite adamant. She—"

The hostile shouts were growing louder. I had to raise my voice. "I have argued with her, but Mrs. Talbot insists that she must make the move for economic reasons—"

"So you're not willing to do a single thing about the worst calamity that Gallop has ever faced?" Mrs. Hipsey bellowed, wearing a look of anticipation as she glanced around at the others.

"I didn't say that. I—"

"But then, of course," she interrupted—*now* she was interrupting, just when it was vital for me to finish, "you're hardly in a position to influence her, are you?"

Even though I knew instantly what she was getting at, I made the worst mistake yet. I exposed myself shamelessly. I stood head and shoulders above the parapet. "How d'you mean?" I faltered.

Crack-bssst. Right through the temples. "Why, isn't it a fact," she cried, so loudly that the pigeons nesting above the blocked Gothic entrance to the town hall arose in panic, showering the Rock Gardens rock with guano, "that you are actually *helping* Mrs. Talbot to move from Gallop?"

Whizbang. The bombshell blew off both shoulders and the top of my head. I goggled, out of what remained of my cranium, hideously aware that the reporters were scribbling like mad— now that I wasn't saying anything.

"Certainly not," I managed at length.

"Oh?" shouted back Mrs. Hipsey. "You deny you're an ally of

Mrs. Talbot's? You aren't helping her to move her products into the United States by air?"

At that, the reporters looked ecstatic. And my morale did not exactly soar when I caught sight of Jim Boyce retracting his head into his raincoat and starting to pack up in a hurry.

"I am merely helping the country's export trade," I said loftily. "I—"

The crowd pressed closer. The few expressions I could focus on seemed more unfriendly than ever, if that were possible. And it were.

"In other words, the Talbot export trade?" Mrs. Hipsey cried. "You're smuggling for Talbots, aren't you? Aiding her, allying yourself with that vile woman," she hollered at a volume quite remarkable in a heptagenarian. But then, of course, she'd had plenty of practice at Temperance League meetings. "Helping that foreign tart to move her supplies and bring poverty, despair, and ruin to Gallop. But then, of course, what do you care? You have money, you won't starve, oh no."

At which there was a loud reaction of umbrage and dudgeon from the crowd. Now a very large crowd; for, from the moment that Mrs. Hipsey had brought up the one subject that I was most eager to avoid, several hundred thousand raincoated, caped, and groundsheeted citizens had immediately swept into the sodden Gardens from all the converging streets. It was as if the old bitch had turned into a magician, effectively substituting the word "Talbot" for "abracadabra." "Hypocrite. Scoundrel. Liar. Impostor," came the shouts, so thick and fast from all directions that even Wattle got caught up in the excitement. "Aesthete!" he cried, before clapping a hand to his mouth as he recollected whose side he was on. And before I could retrieve the situation by slandering Mrs. Talbot like mad, the first rotten egg sailed overhead and thumped into the soggy banner.

It was promptly followed by a mushy tomato. At which point it occurred to me that this Talbot business might be the one unsurmountable obstacle to success. The thought firmed in inverse ratio to the ripeness of the fruit that followed, the third or fourth item of which glanced off my neck, and the fourth or fifth, again a tomato, squelched onto my vulnerable breast, leaving a dreadful wound.

"Well, ladies and gentlemen," I called out, looking around for my supporters Boyce and Wattle—they seemed to be fulfilling appointments elsewhere—"that concludes my address for today." And, holding a hand to my bloodied breast, clambered off the little platform and seized its handles and with great dignity started to trundle it away, determined not to let the side down by actually running for it, despite the howling pack of Hipseys and others that was now forming up and following, tentatively at first but, as I increased speed, at a matching accelerated pace, while various items of overripe fruit continued to arch through the rain, including, for some reason, a perfectly sound banana which nicked me on the neck and ricocheted off like a yellow boomerang; which so startled me that I proceeded up Queen Street at an even smarter pace, though I was not aware that I was running until I was summonsed a few minutes later for exceeding the speed limit in an unlicensed vehicle.

"I told you all along I'd never have a chance in this election, and it would all be a waste of money," I gritted at Karley, the next time we met. "It's all your fault for dragging me out of bed that night."

"I know," Karley said dispiritedly.

From that rally onward, not a day went by without the inevitable question being flung at me: what did I intend doing about the Talbot crisis? And no amount of flimflammery or evasion could obscure the fact that, being impotent, I had no solution.

A Friday night meeting in the Zeppelin-sized armory a dozen days before polling day was the worst experience of all. To begin with, though the turnout was respectable, the audience was surrounded by dismaying acres of dark, chill, echoing space that would have daunted a convention of hashish-besotted Ismailites. Further, the cousins and uncles of the resident bat family were visiting; they kept swooping and chittering overhead, ruining what little concentration on the issues had survived, and making some hatless women very nervous indeed.

By then, of course, the press had utterly abandoned me, except for a junior reporter from the *Advertiser*, who was only there to practice his shorthand; though actually he spent most of the time squeezing his blackheads.

The worst portent was the appearance of the rowdies. We

didn't realize they were present until Karley spied McMulligan's friend Kicker—a nickname derived from the fellow's habit of putting the boot to fallen adversaries—lounging in an aisle seat twenty rows back. A quick scan revealed the presence of another half dozen members of the gang, scattered throughout the cavern. They had insinuated themselves into the audience in the usual way, not in a body but in scattered pairs, establishing themselves in good tactical locations for the disturbance they would later create. As was soon evident, they were carrying tire irons, ax handles, or similar weapons under their coats.

On the platform we held a whispered conference. Wattle suggested calling the police, but Karley felt that the Tories would capitalize on it—"observe how the Grits felt they needed to be protected from the public" sort of thing. Karley did, however, send off an urgent message to some of his construction men, but as it turned out only two of them responded, and were greatly relieved when they arrived too late.

Trouble started even before the meeting convened, when one of the thugs began to demonstrate his sole talent for belching at will—long-drawn-out baritone bursts of a remarkably low aural frequency that caused considerable apprehension among the blacksmiths, navvies, and foundry workers seated in front of him. However, at least two members of the audience seemed to appreciate the respiratory flourishes—a pair of schoolboys, who looked really impressed by the fellow's ability to sustain his eructation.

Luckily the marathon burper had grown tired of it by the time Wattle got up to speak. But it was symptomatic of the general hostility to my candidature that even the introductory speeches, normally lisened to in bored but polite silence, were now being sullenly or angrily received.

It was unprecedented for a man of the cloth to be heckled and badgered, but such was the case after Wattle had been speaking for only ninety minutes. Even our own supporters had grown hostile by then. When he got to the part about "The representative of this noble town of Gallop, which in the past has set such a splendid example of decency, tolerance, and civilized behavior—in this town set in the township of Eden, this 'Garden of Eden,' which—"

"Township of Gloucester, you damn fool," snapped Dr. McKay from the front row.

"Of course—to be sure—Gloucester. That's what I meant—this Garden of . . ." Realizing that his figure of speech was no longer applicable, Wattle changed the subject with his usual finesse. "Now what, you may ask, what does our party, the Liberal Party, stand for?"

"For a lot of nonsense, obviously," quoth another burgher.

"The Liberal Party," Wattle continued, wringing his hands and hanging them out to dry, "stands, in a word, for Liberalism. Now, what is Liberalism? To start with, it is self-evident that it is the opposite of what our principal opponents, the Tory constitutionalists, stand for, which, of course, is the status quo, or, to put it another way . . ."

He continued to put it another way for what seemed like great chunks of sidereal time, until finally I was the only one listening to him. But of course I had good reason to pay attention, for I was still trying to grasp the fundamental difference between Liberalism and Conservatism.

The trouble was that nobody had ever explained it to me, and I didn't dare ask Karley or any other expert because it was obvious that if you had to ask what the party stood for you weren't a genuine Liberal. You had to know instinctively, it appeared. But for somebody like myself who had no instincts, it was like trying to join a club when nobody would tell you who to apply to, or what the qualifications were, or even the location of the club premises. So I had to work it out on my own. As far as I could make out, the only difference between the parties was that the Conservatives felt that they ought to be fiscally responsible, while the Liberals didn't care how much money they printed. Which, presumably, was why the Liberals were usually in power, as everybody liked to have lots of money around.

Anyway, I was still none the wiser by the time Wattle had sat down to a sullen round of relieved applause that he had finally sat down.

Unfortunately he had exhausted the audience's patience by the end of his second sentence. Consequently even Karley, who was generally admired and respected in the community, had a hard time of it. He got no further than "It is now my duty to introduce the principal speaker of the evening, your Liberal candi—" when, "Boo," said a dispirited voice from the gloom.

But the scattered rowdies continued to remain ominously silent, waiting for the right moment—me.

"And it is a duty I perform with genuine pleasure," Karley said stoutly but thinly; and went on to talk about me in the matter-of-fact voice that he had used to inform his infantry company of an impending suicide attack, or to order a second helping of plum duff. "I myself," he plodded, "have been intensely aware of Bandy ever since he first marched purposely through the foot-deep mud up to my company in France, proudly bearing the banner of his face in much the same way that the Roman legions carried their standards into battle. From then on the war was never quite the same," Karley said, faltering as he quite visibly decided not to pursue that line of thought. "Anyway, suffice it to say that over the next couple of years he won so many awards for gallantry that the King finally got tired of receiving him at Buckingham Palace and decided to send the rest of the medals by tramp steamer."

"Never mind the war, what about Talbots?" somebody shouted.

Karley ignored this and all the other interruptions. "I merely wish to remind you," he persisted, "that Mr. Bandy's achievements have been notable, and now that he has embarked on a career in politics, if his past record is anything to go by, his contributions on your behalf are likely to be, uh . . . The point I want to make," he went on, speeding up before he found himself in danger of being specific, "is that Mr. Bandy has the kind of stubborn determination that this country needs, and that he has a considerable talent for getting his own way, despite the most desperate attempts to stop—getting things done, I should say, by trampling down all opp—overcoming, rather, all opposition. I can honestly assert," Karley asserted, averting his face to conceal an embarrassment over his own assertions, "that you cannot do better than to vote for this clergyman's son who, brought up a firm believer in temperance, moral integrity, and service to others, has manifested virtues that have marked him off from the beginning as a man to be watched—"

"Carefully, in case he swipes the silver," somebody called out into the tense hush that was now falling as the time for my speech drew nigh.

I glared out into the gloom, assuming it was a Hipsey who had said this; but apparently the family had decided that I had been sufficiently demolished in the Rock Gardens. There was not one of them present to smite me Hipsey and thigh.

"And now, without further ado, I call upon your candidate to say a few words," Karley concluded, mopping his brow with an impeccable hanky, then putting it to his mouth and saying to me from behind it, "a *very* few words, *please,*" presumably remembering the last meeting in the armory, when I had been unable to wind up my speech satisfactorily and had careened verbally down the icy slopes and ended up headfirst in a drift of irrelevancies. "Ladies and gentlemen—Mr. Bartholomew Bandy."

Whereupon, even before I was halfway to my feet, the rowdies went into action, greeting me with the most frightful hullabaloo of catcalls, hoots, and derisive, cackling laughter; so rancorous a clamor that a group of ladies hastily gathered their belongings together and scuttled out even though they hadn't heard a single word of my speech.

This was definitely not an auspicious start, and it got steadily worse, from the moment I was finally able to make myself heard over the uproar.

"Ladies and gentlemen," I began.

"Sit down."

"Shut up."

"Go back where you came from."

"Piker."

"Nay, nay," bellowed McMulligan, imitating a horse; and the other rowdies screeched with laughter and broadcast similar equine effects. One of the hooligans even jumped out into the aisle to stamp his foot and paw the ground and snort, desisting only when his steel wrecking bar slipped out from beneath his coat and fell to the floor with a ringing clang.

I waited, jittering about on the platform as if practicing for a tap-dance competition. However, the interruption gave me the opportunity to mentally go over my speech in its entirety. Then, as there were still a few minutes to spare, to rehearse my introductory joke. This, of course, was to get the audience into a

receptive mood . . . though, as the minutes stampeded past and
the bats darted about in panic, and as I looked over the apprehensive, gleeful, or antagonistic faces before me, it occurred to
me that it might take more than an amusing anecdote to settle
this particular mob.

So after the hubbub had temporarily exhausted itself I
launched straight into the main theme of my discourse, on the
benefits to be derived from having a Grit in Parliament. "In Ottawa, of course, we have a Liberal administration," I said, "so it's
obvious that our esteemed opponent, Mr. Peel, will not be in a
position to lobby it effectively on your behalf, seeing as he is a
Tory. Whereas if I am elected I will do my utmost to see that
Gallop gets its fair share of federal moneys and projects, such as,
for instance, er, another post office . . ." And I continued for
some minutes to labor this rather distasteful theme, which had
been suggested by Karley.

However, there was one good result of launching straight into
my main theme without any introduction whatsoever. I was beginning to control the audience. Slowly but surely, as a nearby
church tolled the quarter hours, the barracking died down. Even
McMulligan, who had been shouting insults almost continuously
for fifteen minutes, was beginning to slump in his seat, looking
impressed in spite of himself, while his friend Kicker was even
dabbing at his eyes with a soiled hanky—obviously much
affected by one particular example I cited of a poor family in an
unspecified nearby community who had been at its wit's end
financially, utterly destitute, until it elected an unnamed Liberal
and was thenceforth employed on an even more unspecified
public works project. . . . Though it was just possible that
Kicker had tears in his eyes as a result of yawning so hugely.
. . . Presumably he had been up most of the night, booting
people.

Still, there was no doubt that I was finally getting through to
the audience, the way they were becoming so subdued. Of
course, I didn't particularly appreciate it when I saw that one of
my own supporters, Anne Mackie, who was seated in the front
row next to Dr. McKay, was failing to keep the flag of loyalty at
the masthead. Her head kept dipping sharply, then jerking back
to the horizontal, and she kept stretching her eyes. This somno-

lent sequence was causing some mystification in the man behind her, who thought she was nodding in agreement at some of my more telling points, though as far as he could make out I didn't have any.

But then poor Anne was obviously plum tuckered, after setting up five hundred chairs all by herself because no other volunteers had turned up. So I forgave her, and went on to deliver a comprehensive account of the benefits that had been accruing from Liberal rule ever since Confederation, with particular emphasis on the fine neoclassic government buildings that had been erected practically everywhere, thus increasing local employment opportunities, the source of my information being my old schoolbook, *A Picture Book of Canadian History* by Horace Beestley, M.A., with its numerous pictures of exciting moments in Canadian history. Thus I continued to boom onward and onward and onward, interrupted now only very occasionally by a listless bark or nicker from the rowdies and by some heavy breathing on the platform behind me. Until I realized that I had been speaking for over an hour.

My confidence revived still further when, as the heckling and other interruptions died away completely, I realized that I was at last learning how to hold down an audience by the sheer weight of my discourse. For instance, George Garanine in the fifth row, the only person who really believed I could win the election, was even resting his chin on his sternum with his eyes closed, in order to follow my argument with the minimum of visual distraction, while on the platform Miss Rawsthorne was so impressed that she was even making notes of my speech, using the notebook in which she usually inscribed her poems. As for Karley, seated next to her, he was slowly slipping sideways, presumably for a peek at her notes, before hauling himself upright with a palsied start. Meanwhile Dr. McKay on the front row had plugged his stethoscope into his ears and seemed to be searching for his own heart—in vain, judging by his expression—and Jim Boyce, at the end of the tenth row, was obviously so excited by my discourse that his chin kept vibrating like an eccentric motor, and the muscles of his blue cheeks kept rippling, as if he were suppressing an urge to open his mouth wide and cry, "Hear, hear," or something equally supportive. And the reaction

was the same from all the others as well, as they sat slumped in
their seats at a remarkable variety of angles, with their eyes wa-
tering from sheer emotion, or with eyes that were closed altogether, presumably because of the contrast between the glare of
the lights at this end of the cavernous hall and the surrounding
gloom. Until, by the time I had finally found a way to end my
speech, there was scarcely a sound to be heard, even from the
bats. In fact when I finally looked around to locate the thugs individually, I saw that most of them were sitting in a stupor with
glazed eyes and slovenly lips, except for McMulligan, whose
head was resting on his neighbor's shoulder, and who, unlikely
as it might seem, had fallen sound asleep.

The weather that fall had been composed mostly of warm, sunny periods followed by spells of fine weather. Around the farmhouse, black squirrels loped and skittered, making joyful rushes at sky-supporting elm tree trunks, and ricocheted off into yellow-dappled hedge and flaming sumach, or dug and patted at the turf, trying to remember where they had left their nuts. An unusual number of snapping turtles, safe as hawsers, slowpoked across the cinder driveway, and neighbor cats crept into plantain caves and slept until field mouse field day dark. Day after day the dawn-stoked sun had baked the grassland the color of Colman's mustard, and weeds now luxuriated in the flower garden, and flowers in the bent black eavestrough.

This Sunday, however, it was pissing down.

The Talbot lorry driver had just finished helping George and me to load the bonded whisky into the Vimy when the first fat raindrops whacked the terrain. By the time George had finished cranking up the engines the rain was drumming on the top plane and we were both streaming like riverside hippos.

In a hurry to get off before the baked earth flooded, I was lined up at the far end of the field only five minutes later. With the high nose of the huge airplane pointing into the distant gap between the farmhouse and the barn, I ran up, flipping magneto switches and listening attentively to the saturated engines. The rain was sweeping over the field as if a giant hand was drawing French tergal curtains across it. Fortunately it was just a local storm—there was a band of chill blue sky to the east—so I completed the takeoff check confidently enough, then pushed forward the power levers, gradually, to avoid bogging the undercart. The sixty-eight-foot-wide beast trembled, then lurched forward on its four wide-spaced wheels, swishing through the lake that had already formed over the yellow grass.

Forward on the big steering wheel. The aging beast lowered its flat snout. With four hundred and fifty gallons of fuel aboard, and twenty-nine cases of the other liquid cargo, and a sopping field, it was going to be a long run.

For a few seconds the Vimy did its queasy, bouncing act before settling down, the engines straining against the aquatic resistance. We were almost level with the white clapboard farmhouse before the wheels unstuck and the old crate climbed over the rocky, rising ground at the far end of the field, water hissing off the perspex windscreens, straight into our goggled faces.

Minutes later we were in cold, bright sunlight, on our way via Massena and the Adirondack Mountains for the final smuggling trip that would just about pay the last, lost election bills.

By the time we were at eight thousand feet we were both shivering with cold, being unable to dry out in the icy air at that altitude. Our leather coats and helmets had protected us from most of the rain; nevertheless George's slacks were soaked, and about a bucketful of water had streamed down my neck. My combinations were wringing.

However, it was no more than I deserved. The memory of that speech in the armory still hurt. Even now I couldn't help wincing at the thought that I had failed even to rouse McMulligan from his torpor—and he had been *paid* to be roused. At thirty years of age, I had reached the bottom of the ladder of success. I was now the laughingstock of Gallop.

"What's the matter?" George asked, his teeth chattering.

"I'm thirty years old, and an utter failure."

"My dearest Bartalamyeh, that is not true at all," he shouted, pressing my arm. "Thirty years old and a failure, what nonsense you do talk, my dear fellow—why, you are only twenty-nine."

"No. I believe I had a birthday a few weeks ago."

"Oh. In that case perhaps you are right."

I felt too miserable even to glare at him. "Thirty years old and

I have no job, no money of my own, no career, no prospects, and no future."

"Never mind, Bartalamyeh," George said, trying to warm his feet by drumming them on the cockpit floor. "I at least will vote for you."

"That will make two," I said dismally. "Yours and mine."

"Except, of course, I do not have a vote. Still, even though you are down and out, I will still be your friend."

"Wonderful."

"Even after I marry Philippa."

I stared at him. "You're marrying her?"

"I am plainly smitten with her," he said over the drone of the engines. "Even though she often criticizes me for having, what does she call it—no get-up-and-go. Just think, Bartalamyeh, she says I am passive."

"Imagine that."

"But she is so generous," he said dreamily. "She bought me this leather coat. She is charming, honest, loving, sympathetic, rich . . . But she has her good points, too."

It took me a moment to realize he was talking about her redoubtable nipples again. Deplorably frank about such intimate matters, he had mentioned more than once that their coefficient of expansion was quite phenomenal; a piece of information that I had greeted as a gentleman should, with utter restraint, except for a slightly forward-leaning posture, an unblinking gaze, an undulating Adam's apple, and a dribble of saliva, in anticipation of further details.

"They leave dents in my chest—"

"Never mind that now. Has she agreed to marry you?"

"Not in too many words. But I can tell she is willing, the way she looks so meltingly at me, especially when it is time for bed."

"Well, good luck," I said, almost enthusiastically, at the thought of finally being rid of him.

A couple of hours later the Vimy rolled to a halt on the now thoroughly familiar stretch of grass alongside the rusty rails. And then the usual reception committee lurched up: Clutch Revalli and his brutish pal, incongruously attired, as ever, in business suits and homburgs; though this afternoon, making a concession to the chill, cloudy atmosphere, they were also wearing long

black coats of the kind usually preferred by middle-aged lawyers.

If George and I had been in a relaxed mood we should probably have had a good snigger, they looked so absurd. Revalli's
overcoat was so large it kept sliding off his shoulders, while that
of his friend was too small for his massive frame—his wrists, as
thick as garage hoists, stuck half a foot out of the heavy black
material.

"Okay, Pierre, let's get moving," Clutch grated in his usual
superfluous way, but looking uneasily at the black forest that
hemmed in both sides of the field and tracks.

For some reason everybody seemed jumpy that day. Perhaps it
was the weather. Though there were no storm symptoms in the
offing, there seemed to be an ominous pressure in the air, as if
the gods were engulfing us in a brown paper bag and were
about to burst it with a hearty clap.

"Say, yeller belly," Revalli sneered as we unloaded, "I hear
you're quitting after this delivery."

Though I usually returned Clutch's contemptuous serves, he
looked particularly vicious this afternoon, so I decided to keep
quiet—especially as he probably had his automatic tucked under
his arm; not to mention his pal's sawn-off shotgun, which was
propped up against the little two-car freight train.

As I hauled the boxes out of the fuselage and passed them
along I had to admit to being relieved that the job was about to
end; not because it was dangerous—it was the easiest aerial work
I'd done since learning to fly—but because the two subhumans
over there reminded me that my real employer was not Mrs. Talbot but Tony Batt. At one time I had quite liked Tony. The scale
of his enterprises was so great as to transcend censure. But since
leaving the army he had been increasingly involved in much
more than innocent rumrunning. Just a few days previously his
name had been mentioned in the New York papers in connection
with a gangland slaying. That was not the Tony Batt, army en-
trepreneur, anti-Bolshevik, confidant of the literati, and patron of
penniless Russian émigrés, that I used to know. I felt quite indignant at the way he had deteriorated, especially as it was I
who had made it all possible by saving his life in North Russia. . . . Incidentally he had often said that he was indebted to

me for that, and intended to pay me back one day, but never had. . . . A debt not unlike the one I owed George Garanine, come to think of it.

I paused in the offloading to look at George. He was standing on the far wing, busily cleaning the plugs of the port engine. Seeing me looking in his direction, his face brightened as if a ray of sunlight had broken through; and clouded over again when I turned away, looking as surly as ever. I suddenly felt ashamed of myself, wondering why I always behaved so badly with George. Could it be because I was under an obligation to him, after skipping out of Russia in 1920, leaving him to face the vindictive fury of his Bolshevik superiors? I had never asked him why he had fled from Russia so soon after my escape . . . because I was pretty sure I knew the reason: me. In forcing him to flee, I suppose I had done him a grave wrong. I knew how passionately Russians felt about their country. Yet George continued to treat me as lovingly as ever. The man was a saint, the stupid bastard.

"Hey. Hey, Pierre."

Revalli was glaring up at me, his face, sweaty with effort, looking like refrigerated dough. "Thinking beautiful thoughts, are you?" he sneered.

As his brutish pal chortled from atop the homemade freight train, I hauled out the last of the boxes from the fuselage and held it out; but Revalli let me go on holding it, while he grubbed around in his mind for some further derision.

"Or maybe you're composing a tune up there, are you, Pierre?"

"Sure," I said. "Want to hear the lyrics?

"There once was a fellow named Revalli
Who went in for sex far too heavily.
As he pumped night and day
His bollocks gave way,
But a doctor fixed one of them cleverly."

Forgetting that he was supposed to chortle only at his friend's witticisms, Harelip guffawed again; though he stopped soon enough when Revalli whirled on him.

When Revalli turned back he looked so unappreciative that I

hid behind George and busied myself unloading the cases from
the two spare cockpits.

"Be careful of that man, Bartalamyeh Fyodorevitch," George
murmured in Russian.

"Well, he started it," I mumbled.

Just as Harelip was lashing down the last of the cases and I
was tucking the official receipt into my pocket—we became
aware of a peculiar humming sound.

Instinctively we all looked toward the forest. Then, one by
one, we turned to stare at the railway track itself. It was the rails
that were humming—and the humming was growing louder—and
now making a familiar clacking sound. The sound of iron wheels
across track joints.

A train? On this disused branch line?

Next we all turned and stared down the track. We looked in
that direction because that was where Revalli and his friend always headed as soon as they had loaded the train. The track ran
dead straight for about a mile before curving eastward and out
of sight. About another two miles beyond the curve a narrow
dirt road intersected the track. This was where Revalli transferred the consignment into a waiting van. From there the
whisky went by road to its ultimate destination, wherever that
was.

But there was nothing to be seen in that direction. So we all
swiveled and looked in the opposite direction. To the north, the
rusty rails vanished just three hundred yards away, bending to
the left through the scrub pine and brush.

We were just in time to see a linesman's trolley, similar to
ours, come scooting round the bend. And close behind it another
trolley. Both vehicles loaded with blue uniforms.

Because the track ended at an abandoned sawmill half a mile
farther on, none of us had anticipated trouble from that direction. In fact none of us had anticipated that the authorities
would use the track at all. We had thought in terms of, at worst,
an irruption from the woods. But even if we had considered the
possibility that the law would use our own line of communication, we would certainly have assumed that they would
approach from the south, to come between us and the transfer
point three miles away. That made sense—a tactic designed to

cut off our escape. It was quite disorienting to find them attacking from the wrong direction.

So we all just stood there for a frozen moment, gaping up the track at the rapidly approaching linesman's trolleys. The one in the lead must have been fairly capacious, for it held five men in uniform. There were only two men in the one behind, pumping away furiously at the trolley operating lever.

All four of us reacted simultaneously. Revalli and his friend dived for their own vehicle and scrambled aboard, uttering meaningless yells; George bolted toward the bomber; while I, who was inclined to panic where human relationships were concerned but who in a physical emergency could sometimes be quick-thinking enough, decided instantly that we would have to abandon the Vimy. Even with the most efficient coordination between pilot and mechanic, it took at least three minutes to wind it up and get it moving, even with warm engines. But the customs and excise men, who were now yelling as well and waving their weapons in the air, would be upon us in less than a minute.

I caught up with George as he was clambering onto the lower wing, and hauled him off, and started dragging him after the others.

"But we must fly," he said bewilderedly, as if that was not precisely what we were doing, as we hurtled over the gravel along the track, chasing after the bootleg special.

Revalli and his friend had already overcome the inertia of their rolling stock and were moving off, though still at only three or four miles an hour. Had I not been suffused with a certain amount of anxiety, I might have guffawed at the sight of the two flapping-coated thugs frantically hauling back and forth on the trolley lever, with Revalli exhorting his pal to greater efforts in a voice like fingernails on a blackboard, while his massive companion lowed in panic like a stuck ox.

As George and I scrambled aboard the hoodlum-powered engine, it started to pick up speed. By then the pursuit was less than a hundred yards away. As I peered, panting, around the little freight truck we were towing, I was surprised that the leading trolley was no closer. While the one behind it was actually slowing down.

A moment later I saw why: as it drew level with the Vimy it

braked to a halt, and the two men on it jumped down and, crouched over, cautiously approached the airplane with leveled rifles, as if expecting it to take off on its own.

So that was that, I thought: the end of the Vimy after three hundred hours of flight-testing, movie work, joyriding, electioneering, and smuggling. I'd never get it back now. It would undoubtedly be confiscated. Oh well. At least I wouldn't be confiscated as well—provided Revalli managed to keep ahead of the customs men.

Surprisingly, considering the weight we were towing, the customs and excise men did not appear to be closing the gap. Of course, we ourselves were now racing along the track licketysplit, with Revalli and his pal jerking the crossbar back and forth so rapidly that the former looked as if he might lose the rhythm and be hurled overboard.

Perhaps realizing this himself, he let go and, gasping for breath, picked up the shotgun, and peered back over the top of the homemade freight car. Harelip continued to pump, his black coattails flapping violently in the wind. He had long since lost his homburg.

Crouched at the rear edge of the trolley, I said hurriedly to George, "We'd never have gotten off in time."

"No, of course not," he replied with a smile that was remarkably serene in the circumstances. "You always know best, Bartalamyeh."

Again I peered cautiously around the edge of the swaying whisky wagon. The pursuing trolley was no closer. For some reason, this made me feel more unsettled than ever. It was almost as if they were content merely to keep us moving along the track. They weren't even shooting at us.

Before I had a chance to work it out I caught a scrabbling movement from Revalli. Bracing himself against the yawing motion of the trolley, standing just clear of the wildly oscillating handle, he was aiming the shotgun. Before I could get to him he had fired.

The gun banged. A puff of smoke shredded in the wind. With a bellow, I snatched at the barrel and wrested it from him, and flung the shotgun over the side. But his futile gesture had gratuitously worsened the situation; for now the customs men began to shoot back; and they had at least one high-powered rifle. Even over the racket of the wheels we heard the bullets cracking overhead, and others smashing into the cargo behind us.

"You cretin," I shouted, huddling down. "*Now* see what you've done."

Half crouched, Revalli looked at me out of his soulless eyes. Harelip stared as well, though he continued to pump away, his fists, clamped around the handle, the size of prime red cabbages.

I snorted, and turned away to examine the coupling between the trolley and the homemade freight car. I was considering unfastening it, to increase our speed or slow the pursuit. But it was not a standard coupling. It was a welded arrangement of steel bars.

Perhaps it was just as well that it didn't detach. We would lose the protection that the cases of whisky afforded, and expose us to the enemy fire. The customs and excise chaps could hardly miss at this range.

I became aware that George was trying to attract my attention. When I looked at him, he gestured with his head. I looked around. Revalli had taken up another weapon, his automatic. Only this time he was pointing it at me.

"Jump," he said.

"Eh?"

He jerked the automatic. "You too, sap," he said to George.

I looked down at the track. From this low elevation the gravel was a gray blur.

"But that could be dangerous," I faltered.

"Jump," he screamed again. "Or I'll put a bullet in your goddam hide."

He was lurching about on straddled legs, but the automatic was steady enough. He jerked it again and shouted, "It's alla same with me, Pierre. It would suit me just fine to plug you." His face was swollen with rage, and spittle was forming in the bristles at the corner of his mouth. "Maybe I will anyways. Yeah."

The thought transmitted itself to his finger. As it tightened on the trigger, George scrambled to his feet, shouting. The movement distracted Revalli. He whirled and the automatic jumped. There was a flat report. George staggered back and pitched over the side.

As Revalli turned the weapon on me again, his dough-colored face glistening, I decided not to argue, and followed George over the side. Unfortunately I was facing the wrong way. My feet struck the gravel and I somersaulted backward.

I saw my feet walking on the clouds, quite slowly, it seemed, and thought that surely it ought to have been my head in the clouds, not my feet. Peculiar.

After the first impact of fleece-lined flying boots on gravel, I seemed to be in the air for the next several minutes. This gave me ample time to think about the election. When they heard I was dead, they would have to postpone it a third time. Unless they propped up my lifeless carcass on the hustings platform and went ahead anyway, on the assumption that nobody would know the difference. Yes, that was probably what they would do. Otherwise, at this rate, Gallop would be left unrepresented in Parliament for years.

Funnily enough, hurtling backward also inspired several vivid memories of childhood. Nothing particularly significant, just odd flashes, like the memory of falling off a stool while reaching for a copy of the *National Geographic*, which I had hidden on top of the mahogany cupboard in my room in Beamington. It was a tactile memory—the smooth feel of the paper—as well as visual: the sight of Papa's face when he came in and picked up the magazine, and it sprang open at a picture of a bare-breasted Zulu maiden. And various other memories and thoughts of a distinctly uninspiring nature, before I finally landed on my back with a loud smack, and almost immediately felt the blood gushing down my back.

I realized that my head had been wrenched off. I was obviously about to croak. I could even hear myself croaking.

A moment later I noticed the frog sitting on my chest. Which explained why the blood felt so cold. It wasn't because it had cooled during my passage through the cold air. It was swamp water. I had landed in the swamp, ten feet from the track.

I lay there for what seemed like many minutes, afraid to learn the extent of the damage, to discover that only the mud of the swamp was holding me together. Until I thought of George. He might similarly be sharing the swamp up the track, and drowning in it—if he was not already dead. The thought encouraged me to stir, and I soon perceived that I was unhurt. Remarkable. A moment later I emerged from the primeval slime.

I crawled onto the firmer ground near the track and was just about to stand up when the pursuing trolley appeared and rattled past, crowded with uniforms, all shouting and firing rifles and yanking their propulsion bar back and forth. I gaped after them as they continued round the bend and out of sight. I was astounded. Between the time I had abandoned the trolley and the moment that saw me rising shakily and squelchily to my feet, only seconds had passed.

Much later I learned why the pursuit had not appeared to be overly determined. The customs men had been driving us into another ambush. The rumrunner's van farther down the track had already been captured and placed across the rails, and a car loaded with an extra supply of excise men had been positioned on both sides of the track. So in a way Revalli did us a favor by forcing us to abandon ship before we, too, could be shot up at the ambush.

I found George only a minute later. He was lying at the edge of the swamp only a few yards away, sitting up and looking extremely surprised. Apart from the blood seeping out from under his flying coat, he was quite dry. He had missed the swamp and thumped onto the hard ground. Presumably his relaxed state, caused by the impact of the bullet, had saved him from further injury.

He was mumbling to himself as I pressed him back into a supine position and opened the jacket to examine the injury. The bullet appeared to have entered at an angle, just above the hipbone. When I slipped a hand behind his waist, it came away dyed with blood.

"You are all wet, Bartalamyeh."

"M'm," I said, wrenching off my coat and woolen sweater.

"You must get out of your wet clothes," he said, "or you will catch pneumonia."

As I tore off my shirt, I stared at him. A bullet had plowed right through his waist, he was bleeding like a stuck pig, and he was worried that I might catch the sniffles. The man was incredible.

I applied the two halves of wadded shirt and bound them

tightly round his waist with my leather belt. "Do you think you
can walk?" I asked as I maneuvered his flying coat back over his
shoulders and fastened it.

But he was regarding the bullet hole in his coat with dismay.
"Oh, look at my coat. It is quite ruined." He was almost weeping
over the damage.

"She can always buy you another. Come on, see if you can
stand."

"Where are we going, Bartalamyeh?"

"Back to the airplane."

I had no idea how we were going to get past the two guards
who had dropped off near the Vimy. I set off anyway, to walk
the mile or so back to the landing field, spurred on by a distant
fusillade of shots. Our erstwhile colleagues had reached the
roadblock.

Though the government men did not appear to have noticed
our abrupt departure from the trolley, I wondered how long it
would take them to realize that two of their quarry were
missing.

For the first few hundred yards George managed quite well,
though it was obvious he was uncomfortable. I saw how much it
was hurting when he stumbled over a rail tie and sank to his
knees. His handsome face was so twisted that his pencil mustache was almost vertical. To make things more difficult, I
couldn't support him round the waist because of the injury, but
had to hold him under the arms.

He managed to force himself up again and lurched off, but
sank down again a few minutes later, gasping.

"George?"

He looked up at me, trying to make room for an inquiring look
on his distorted face.

"We'll give in."

"No, I will be all right, Bartalamyeh. We should get away if
we can."

"It won't be so bad. Smuggling isn't such a crime. And they'll
get you to a hospital," I said; though admitting to myself that,
because that employee of Tony Batt's had fired on the United
States Government, we were not likely to be treated too le-
niently.

But George became so agitated that I was afraid he was going to faint from sheer emotion. "All right, all right," I said. "In that case I suppose I'll have to carry you."

Gad, he was heavy. I barely managed a hundred yards before it was my turn to sink to my knees—crunching a patella right on top of the shotgun that I had thrown from the trolley.

I picked it up with the ridiculous idea of using it as a crutch, until I discovered that it was only a foot long, and staggered onward, wondering how long it would take the enemy trolley to return. It was now a quarter hour since we had heard the shooting.

By the time we reached the end of the landing field I felt as if I'd just completed all seven of the labors of Hercules. As we lay gasping in the long grass, I could see the big biplane tantalizingly close, only about two hundred yards away. But one of the guards was standing on the wing, leaning over into the pilot's office. Presumably he was taking an interest in all the knobs, levers, dials, and switches in there.

But where was the other man? A moment later, as I pushed aside the reeds, I caught sight of him. He was sitting on the linesman's trolley, his rifle propped up against one of the wheels.

"George?" He was lying on his back, shivering in spasms; but he opened his eyes immediately. They widened still further when he saw me breaking open the shotgun.

"I have to leave you for a few minutes. I may be back soon or the customs men will."

"You are not going to shoot them, Bartalamyeh?"

I showed him the breech. "Empty. Try and keep warm, all right?"

I started to crawl away, but then returned, took off my flying coat, and wrapped it around him.

"You are always so kind to me, Bartalamyeh."

"I know," I said. Actually I had only removed my jacket so that I could run and abandon him more speedily. Perhaps forever. This was an excellent opportunity to get away from George Garanine once and for all.

It was hopeless to try and approach the airplane on this side of the track. On the far side, though, the forest came to within thirty feet of the permanent way. So I crawled to the lines and rolled over them, and down into the ditch on the far side, and waited to see if either of the guards had spotted the movement. But they were now seated side by side on the trolley, one of them smoking a pipe. They were obviously waiting for the rest of their colleagues to return.

A minute later I was in the trees and darting through them, slipping and sliding over hills of slippery pine needles. I was taking risks by moving so incautiously, but I had little time to spare. The others were likely to appear at any moment.

It took two minutes to reach the part of the forest opposite the trolley. The two men were still there, the older one puffing away at his pipe, the younger holding the rifle, the butt resting on his thigh. But they were a good fifty feet away at this point. I would have to get much closer, before rushing them.

I was halfway across, near the top of the ditch, when they both arose and turned.

I froze on one knee, staring back at them. The younger man snatched up his rifle. He aimed it. And the other called out sharply.

So that was that. They had observed me just a few seconds too soon.

I was just about to stand up and raise my hands when I realized that they were not quite looking in my direction. Which was absurd, as I was only twenty feet away, only half concealed, conspicuous in a blue sweater and large white face below a light brown flying helmet with the straps dangling stupidly, and sodden, swamp-colored breeks.

A second later I heard the rails humming again. That was what had alerted them. The others were on their way back.

I swiveled my eyes to the left. The trolley was just rounding the curve, two miles away.

The guards exchanged words, visibly relaxing as they recognized their friends. The rifle barrel dipped. As they turned back toward the Vimy I tensed, then charged forward and leaped onto the track with shotgun at the ready, before they had fully turned.

"Drop it."

The rifle clattered to the gravel. Four hands shot into the air. The older man's pipe fell from a slack mouth.

"Get onto the trolley. Both of you. Quick, quick."

"What are you going to do?" one of them faltered.

"Send you to blazes," I said, waving the shotgun, "if you don't hurry."

As I picked up their rifle they scrambled aboard, shaky with shock.

"Take off. Start pumping."

They stared goiterishly.

"Right," I said, and aimed the shotgun.

They started pumping.

"And if I see you slow down it'll be just too bad," I added.

Half a minute later they were well down the track, heading toward their companions, frantically hauling the bar back and forth as if bailing out the *Titanic*.

By then I was leaning into the flying cockpit of the Vimy, priming, pumping, opening cocks and clicking switches like mad, and inching forward the fine adjustment, and wishing with all my heart that I had followed through on the idea of hooking starter batteries to the engines while I had the chance.

It was hopeless, of course. I'd never get the engines started in time. Still, it would be good exercise, and better than tamely surrendering.

Still standing on the wing, I turned to the port engine and snatched the inertia starting handle sticking out from the scarred crimson cowling of the Rolls engine, and began winding. It was so long since I had started an engine myself that I had forgotten what an effort it took. It felt as if it were attached to a steam roller; or perhaps I was enfeebled by funk and exertion. I'd never yet gotten into the air from scratch in under five minutes. Still, the alternative to the attempt was at the very least several months in jail, and perhaps a lasting notoriety, when they learned that their captured rumrunner was also currently standing for Parliament. The newspapers would have a field day. Practically any risk was better than subjecting myself to that ordeal.

So I hauled on the handle with as much horsepower as I could summon, and gradually the resistance lessened, and the sound of the generator rose in pitch to a craven whine. Whereupon, sweating and trembling, I stabbed the button to engage the crankshaft and rushed back over the wing to the flying cockpit, and leaned in, ready to stimulate the engine with a proper flow of petrol.

The four-bladed propeller started to turn, the engine spluttered. Then stopped abruptly with a huffy sigh.

Oh, God, missed. And now in the silence I could hear the rails not only humming but clicking as the linesman's trolley—trolleys, there would be two of them—rapidly approached.

Back to the starter, gasping for air as if the airplane were perched on a twenty-thousand-foot peak. Once again I shoved on the handle, gripping it with both hands, feet braced on the wing, forcing the handle, faster and faster, determined this time to wind it up as high as I could get it. The pitch rose to a most frightful keening.

For a moment I thought the huge 360-h.p. engine was going to wrench free. The propeller jerked round unsteadily for a couple of seconds, then caught, and by the time I had skittered back to the cockpit it was bellowing in pain. I reached in and hurriedly whacked back the fine adjustment lever on the throttle pedestal. With the result that the engine started to die again. I was barely in time to catch it before it gave up.

Precious seconds streaked by while I adjusted the controls, then leaped frantically over the fuselage to get to the other engine. This time I got the cranking more or less right. Twenty-five seconds later I flung myself into the cockpit, making sure the starboard engine was being fed properly before shoving forward both throttles.

With the throttles dangerously far forward I wheeled the huge airplane around and drove it as fast as I dared down the field. Though high up in the cockpit, I could not see along the track; but it was obvious that the excise men would be upon me at any moment, and I was actually helping them by hurrying in their direction. I could hardly believe it when they had failed to appear by the time I reached the far end of the field, or even by the time I had swung the machine around, ready for the takeoff. As I dropped off the wing, leaving the engines turning at the highest revs possible without causing the machine to move, I could only surmise that the trolley I had sent back had gotten in the way. Unless they had all stopped for a chat. And indeed, as I reached the spot where I had left George and was able to obtain an unobstructed view down the line, I saw that the two trolleys, though clearly in sight, were traveling in company at a reduced speed, judging by the cautious seesawing motion as they pushed and pulled at the trolley handles. All the same, it was obvious that I would never manage to carry George to the aircraft and get him aboard in time. Especially as he wasn't there. He had disappeared.

I had left him lying near the track in deep grass, I was sure of it. Yes, there was the grass, flattened. But he had vanished. I looked around in bug-eyed desperation, thinking he had wandered off in delirium and been sucked into the swamp. Then with a wave of relief mixed with incredulity, I saw him staggering out of the undergrowth only a few feet from the box-kite-shaped tail of the Vimy. Hearing the airplane approaching, he had dragged himself forward to meet it, perhaps to save himself from another painful piggyback ride—or, more likely, to save me a few steps.

I got to him as he was trying to climb onto the lower wing. By the time I had stuffed him into the cockpit his face matched the cloud-gray color of the fuselage, a sunken garden of pain.

I had to clamber over the fuselage to reach my side of the cockpit. I was perched right on top of it when the trolleys finally appeared and started grinding to a halt only thirty yards away. Frantically I shoved my bum forward off the fuselage and down onto the wickerwork bench in the cockpit, and promptly sat on my scrotum.

With a face almost as twisted as George's, I was still able to issue a stream of profanities mixed with my entire range of short though strangled Saxon words, while getting down to business, greatly encouraged by the cries of the revenuers, and even more so by a volley of shots. Several bullets passed overhead with that all too familiar whip-cracking noise. One came even closer. It hit the shield at the side of the cockpit, six inches away. This was supposed to protect the pilot from lumps of ice that might be flung off the propellers. On this occasion it saved him from a high-powered bullet, which struck the shield and ricocheted off with a warbling howl. Then we were moving forward, bouncing over the rough ground beside the track, the engines bellowing almost as loudly as I was.

As the elevators bit into the slipstream and the nose dipped, I risked a quick sideways glance, then wished I hadn't. The excise men in the two trolleys, red with exertion in their thick blue uniforms, were actually drawing ahead of the Vimy, oscillating along at a furious frequency. The two in the first trolley were not shooting but were expending their energy in keeping ahead of the second vehicle. Had the others not been behaving so vindictively with their armament, the sight might have provided a spot of comic relief, what with the two men in front pumping away faster and faster to avoid being run down. But the spare bodies in the following trolley were shooting in deadly earnest. From a hundred feet they were clearly frustrated by their inability—so far—to stop us, despite the ridiculous slowness of our getaway. They were shooting their rifles as if competing to see who would be first to exhaust his ammunition. Had they been less infuriated they would almost certainly have hit our exposed heads or hunched shoulders.

Even so, they could not fail to miss such a huge target at such a range. Bullets were slashing through the wood and canvas body. I was rigid with fear that they would hit the main tank in the fuselage. They were doing plenty of damage as it was. One bullet struck the red cowling of the starboard engine, leaving a jagged hole that whistled in the wind. Another hit an engine support strut, almost, but not quite, severing it.

We were still doing only twenty miles an hour. I trod on the rudder to veer farther away from the railway track but had to resume the former heading when the tall trees of the forest swung slowly into view. Too high to climb over. But gradually the giant biplane began to draw away from the pursuit. At last, minutes, it seemed, after starting off, the control column stiffened. I gave the old beast another few seconds before hauling back on the wheel. As the airplane was lightly loaded, and as a considerable weight of fuel had been burned off, the four landing wheels plucked free readily enough.

I waited, holding my breath, half expecting one of the engines to falter and die. At twenty feet a rude crosswind began to push and shove at us. A series of bumps jerked George about in the cockpit. I had not, of course, had time to fasten his safety belt. He turned his white, sunken face away, fists clenched in his lap.

The bumping smoothed out as I canted into the wind. A second later we were straining over the trees, scattering a fluster of wood pigeons. Then the engine quietened slightly as I adjusted the throttles and flew up toward the clouds.

I could hardly believe that we had actually gotten away and were still alive. Shot up, racked, sweating, shivering, corroded to the marrow by adrenaline, and, in my case, probably rendered impotent for life by that frantic leap into the cockpit, but free, and flying.

For most of the flight back, I sat in a frozen stupor, barely able to rouse myself to navigate the craft the easy way home up Lake Champlain, with George huddled and silent against my left shoulder. We were approaching Montreal before I reached the second great turning point in my life.

The first had occurred after a few months in the army, with the realization that I was being untrue to my real character, such as it was. All my life I had been listening to people with varying degrees of respect, accepting their orders, their guidance, and their prejudices as if these represented immutable moral standards as fixed as that of a yardstick; until I finally acknowledged that the yardstick varied in length according to the half-witted, self-seeking, or malicious feelings of others. From then on I had determined to act independently rather than like a living proxy vote, even if the individualism produced results that alarmed even me.

Now, two thousand feet over the St. Lawrence, came this second resolve, to fight this arrogant prohibition measure that had switched the country onto the siding of dishonesty, graft, and hypocrisy. I mean, look at Jewell, a decent enough fellow, I supposed, until placed in a bribable position by a presumptuous law. And look at Toombs, made ferocious by his experience of authority. Look at Mrs. Talbot, corrupted by a power awarded her by authoritarian governments, quite possibly bribing the most senior officials of Customs and Excise, judging by the otherwise inexplicable freedom with which she dispensed her bottles and flagons. And most important of all, look at me, formerly the most upright, decent, honest, accommodating chap imaginable, now breaking and entering the house of our American neighbor and threatening the householders with shotguns, and adding to

the profits of a racketeer, and risking lives in the process. By
God, I *would* get into Parliament and do something about it. Not
this time, but next time, sometime, somehow, and undermine, if I
could, this bureaucratic disdain that asserted the right of governments to deny the individual the right to take his own route to
perdition or self-discovery, with their supercilious measures designed to protect the citizen against the excesses and uncertain-
ties that helped him to thrive as a human being. Right from the
beginning, Canadians had been stifled by authoritarian thinking,
by a third-rate oligarchy. What right had the rulers to impose
their sanctimonious standards on us common anarchists and de-
value the individual in the name of security? The process was
still continuing, to the extent that people were getting used to
being anesthetized by the law. But then, of course, to be torpid
was to be safe.

Admittedly, the narrow escape from the customs men was not
a particularly worthy inspiration for such a re-evaluation. After
all, I had placed myself in this situation. But the fury was also
the result of a dawning awareness that the war had been a gigantic fraud. Throughout the conflict, despite a knowledge of its
excesses and the abominable way it was being conducted, I had
jousted under a banner I believed in, knocking off the heathen
Hun with a crystal conscience borrowed from Frank Merrivale.
But since the war, when every selfish political maneuver became
manifest in the capitals of the world and in the League of Nations, it had become more and more evident that the war had
come about purely through the confrontation of rival power
structures and greedy commercial interests. It had had damn all
to do with democracy. Ten million of the most intelligent, vigorous, and valuable men in the Empire and Europe and America
had been gutted in the name of abstract concepts and concrete
avarice. In the city of Montreal—which was now spreading
around the snout of the Vimy—when I visited Liberal headquarters that time, I had seen a chauffeur shooing away a crip-
pled, pencil-selling veteran so that the chauffeur's boss could
march unobstructedly into his neoclassical head office, so that
the boss need not be disturbed by the sight of one of those
whose lost arm and leg had perhaps enabled him to become a

millionaire. I knew at last how people like Fred Toombs felt, and how the Lost Generation felt.

As it turned out, these molten ruminations solidified still further when, just as I was about to turn upriver below Mount Royal, the starboard engine caught fire.

If I had not been as numb with cold as I was hot with unrighteous indignation, I might just possibly have noticed something wrong and been able to do something about it. But I had been flying just below cloud level all the way up Lake Champlain with little protection above the waist but a sweater and a woolen vest, my expensive flying coat having been left behind. I had also lost my goggles during that dash through the forest, and it was no fun flying in an open cockpit without eye protection. At times even George looked blurred as he leaned, half fainting, against my left shoulder, so I certainly didn't have a clear view of the engine a few feet to my right.

The engine was fed from a tank in the leading edge of the top wing, which in turn was supplied from the main tank in the fuselage. Judging by what happened now, a bullet had nicked the feed line from the wing tank, not enough to sever it, but ultimately to cause fuel to leak down the outside of the fuel line onto the engine surfaces. Just as I was starting to bank to the left, to follow the Ottawa River back to Gallop, I saw smoke wisping from the red cowling. A moment later there was a *woof* audible over the mechanical racket, and in a second the entire engine was ablaze.

The distillery was only a few miles to the right, but I didn't dare turn in that direction, otherwise the flames would play over the highly inflammable wings. So I turned left instead, and kept turning in a circle until I was steering in the right direction. Though I had now shut off the fuel supply, the engine continued to burn. Black blisters were already bulging and popping in the red cowling paint. When I pushed the wheel forward toward the wetness below, the flames altered direction and started licking the trailing edge of the upper wing. I hurriedly pulled the wheel back again. If any other part of the aircraft caught fire we would be a flamer within seconds. We should already have gone down in flames had the engine not been isolated from the wings by its special struts.

Roused from his own preoccupations by the unfamiliar motions of the aircraft, George finally raised his head. His eyes widened.

"Bartalamyeh, the machine is on fire," he said, as calmly and obviously as if quoting one of his proverbs.

"Yes, George, I know," I replied, straining to maintain the pressure on the left rudder. The torque from the port engine was practically bending the bones in my leg. But I had to keep that engine at full throttle. Even so, we were losing height. The river was only six hundred feet below.

Though the wings with the incendiary dope and varnish were not yet affected, it was only a matter of time, now, before we were cremated, for the wooden fairings covering the tubular steel engine struts were burning as well. One of the rear supports had already parted—though I remembered, now, it was the one that had been struck by a bullet. Until then I had hoped to reach the distillery, which was only a couple of miles ahead. I could see its distinctive buildings clearly, outlined against a bright band of yellow sky that was flaring across the horizon between the darkening earth and the gray cloud above. No land pilot pancakes into the water if terra firma offers an alternative, and I shared that hydrophobia. Even though the open ground at the distillery was hardly adequate, I still preferred to smack down on that rough ground rather than risk the unknown effect of digging four landing wheels into a swirling river. But now, with the fairings afire and the tubular steel twisting noticeably, not to mention the roaring flames below the wing fuel tank, I decided that I would have to dunk.

Then, just as I was about to draw back the left-hand power lever and wallow downward, the engine fell off.

One moment it was there, its cowling scorched and blackened, flaming away merrily; then it was sagging, wrenching loose with a sound like wet kindling on a blaze, and in the process tearing away a great chunk of the lower wing—and the windmilling propeller slashing at the upper wing. Then it was gone, leaving a trail of smoke as it curved down to the drink and smacked into the brown water four hundred feet below.

I waited for the Vimy to complete its self-demolition. After all, a great chunk had been bitten out of the lower wing, exposing ribs and spruce and plywood spars, and the fabric was torn and flapping and rattling like a Spandau; while at least six interplane and support struts had gone; and in the upper wing the whirling propeller had chopped a four-foot hole, and the wing was groaning and straining against its remaining supports.

Astonishingly the huge biplane kept on flying. Even the pull to the left, caused by the wind resistance to the now silent engine on that side—I had cut it instinctively—was being compensated by the drag on the opposite side. The airplane was drifting down as steadily as if it actually enjoyed being tortured. And the falling engine, moreover, had taken the fire with it. And when I saw the pump house of the distillery coming up on the left, and I turned the wheel in that direction, the horn-balanced ailerons actually responded—somewhat erratically, but effectively enough.

So that only left the landing, on the stretch of rough ground within the L formed by the distillery buildings. As the field drew closer, though, I was reminded again of how inadequate it was. We would likely be piling into the building at the far end. Still, after what we had just been through, this seemed a minor consideration. Especially as there was still that archway in the middle of the building. Fifteen feet high, it was not all that much wider than a motor vehicle. But as a last resort I might be able to shoot through it, using the Vimy's wings as brakes when they were wrenched off. Well, at least it was better than charging headfirst into the brickwork.

It being Sunday, there were no construction workers about, so the ground was clear, apart from the usual building site clutter: tar paper, lengths of discarded lumber, drums and sacks and small heaps of rubble peeking out of the longish grass.

But now as I aimed cautiously at the riverbank to the left of the pump house, I saw that I had miscalculated. I was too high.

The emotional reservoir having long since gone dry, I considered sideslipping; but thought better of it. The upper wing was already tearing at its remaining struts. A sideslip would wrench it off completely, and even this tolerant aircraft was not likely to put up with that sort of nonsense. So the last resort was upon us. I would definitely have to get through the archway somehow, or George and I would end up as mangled as the wings.

Now that the only sound was the whistle of the wind in the

wires and the flapping of canvas, I was able to talk to George
without hollering. It was practically the first time I hadn't
shouted at him since Petrograd.

"George, can you manage to tighten your safety belt? There's
going to be a bit of a jolt."

He looked dazedly at his lap, then fumbled for the straps. I
couldn't help him, as I needed all four hands and feet to keep
the nose straight. Besides, the trees along the riverbank were already swishing below the fuselage so there was only ten seconds
to go.

As the details of the ground, the debris and tufts of grass,
sharpened into focus, George raised his head to look through his
perspex windscreen. His mouth fell open when he saw a brick
wall rushing to meet him. By the time I had leveled out, it was
only a couple of hundred feet away, and to make it look even
worse, we were traveling faster than usual because I could no
longer assume that the stalling speed still applied.

George lowered his head again, in prayer or exhaustion, swaying as I trod on the rudder. I was still trying to line up with the
high, narrow Roman archway in the wall, even as I pulled back
on the wheel. But the Vimy was now so lightly loaded it was taking an age to settle. By the time it had decided to do so, we were
only thirty feet from the wall. The gear banged down, the building reared up. By a miracle, the aircraft failed to slew in the
rough ground. As we hurtled into the archway there was a splintering crash as the wings were wiped off, and the fuselage, on
four wheels, with the tail skid still high in the air, charged onward through the short passageway and out into a courtyard.
And came to rest just a few feet short of a line of trucks that
were busily loading bonded whisky for onward transmission to
the thirsty citizens of Canada.

I knew it was bonded whisky because the red seals on the
cases were naturally a familiar sight, and I knew it was going to
the domestic market because one of the trucks that was loading
it belonged to Fred Toombs. Besides, he told me so, while we
were waiting in the lobby of the Montreal General Hospital,
and, convinced that I would keep quiet about it, also confirmed
my conjecture that Mrs. Talbot had been "switching back" liquor for a good many months; a revelation that would make
quite a difference to the outcome of the Gallop by-election.

I spent most of polling day hanging around our headquarters on Queen Street, trying to look busy; but we had so much help by now that there was little for me to do except give the occasional preoccupied nod, as if my mind was already on affairs of state. For our small, overworked band—Jim Boyce, Anne Mackie, Mr. Wattle, Miss Rawsthorne, and Captain Karley—had now been supplemented by a rush of last-minute volunteers, all clamorously willing to help, to canvass, carry messages, drive vehicles, agitate typewriters, or act as D.R.O.s, scrutineers, or poll clerks. They had been turning up in droves ever since the Announcement.

As they swirled around the shop, Jim Boyce regarded the volunteers with amused tolerance. "They're only here because they think you'll be able to bring influence to bear on their behalf," he said, rasping his hand judiciously over his blue chin. "Altruism is in short supply these days, isn't it, or dedication to the honorable tradition of putting back into the community what one takes out of it? By the way, old man, when you get around to finding a job for me, I'd prefer not to go back into External Affairs, if you don't mind. I hear that Rankin is now the assistant under secretary."

"He the one who caught you with your socks down?"

"H'm? I thought perhaps something in Health. Or maybe Mines—there's this gorgeous bookkeeper in the Assay Office I met once," Boyce replied vaguely, ignoring Anne's snort of disgust.

"And when you're in, don't forget to use your influence with

the publishing business," Miss Rawsthorne said. "Don't forget
my poems."

"And my bill of divorcement," Anne said. "I want to get rid of
Gordon's name forever, and go back to the family name."

"What name is that?"

"Oliphant."

"You actually want to go back to being called Anne Oliphant?" Boyce inquired. "That could be a terrible temptation to
a punster. Never forget that, Anne."

Anne glowered and there was an antagonistic silence. To
break it, I put my arms around Anne and Miss Rawsthorne and
said soothingly, "Gad, it gives one such a warm feeling, being
surrounded by such selfless, disinterested people."

Just then Mr. Wattle came up to discuss the Tories' latest
counterattack and the effect it was likely to have on today's voting. Over the past week the Conservative Party had brought in
practically every member of the shadow cabinet in a desperate
effort to recoup the situation. But our discussion was desultory,
almost complacent, for we were certain to win regardless. We
had finally found our issue.

After the crash and after settling George Garanine in the Montreal General Hospital, I had continued on to Gallop on the following day. I had barely had time for a wash and brush-up and
a change of clothing before Mrs. Talbot telephoned and asked
me to call round as soon as possible.

"What's happened?" she asked the moment I stepped into her
office. "They tell me there's an airplane wreck at the distillery. Is
that yours?"

"Yes."

"You crashed? Was the whisky aboard?"

"No. We'd delivered it."

"Thank God for that. But I had a call from New York. They
said they haven't heard from Revalli."

"Tony Batt called?"

She hesitated, snatching up a cigarette and inserting it into her
long ivory holder. "You know Tony Batt?"

"Naturally. Didn't you get Anne to pump me—to make sure I
wasn't in cahoots with Tony?"

"Did I?"

"Didn't you?"

"I don't think we'll get anywhere, honey, if we both keep asking questions—do you?"

"So Revalli hasn't been heard from, eh?" I said contentedly. "That's too bad."

However, when Philippa's smooth, watchful face hardened, I took out the receipt. "Nevertheless, I have his receipt," I said, smoothing it out on her desk. "So you owe me eight hundred and seventy dollars, Philippa."

"Yes, yes, you'll get your money. But what happened?"

"I told you on the telephone that George was hurt. You haven't asked how he is yet."

"How is he?"

"They said he was all right. Resting comfortably."

"I'm so glad. Poor darling George. But how did you come to crash? And where's the consignment?"

So I told her everything that had happened, concluding the account with my discovery that she had been shipping duty-free liquor to the domestic market. "And obviously on a pretty hefty scale," I said. "Five truckloads of bonded booze in that one operation yesterday, to five different locations in southern Ontario. And I gathered it's been going on for quite some time."

With admirable calm considering the shock I'd administered, she rose and walked to the window, and looked out, the brilliant sunlight committing arson on her auburn topknot. It was at least a minute before she spoke. She even blew a smoke ring, and watched it waver across a sunbeam and slowly turn into a pretzel.

Finally: "So you've found out I've been supplying the home market as well, have you? Oh dear. What are you going to do about it, Bartholomew?"

"Smuggling across the border might be quite legal here, Mrs. Talbot, but importing liquor that your friend Jewell has exempted from duty, that's quite a different matter, isn't it? You must have denied the country a good many hundred thousand dollars over the years."

I expected her to protest at this estimate, which I thought was a gross exaggeration. Instead she fell silent again, still standing at the window, half turned away from me so that I could see only her thoughtful profile.

Somehow I rarely viewed Mrs. Talbot from a decent perspective, as it were. She was the sort of person who tended to edge close, to touch, or press, or talk straight into your earhole, or lock kneecaps like train buffers. She crowded you, except when exciting customs officers or when in disguise—though of course there was plenty of tactile communication there, too.

This was one of the rare occasions when I had a chance to study her from a more objective distance, and it was like viewing a different person. Head on and close to, her face looked warm and pleasant, with hardly a wrinkle to underline her forty years, her darkish gray eyes as bold as beaten brass. But seen in profile, her head would have been the despair of a numismatic designer, it was so crumpled. And I could have sworn that her waist was as narrow as that of an underfed Swahili. Now, outlined against the window, her stomach noticeably bulged below the almost equal curve of her blousy bosom, as if she were playing charades and illustrating the letter B. How could she have put on so much weight in such a short time? Had she been eating bananas and cream? Not getting her exercise with Jewell? Forgotten to wear corsets? Or wearing a money belt or a rope ladder?

She even had a habit I'd never noticed before, of drawing in a lungful of cigarette smoke and allowing the smoke to trickle thoughtfully out of her mouth and straight up her nose, as if thriftily recycling it.

But then she turned, and the old Philippa reappeared, complete with smooth, physiognomical facade and dark eyes like invitations to an *exhibition*.

"You still haven't told me what you're going to do about it," she said expectantly.

"Do about it? I'll tell you what I'm going to do about it," I said indignantly. "I'm through with smuggling. Apart from anything else, I've lost the Vimy. It's totally destroyed."

"And what else?"

"What d'you mean, what else? Isn't that bad enough?"

She wandered back to the desk and stood there, riffling a sheaf of crackling documents with one hand. The nails, I noticed, were gnawed almost to the cuticles.

"It seems I'm completely at your mercy, Bartholomew," she said despairingly.

"You are?"

"I'd be in trouble if the government learned I was switching back liquor and depriving them of a fortune in revenue."

"You sure would."

"So what do you want, Bartholomew?"

I stared at her, feeling disoriented by her downright unnatural reaction to practically everything I'd said so far.

"Want?"

"You've got me just where you want me."

"I have?"

"So there's only one thing for it."

"There is?"

"We'll have to do a deal."

"We will?" I began. But then, growing tired of practicing to be a parrot, I said firmly, "Absolutely. Er . . . what sort of deal?"

"Would it satisfy you if I gave up the move to Montreal?"

"Eh?"

"If I canceled our move to Montreal?"

"You—you mean . . . abandon your brand-new distillery there? Why would you do that?"

"Oh, you're so subtle and cunning, Bartholomew. I see I've greatly underestimated you. You know perfectly well I've no option but to give in to your ruthless ultimatum."

Saliva dribbled from the corner of my mouth. I wiped it with a sluggish hand, producing a sound like false teeth being extracted from a cadaver. "You mean—abandon the distillery move? Keep your operation in Gallop?"

"After all the work we've done on the new plant, too," she said, slumping into her chair behind the desk, the despair on her face undoubtedly genuine. "But what else can I do but give in to your ruthless demands?"

"Uh . . ."

"While you," she went on tonelessly, "will no doubt insist on taking all the credit."

"How?"

"Don't play with me, Bartholomew. You know perfectly well

you intend to make the public announcement that you've 'persuaded' me to stay in Gallop."

I gaped at her. Then slowly a look of subtle cunning appeared on my face. I gave a cynically twisted smile. "Of course," I drawled, stretching out my legs and hooking a couple of thumbs into my armpits. "Naturally."

Then, emboldened by the unfamiliar experience of being in the ascendant where Mrs. Talbot was concerned, I added, "And there's a further condition that must be met, my dear Philippa."

"Yes?"

"There must be no more of this wholesale selling of duty-free liquor on the home market," I said pompously. "Depriving the country of a fortune in desperately needed revenue."

"You sound as if you're in Parliament already, Bartholomew."

"I'm practicing. Well?"

"All right," she said immediately. Then, with a rueful smile: "I'm putty in your hands, Bartholomew. You've won hands down, I'm afraid. I agree."

Twenty minutes later I parped into Karley's driveway and braked to a halt at the front door in a shower of gravel and dried brown leaves.

"Where the hell have you been?" Karley demanded as, feeling as if I were on cotton-wool roller skates, I drifted past him into the chintzy living room. "Where've you been for the last two days?" he shouted. He was actually shouting at me.

"Oh, flying here and there."

"God damn it, I know your campaign's in a shambles. But to vamoose for two days one week before polling day— In case you've forgotten, you were supposed to be at the unveiling of the war memorial this morning. I mean, Christ, man, if there was one occasion when you ought to have been present, that was it. How do you think it looked when you of all people failed to turn up?" Red in the face with fury, he tore off his jacket and hurled it into a chair. For a moment I thought he was about to challenge me to put up my jukes.

"I come bearing glad tidings," I said.

"Oh yes? You've been arrested for smuggling, so we can start the election again with a new candidate?"

"Nothing like that, old bean. No, I've persuaded Mrs. Talbot not to move out of Gallop."

Kitty entered the room with a welcoming smile and held out her arms. "Hello, darling," she said.

"Not now, not now," Karley said, waving her off. Then: "What did you say?"

"Talbots aren't moving out of Gallop," I said as Kitty stood for a moment, looking a bit miffed, I thought, then turned and walked out again. "And she's leaving the announcement to me."

Karley twitched as a door slammed in the distance. Then another door slammed. He sank slowly into an armchair.

"She's not pulling out after all?"

"No."

"And you persuaded her?"

"Absolutely."

It took him another two or three minutes to absorb the significance of it. He kept asking in one form or another, "And she's definitely agreed not to say a word until you officially announce it? You personally?"

"That's right."

"My God . . . My God . . . But that means—it may not be a disaster after all. If you can really show that it was you who pulled it off . . . But how? How did you get her to change her mind?"

"I think we can leave that aside for the time being," I said in a lofty sort of way, "and concentrate on the fact that we can get the full credit for dissuading her from moving."

"In which case," Karley said dazedly, "we might, just possibly —with good timing—provided you've got it right—and you don't make any more speeches—or get caught in flagrante delicto with a sheep—and Mrs. Talbot confirms it unreservedly—we might just possibly—quite conceivably—almost certainly—win this election."

PART III

Looking Horribly Conspicuous

When I approached the bar of the House before taking my seat, I was subjected to a thorough scrutiny from all sides, in which curiosity predominated. Who was this fellow Bandy who had gotten himself caught in the electoral starting gate and who had floundered far behind the rest of the field, only to surge forward at the last moment and win by a horse's rump? The little that could be learned of him was decidedly suspect. If, as some press gallery snoop had reported, he had cut such a figure in the Great War, ending up with a C.B.E. which was said to have been approved strictly on the understanding that it was to be awarded posthumously, and which had aroused chagrin in imperial circles when it was discovered that the recipient had failed to get himself killed in Russia after all—if he was such a warrior, why had he been relegated to martial obscurity, compared with, for instance, those national heroes, Billys Bishop and Barker? And if he had risen to field rank, why had the Defence people striven so desperately to prove that it had all been a dreadful mistake? And what was this rumor about some involvement or other in the filums? Good God, surely that couldn't be true?

Most disturbing of all, where were his credentials? Where was the evidence of that arduous struggle from the grass roots to the flourishing crabgrass of national politics? Damn it, the fellow didn't even look like a politician. Just look at him, with his great, blank mug and large, windburned hands like those of a professional strangler, stuck on the end of an unseemly stretch of wrist, as they emerged from a pinstripe sleeve and from, horror of horrors, a shirt with a soft collar? Was that a fitting suitor for the daughter of parliaments? What the goldurned Helsinki were the voters of William and Mary Counties thinking of?

Still, there was no doubt he had won the election, albeit by a fluke and with an unimpressive majority, so he had better be given the desk-thumping welcome traditionally accorded a candidate who had wrested a seat from another party. He would find out soon enough that a new member was of little consequence, with about as much real power and influence as a school janitor. The poor fool would receive his first few lessons in parliamentary deflation soon enough; that would etch a few lines on that shockingly unorthodox countenance of his, all right.

Actually the process of humbling yours truly had started from the moment I signed the register and became an official Member. When I asked for directions to my office: "What makes you think you're entitled to an office?" replied the clerk with a superior smile. So, though there were four hundred and eighty-eight rooms in the Centre Block, not including the Commons and Senate chambers, initially I had to make do with a battered locker in the basement and a loose hook for my new overcoat and my new fedora. It reminded me of when I was at the Air Ministry in London, and they had installed me in a converted gentlemen's convenience, with ling cabinets permanently at attention in the porcelain stalls.

Snooty officials were to be expected, of course, but my colleagues seemed just as eager to put me in my place. The one who had been delegated to introduce me to as many members of the three main political parties as would slow down for the encounter said, "From the moment you first bow to the Speaker, you will be entering an obscurity that will make your former insignificance seem like papal eminence." And another remarked, "You may be noticed only once in public, Bandy, and that's when you make your maiden."

"If I did *that* in public, I'm sure I would *definitely* be noticed."

"Your maiden speech. But after that you are never likely to be heard from again. Look at me. The last time I managed to catch the Speaker's eye was during the Chanak Affair."

Entering Parliament in the middle of a session was like going to a new school. Everybody had already acquired a friend and had no desire to cultivate a newcomer, especially one who had come out of nowhere and who quite plainly did not fit the mold. Perhaps if I had been as self-effacing as a possum I might have got by, but it was the curse of my life that I stood out like a lighthouse and sounded like a fog warning. And immodesty, either in appearance or manner, was as suspect in Parliament as in any grammar or reform school. If there was the slightest hint of the unconventional, or self-importance, or any sort of excess in his demeanor, the new boy was likely to be punctured as loudly and rudely as a pricked balloon, and end up as a short length of wizened skin. In my case, the process was perhaps more thorough than usual, because I had defied the hierarchy by running in the first place and, worse, had failed to live up to their confident expectations that I would lose handsomely. When I was introduced to the sergeant at arms, for instance, his manner was so remote as to suggest that I was the Ghost of Christmas Past.

I did, however, make a favorable impression, to some extent by proxy, on one official, and that was the Government Whip. At the time I didn't realize what a stroke of luck this was. Several days hiked by before I fully understood how powerful a figure he was in the hierarchy. At first I thought that, as he was the man responsible for things like office space, he was hardly more than a glorified caretaker, so I wasn't even particularly respectful when I finally tracked him down in the lobby.

He was buried in one of the vast leather armchairs in the long room adjoining the Commons chamber, making notes with a silver propelling pencil when I ambled up and wheezed into the chair alongside, and forced him to look up by staring at his nose.

"Yes, what is it?" he asked sharply; though his expression changed when he saw who it was. To my surprise, it actually changed for the better.

He was a highly distinctive-looking man in his early fifties, with hunched shoulders, light brown hair through which valuable veins of silver ran, and an authoritative beak borrowed from a snowy owl. He had an alert, confident air, as if he had spied several field mice and was trying to decide which one to pounce on.

"Oh, it's you, Bandy," he said, his tone actually softening.

"Yes. Somebody has finally informed me," I said sharply, "that you're the person to see about getting a noffice?"

"Yes," he said, looking me over. He even turned his head like an owl, in a slow panning movement. I half expected him to hoot at any moment.

Instead, he apologized for the fact that my name had not registered on him when I first arrived.

"Oh? Have we met before?" I queried.

"No, but my son knew you. He was in your Dolphin squadron in France. Eddie Holland?"

"Yes, of course," I said, flicking rapidly through the old memory. Holland, Holland. Yes, one of the new pilots. I remembered his nose. He had lasted about two months.

"Yes, I remember Eddie," I said. "We were very sorry to lose him, sir. Everyone liked him."

"Did they? We did too. He was always talking about you, Bandy, in his letters."

"Not too libelously, I hope."

"Pages and pages about you, as a matter of fact, and how decent you were to him and the other new men."

"Yes, I've always been very decent."

"I suppose hero worship was natural, in the circumstances, but I must confess we were getting a bit fed up with hearing about you," the Whip said, smiling wryly. "We wanted to know how things were with our son, not this very odd-sounding C.O. of his. But when he—went west, I believe the term was?—we had a very nice letter from you. His mother still has it."

"I'm sorry."

"You must dine with us sometime. I've told her about you in your present role, but she still wants to meet you."

"M'kew."

After quite a lengthy and rather sad chat about his son, he informed me that office space was now available on one of the upper floors on the west side of the Centre Block. So with indecent haste, pausing only to snatch my fedora from the loose peg in the basement, I hied me thither, expecting, after the way I had been treated so far, to find a windowless cupboard occupied by a peevish janitor who would object to moving his mops.

Instead, I opened the door on a room so clean, bright, and spacious that for a moment I thought I was back in a gentlemen's convenience. But it was a regular office, all right, with a bookcase, a water cooler, a view, and everything. There was even a fireplace, spotlessly black-leaded. And, by Jove, they had provided me with not just one desk but two. Obviously they were beginning to realize that one desk would not be sufficient for a resourceful, energetic, ambitious chap like me.

My new bumper sanctum had even been freshly painted in cream and green, and the view of the car park was just splendid. And for at least three minutes as I sat beaming around at the uncluttered space, I couldn't understand why nobody else had claimed it; until I began to feel more light-headed than ever, and realized that it was the smell of the paint. It was so powerful I could almost feel the leaden emanations decelerating my synapses. And the tall windows were not designed to be opened.

However, by keeping the door wide open and by dashing into the corridor every few minutes for emergency oxygen, I managed to avoid losing consciousness. In the process I met Cyril Hawkspat again—the Liberal M.P. whom I had met in the Prime Minister's outer office that time.

Actually I could hardly have missed him, as he was seated at a card table in the corridor right outside my room.

"They haven't given you a noffice yet, eh?" I said in a superior sort of way. "Tell you what, Hawkspat—you can use mine until the smell subsides."

It turned out to be his office as well. M.P.s shared offices in the Centre Block, and he had been occupying this one for several months until it was redecorated.

So I dragged out one of the desks and joined him out there, much to the annoyance of the staff, who regarded the corridors as their territory.

"Aren't you the fellow who forged that appointment for me with the P.M. earlier this year?" Cyril asked after peering at me in a doubtful sort of way for two days.

"M'm," I said, still feeling a bit guilty about it.

But apparently it had turned out satisfactorily. The P.M.'s secretary, convinced that he had recorded the appointment himself, had been full of apologies when his master failed to turn up.

"It put the fellow in my debt, you see," Cyril said as a very loud bell rang in the distance, and went on ringing and ringing. "It's always useful to have people's secretaries on your side."

Suddenly, fourteen well-dressed men of assorted sizes and ages came galloping along the corridor. Panting, cursing, and complaining, they squeezed past our desks and scrambled onward into the distance.

I gaped after them. "What on earth?" I asked.

"Tory M.P.s," Cyril explained, replacing his decanter of sherry in the wastepaper basket and covering it with bumf.

"Late for dinner, are they?"

"No, they've been hiding in somebody's office all afternoon, to fool us that they're not here for the debate. That was a division bell you just heard, announcing a vote. They're hoping to catch us with not enough of our fellows on hand, so they can outvote us and bring down the government."

"Oh. Uh . . . hadn't we better go down, then?"

"Yes, I suppose so," Cyril said, and led the way to the Commons chamber at a dignified trot.

Despite his donnish air, Hawkspat was a useful archive on the follies and foibles of his fellow parliamentarians, and after he had gotten used to me, he gave me a list of the stuffed shirts, bores, and heavy drinkers who should be avoided, and another list of those who should be cultivated. "Though of course," he said, "I can see you've already got the right idea, by insinuating yourself into the good graces of the Whip."

"Why? Is he useful?"

"Useful? It's almost more important to be on good terms with the Whip than with the House leader."

"Really?"

"Oh, come now, my dear fellow," Cyril said. "As if you didn't know."

Well, I did now. Apparently in earning the goodwill of the Government Whip I had secured a considerable advantage. He was not only the bloke responsible for most of the housekeeping, and the chief disciplinarian in the party, but had much influence with the Speaker. A word from the Whip could make all the difference between a Member's being invited to contribute to a debate or being allowed to languish unrecognized on the back benches until his teeth turned moldy. Actually his location in the House should have alerted me to his importance. He sat directly behind the Prime Minister.

"If he's as friendly to you as he looks," Cyril said enviously, reaching into the wastepaper basket for his sherry, "you'll have no difficulty in being called, lucky devil." He held up the cut-glass decanter and raised his thin eyebrows inquiringly, obviously hoping I would refuse. It was very expensive, imported sherry.

"So tell me, Cyril," I said, sipping the Amontillado, "who else is worth sucking up to?"

"Well, the P.M., naturally. You'll never get on without a nod from him, of course."

"He hasn't nodded yet. I haven't even been officially introduced to him."

"Haven't you? That's unusual," Cyril said, cheering up slightly as he recollected how thoroughly the P.M. disapproved of me. "Then there's the cabinet ministers, of course, and their secretaries." He winced as a fold of skin caught in his starched collar. "You'll know that you're one of us, Bandy," he said, jerking his chin up and down, "when you reach the point where you'd far rather talk to a cabinet member at a party than a beautiful and interesting woman."

"That's how far things have gone in Ottawa, is it?"

"Of course. You may think that you're here selflessly to serve the interests of the nation, my dear fellow, but what it's really about is the pursuit of power. If you're unable to attain it yourself, the next best thing is to rub up against those who have, so you may gain at least a modicum of prestige by osmosis. If you're looked upon benignly by a minister, or even his P.P.S., you won't go far wrong. I've been cultivating Jacques Gassien myself—the Minister of Customs and Inland Revenue, you know. Not so much because of his bailiwick, but because he's a crony of the P.M.'s." He lowered his voice, glancing guiltily at the filing cabinet as if a midget spy might be hiding in the top floor of its wooden apartments. "You'll hear lots of stories about him and his wife, by the way."

"M'o yes?"

"He has a problem. His wife is . . . well, you know?"

"What?"

"She's . . ." He twisted embarrassedly, and colored. "She appears to be excessively demanding."

"Money or sex?"

"Both—and he doesn't have much of either. But mostly the latter."

"She's demanding in bed?"

"In bed, out of bed, in trains, boats, hotel bathrooms, everywhere, I hear," Cyril said in a burst of excited candor. "Not to beat about the bush, old man, he's married to an insatiable woman."

"And so he's forced to beat about the bush himself, eh?" I said coolly. As a man of the world I felt it incumbent upon me to balance Hawkspat's pruriently flushed attitude with a reserved one of my own.

Cyril squinted guiltily up and down the corridor but there was nothing in sight except for an abandoned floor polisher. The floor polisher was having a quick drag on his cigarette. "He married the daughter of one of Quebec's richest and most influential Liberals not long ago," he began.

"Go on."

"Which was a mistake for a start, as she was used to all the luxuries—food, clothes, Europe—whereas he had little money of his own."

"Never mind that, what about the sex problem?" I asked indifferently as I leaned halfway across his desk; and bit by bit I learned that Gassien, who was in his early forties, had married the lady only three years previously. She had immediately proved to be as demanding in the boudoir as in the marketplace, draining his energies as assiduously as his pocketbook. On his seven-thousand-dollar salary, Gassien managed to pay a few of the bills she racked up at all the best stores and resorts, but it was soon obvious to his colleagues that he was not coping with the sexual invoices. Within weeks of his marriage he began to lose so much weight that his spare folds of skin could have provided him with a spare overcoat, and he seemed to float rather than perambulate from meeting to meeting, as if suspended from invisible hydrogen balloons.

Gassien had tried to solve the problem by buying a house in

Montreal and persuading his wife to move into it on the grounds that that city's social life was infinitely superior to Ottawa's. Secretly hoping that she would take a lover, or preferably several, he had since sold their Ottawa home and moved into an apartment, and now visited Madame Gassien only when he could get away from his pressing ministerial duties or ran out of other excuses.

Though even the occasional weekend visit appeared to be too much for him. His colleagues could always tell what day of the week it was by his appearance. On Mondays he could barely rise to his feet to answer questions. It was usually Wednesday evening before he was able to carry a dispatch box all by himself. As for Friday, that was when he started to look apprehensive again.

Actually I was disposed to sympathize with Gassien rather than to titter at his connubial predicament—that Russian woman had been inclined that way, too. Nevertheless I must admit I looked forward with a certain tingling interest to meeting him; which I did one morning, on one of Parliament's marble stairways.

I expected to see a wasted figure composed of a few sticks nailed together and covered with the pepper and salt suiting that he favored. I was quite disappointed to find him looking almost normal, just another middle-aged, rather self-important little man with bags under his eyes resembling theater curtains that had been raised to set the scene for the minor character of his nose. He wasn't even clinging for support to the marble rail of the staircase—and it was a Tuesday, too. Even his darkish gray hair looked fairly jaunty, with that well-known quiff of his sticking up like a pad of steel wool. I could only assume that he had not been home for the weekend.

At least his opening remarks were unconventional enough. "You are duh one 'oo crashed on Madame Talbot's property, aren't you?" he asked abruptly. "In Montréal?"

"Oh yes. Do you know her, sir?"

Apparently he didn't consider the question worth answering, for he replied with one of his own. "Dey say you are a troublemaker, Bandy," he said with a sideways smile that exposed his sallow teeth. "Is dat so?"

"Certainly not, sir. There's nobody in the world who's more reasonable, conventional, and accommodating than I. Ask anyone."

"I'm glad to 'ear it," he said in a dry voice that, for a politician, had remarkably little projection. "Don't forget, my friend, you may 'ave impressed duh country voters, but duh only t'ing dat will impress us 'ere is dutiful silence. If you want to let off steam, dere is nutting to stop you doing so in caucus. Dere you can say what you like, as long as duh Opposition and duh papers don't 'ear about it. Udderwise, if I were you, I would just sit quietly at duh back and listen and learn, my friend. You will find dat you don't do too badly, den."

"Thank you, sir," I piped, bobbing. "By the way, you're a friend of Mr. King's—can you tell me when I'm finally going to be presented to him? Surely it's customary to introduce a new Member to the party leader. I mean—"

He seemed to have a habit of not listening—unless his wife's importunate cries had deafened him as well. "And if I were you," he went on, moving a couple of steps higher up the staircase so that he could look down on me, "I would do somet'ing about dat face of yours, Bandy. It 'as already been remarked on unfavorably in duh rapeseed committee. I would not go around looking like you consider duh rest of us to be beneat' your contempt, eh?"

"Sir, I don't in the least consider—"

"I am aware, of course, dat you cannot change duh individual features—unless, perhaps, you considered plastic surgery. . . ." He paused to see if I was receptive to the idea, before continuing. "But surely a modest adjustment to duh overall expression of 'aughty disdain would be a good start, eh?" And he smiled complacently, patted me on the shoulder, and continued up the stairs, obviously believing that he had done me a good turn by offering such valuable advice free of charge.

And that was one of my friendlier encounters with the brass.

Actually I found myself getting on better with the Opposition than with my own side. Mr. Crerar, the leader of the Progressive Party, even put an arm round me and, after congratulating me on my win, said, "That'll show them big business interests they can't do down us farmers, eh?" He seemed to think that I was a farmer myself. Perhaps it was my sandblasted appearance, after all that flying in open cockpits.

A good boy was usually expected to be seen but not heard, but in my case I was obviously not expected to be seen either. When I took my place in the House, I was given a desk that was as distant from the Speaker's throne as it was possible to get, in the farthermost corner of the chamber, near the main entrance. Any farther away and I should have had to fire a Very light to attract attention.

None of which had the slightest effect on a beaming pride in my accomplishment, nor did it dampen my eagerness to deliver my maiden speech as soon as the opportunity arose. To that end I sat in the corner for day after day, from prayers to adjournment, trying to make sense of the procedure. But even by November I was still feeling like Little Jack Horner, though without the plum; for none of the debates I attended dealt even irrelevantly with a subject that I knew anything about. A further difficulty was that, even had I been familiar with the subject, I would not have known whether to be for or against it. I had not yet entirely grasped the difference between the philosophies of the three principal parties, except that the Liberals stood for medium-sized tariffs, the Conservatives for high tariffs, and the Progressives for no tariffs at all.

Gradually, however, I perceived that, while the Conservatives were angrily loyal to the Crown and favored a strong state that would somehow remain dedicated to private enterprise, the Liberals, less impressed by the British connection, were veering toward economic and social reform and the extension of public ownership, while simultaneously marching under the banner of economy in government, less government interference, and low taxation—a position, it seemed to me, like that of a general who had close relatives on both sides of the front line.

Still, on the whole, I felt more sympathetic toward the Liberal than the Tory philosophy—which was just as well, I suppose, as I happened to be a Liberal. The leader of the Opposition, Arthur Meighen, seemed much less concerned to hold the disparate, quarrelsome, and self-interested elements of the country together than our leader, Mackenzie King. The only trouble was that Mr. King seemed to be holding the country together by first render-

ing it inert. Though generally considered to be an effective politician, one who aimed unswervingly at those objectives that
would sustain him in power—which was what politics seemed to
be about—he was paralyzingly dull in both appearance and delivery. When I first heard him addressing the House I could
hardly believe that this was the nation's leader. He sounded
more like a schoolmaster who had heard his own dissertations so
often that even he could hardly be bothered to listen. "We have
an urgent need for a solid manufacturing base," he said during
one debate, "a diversified economy for a country that has for far
too long been a mere hewer of wood and drawer of water. It is
all very well being a treasure chest of raw materials for other nations to transform into cheap goods, but it is not the basis for a
sound economy. We must produce our own cheap goods. We
must mine our own tin, process our own iron ore into steel products, such as girders, reinforcing rods, and copper pipe; we must
melt our own nickel into, uh, suitable shapes, forge our own
wheat, weave our own cotton, if we have any, shape our own
pine forests into good solid hardwood furniture, knit our own
socks, and so forth." The Opposition leader, Arthur Meighen,
was infinitely more effective in debate: cold, cruel, and cutting,
but also logical and stylish. The first time I heard him, I was so
impressed that I started to bang my desk lid in Parliament's ju-
venile version of applause, until several colleagues twisted
around and glared; whereupon, remembering that Meighen was
on the other side, and that he had made several contemptuous
references to Mr. King, I hurriedly converted the demonstration
into a toneless cry of "Oh, oh." But this didn't seem to please my
colleagues much either. I had employed that interjection, which
I had come across in Hansard, several times before I learned that
it was not a protest at all, but was the official reporter's shorthand for "Laughter."

I was also all at sea over the rules. "I don't know," I said to
Cyril. "There seem to be so many of them. All this protocol and
precedents and procedures and rules of order, and things. I'm
sure I'll never get the hang of it."

"Don't worry, nobody else does either," Cyril said, gazing hazily through our office window (we were back in the office by
then), "except the chief clerk, and even he has to consult
Bourinot every few minutes."

"On the one hand the House of Commons seems to be full of rules," I muttered gloomily, "while, on the other, the caucus meetings don't seem to have any at all."

Actually I had been shocked when I attended my first Wednesday morning caucus—the party meeting in the big room overlooking the front gardens of Parliament Hill. Something very close to chaos had reigned, a free-for-all that would have awed a teacherless classroom filled with backward rugger players. I was only just beginning to understand that it was the only opportunity the Liberal Members had to express their feelings. For while the Tories and Progressives could criticize like mad in the House, subject only to the official list of proscribed phrases (No Member will be permitted to say of another that he could expect no candor from him, etc.), the government supporters were expected to keep their cavils and quibbles to themselves, to enable the legislation to sail through as smoothly as possible. The caucus meetings gave the ordinary Liberals their only opportunity to express their ire or dissatisfaction with their leaders' performances or conduct of affairs. I was quite amazed at the rowdiness of the meetings—though it seemed to me that even there there was an ultimate restraint, that my colleagues were reluctant to tangle too determinedly with the brass, in case it jeopardized their futures.

I felt that when I settled down and got the hang of it I could do a lot better than that.

"By the way," I said to Cyril Hawkspat one morning, apropos of absolutely nothing at all, "I'm glad I was able to do you a favor." I wiggled my empty sherry glass at him. "Perhaps you can do me one in return."

"What favor did you do me?" he asked.

"I put the P.M.'s secretary in your debt, remember?"

"Oh yes," Cyril said doubtfully.

"So now maybe you can help me, if it's true what you say, that you're a publisher in real life."

"Of course it's true. Who on earth would claim to be a publisher if he wasn't?"

"I wondered if you'd consider publishing a book of poems."

"Oh, God, you're a poet."

"Not me," I said, still holding out my glass for a refill. "A Miss

Rawsthorne." And I informed him that I was in the amazing position of owing favors to only three constituents: Miss Rawsthorne, who wished to earn just enough money from a real publisher—say ten dollars in royalties—to enable her to qualify as a professional poet; Jim Boyce, who wanted a civil service job; and Anne Mackie, who wanted a divorce.

As an act of Parliament was the only way Anne could obtain one, I was now in a position to oblige her. "Provided I can make head or tail of the divorce bill procedure," I said.

Giving in with a twitch of annoyance, Cyril poured me a fluid ounce of sherry. Then, obviously hoping to change the subject, said, "By the way, have you applied for your subject yet?"

"Subject?"

"To get on, every M.P. should have an area of expertise. Take me, for example. I was offered Mexico or a ten percent share of Reciprocity. Ultimately I persuaded them to let me have Penal Reform. I'd found out that there was only one other Member, a Tory, with an interest in it. So we tossed up to see where we stood on the issue, so now he's calling for more severe punishment for offenders, while I specialize in calling for leniency. And calling for it passionately, I might add," he added, frowning at the low level of sherry in his cut-glass decanter. "Prisoners are treated with an abominable lack of consideration, you know. I visited a prisoner once—it was one of my authors, actually—on Christmas Day, and do you know, hardly any allowance for that festive occasion had been made within those bleak prison walls— no plum pudding, no holly or mistletoe, not even a turkey."

"No jailbird, eh?"

"They had to make do with boiled ham and custard. And there were prisoners there who were serving as much as twenty years for crimes for which they should merely have received manly advice from a clergyman. For instance, murders that had merely been committed in the heat of the moment, and were never likely to be repeated, that is, crimes of passion. One of the prisoners, for example, had been convicted of killing his mother-in-law. Now I ask you, what's the sense in putting away somebody who had given in to a single moment's passion in his life— would he ever be likely to kill another mother-in-law? Of course not. Yet the jails are filled with people who merely lost their heads on account of one single moment of irritation in an otherwise blameless span of years.

"Then there's the question of bail, an appalling situation where accused persons are kept in prison sometimes for months before coming to trial, despite the fact that every one of the accused I talked to was innocent. Why, I heard of one man wrongly accused of rape, who was so driven to despair by his incarceration that he attempted to have his way with the prison chaplain. That would never have happened had he not been languishing in jail for such a protracted period. I intend to work for the day not only when bail will be automatically available for all but the most serious crimes, such as political assassination or misusing party funds, but for an enlightened parole system to counter the present situation where years in jail exacerbate the very hatred of society that led to the imprisonment in the first place, as in the case of my author's cell mate, who was convicted of robbery and had spent eighteen years in jail, though in fact there was hardly any loss of life involved in his crime. So that, when he was finally allowed out on parole, he was driven to killing three innocent cyclists when one of them ran over his foot. What good did those years in jail do him? I ask you. So I will work with every fiber of my being for the day when we will see such unfortunates properly protected from our present vicious system."

So far, Cyril Hawkspat was the only Member, apart from the Whip, who had treated me in a reasonably friendly fashion. So naturally when I next encountered him in the government lobby I loped forward to join him. He was chatting to a group of friends, and I was hoping that he would put in a good word for me with them.

But as I was approaching, the welcoming smile that had suddenly debauched his ascetic features just as suddenly went all crooked, then vanished completely. Snatching nervously at the tight little knot of his private school tie, he looked away quickly. A moment later he was shooting furtive glances through his eyebrows, to make sure that nobody had noticed the labial riot before he suppressed it.

Apparently it was all right to talk to me in private, but I could not be advantageously acknowledged in public.

As it was too late to veer onto a new course, I pretended that I hadn't seen him either but had been making purposefully toward another group of M.P.s just beyond him. The group, all wearing wing collars, were clustered near the open door to the Commons chamber, as if they had been about to enter it but had paused for a last-minute consultation on imperial preference, or to make sure their flies were done up. But as I reached the perimeter of the group I saw that they were all cabinet ministers, with the Prime Minister at the center. He was listening attentively to the Minister of Defence, nodding his head as gravely as if he had just been informed that the Russians had reclaimed British Columbia.

As there was nowhere else to turn, I found myself trapped on the immediate outskirts of the group, and immediately became the focus of attention of a dozen other lowly souls, who had been eying the elite as if they would have loved to join the circle as well.

Worse, my purposeful march down the long room had attracted the P.M.'s attention. He turned, a smile forming as if he were expecting some sort of emissary. But when he saw who it was he frowned, possibly in annoyance at himself for noticing me in the first place. Then he turned his back. And, observing this snub, his cronies also turned their backs and closed ranks around their leader, as if to spare him a sight too ghastly for words.

I could, of course, have continued onward into the chamber via another entrance, but it had looked as if I had been making a determined approach with a message from Garcia. As several embarrassed seconds hobbled past, I couldn't decide whether to accept the snub or ignore it. Which made things all the worse, for practically every other M.P. in the place began to watch me slyly, as if mentally speculating on how long it would take before I gave up and shuffled off, leaving behind a large quantity of lost face. In fact, I actually started to snap my fingers as if I had just remembered an appointment in Dawson City, before drawing the cloak of resolve about me.

So, as the conversation languished, I took a step forward and insinuated myself so neatly between the Minister of Defence and Jacques Gassien, the Customs Minister, that they had either to move aside or look as if we were forming up for a football scrum.

"Well, well, if it isn't Mr. King," I cried jovially. "Good to see you again, sir." And, to show how respectful I was prepared to be, and how determined to make a fresh start and let bygones be bygones, I even stood to attention and bowed to him, as if he were somebody really worthwhile.

It didn't do a bit of good. Mr. King merely treated me to a froglike stare. Nevertheless, I pressed on, ignoring various scandalized looks and the affronted face of the Defence Minister who had not appreciated being shouldered aside, however tactfully. "Bartholomew Bandy at your service, sir," I continued, unabated. "Now a fully accredited M.P., and more than ready to carry out my duties and responsibilities to the great party to which I have the honor to belong," I said, treating him to one of my sincerest smiles.

As my teeth bared themselves shamelessly, he recoiled as if he expected me to sink them into some exposed part of his pudgy frame—especially as I was now leaning forward confidentially. "And don't you worry, Mr. King," I went on reassuringly, "I'm sure your protégé, what'saname, Sharp—you know, the man you were backing in the Gallop by-election? Don't you worry, I'm sure he'll manage to get into Parliament somehow, sooner or later." And I bowed again. "Anyway, that's all I wanted to say, Right Honorable. Just wanted to start off my career on the right foot, as it were."

Mr. King was already well known for being distantly polite to even the most insignificant Member. He avoided the slightest confrontation by hurriedly agreeing with everything that was said, however extravagant or pedestrian the viewpoint expressed. Instead of manipulating human beings like any ordinary politician, he tended to achieve his ends, which he usually did with consummate skill, by pulling strings from a safe distance, or by averaging majority opinions.

Nor did he make an exception in this case, despite his being quite plainly annoyed at the interruption. In fact his head was swelling with rage so markedly, further increasing his resemblance to a bullfrog, that I half expected him to reply with a "rivet, rivet."

No, but honestly, he was positively bloated with fury, as if we had suddenly reached the climax of a series of quarrels extending over several months, despite the fact that this was only the second time we had met—not counting the encounter on Long Island, which I hoped he wasn't able to count.

Yet even now he looked not at me but at the Defence Minister, who looked like a former army general, possibly because he was—an angry-looking chap with giant hips and a yellowing mustache. Who, as if he had been audibly prompted, promptly turned on me and in a deadly quiet but nonetheless carrying voice said, "You think this is starting off on the right foot, do you? Interrupting an important conversation?"

As the conversation had definitely been languishing when I spoke up, I raised a pair of surprised eyebrows at him. But this engendered a heat that had formerly been lacking, for the minister immediately seethed, and launched into a diatribe of short, army-type sentences in which accusations of opportunism, troublemaking, impertinence, arrogance, and conceit scrambled for precedence.

As usual, when somebody was castigating me, I listened attentively, nodding appreciatively at some of the more telling épée strokes, remises, redoublements—or just plain bludgeonings—for it was one of my virtues that I could rarely take a verbal, or even adjectival, assault too seriously. It seemed to me that the passion behind the words was often inspired more by what the attacker thought was expected of him in the way of passion than by spontaneous emotion, man being, on the whole, a pretty synthetic creation.

Besides, I thought that, at heart, nobody could *really* be angry with such a decent, sensitive, civilized person as myself.

Of course I may have been wrong about that, for as I continued to nod at the minister appreciatively when I thought he was summarizing the position fairly, or looking dubious when I thought he was exaggerating just a teeny bit, he appeared to become angrier than ever.

"You come in here. Acting as if your miserable majority. Gained by a bloody fluke. Entitled you to behave. As if you owned the place and we were paying rent. Hear you're already pestering officials. For divorces for your women. Jobs for your disreputable friends. And your bloody poems. All the while sitting in there"—he gestured violently at the open doorway, through which the drone of an Opposition speaker could be heard through the gold curtains beyond the doorway—"in your corner. With a sneer on your face. Just. Just who do you think you are? Behaving like a. Like a."

"A pushy Jew?" Mr. King prompted; then nodding in agreement as his mouthpiece repeated the words.

The minister was so angry, in fact, that it was some time before his operator, the Prime Minister, could recover. But even as the P.M.'s swollen fury subsided in inverse ratio to his proxy's outrage, it was replaced by something even worse, an expression of quite alarming vindictiveness.

I began to suspect that Mackenzie King was not as ordinary a person as he looked. Now even his cabinet colleagues were looking away from the P.M.'s malevolent ventriloquism, as the Minister of Defence came to a heavy-breathing halt with the words, "We've looked up your record, Bandy, and it was just as we suspected. A troublemaker throughout the war. Not least being very nearly court-martialed for a treasonous speech you made while at the Air Ministry."

However, at this point the Prime Minister turned away, to indicate that he had said enough; and immediately the minister concluded his remarks with, "So I'm warning you, Bandy. Put one foot wrong. Just one foot. And it will be the worse for you."

With a nod, as if he had said this himself, Mr. King turned and disappeared through the open doorway into the chamber, followed by the others, leaving me standing there with a horribly wide space around me, hideously aware of the breathless silence through the lobby, and with everybody looking at me as if I had broken out in pustules.

"Yes, well," I said into the awful silence. "That's all I wanted to say." And, clearing my throat, I followed them into the House as if I were part of the group, but no longer wearing the equine features of a noble thoroughbred so much as the leonine ones of a leper.

My Apartment

When anybody asked me where I was staying while Parliament was in session, I was able to answer in an offhand way, "Why, the Château, of course." Naturally they assumed that I was referring to the Château Laurier Hotel, where all the best people stayed—except that the best people never came to Ottawa. Actually I was staying at Le Château McTavish, much farther along Rideau Street.

Despite its Scottish appellation it was owned by a French-speaking Syrian, who had built a squat apartment block with a Moorish archway entrance and Tudor windows. To save money he had built it with a flat roof, and annually spent twice the cost of a set of roof trusses in repairing the damage caused by the winter snow. (His flat-topped fez tended to sag under the weight of snow as well.) It was not the most luxurious of abodes, but it was the best I could afford in the way of a two-bedroom apartment. For now that I had reached the heights I was practically impoverished. An M.P.'s salary, I had discovered to my dismay, was a measly twenty-five hundred a year.

The reason I needed an extra bedroom was because George Garanine was living with me again. Though he had been out of the hospital for nearly a month, there had apparently been more damage to his hip than was at first thought, and he was still using a cane to get around—when he felt like getting around, that is. Often he had not even risen by the time I had left for work after lunch. Shopping for loaves and fishes and trimming his mustache seemed to be the high points of his day.

By now I was beginning to wonder if it was my destiny to be linked forever with George Garanine. I had tried really hard to get him and the voluptuous Philippa together again, in the hope that she would make an honest man of him by marrying him, or at least set him up in a pied-à-terre. But she wouldn't have him back. She had taken one look at his ravaged face and twisted hip, and had immediately matched his pallor and recoiled as if he were something under a heap of stained sacking.

Her refusal to employ war-damaged veterans at the distillery had contributed substantially to the hatred with which she was still regarded in Gallop; which was perhaps not entirely fair, for apparently she couldn't help this reaction to physical injury or impairment of any kind. She was quite plainly distressed on George's account, though it didn't stop her from turning him away from her doorstep. Even Jim Boyce, whose affection for women incorporated an almost limitless tolerance for their foibles, was a bit shocked at this callousness, though he excused her by surmising that she was attempting to create for herself a world free of the intimations of morality. "For her, people don't die, they sort of emigrate," he said when he heard about her reaction to the demise of Mr. Riddle, her principal farm produce supplier. When she was informed that Riddle had expired while loading a corncrib, she had made no comment until a week had gone by, and thereafter referred only to him in passing as having given up farming.

Anne Mackie had learned to accommodate these pathological evasions. When, unknown to Philippa, one of her pump-house workers drowned, and she asked where he was, Anne had hesitated, then replied that he had "gone away." As if Philippa were three years old. "Gone away up a kye."

Anyway, when she saw George's twisted figure and hospital pallor she made it plain that she wanted nothing more to do with him until he had regained his health. "I don't run a convalescent home," she informed me when I turned up on her doorstep with a hopeful expression and George's suitcase. And, getting her own back, perhaps, for the way I had blackmailed her into canceling the Montreal move, she added, "He can live with you. You did this to him, you take care of him."

Even George was taken aback by this despicable rejection, but to my fury he accepted it with even more despicable resignation. "Haven't you even any sexual ambition?" I'd shouted. "Damn it, you've said often enough she's terrific in bed—are you just going to take it lying down?" But he just murmured with a rueful twist of his natty mustache that he could hardly importune her if she refused even to see him again until his former vigor was restored.

"Besides," he said, "I cannot leave you now, after your heroic efforts to rescue me. You saved my life."

"I did not. How dare you say such a thing?"

"But of course you did."

"I did not. I just—I just gave you a lift, that's all. I was going your way anyway."

"Oh, Bartalamyeh."

"You're always accusing me of things like that," I stormed. "Well, I'm warning you, if you say another word I'm packing my bags and leaving this apartment."

George looked really concerned as he stood in front of my army valise, as if to prevent my leaving. "I can't let you go, Bartalamyeh," he said.

"Just try and stop me."

"But where will you go?" he asked, opening the valise and gazing into it unhappily. "You have no money left."

"I don't care," I said, stuffing in my shirts, combinations, and hair restorer. "Anywhere, to avoid the fate of living with you forever. Otherwise I can see us still together at the age of ninety, bickering, slavering, and jockeying for the best position by the fire."

"You will write, won't you?"

I snarled, and started to empty another drawer; but then stopped dead and said, "What is this, anyway? Who said I was leaving?"

"You did. You said you were packing your bags."

"I didn't say I would definitely. I said I would leave if you said another word."

"But I did say another word, Bartalamyeh."

"Damn it, I was using the conditional tense. Haven't you grasped the conditional tense yet, you slavering Slav?" I shouted, defiantly unpacking my bag—and was furiouser than ever when I caught him smirking to himself and realized that he had been ragging me.

It was rather a shock to discover that he was capable of humorous disrespect. I kept glancing at him uncertainly, and suddenly wondered if he had been twitting me ever since Moscow—purposely misinterpreting the perpetual indignation with which I regarded him.

However, I soon convinced myself that this could not possibly be the case. I was much too sober and dignified a person to warrant being made fun of. Even His Majesty the King had taken me seriously. So I contented myself by warning him that as soon as he was well again he would have to make his own way in the world, and tried to ignore him when he merely smiled lovingly, as if he thought I didn't really mean it.

"You see what I have to put up with?" I said to Anne one evening in early December. She was in town on distillery business and was staying overnight at the apartment. "No matter what I do or say, whether I curse him or slander him or get him shot or betray him, he continues to regard me as if I were an adoring relative. I swear I'm going to walk out on him one of these days. I've had just about enough of his filthy, saintly behavior."

"Betrayed him?" Anne asked alertly. "How do you mean?"

I reminded her that I had compromised George by fleeing from Russia, after going back on my word of honor.

"Oh, honor," she said, shrugging dismissively. "You don't want to bother about that."

"I forced him to flee from Russia, didn't I?"

"Considering the state Russia is in, you were surely doing him a favor."

"You don't understand—Russians are devastated when they have to leave the motherland."

"Yes, I can see how utterly devastated George is," she said, looking pointedly at the exile as he sat atop the living-room radiator in his Fair Isle pullover, idly swinging a carpet slipper from his bare toes.

Anne was still the only person I knew who refused to be converted into bran mush by George's lazy charm and his matinee-idol face; especially now that he was once again as idle as an Oblomov. Belayed from the slopes of the work ethic herself, she

felt little but indulgent contempt for George's passivity and had
let him know it on every possible occasion.

As she did now. "I think it's disgusting, the way you deny
your God-given talents," she said to him. "I mean, you're obviously smart enough. Look at how well you've learned English in
only a few months. This idleness of yours is such a waste of your
abilities, you half-wit."

Finding the tines of the radiator not nearly as comfortable as a
Russian stove, George eased down from the hot, rough metal,
wincing as his hip took the load, and limped over to the side-
board to pour himself another slug of Gold Bullion. He had been
drinking the stuff in ever increasing quantities since his arrival in
Canada, but it was not until recently that I realized how much
he was tucking away. No doubt it was to anesthetize the pain I
had caused by forcing him into exile, not to mention getting him
shot up in the wilds of New York or Vermont.

Returning to the radiator and leaning against it, he smiled simply at Anne. "I am not nearly as clever as Bartalamyeh," he said,
sipping. "*He* learned Russian in only a few weeks." About to
polish off the rest of the glassful, he stopped, as another thought
occurred to him. "In fact, my dear Anne, have you ever considered how extraordinary he is? He is truly an original, broadcast-
ing his personality like human radio station. And such quick
thinking behind that frozen face of his, such energy, such drive,
such . . ." And the dreamy veils of his eyes were swept aside as
he proceeded to extol my virtues, in a brief revival of the ecstatic
enthusiasm that had once been so characteristic of him.

But Anne interrupted him—rather to my annoyance, as I had
been getting quite interested. But of course he was just match-
making again. Though he did not seem to be overly fond of
Anne, he was convinced that I needed female company, and so
rarely missed an opportunity to fan our affair with puffery.

"We're not talking about Bart," she snapped, "we're talking
about you. Why don't you get out and do something with your
life? I can think of a dozen jobs you could do, as a mechanic, or
a Russian or French translator, or . . . or . . . With your looks
and personality, you could even be a salesman."

"But, my dear Anne," he said gently, "I have a rich life. Why
should I change it?"

"Rich? When all you do is sit there like a loofah?"

"That's a sort of sponge," I explained when George looked puzzled.

"But that's exactly it," he exclaimed, tugging down his Fair Isle pullover. It was too short for his muscular frame, and tended to ride up. "I soak up experience. When I do the shopping for Bartalamyeh, I meet all kinds wonderful people—grocers, policemen, peddlers—French, English, many nationalities." He turned to me, his eyes vivid with excitement. "Do you know, in the next street there is an Arab who has a slave? It's true, she is a Nubian girl, only twelve years old, but she is an erotic expert. She spits into his mouth when he is at pitch of sexual excitement."

I looked at him incredulously. Anne looked absolutely revolted.

"Some people I meet are quite amazed to hear themselves telling me things about their lives that they would never tell their husbands or wives, or mothers," he continued, more calmly. "Even in this so ordinary district there is such a richness of humanity. But if I worked for a living, what time would I have for exploring it? Be reasonable, Anne."

Anne exclaimed in disgust. Seeing that she was determined not to be reasonable, George subsided, gulped the rest of the whisky and, giving me a wink, said, "Anyway, as we say in Russia, *The man who feels under the hen for the egg is likely to get his hand covered in chicken shit.*"

Anne flushed, snatched up her overnight bag, and turned to the bedroom door. "You and your stupid proverbs," she muttered.

"But for once, apposite enough," I said, now feeling quite cheerful. For once, somebody else was mad at George. "It perfectly illustrates his attitude to life."

"But if you don't reach under the hen for its egg, how would you ever have egg for breakfast?" Anne snapped, rattling the doorknob in her agitation—unless she was hinting to me that it was time for bed.

"He doesn't need an egg," I put in. "He's never up in time for breakfast."

"Then I suppose he'd wait until the egg was hatched, and the chicken wandered over—so he could grab it and have it for dinner."

"Even then, it would have to pluck and stuff itself—"

"And then climb into his bloody oven and baste itself," Anne finished hotly.

There was a moment's silence as she glowered at George and looked more annoyed than ever when I caught George's eye, and we both burst out laughing.

But not more than ten minutes later, while Anne was performing her ablutions in the bathroom, George descended without warning into one of his black moods.

It was quite a recent phenomenon, this sudden withdrawal into a cavern of despondency, and it never seemed to have any particular cause. In Russia he had never once evidenced symptoms of that well-known Slavonic-type melancholy. In fact it was his perpetual optimism and cheerfulness in the face of adversity that had most infuriated me. But since his arrival in Canada he had been subject to increasingly dark fits of depression.

However, I assumed it was just the belated arrival of the oriental despair that uplifted so many of his countrymen; and as the clouds usually passed after a day or two, leaving him as hatefully sunny as ever, there seemed to be no particular cause for concern. So now I just turned away from his dulled eyes, sagging features, and hunched posture and told him to pull himself together. Then I went to bed.

Shortly after Anne and I had disentangled ourselves from the sheets, pillows, springs, etc., having raised the temperature of the chilly bedroom with our frictions and loudened it with our fricatives, I whispered suddenly, "You know, Anne, making love is supposed to be a celebration of life, not a duel to the death."

"H'm? How d'you mean?" she murmured lazily.

"You seem to be struggling for supremacy the moment you hit the hay."

"Do I?"

"Damn it, it's a cooperative endeavor, not a fight to the finish. I'm not at my best when you're trying to strangle me."

"I don't see why I shouldn't be on top now and then," she murmured complacently, "literally or figuratively."

"That's all very well, but too often you end up with your elbow in my throat, or your toenails in my hair. I'm losing quite enough hair as it is."

"M'm," she said, yawning. "I suppose it makes me feel more secure if I can dominate the proceedings. . . . Just because I'm a woman doesn't mean I have to lie there and take it, you know."

"I'm not asking you to lie there and take it—just don't take it and tie knots in it."

"Well, you're so slow, Bartholomew."

"Don't you understand, I'm just trying to draw it out—"

"I know."

"—as long as possible, for your sake," I hissed.

Though perhaps this was not strictly true. I suspected that on this occasion at least I had extended the bout into the early hours so as to leave no time for a rematch. I had to get up at seven-thirty. I had been dragooned onto a ways and means committee—more to make up the numbers than because I had anything to contribute—that was meeting at the unusually early hour, for parliamentarians, of nine o'clock.

"I suppose I'm just a plaything to you," I said sullenly.

"Ra-ther," she said, giving me a pinch.

She didn't even seem to care that I found her lovemaking overly muscular. A couple of minutes later she changed the subject through a yawn, saying, "What's up with Georgy Porgy tonight? Going all broody, all of a sudden."

"Another of his depressions."

"No wonder. Doing nothing would make anyone depressed."

"It's never bothered him before."

"I don't know what everybody sees in him, to be frank," she said. Even heavy with sleep, her voice sounded contemptuous. "He has no pep."

For a moment I was tempted to defend George against her waspish conditioning; but it might have led to a quarrel, and I was anxious to go bye-byes. So I just wished her good night, and turned over, and settled down to sleep.

An hour later I was still awake, listening jealously to Anne's deep breathing. Having nothing else to do, I mulled over what George had said one evening, when he remarked that the only person Anne really cared about was Philippa.

At the time I'd expected him to add the words, "Present company excepted." But now I wasn't so sure that I was an exception. When we first got together I suspected that Anne had a motive for cultivating me that had little to do with my inherent qualities, assuming I had any. It occurred to me now that she was still using me, that she only loved me for my divorce bill. Which was rather disappointing, as I now loved her. I could tell, because I thought about her even more often than about that humiliation in the government lobby, and that was saying something.

Actually just a week previously, when I treated her to an inexpensive but ghastly dinner at the Auberge McTavish (*morue salée avec pommes frites, haggis à la mode*), I'd asked her why she was so anxious to obtain a divorce, when Gordon was giving her no trouble whatsoever.

"You're not thinking of remarrying, are you?" I'd asked coyly over candlelight and ninety proof wine.

"Erch, no. Anyway, who on earth would I marry?"

"Say a certain stalwart high flier, spellbinder, and all-round good egg?" I suggested, smugly smoothing my de luxe tux.

"Well, of course, if I met somebody like that I might consider it," she said, pushing aside the ghastly coffee with a twist of her sublime lips.

I had been a bit affronted to learn that her intentions were strictly dishonorable. And the fact that she had not been the least upset an hour ago when I practically accused her of brutality suggested something even worse: indifference.

As she sighed and turned over convulsively in her sleep, she pressed a long leg against mine. I found the contact not the least comforting. This was partly because I was seeing her in a new light in the darkness, partly because her leg prickled—she must have shaved it since her last visit—but perhaps mostly because she was asleep and I wasn't. I was quite tempted to jostle her accidentally, to give my insomnia some company. It wouldn't have taken much to waken her, as she was a light sleeper. But I didn't dare, in case she demanded another bout of all-in wrestling.

Ah. I could feel myself drifting off at last. Must be at least 3:30 A.M. by now. . . . I would be yawning all through the meeting tomorrow . . . today . . .

Glorious sleep . . . relieving slumber . . . Any moment now would come that violent twitch as the last line to consciousness parted . . . Beautiful silence, too, not even the occasional rattle of traffic from the main street outside . . . And I was just a hairsbreadth from sleep, when the worst thing that can happen when you're just drifting off to sleep happened. A bogey in my nostrils started to sing.

Roused instantly to full consciousness again, I listened to it in mounting fury. It was vibrating in a liquid sort of fashion with every suspiration of forced breath.

I sniffed loudly to clear the passage but all this achieved was to disturb Anne. She uttered a deep sigh and turned violently onto her other side, barging me in the behind as she did so. As if aware that there were other people to consider besides itself, the bogey considerately fell silent—for about another fourteen breaths. Then, just as I was relaxing, it started to chirrup again.

With suppressed rage, I fumbled under the pillow for a handkerchief and, not caring now whether Anne awoke or not, blew great guns. After which, still leaning up on one elbow, I tested. Silence. I waited, sniffing in the darkness. Nothing.

Naturally, the moment I had stuffed the hanky back under the pillow and lain down, the gocky began to warble again—brief, angry, high-pitched whinings like a frustrated mosquito at a screen door. In a bursting fury I tried expelling air at high velocity in an attempt to either blast the gocky from my nose or to raise the sound above the audible range, like a dog whistle. But the moment I breathed normally again, the thin, wailing sound returned.

Next I tried to subdue the twittering by grinding a thumb into the side of my nose, but all this achieved was to alter the pitch. It was now producing a rough, cheeping sound like an asthmatic thrush.

Becoming more violently alert with every ululating note, I kept one nostril closed with a thumb and fired a burst through the other nostril into the handkerchief, then did the same with the other, with such force that my ears joined in and blocked themselves.

Surely it couldn't survive such treatment. No. My nose fell silent again. Until I sank back onto the pillow; whereupon the nasal trill started up again, then modulated to a twittering wail, as if the obstruction, too, was beginning to despair of ever getting any rest.

Beginning to suspect that it might not be a bogey at all but a hair—with an unusually stubborn root—I grabbed the handkerchief once more and did a thorough excavation job on the offending organ, reaming out each nostril like a demented plumber. But within the space of two minutes the twittering had changed to a squealing wail and then to a peeping whiffle. *Jesus Christ.* It was driving me *mad.* No longer bothering with the hanky, I rammed a stiffened digit deep into the cavity and ran it around the walls in so thorough a fashion that I thought my forefinger was going to emerge from an earhole and wiggle like a liberated tapeworm. Surely that would spring-clean the interior, or at least crush the hair, or mash the gocky, or whatever the obstruction was.

After which I lay back rigidly, waiting for one or either or both nostrils to start buzzing, chirping, twittering, or puling again. But I had finally done the trick. My wide-open, spotless beezer had finally settled down for what remained of the night.

Then I realized that all that frenetic activity had built up an air pressure at the other end.

I waited, with sinking heart, stomach, lights, liver, etc., lying there with wide-open eyes and tightly closed sphincter, hoping that the pressure would die down of its own accord, or at least reverse itself and pulse back all the way to my duodenum. But the pressure gradually increased, as if the bacilli had decided to go for broke.

It must have been that fresh-baked bread that George had brought back from the *boulangerie.* And I couldn't release the air because the nasal hubbub had already brought Anne close to the surface of consciousness. She was now almost as restless as I was. If I let go, the sound would almost certainly issue forth as a veritable trumpet voluntary. The bedclothes would probably billow as well, assuming they weren't blasted off entirely with a rending of sheets and a cloud of feathers. Anne would be absolutely disgusted—or worse, asphyxiated, for I knew how noxious dough-created fumes could be. I tried to think beautiful thoughts, hoping to tap the tranquil mind's ability to subdue its

own functions, but I had reckoned without the intestinal forti-
tude. It was either let go or confirm Robbie Burns's *Let wind
gae free where'er you be, for 'tis wind that was the death of me.*

There was only one thing for it. Carefully reaching over
Anne's sleeping form, I covered her face with the sheet; then,
inch by inch, hauled out the bedclothes on my side, cursing myself for having tucked them so firmly under the mattress; then
slowly maneuvered until my bare behind was exposed to the
chill air; and with bated breath, so to speak, concentrated intently on loosing the appropriate valve a quarter turn at a time,
releasing the pressure as slowly and discreetly as possible, in a
long, tightly controlled flow.

The faint hissing went on for so long that I began to get
worried, imagining my entire form slowly deflating like the
world's largest sausage balloon. I had a frightful picture of Anne
waking up in the morning to find nothing left of me but a puck-
ered end—assuming she was not found dead in bed from fresh
bread.

But the emission finally ended, concluding its efforts with a
stertorous burst and a faint bubbling.

Five minutes later, after I'd finished waving to somebody in
the darkness, and was just settling down again, another mis-
shapen bubble of air started to build up, and by the time I'd
dealt with it I was so thoroughly chilled in the exposed region
that I even considered warming it up against Anne's naked back;
except that the shock of contact with a pair of icy buttocks
would probably have shot her out of bed and embedded her in
the far wall. Nor did it help in the least when I remembered the
brand-new Russian proverb that had been going the rounds
while I was in Moscow, to wit, *If there were no birds, a commissar's fart would sound like a nightingale.*

By then it was nearly five in the morning; but at least I would
get a few minutes' sleep before the horse-drawn milk trucks
began to clatter past at their usual ungodly hour. And I was just
about to claim those few minutes when the next and final distraction occurred: the bedroom door slowly opened and a form,
discerned in the faint light from the apartment corridor beyond,
appeared and stood there glaring toward the double bed.

As it wasn't me and it wasn't Anne, I guessed right away that
it must be George. But what on earth did he want to talk about
at five in the morning? I was just about to lean up and ask him
when something stopped me. Possibly the tension in his posture.
As if he did not want us to wake up—ever.

Now he was advancing, approaching my side of the bed,
lurching at one point and putting out a hand as if to support
himself against an invisible wall. Good Lord, he was still in his
Fair Isle pullover. He must have been drinking all night, ever
since we left him at midnight. But why was he behaving so surreptitiously, so tensely? Walking in his sleep? Or perhaps he had
left something in the room, something he didn't want us to see,
and had come to fetch it.

But no—he was hovering over me, one hand resting on his
thigh, the other loose by his side, but with the fingers curled in a
curious way.

I wasn't sure if he knew that I was awake or not. Probably not.
I was in darkness—he was visible only because of the light from
the corridor. And he was probably too stewed to notice that I
wasn't breathing. I hadn't noticed it myself until now. And there
was something so strange about his posture that my heart started
thumping loud enough to create a crunching sound in my ears.

He must have stood there for at least two minutes, oscillating
back and forth like an erratic metronome, disseminating clouds
of whisky fumes. But just as I was getting ready to shoot up,
switch on the bedside lamp, and demand an explanation for this
shocking invasion of our privacy—he uttered a strange, unin-
terpretable sound, then turned away and stumbled off across the
threadbare carpet, and out through the open door, hitting the
jamb with his shoulder as he went, leaving me in such a cold
sweat that I had to get up half an hour later and have a good
scrub in the rusty, claw-footed bathtub next door. So I never did
get any sleep that night, and received some very disapproving
glances when I turned up for the meeting at nine o'clock with a
dissolute face, including a pair of eyeballs like cross sections
from a hot dog that had been boiled in alizarin dye.

The Day of My Speech

In my corner of the House, I found myself jammed against Hormidas Talleyrand, M.P. for St. Leon, Quebec. A sallow-faced lawyer of thirty-five with a long chin and weary eyes, he had had the corner to himself for months, and appeared to resent the intrusion. Nevertheless I attempted to curry favor and asked him if he was related to the great Talleyrand.

"But naturally. He is my father."

"The great statesman?"

"The chiropodist."

As most of the scenery—throne, clerks, press gallery, and so forth—was to his left, he had a good excuse to turn his back and give me zee cold shoulder. Two or three days passed before he swiveled back again.

"I do not like the English," he said.

"I know what you mean," I replied. "It's that awful weather they have over there. It makes them cross."

"I meant you English over here."

As an Opposition speaker droned away about the supplementary estimates, he turned his heavy-lidded eyes on me and continued, "A member of my family, who had a medical degree from Harvard, had been practicing in Quebec for years when you English insisted on his taking another exam, to ensure that he was competent. But, though they licensed several English at the same time, they refused to license him. But of course that is the kind of discrimination we in Quebec have come to expect of you types."

"That's terrible," I said. "We should look into this. When was this?"

"Seventeen eighty-nine."

As Talleyrand's bored eyes drifted over my third-best suit, the gray woolen one with the slipped shoulder pad, I made a mental note not to mention that my middle name was Wolfe—the red-haired, rat-faced general who had demolished Talleyrand's ancestors on the Plains of Abraham.

Meanwhile Talleyrand continued to regard me gravely, but with just a soupçon of humor in his tired eyes. "You are this new man who fought with questionable distinction in the war?" he asked at length, switching to English.

"Uh, yes, I guess that's me."

"I myself refused to join the army."

"Very sensible."

He looked at me suspiciously. "Why do you say that? Most of your kind are contemptuous of people like me." He gestured to the left. "Like him," he said, indicating Arnold Bulmer, M.P. for Hay County, Ontario, who was seated a few desks away. A bulky, fiercely mustached gent, Bulmer was busily tickling his face with a pen as he listened to an Opposition speaker. "He treated me most disrespectfully," Talleyrand continued, "when I told him that I had refused to be conscripted; though I believe he himself saw nothing of the war but only the walls of a recruiting office."

"The most loudly patriotic are invariably the ones who have not had to put their patriotism to the test," I said. "You never find jingoists among those who did."

"Besides, I am pro-German," Talleyrand said challengingly. "I believe that the Americans and the Germans could carve up the world between them, if only the former would learn to obey orders and the latter to disobey them."

He looked quite disappointed when I failed to rise even to this bait. "Personally I prefer the English," I said, "even though they will never be truly civilized until they have learned to remain cheerful and optimistic in the face of good fortune."

Before you could say De Rochefoucauld, we were engaged in a duel of maxims and aphorisms. "You were in Russia too, they say," Talleyrand said. "Their motto, I believe, is that there is only one fate worse than death, and that is life."

"At least that belief gives them something to live for," I riposted. "Unlike the French with their motto, *Toujours la logique.* The logic on which the French pride themselves has brought them their greatest achievements in peace and their greatest disasters in war."

"At least they have a system. The British have neither system nor logic, only a sense of duty, which is their substitute for thought."

"That's why they conquered you French," I said. "They felt it was their duty to do so, to save the world from logic."

"They defeated us only because we were sensible enough not to fight to the end," Talleyrand said, brightening still further. "A soldier who fights to the end does so only because his side has eliminated the alternatives, usually through incompetence."

I opened my mouth to reply, but he was too quick. "Anyway," he said, "duty is a fraud perpetrated by people who have been taken in by their own utterances. Duty is what others expect of you after they have failed to do theirs."

Bleeding profusely, I threw up my hands to show that I had the sense not to fight to the end. Talleyrand smiled. "Now we can get to the important matters," he said, pressing my arm. "Gossip. To understand Parliament you must first become acquainted with the weaknesses of the parliamentarians. Monsieur Bulmer over there, for instance—the recruiting officer? Do you see the way he is thoughtfully biting his pen, while pretending to take notes?"

"Uh-huh."

"And the way he is now dipping the pen into his large inkwell? Well, the pen is hollow, and the inkwell is filled with whisky. He is sucking it up through the hollow pen."

"Really?"

"I am the only one who knows that he is drinking steadily from an inkwell from early afternoon until late at night."

I watched openmouthed as Bulmer leaned forward to dip his pen in the inkwell, then thoughtfully tap his teeth with the other end, before applying his mouth to it, as if it were just a habit.

"Good heavens," I said; then changed to a whisper as the current speaker stopped talking for a moment and looked in our direction. "Have you ever thought," I tittered, "of filling his inkwell with real ink?"

"But that would stain his tongue a permanent black."

"Not if you used blue ink."

"Blue ink, black ink, what difference would it make?" Talleyrand said severely. "It would be disgraceful. I do not approve of that sort of thing. Practical jokes are an expression not of humor but of hostility."

"But you *are* hostile to him."

Talleyrand thought about it for a moment, then nodded slowly. "But you are right, Bandy," he said, looking surprised. "It's true, I am hostile. So, logically, that is what I should do."

He considered the idea for a moment before continuing. "Then there is Monsieur Chew on the Progressive benches opposite. The one with the bald head that is pointed?" And he proceeded to tell me all about Charlie Chew, who had been caught smuggling a camp bed into his office after his wife had locked him out once too often. M.P.s were not allowed to sleep in their offices—not even alone. In Charlie's case he had been caught smuggling in not just a camp bed but a camp follower.

Then there were Jacques Gassien and his wife; but I already knew about him. And Tudhope, the government's principal work horse, who introduced most of the legislation, and who had once been challenged to a duel by a Tory and, being given a choice of weapons, had selected Volume II of Arbuthnot's *History of the Royal Artillery* and thrown it at his opponent. And Francis Doherty, who, Talleyrand said, was particularly adept at emptying the chamber.

"Emptying it out the window, you mean?" I asked; then, when Talley looked at me blankly: "I suppose he needs a chamber when there's a long sitting."

"Pardon?"

"Never mind."

"I meant that people scramble to leave whenever he speaks," the other said, regarding me curiously, "because he has such a discordant voice."

Apparently the Speaker would go to almost any lengths to avoid calling Doherty, for the moment he spoke the entire chamber would start shifting about in agony, wincing and cringing as if somebody were drawing a razor blade over glass, or a piece of chalk with a stone in it over a blackboard.

And then there was Edmund Jasmine, who— "But I will introduce you to him," Talleyrand said, "and then you can tell me what you think."

Jasmine, a Manitoba representative, was a slender man of indeterminate age with a high white forehead and the smile of a simpleton. The smile battened itself to his mouth whenever you caught his eye, as if to disarm you as a potential critic.

After talking to him for a few minutes I felt quite bemused, though I hesitated to say why, until Talley insisted.

"Well, I hate to say it but he seems kind of, well, dense."

"Stupid. Exactly," he said.

"I had to tell him three times where Gallop was."

"His constituents," Talley said, "are mostly East Europeans— Galicians, Ruthenians, Dalmatians. When he first appeared, we all thought they'd elected an idiot because they didn't know any better. No doubt," he added, fixing me with his sly, hooded eyes, "they assumed that all the English were like that.

"Naturally we were affronted when this half-wit appeared among us two years ago; this agreeable but distinctly unintelligent railway clerk—for that was his job before he was elected —with his vacant eyes and his loony, obliging smile and strangely irrelevant commentary. It was as if the population of a large area of Manitoba had conspired to satirize us; as if they were saying to us, 'You all behave like idiots, so we might as well be represented by one.' How were we to know that he was merely drunk?"

"Drunk?"

"Constantly, even during the morning sessions."

"You mean he's drunk right now?"

"Of course. He is an alcoholic, drowning himself in bathtub vodka. We didn't realize it until last spring, when he disappeared for a month, then returned, his nerves electrified, his face haggard, his gait unsteady—for now that he was sober he walked quite unsteadily. And over the next two weeks we slowly realized that he was in fact a very clever man, quiet, modest, with a depth of political and historical knowledge. A Cambridge scholar no less, until forced for some reason to emigrate. It was probably the academics who were responsible for his condition—you know what those Cambridge scholars are like, with their vinous carousals."

"I gather the cure didn't take."

"Obviously. He is no use, of course, but now that we know, everybody protects him from a scandal, even the press gallery. It is not easy, especially after Jasmine delivered his one and only speech. Maiden speeches are invariably horrible, but his was so incoherent and repetitious that the official reporter had to seek special permission to omit it altogether from Hansard, an unprecedented event."

Talleyrand's heavy eyelids rose a fraction, exposing a gleam of malicious inquiry. "Which reminds me—when are you going to deliver *your* maiden speech, Bartolomieux?"

Actually I already had a date. In November the Minister of Customs, under pressure from commercial interests, had proposed that the laws relating to the smuggling of goods into the country be more strictly enforced. Which was just what I had been waiting for, a subject that I knew something about, and that would give me an opportunity to lick the government boots until they shone like slugs.

Accordingly I sent a note to the Speaker, informing him that I wished to be called during the debate, this being one of the few occasions when one could use that alternative to catching his rheumy eye.

It was the custom that a maiden speech should be noncontroversial, and I was determined to uphold it, not so much out of respect for parliamentary tradition as to ingratiate myself with the hierarchy and rectify the rotten impression I had made so far in their leather lobbies and marble corridors. So on the great day I took my place in the farthest recesses of the chamber and listened with nods and sycophantic cries of "Hear, hear," as the minister, Jacques Gassien, busily whitewashed his department while acknowledging in a vague way that smuggling had increased substantially during the last three years.

Through my researches I happened to know that he was being pressured by the newly formed Commercial Protective Association. They were demanding that he do something about the flood of contraband that was pouring across the border and severely affecting domestic commerce. Accordingly, Gassien was proposing to increase the penalty for smuggling by ten percent, while assuring the House that his department would continue its determined efforts to resist the nefarious trade to the utmost.

It was then the turn of the Conservative Opposition, and their spokesman promptly accused the minister of not going far enough in combating this menace. The spokesman was exceedingly scornful of a mere ten percent increase in fines. He felt that the main problem was the inefficiency of the minister's department in suppressing the illicit trade, which, if allowed to continue at the present rate, would bankrupt many Canadian companies.

Though the criticism sounded severe, nobody seemed particularly concerned, judging by the tone of the debate and the reaction to it. After both the Opposition spokesmen had addressed the House, the chamber quickly emptied, especially as Francis Doherty was trying to catch the Speaker's eye. Half a dozen speeches and two hours later, there were only about twenty people left, and that included the clerks, official reporters, doorkeepers, sergeant at arms, and the bewigged Speaker.

I didn't know whether to be happy about it or not. On the one hand I had worked up my speech with some care, and, with the help of the Commercial Protective Association, had devoted a fair amount of research to it. On the other hand, as the inevitable moment drew nigh, I found that I was not quite as calm as I had thought. My heart was beginning to work at time-and-a-half rates, and my mouth was as dry as iron rations. So perhaps the smaller the audience the better.

Finally the dreaded moment arrived. As a Progressive Member sat down, the Speaker paused, consulted a piece of paper, looked in the wrong direction, and said, "The Chair recognizes the Honorable Member for William and Mary."

Immediately I realized that I had failed, through nervousness, to listen attentively to the other speakers; which meant that my entire argument had probably already been anticipated, discussed, and dismissed as irrelevant or inconsequential.

But that was all right, because when I arose, as if being

hoisted against my will by a cunningly concealed arrangement of ropes and pulleys, I found I couldn't remember my speech anyway, not even my carefully rehearsed opening remarks.

My mind was as blank as a spare domino. To make matters worse, the moment I was called, the lobby curtains swished back, and a host of Members from both sides of the House trooped into the chamber—dutifully if somewhat reluctantly. I knew they didn't want to hear what I had to say—it was just that it was customary to give a maiden speaker a polite and reasonably well-attended hearing, however ghastly his performance.

I watched them with staring eyes as they scattered through the ranks of deserted benches, plumped themselves down, and looked at me expectantly. For several seconds all I could manage was to clear my throat; which I did somewhat startlingly, it seemed, for an elderly colleague farther along the back bench jumped, stretched his eyes wide, and called out, "Hear, hear," before realizing that nobody was actually speaking.

As he cupped a hand over his brow to hide his embarrassment, I managed to croak out the words, "Mr. Speaker," hoping that somehow this would galvanize me into action. It did. Unfortunately it galvanized me halfway into my speech. "And so," I heard myself say in a shaky voice; and then stopped in further confusion, realizing that I had started not only in the middle of the speech but in the middle of a sentence.

This was ridiculous. By now I was used to speechifying. Why should this occasion be any different? For God's sake, say something, anything.

Then I remembered my dramatic introduction, an arresting start that would transfix the entire multitude and cause a profound hush to settle over the rapt representatives. So: "Mr. Speaker," I repeated, "the subject of this debate is smuggling, and I feel reasonably competent to speak on the issue, for I was a smuggler myself." And I looked around expectantly.

There was no reaction whatsoever. I might just as well have said, "Unused as I am to public speaking," for all the stir it caused. In fact, a Member, who was just about to enter through the lobby curtain, changed his mind and backed out again, and a couple of Tories glanced up only briefly before going back to their game of cards.

So much for my dramatic opening.

"I am declaring my interest," I faltered, "so that I cannot later be too convincingly accused of hypocrisy. I was a smuggler. I transported liquor across the border on half a dozen occasions only last summer."

The usual Commons sounds—chitchat, yawns, scraping noises, rustling of papers, and cries of "Snap," diminished only slightly. Another three or four Members entered from the lobbies and bowed perfunctorily toward the Chair.

"I did not, however, smuggle any merchandise into this country. So none of our laws were broken, Mr. Speaker. Merely American laws."

Now that I had finally started, a certain degree of confidence returned, especially as nobody except the official reporter seemed to be listening, and he only because he was being paid to listen. "Through contacts made while I was engaged in the trade and through subsequent investigations," I went on, "I learned a bit more about the smuggling racket and its extent. From what we have heard so far in this debate, few Honorable Members seem to be aware of just how extensive the trade is. I have a few figures, and perhaps I might be allowed to refer to them," I said, taking out a tiny notepad, which was plainly in a funk, for it was trembling uncontrollably. And I proceeded to quote a few statistics, some of them quite accurate, which promptly deepened the general apathy. "In British Columbia, when the trade began in 1920," I continued, "the ships smuggling liquor down the coast and into the States returned empty. Until one day it occurred to the ships' masters that it would be a good idea to bring back U.S. merchandise rather than, uh, returning empty. And naturally, while they were on a clandestine mission, they might as well smuggle the goods past our customs, just as they had smuggled the liquor past the U.S. customs. It seemed only natural. The result: U.S. manufactures being sold on the Canadian market and undercutting the domestic producers."

A similar pattern had emerged in all the other provinces, with great damage being done to domestic industry by the return traffic across the rivers, lakes, and coastal waters, and along prairie back roads. For instance, as many as a hundred smuggling

trips a day were being made by power boats across the river between Windsor and Detroit: liquor one way, contraband the
other. Increasing amounts of American textiles, clothing, cars, tobacco, drugs, appliances, and masses of electrical equipment
were being sneaked in this fashion into the country. "A conservative estimate of the value of the imports on which no duty is
being paid," I said, "is a staggering fifty million dollars."

I paused to gaze around, suitably appalled; but nobody looked
the least staggered. Though there were now sixty or seventy
Members present on both sides of the House, not a single face
was turned in my direction.

I was not used to being ignored, nor was I yet accustomed to
the distracting perambulations of my colleagues; the way they
tended to saunter in and out of the chamber every few minutes,
or to meander, chitchatting, from bench to bench. Even when
they remained seated they seemed to pay scant attention to a
speaker, but gossiped over their shoulders, read newspapers, or
snoozed.

Forgetting that Talleyrand and I had talked loudly while
others were on their hind legs, I was quite distracted by this behavior; and again forgot what I was going to say. Hot flashes of
panic instantly set fire to my face, and smoke and flame coiled
from my receding hairline and incipient bald spot. It was only
with an effort that I repressed the impulse to flounder. Fortunately I had learned as far back as 1918 during that speech at
Fallow that it was fatal to give way to the temptation. Far better
to let the silence stretch to the utmost than to dissipate it with
gibbering sounds. That way the tension would seem deliberate.
As was happening now. Heads began to turn, an uneasy silence
settled over the House.

So that when I finally joined up the next sentence I had, for
the first time, the full attention of the now quite crowded
chamber.

"But, Mr. Speaker," I said, lowering my voice now that there
was no longer a dim hubbub to override, "the country is being
damaged not just through the loss of duty on fifty millions' worth
of such contraband. Though Honorable Members do not seem to
be aware of it, an increasing quantity of our own liquor is coming onto the home market without a penny in excise tax being

paid. Liquor that is being switched back, as they call it in the trade; leaving the distilleries under bond for export, but somehow pouring into the home market. There is no way of estimating how much of it is defeating the admittedly arrogant prohibition laws of the provinces, but it is obviously available in quantities ample even for the most dedicated tippler. It must be equally obvious," I went on rather more emphatically, "to—" What was Gassien's constituency again? "To the Honorable Member for Three Rivers and St. Maurice and to his Customs Department that the country is losing huge sums in this area of desperately needed revenue as well. Desperately needed, to give just one example, by the air force, which is so short of funds that it has not been able to train a single mechanic or pilot since last February, and at its main training base at Camp Borden has not been able to afford a gallon of fuel for the past nine weeks."

"Hear, hear," the Opposition defence critic called out. But though heartened by this support, I thought I had better get back to a spot of toadying, just in case I upset the front bench— even though the front bench was almost deserted. After all, it wasn't done to make a controversial maiden speech.

However, I couldn't just leave my argument suspended in the air. It wouldn't look at all good in Hansard if I petered out without rounding off my ingratiating arguments. "So the situation is plain enough, Mr. Speaker," I went on. "As a direct consequence of our rumrunning efforts into the United States, we are rumrunning into our own country, without benefit to the Treasury. And when, for example, an estimated two thousand automobiles a year are entering the country when they shouldn't, and thousands of cases of bonded liquor are not leaving the country when they should, one cannot help wondering what the customs people at the border points are being paid for."

At that, everybody glanced surreptitiously at Jacques Gassien; but it was all right. He obviously wasn't the least annoyed with me, though the chap behind him with whom he was conferring so tensely was glancing at me in an unpleasant way. But that was all right, he was only a parliamentary secretary.

"But even that is not the full extent of the damage we are doing to ourselves," I continued. "We all know that rumrunning into the States is perfectly legal. Our rumrunners might be re-

sented by American authorities, but here they are quite the
heroes, twentieth-century buccaneers, who do no real harm, eh?
and keep our distilleries operating, thus providing employment
in this country. And also, is it not exceedingly satisfying, this
business of plucking feathers from the bald eagle and defying
the infamous Volstead Act? Why, in succoring our parched kin
to the south, rumrunners are positive benefactors, are they not?

"Except, Mr. Speaker, the question inevitably arises—" That
phrase sounded so splendidly parliamentary that I couldn't resist
repeating it. "The question inevitably arises: how long can we
go on being unaffected by the crimes we are committing so complacently in another country? For one thing, we are actively encouraging gangsterism in the United States."

There was a murmur at that, and the reporters in the press
gallery were now actually scribbling. "Rubbish," somebody
snorted.

"'S not rubbish," I retorted tartly. "Do you think our export liquor is enriching ordinary American citizens? We are aiding and
abetting the corrupt elements, killers and gangsters; and I have
the names: people like Al Sapphire in the state of Washington,
Izzy Tormac in Minnesota, Jay Spinelli in Illinois, and Tony Batt
in New York."

At this there was such a hush that I started faltering again.
"Uh . . . uh . . . and when we add to that the damage we are
doing to our own commerce and to our Treasury by a criminally
feeble enforcement . . . Well, the Prime Minister was going on
the other day about building up domestic industry, but it's
hardly the way to do it, is it, when, according to the C.P.A., only
four percent of the smuggled goods that are endangering our industry are being intercepted, and hardly a single bottle of
switched-back liquor. From what I have learned so far, there appears to be something very suspicious about this lack of exercise
by the excise, this unaccustomed customs lassitude."

At that point I noticed that, though he was still not looking at
me, Mr. Gassien's neck was becoming sort of inflamed, so I
thought I had better wind up my speech before I said anything
damaging to my prospects. So I finished off by saying that my
entire speech could really be summarized in just one sentence, to
wit: "In breaking U.S. laws we must inevitably lose respect for

our own." Then I plumped down, making a face at this rather
lame and abrupt finish, but otherwise feeling satisfied enough
with my performance. And in fact there was a fair bit of desk-
thumping from the other side, and the next speaker to be recognized, a Liberal, began, "Mr. Speaker, it is customary in this
House to congratulate a maiden speaker, and I do so."

I must admit, though, that, suffused with relief as I was, I
thought I could detect a certain chilliness in this response. And
the page boys delivered remarkably few notes of appreciation
from my colleagues. Actually there weren't any at all. Which was
a bit disconcerting, as I had understood that a maiden speaker
could usually expect twenty to thirty handwritten notes of con-
gratulation from his colleagues. And though the next two
speakers were most enthusiastic about my speech, somehow this
didn't entirely reassure me, as they were both Tories.

So that later that day when I strolled into the great parliamentary library to see if there was anything to read, and caught
sight of the Prime Minister in one of the alcoves, I thought I had
better have a word with him and set the record straight.

Though he had not been present for the speech, I supposed he
had heard about it because the moment I had sat down Jacques
Gassien had stalked out and Cyril Hawkspat had whispered that
he had marched straight to the P.M.'s office.

So, after no more than a few seconds' hesitation, I padded
over, hoping to convince Mr. King that I had been trying to
make a fresh start, and that it was time to let bygones be bygones.

He was ensconced in one of the book-lined alcoves around the
perimeter of the circular library, his lumpy figure and shapeless
black suit diminished still further by the size of the oak table at
which he sat. The table was deep in typescript, minutes, letters,
and numerous books with their tongues out.

"Ah, Prime Minister," I cried into the muffled hush, and clicking a cold pipe against my teeth.

Perhaps I had spoken a trifle loudly, or possibly he mistook my
orthodontal tattoo for the release of a Lee-Enfield safety catch,
but he started so violently that the tome he was consulting
slipped off his lap and fell to the floor. Actually it didn't quite
fall all the way but landed edgeways on some obstruction or

other with a peculiar crunching sound. However this was just as well, for had the deckled volume landed flat on the bare floor it would have made a very loud slamming noise, and, as everyone knew, you were supposed to keep quiet in a library.

Thus reminded, I lowered my voice before leaning over and breathing all over him. "Just wanted a word, sir," I hissed. "Hope I'm not disturbing you."

When he looked up his face was working like an ant heap. "What?" he said; then: "Yes. No." And for some reason he slowly brought up his right foot and placed it in his lap, as gently as if it were a small baby in kinky leather. As a matter of fact he actually started to nurse it as if it were, his lips drawn back from his teeth as he regarded his boot with a fond smile.

His fully exposed teeth, I noticed with admiration, were amazingly clean and even for a man of his age. It was not until the following spring, when I ran him down with my floatplane, that I realized they were false.

Holding his boot affectionately in both hands and rocking back and forth, he darted a look at me which suggested that his mind was elsewhere and he was not yet entirely ready for my oratorical explications. So I thought I would start with a little social chitchat, to establish at least a modicum of rapport. I said, "Beautiful library this, isn't it?"

As his lips slowly retracted over the porcelain, he looked around wide-eyed, as if searching for help. But this time there was nobody to speak on his behalf.

"What? Yes, it is nice," he said in a voice that sounded as if it were being strained through a colander.

"The library, I believe, was the only part of Parliament to escape the great fire," I said, still leaning over confidentially. "The rest of the building, including the Commons chamber, was burned down in 1916."

"Yes, I know," King mumbled, closing his eyes and breathing shallowly as he continued to cuddle his boot. "We moved to the Royal Victoria Museum."

"Indeed, some people probably thought that a museum was where parliamentarians really belonged," I said, but uttering a light laugh to show that I was just joshing.

As he was becoming more hunched than ever, as if attempting

to tuck his head under his arm, I sat down at the table so that he
could see me clearly without having to rotate his round napper.
"But to return to the library: the floor here," I explained, "is laid
in an intricate pattern of oak, ash, cherry, and walnut. If you
raise your eyes to the galleries you will see around you the coats
of arms of the various provinces. The paneling is of white pine.
Of the hundreds of hand-carved rosettes, gorgons, and crests, no
two are exactly alike."

"Is that right? Look, Mr. Bandy, if you wouldn't mind—"

"The overall style of the library," I went on enthusiastically,
"which houses approximately 121,242 volumes, is in Italian
Gothic. In the center of the floor is the massive white marble
statue of Queen Victoria, sculpted by Marshall Wood in 1871."

"Yes, I knew that, too. I knew it was Queen Victoria," Mr.
King said, still looking around a bit wildly.

"The idea for the library originated in 1791," I continued,
warming to my theme, "when John Graves Simcoe—"

But at that moment Mr. King lurched to his feet and, with
staring eyes, limped, almost on hands and knees, up the nearest
flight of stairs. The stairs led to the circumambient gallery that
was segmented by other walls of books into still more alcoves.

Discerning that the time for social chitchat was now over and
it was time to get down to business, I followed him up the stairs,
saying, "However, that wasn't what I wanted to talk to you
about, Prime Minister. I just wanted to explain that in the
speech I made this afternoon, which you have no doubt heard
about, I was being as loyal and dutiful as anything, you see, in
the best sense of the word, or words. I was just following
through on what you said in your speech the other day, sir,
about your being prepared to stand foursquare—your very word,
sir, foursquare—behind the manufacturers"—as I trampled after
him, treading on his heels, I plucked at his coattails to gain a
rather more complete attention—"who're attempting to rectify
the nation's economic disequilibrium," I said, following him
round and round the upper gallery, "to provide the industrial
base on which the country as a whole depends for its future. All
I was doing was speaking up for the industrial base, who—which
—is being seriously hurt by the smuggling racket," I said, follow-

ing him down the stairs again, and back to his original alcove, and then following him around the big oak table.

"Yes, yes, I quite understand," he panted, but now looking quite frightened, for some reason, as he found himself trapped in a corner. Perhaps he had claustrophobia. In case he had, I moved away a couple of inches.

Meanwhile a group of librarians and a few Members and people had gathered at the long table that faced the main entrance and were conferring in an agitated sort of way, while darting anxious glances toward our alcove, almost as if they were contemplating a rescue mission. Which was quite unnecessary, as I didn't in the least need rescuing from my own leader, for heaven's sake. He was being most understanding, the way he kept nodding spastically and repeatedly agreeing with me, manifesting that well-known propensity of his for avoiding controversy by concurring with everything that was said.

"So you see, in venturing a minor criticism or two of the Customs Department, I was being particularly loyal to you," I said. "Indeed, to quote my own speech . . ." I said, looming over him as he stood there with wide-open eyes while he clawed at the wall of books behind him, as if seeking a hidden spring that would open a secret passage. Indeed, his nails were rasping quite unpleasantly over the colorful bindings.

But before I could quote from my own speech one of King's aides came up and started to clutch at my sleeve and whisper anxiously in my earhole, while a number of library readers, who had long since given up any pretense at doing their homework, were practically standing on the various seats, benches, and tables in an effort to see what was going on. What actually was going on at that particular moment was rather peculiar. Temporarily relieved of the pressure by the intervention of his aide, Mr. King, perhaps as a result of disorientation, or to justify his scrabbling activity, plucked another large book from the shelves behind him, and, opening it at page 1198, began to read with a concentration as intense as if it were a work on witchcraft and he had found a hex particularly effective against backbenchers; though in fact he had plucked out a work in some foreign language or other.

As he had been making notes for a speech on the Industrial

Disputes Act in which the motivating force would be love of God and an issue of rifles to the Mounties, it was hard to see why he needed to refer to a copy of *Der Grundriss der Indo-Arischen Philologie.*

A strange man, Mackenzie King, I thought as the worried aide tactfully nudged and butted me out of the alcove like a tugboat, and towed me into the mainstream in the corridor outside, and then hurriedly closed two or three sets of library doors, thus trapping our leader inside, with his eyes still rigidly fixed on the Gothic print as if there was something in the text he couldn't quite understand. A very strange man indeed.

Me and My Chauffeur

Toward the end of the year I was delighted to receive a last-minute invitation to a December 29 reception at the Governor General's joint on Sussex Drive, and even more pleased when the engraved invitation specified that I could bring a guest. So I invited Anne. And my happiness was complete when George volunteered to drive us there and back in the Pierce-Arrow.

I was really grateful to him for the offer, for it would never have done for me to be the only guest to park his own car at the back of the house and trudge ignominiously round the side of the house and back to the front door, especially as the snow was six feet deep and it was viciously cold that supernatural Saturday.

Unfortunately the effect was rather spoiled by the fact that our chauffeur looked much more impressive than we did. Anne had blown her budget on a new evening gown and so had to make do with her father's old cloak with the silver chain, while I was wearing a black China dog coat, which, though new, had cost only eighteen dollars at Eaton's, and looked it. But George was togged out like the Grand Duke Michael, in a magnificent astrakhan and a Russian fur hat that raised his height to six feet six inches. With his noble bearing and that face of his, he looked so spectacularly beautiful that the shivering servant at the front entrance rushed over to help him, instead of scurrying to the rear passenger door. Even the Mountie on duty came to attention as George drew himself to his full height and looked around in naive curiosity. The Mountie was just starting to salute when

the crumpled couple in the back seat emerged, blinking, into the
icy moonlight. He had to pretend that he had merely been adjusting his hat.

Aware that the attention of the other newly arrived guests was
still exclusively on George, I attempted to recoup the situation
by saying, "That will be all until midnight or so, my good man."
But George, who seemed at last to be skirting the latest swamp
of depression, smiled and saluted with such grave dignity that all
eyes returned to him as he got back into the car and drove off
round the side of the house through a deep gully of snow.

So, with kneecaps rapidly icing up and with plebeian knuckles
thrust into the maws of our low-class topgear, Anne and I scuttled, disregarded, under the portico of the main entrance. But
our entrance was spoiled there as well, for there was a jam of
guests at the front door, all shifting about from one foot to another and emitting clouds of steam.

"You'll stay with me all evening, won't you?" Anne whispered,
shivering and clutching her cloak closer to her throat. She had
needed a good deal of persuading before agreeing to come. Distillery employees were not usually to be found at Rideau Hall,
even in this most festive and tolerant of seasons.

"I may have to take a minute to go to the bathroom."

"I'll come with you."

After a couple of minutes of shuddering, we were allowed inside, and were soon being divested of our coats by an excessive
number of liveried servants and being steered in the direction of
the reception room.

Though the invitation had ordered us to arrive at eight o'clock
sharp and it was now only ten past, the room was already
packed with nobs: senior civil servants, diplomats, judges,
officers in magnificent dress uniforms, and even a politician or
two, together with their ladies. And the Governor General, Field
Marshal Lord Byng, in his cockaded outfit, standing at the entrance and shaking hands with not the slightest sign of pleasure
on his carved ivory countenance.

His aide, a young Guards lieutenant in dress blues, was checking names against a list. As he introduced us, Lord Byng took a
not unappreciative inventory of Anne, appropriately enough as

she looked quite stunning in her sweeping blue silk gown, which had cost her two months' salary.

The G.G.'s eyes even snuggled momentarily into her pearly cleavage before snapping in my direction.

"Bandy. We've met before."

"I didn't think you'd remember, sir."

"Not likely to forget you, Bandy. You told me how to run the Third Army."

"Ah," I said. "I was a cocky lad in those days, me lud."

"M'm." He studied me piercingly for a moment, before looking away along the waiting line of toffs. "Next," he snapped, as if holding a pay parade for a battalion of conshies.

"You never told me you'd met him before," Anne said, staring back defiantly at a couple of dowagers in chokers, who were regarding Anne's half-exposed tits with outraged envy.

"I met the G.G. in '17," I said. "My G.O.C. introduced him at G.H.Q. when I was O.C. an SF.1 squadron."

"Oh yes?" Anne said, her sublimely sculpted lips stretching satirically. "By the way, B.W., get me some COOH, would you, O.B.? O.B., that stands for old bean, you know."

A silver trayful of champagne glasses was being ported past by a servant. I deducted a couple and handed her one of them, watching interestedly as she glanced around to see how the glass should be held. Within seconds she had correctly adjusted her own grip.

Anne would have no trouble adapting to this mob, I thought, and hoped that I would have no trouble myself. There were at least two cabinet ministers present, including the Minister of Customs. He was just walking past, supported by his famous wife. He was looking me over, his face a study in conflicting emotions, including chagrin that I had managed to wangle an invitation to this do as well.

He slowed as if about to speak, but then thought better of it and merely nodded distantly, from a distance.

"I should have gotten my diamond cuff links out of hock," I whispered to Anne as I tugged down the sleeves of my tux. "Do you think he noticed the paper clips?"

She wasn't listening. She was staring after the minister's wife.

"Is that Mrs. Gassien?" she asked. "The bloodsucker—so to speak?"

"It must be. He wouldn't have the strength to bring anyone else," I replied as I, too, stared after the lady. She wasn't at all what I'd expected. She was so thin that her hipbones threatened to slice through her gown, and she had thin lips. Somehow I'd imagined her with great, wet, mushy, sensual lips, and eyes like powdered rhinoceros horns, or some such aphrodisiac. Even her bust was a bust.

"It just goes to show," I said wonderingly.

For nearly an hour nobody spoke to either of us, which gave us rather too many opportunities to sample the Veuve Clicquot, the only drink that was being served that evening, presumably in deference to prohibition. By nine o'clock when the Prime Minister arrived from Laurier House, Anne was quite flushed and bright-eyed, and holding onto me as much for support as for protection against the nobs.

I didn't realize that the chief had arrived until I became aware of a swirl of movement toward the entrance and caught a glimpse of his balding pate. He was talking to the Governor General, who was not looking too pleased, perhaps because the Prime Minister was not wearing evening dress. The Right Hon. had come in a dark business suit, complete with the inevitable chain across his waistcoated midriff, as if to restrain the bulge in that region.

"He's much smaller than I thought," Anne said. "Who's that on his arm?"

"Joan Patteson."

"I didn't know he was married."

"He isn't."

"He sure looks it," Anne murmured, her female eyes drawing and quartering Mrs. Patteson, who was a pleasant-looking woman of fifty-four, five years older than Mackenzie King. She was hanging onto the great man's arm and gazing rapturously at his glowering eyebrows.

"That's her husband, Godfroy, the bank manager, bringing up the rear."

"Golly. Doesn't he mind?"

"I doubt if there's anything to mind. She's probably just taking the place of Mr. King's mother. They say he was very close to his mum. Good Lord, here's Boyce. Who on earth let you in, Boyce?"

But even Jim Boyce, who looked quite personable in his evening jacket despite the soft anonymity of his features, could spare us only a few minutes. He was hot in pursuit of the Belgian ambassador's wife.

"God, isn't she gorgeous?" he said, gazing lustfully across the floor. "She's a baroness, you know. She was asking me why it was that when a Canadian woman meets a couple she always inspects the female first, whereas in Europe a woman looks first at the man; while Canadian males take no particular interest in either."

"Nobody could say that about you," Anne said recklessly. "You go after every frail with her bumps in the right place. Incidentally, how come you've never tried to seduce me? I ask not out of resentment but purely out of interest," she added loftily.

"Don't think I haven't been tempted, my love," Boyce said, kissing her hand and incubating it in his, "but you look too intelligent."

"That's a filthy thing to say to a girl."

"I've never had much success with overly intelligent women."

"Or ones with taste," Anne said, withdrawing her hand.

Boyce's brown cow eyes swiveled as he watched the ambassador's wife. She was in the far corner, talking animatedly to another lovely woman.

"Look at that," Boyce said disgustedly. "In any other town but Ottawa she'd be surrounded by admirers. Men would be fighting to get near her. Here . . . Well, look," he said, jerking his head toward the Minister of Justice, who was surrounded by men, all of them hanging onto his every word as if he were dishing out appointments right and left.

"That's why you pursue women so dedicatedly, is it?" I asked interestedly. "To set the rest of us a good example?"

"Somebody's got to care about women," he muttered.

"What are you waiting for, then?" Anne asked. "There's two pretty women in that corner."

"The one the baroness is talking to is an old flame," Boyce

mumbled embarrassedly. "One of the few I didn't part from on good terms."

Wrenching his eyes away, he looked at me. "By the way, Bart," he said, "thanks for the job."

"How's it going?" I asked. Somewhat to my surprise, I had managed to get him a post with the Finance Department.

"I'm on the investigation side."

"Checking into people's income tax?"

"No, it's a special team. Incidentally, we're starting to muscle in on your territory."

"How d'you mean?"

Boyce lowered his voice, glanced around, and shuffled closer. "My chief has been given the job of investigating the Customs Department," he murmured.

"Oh?"

"Apparently the P.M. has been compelled to order a confidential inquiry."

"Really? And I never knew he cared."

"I guess it was all the editorials. You've really shaken them up, you know, especially about the switching back. I don't think anybody realized how—"

He stopped as he became aware of the hush that had descended in the vicinity. For a moment Boyce looked quite alarmed, thinking that he had been overheard.

But then we both realized that the cause was the Prime Minister. He was only a few feet away—staring at us rigidly.

Apparently he had been progressing through the reception room with his entourage when he caught sight of us. But he had not merely stopped dead. He was actually recoiling. And his face had turned white with shock.

People were looking at him curiously, and Mrs. Patteson was murmuring to him; but he didn't seem to be listening. His brow, illuminated by the chandelier, was sequined with sweat. It was as if he had seen a really ghastly sight, which was hardly very complimentary to Anne, I thought—until I realized that it wasn't Anne he was looking at. He was gaping at Jim Boyce and me . . . as we stood there in something like the posture we had adopted on the sandbox by the railway line on Long Island: both of us leaning forward slightly, Boyce because he had been trying to keep the baroness in sight, and I because of a surfeit of champers.

Slowly the level of conversation rose again as the P.M., with an obvious effort, wrenched his gaze away and continued onward, his gait decidedly unsteady, as if the sight of us had quite intoxicated him. He was holding tightly onto Mrs. Patteson's arm, with a concerned-looking Mr. Patteson supporting him on the other side.

"Golly, what was all that about?" Anne whispered as a mystified hubbub arose.

Boyce and I just looked at each other.

"You don't think he . . . ?" Boyce faltered.

"I don't know. I think it may have suddenly come back to him."

"What?" Anne asked.

"Christ . . . I hope he doesn't find out who I am, or bang goes another government job."

"What, what?" Anne hissed, nipping my arm.

Half an hour later the Governor General approached. He was listening impassively to a lady in a white silk and lace gown which was gathered, rather suggestively, I thought, in the groin area around a small white button.

"Well, young lady," he said to Anne. "Enjoying yourself?"

"Lord, yes—my lord," she replied recklessly, and hunched her shoulders to give him a better view of her cleavage.

"Excellent," said His Excellency. Then, to me, abruptly and sternly: "Look here, Bandy, I didn't mean to embarrass you. About the Third Army. Actually I quite appreciated the encounter. Especially as you were flattering me, what?" He uttered a Sandhurst laugh, somewhere between a dog bark and a costermonger's exclamation. "The topic, as I remember, was the Battle of Cambrai."

"And I was going on about your original methods, sir." I turned to Anne. "Lord Byng attacked at Cambrai without a preliminary bombardment."

"You mean, you attacked personally, Lord Byng?" she asked mischievously, widening her eyes. "All by yourself?"

"No, no, my dear. My army did."

"The attack came as a complete surprise to the enemy," I continued, giving her a surreptitious kick. "Nobody had ever thought of doing that before. It was a truly original idea."

Doing his best to conceal his pleasure, Lord Byng ran a forefinger under his army-type mustache as if collecting dewdrops. "Except Dougie had no more men to follow it up, so we ended up back where we started," he humphed. He stared at me fixedly for a moment, then, excusing himself to Anne, gripped my arm and said, "Let's sit down. My bunions are giving me the devil." And the next thing I knew he was leading me to a sofa in the window bay, where the Minister of Justice was now seated, holding forth to a small audience.

Lord Byng stood there looking expressionlessly at the minister; who, after a moment of confusion, arose hastily and moved aside, weaving, bobbing, and apologizing profusely. The Governor General promptly took the vacated space and gestured for me to sit beside him; which I did, smirking at the minister.

"Handsome woman, that friend of yours," he said.

"Yes."

"Bit naive, perhaps. . . ." Then, the social amenities having been dispensed with: "You were in Russia at the end of the war," he said.

"Yes, I know."

"Ironside was talking about you at a dinner party not so long ago."

"Hope the subject didn't upset too many digestions," I replied, adopting his gruff manner of speech.

"Quite a bit of merriment, as I remember. And now," he added heavily, "you're a politician, eh?"

"Yes, sir."

"Yes, well, can't be helped, I suppose. Read your speech, by the way. Or actually just the bit about the services being short of money. Couldn't make head or tail of the rest of it, I'm afraid. Still, attracted quite a bit of attention, didn't it? Where was I? Oh yes—high time somebody spoke up for the services. Though you won't get anywhere, of course. Just the same in England. Treat the services like dirt until they're needed to shed a few spots of blood."

Five minutes later he was saying confidentially, "This fellow

Mackenzie King. Can't make head or tail of him. Fellow has no personality, no spirit, no conversation. In rotten shape, too," the G.G. added, sitting up straight and patting his own stomach. "Confidentially," he said, leaning close, "I've a feeling I'll have trouble with that fellow."

"Oh, I wouldn't worry about Mackenzie King, me lud," I said expansively—but not too expansively, in case some snitch overheard and reported me to the beak.

"Don't call me 'me lud,' I'm not a damn magistrate. Why not?"

"He'll never last," I said with a wink and a knowing nod.

Twenty minutes later he got up, muttering that he supposed that it was his duty to mingle a bit, adding, on an afterthought, "Perhaps you would care to see my collection, Bandy."

"I'd like that, sir," I said, wondering what it was a collection of.

"Get Bakewell-Tarte to show you. Tell him I said so."

"Which one's Bakewell-Tarte?" I began, but he was already out of range, using his sword to clear a way through the jeweled rabble, by tilting the scabbard forward.

I looked around for Anne, in case she was wallflowering up the paneling, but she had been absorbed into the younger crowd in another alcove.

As I started toward her, people actually made way for me, as if I, too, had a sword. After only a few paces across the parquet I was intercepted by a lady who asked if I'd take her for a joyride. I'd explained at length that, owing to the deep snow, there was very little aerial activity in winter, before I realized that she wasn't talking about flying. By which time Anne had been swept off to the ballroom, or wherever the music was coming from.

"You got to watch out if he has it in for you," somebody was saying. "They say he was doing it deliberately." While somebody else was complaining about the Post Office's recent decision to reduce its Saturday service to only one delivery.

Fortunately all the chatter had made it impossible for me to guzzle any more champagne, so even by eleven o'clock I was still sober, though I was exceedingly cheerful by the time the Minister of Justice came over.

After some inconsequential talk he said casually, "Known the Governor General long, have you, Bandy?"

"Oh, about four years," I said airily. "Good chap, Byng. He's going to show me his collection."

"Collection?"

I raised an eyebrow at him. "You know? His collection."

"Yes, of course," the minister said. "He showed it to me just the other day."

"What did you think of it?"

"Remarkable. Quite remarkable. Look here, Bandy, what exactly is this between you and the chief?"

"How do you mean?"

"Well, he's been going on and on about—something about Atlantic mists and green slime. Does that mean anything to you?"

"*Atlantic mists and green slime?*"

"I know. It's very strange. We were getting quite worried."

"Do you think I should go and straighten things out?" I asked.

"No," the minister said quickly. "He seems to be all right now."

"Perhaps I could reassure him—"

"No, I'm sure you couldn't—"

"Perhaps talk about something else, say about my Gander?"

"No, Bandy. You always seem to have a rather unfortunate effect on him, regardless of the subject," the minister said. A couple of minutes later I heard him say to somebody, "He wanted to discuss geese with the P.M. but I dissuaded him."

Shortly after, Jacques Gassien came over as well. He was carrying two glasses of champagne. The starched front of his shirt was bowed, as if he had stuffed several napkins behind it.

"One of dese was for my wife," he muttered, waving a glass and looking everywhere except at me. "But I can't find her anywhere."

Gazing over the top of his steel wool quiff, I espied his wife in the distance, near a picture entitled *The Burgher of Hamm*, by Jan van Egg, or somebody. "She's over there, Minister," I said helpfully. "Below that portrait of a Hamm burgher."

"So you might as well 'ave one of dese," Gassien said abruptly, holding out one of the glasses.

"Ta."

"You know duh Governor General quite well, I see."

"M'm."

"Look 'ere, Bandy," he began in an undertone; but then
stopped and straightened. So did his boiled shirt.

"Yes, sir?"

"Never mind. It's not duh time," he muttered, and turned
away.

Two glasses of champagne later I caught sight of the young
officer who had been standing next to Lord Byng when we first
entered. Thinking he might be Bakewell-Tarte, I hurried toward
him, but by the time I had snaked through the throng and
waded through a couple of chambers he had disappeared.

Rideau Hall seemed to be much larger than it had looked from
Sussex Drive. Soon I was completely lost in a maze of corridors.
I could no longer even hear the music from the ballroom.

After a while I got so confused that I even considered
reorienting myself by going outside into the garden and floundering along the side of the house and back to the front portico.
I must have been more stewed than I'd thought, to even contemplate such an idea. It was a bitterly cold night, and I could very
easily have been converted into a public statue.

Nevertheless, I walked into one unlit room with just such a
journey in mind, assuming it might give onto a side garden; and
in fact it did. It was a small sitting room with a french window
along the far wall. But fortunately the snow on the patio outside
was so deep that the french window wouldn't open.

"Oh, *figgen*," I said, stumbling over some furniture—a wine
table, appropriately enough—and then giggled a bit, as for once
this was not exactly an emergency—I knew I'd be able to get
back to civilization sooner or later.

At least it wasn't an emergency until I heard noises in the corridor outside. Then the rattle of the doorknob. And William
Lyon Mackenzie King's voice.

Instinctively I sidestepped behind the velvet curtains that
lined the entire window wall. Suspended from pelmet to blue
Persian carpet, they were drawn back from the french windows
but they were so wide that there was ample space for conceal-
ment.

The moment I had done so, I knew it was a mistake. If I had
remained where I was, it might have been a trifle embarrassing,
but I could easily have explained that I had gotten lost. Then all

I needed to do was ask for directions back to the upper-class up-roar.

They might have wondered why I was skulking in an unlit room when it was obvious that there was no party going on in there, but by then I should have been a hundred yards away with my dignity more or less intact. But now, if I was discovered, no eloquence would suffice to explain this guilty conceal-ment.

I suppose it was because the Prime Minister was in the party, and it might have reminded him once again of the Long Island incident, assuming he needed reminding. But, oh, God, hadn't I learned by now that these panicky reactions of mine invariably led to disaster? Why did I behave this way when normally I was quite equal to the task of brazening things out? But then, of course, my normal behavior was usually deliberate—perhaps a defence against being taken for granted, or exploited, demeaned, or imposed upon. But when it was a matter of a split-second de-cision, and the conditions were right—feelings of guilt, usually—too often I took precisely the kind of action I was taking now.

Even so, I very nearly stepped out again, to explain that I'd just been studying the mechanism by which the curtain was hung, or something like that. A second later it was too late, when they switched on the lights and entered the room.

"Oooh," said a shivery voice. "It's cold in here." It was Joan Patteson. Who added, a moment later, "Draw the curtains, will you, John?"

Well, that was it. Any moment now I would be exposed. This would really finish me off. I'd be lucky if I lasted past the Christ-mas recess. I'd be accused of being an apprentice Polonius, spy-ing behind the arras. In fact, as John approached the window, I was sincerely hoping to be run through with his sword like Po-lonius, or, if he didn't have one, he could borrow the Governor General's sword.

Any moment now. A fist appeared at the edge of the brown velvet curtain. I clamped my eyes shut and stood there rigidly, without breathing. There was a jangling of curtain rings. I even smelled John's breath. He had been eating cheese.

When I opened my eyes the curtains were drawn. And I was still undiscovered. Not only unexposed but provided with a rea-

sonable amount of space in which to maneuver, for there was a
good two feet of space behind the curtain. I even had my own il-
lumination, the moonlight through the french window.

Several minutes elapsed before I began to work out what was
going on in the room beyond. At first I thought there were only
three of them out there: King, Mrs. Patteson, and John, who had
an English voice and a stammer. Until Mrs. Patteson addressed a
Madam Bite—Bight? Beidt? Madam Bite was obviously some sort
of brothel keeper. Except, what on earth would Mr. King be
doing with a brothel keeper?

I was even more puzzled when they began to shift the furniture around. Good Lord, were they going to play musical chairs
or something?

The one called John seemed to be doing most of the work,
judging by the strain in his voice. "Guh, guh, Godfroy doesn't
guh, go for this sort of thing, eh?" he was asking.

"No," said Mrs. Patteson, adding quickly, "not that he's a
skeptic, or anything. It's just . . ."

"Ow, ow!" cried John. God, what were they doing now? Vio-
lating him?

No. Apparently he was straining after a syllable. "Ow, ow, ow
does the jolly old thing work, anyway?"

"Grunt." That, presumably, was Madam Bite.

"Rex, would you like to sit there? Mrs. Bite, will this table be
all right?" Grunt. "Oh, fine. Close the door, will you, Johnny
dear? We don't want people looking in and seeing . . ."

Mrs. Patteson had an annoying habit of not completing her
sentences. Seeing what, for God's sake? Illegal gambling? A bac-
chanal? Or were they going to play doctor?

"It works amazingly well." That was Mr. King's toneless voice.
"On the last occasion, I heard from dear Mother."

Mother? From his mother? Surely his mother had died in 1919.
What the hell was he talking about?

"Won't I spuh, spuh, spoil things, Joanie? I don't know anything about this luh, luh, lark."

"Lark?" said Madam loudly. "Young man, I do not indulge in
larks."

"Sorry, sorry."

"Communication from the beyond is not a lark."

Beyond? Beyond what?

"It's quite simple, Johnny," Mrs. Patteson said. "You just put your hands on the table like this and ask questions of the spirits." The what?

"Ow, ow!" John cried. I started, thinking that King had clubbed him or something. "Ow do they answer?"

"With knocks. They knock on the table."

"Responsive raps," said Mackenzie King.

"Sir?"

"Responsive raps," the P.M. repeated, in so dead a voice that I thought for a moment that the spirits had already arrived.

Gosh. I never knew that Mr. King was interested in spiritualism.

"One rap means yes, and two raps means no," Joan explained. "Otherwise they spell out their answers in the usual way. One knock then stands for *a*, two for *b*, three knocks for the letter *c*, and so on."

"Ow, ow, ow do the spirits know ow many knocks to muh, muh, make, Joanie?"

"Let's get on with it," Mr. King said impatiently.

"I must say it was very good of Baron Byng to let us have this room," Joan said, "after we heard that Mrs. Bite was willing to . . ." Once again she trailed off, before reviving with, "Well. I have a paper and pencil, when you're all ready."

A moment later: "Do you wish to get in touch with your mother again, Rex?"

"No. I want to find out if the spirits had anything to do with . . . the incident on Long Island."

"Oh, Rex. Do you think you should go into that, my dear? You know how upset you get when . . ."

This time, instead of petering out, she was interrupted by Madam Bite, who asked in her grumbly voice if they were ever going to start, because if they weren't she was anxious to get back to the buffet.

A couple of minutes later, scarcely able to believe it was really happening, I heard Mackenzie King ask in a low voice, "Is anybody there?"

God, if he only knew.

There was a long silence. Johnny started to say something but was hushed by Joan. And then came two knocking sounds.

"Guh, guh, guh, gosh," Johnny said faintly, echoing my sentiments exactly. For the sound had sent a shiver down my spine. It had not sounded the least like a physically produced sound.

"Somebody must have, kuh, kuh, kicked the table," John said uneasily.

"Shhh. Nobody did any such thing."

"But everybody's uhuh, uhuh, hands are on the table. It must—"

"Will you hush up? Somebody's trying to get through."

"Who is it?" Mr. King asked, sounding as matter-of-fact as if he were answering the butler.

A pause. Again came two slow and decidedly chill-making knocks.

"Two knocks? That means no, does it? I guh, guh, guess there's nobody there, then. Let's go," Johnny said with an uneasy chortle.

"John. You are at liberty to leave at any time," King said quietly; but he must have accompanied it with a nasty look, for an embarrassed silence ensued.

Next Mrs. Bite asked in a grave voice, "Who is there from the beyond? Is it somebody I know?" Another two knocks. "Is it somebody for Mr. Mackenzie King?" One knock. "It's for you, Mr. King."

"Thank you. Who's that? Is that you, Mother?"

As a series of raps followed, I wished I could see them all gathered around the table; but the only place that I could have peered through was where the heavy curtains came together opposite the french windows, and I didn't dare move, in case the material billowed.

"*M, k, e, n* . . ." Joan read out. "I suppose that's Mackenzie. It's your ancestor, Rex. William Lyon Mackenzie."

"The very person I wanted to speak to," I heard the Prime Minister say. He cleared his throat. "Mackenzie, here is my question—"

"Shouldn't you be more polite, Rex?" Joan said softly. "After all, he is your grandfather."

"Mr. Mackenzie, then. Here is my question. Does your world

know anything about what happened on a certain train on Long Island last Easter?"

Two raps. No. I breathed a sigh of relief. But the reaction was premature, for another rap followed, then several more, in rapid succession.

"B . . . a . . . n . . . Bandy! I knew it," the Prime Minister cried agitatedly. "I had a suspicion all along but I knew it as soon as I saw him tonight with that other man."

Obviously choking down his agitation, he went on, "What was Bandy doing on Long Island? Was he spying on me? He had some nefarious purpose, is that it?" he said, his voice rising.

"That's three questions," Mrs. Bite said. "You should just ask one, sir."

"You're right, Mrs. Bite. I must . . . Yes, well—my question is, What was Bandy doing there?"

A moment later the raps spelled out the word, *F-l-y h-a-m-e.*

"Fly hame?" Joan asked. "You mean he was flying home from there?"

"*T-o b-l-a-k-m-a-l-e T-a-l-b-t* . . . Your grandfather never could spell too well," Joan said. Then: "Does that mean anything to you, Rex?"

"Yes, it does," he answered grimly.

My God. How could William Lyon Mackenzie, the leader of the 1837 Upper Canada Rebellion, know about Mrs. Talbot?

I began to feel quite faint. I started shivering.

The knocking sounds started up again. Now they were speeding up, becoming agitated, sounding hollow and frighteningly close, like bursts of machine-gun fire just over a rise. Chills were running down my back, right to the very coccyx.

This was only partly caused by the draft from the french windows. I'd never experienced the supernatural before. I must admit I was really quite scared, especially when Johnny, sounding subdued, whispered, "I uwah, uwah, watched everybody's feet. Nobody was kicking the table at all."

"Be quiet, John. You're disturbing Mr. Mackenzie's train of thought."

"Mackenzie," the Prime Minister said with an uncharacteristic and, it seemed to me, distinctly unhealthy intensity in his voice, "have you a message for me about Bandy?"

"*C-o-n-s-*," Joan read out. "Constipation?"

"No, no, it was conspi. Conspi, conspi . . . Conspiracy? Conspiracy! That's it. Bandy's conspiring against me, is that it?"

One knock. "Yes."

I had the distinct feeling that the rest of his grandfather's message was going to be even more hostile or, worse, revealing. Whether or not there was anything to this spiritualism business, whether the sounds were being physically produced or otherwise —and I couldn't see Mr. King deliberately involving himself in fakery, he was much too sincere and religious a person, always quoting God, and claiming to be divinely guided in his political maneuverings—the fact was that somebody was passing messages, and they didn't appear to be at all friendly toward me.

I thought it was about time I took a hand in the affair before it got out of hand—or to make sure that it did. So, as the rappings started again, I looked around the confined space between the curtain and the wall. There was a radiator a few feet to my left. But it was made of iron, and the sounds from beyond the curtain —or the grave—had not been metallic.

Now it was Mrs. Bite who was translating. "*H-e n-e-m-e-s-i.*"

"Nemesis?" King asked in a dead voice.

"Somebody who wreaks ow! ow! havoc," Johnny explained, "and who is usually victorious."

There was a brief silence. I had the impression that the others were glaring at Johnny, despite his helpful definition.

The wall behind me was of plaster, so that was no use. That left only the floor under the Persian carpet.

My knees buckled. I settled into a crouch, wiggling out a fifty-cent piece and pulling back the edge of the carpet; and hurriedly, while the beyond was still thinking things over, I started to tap on the parquet.

Thirteen raps with the coin. Then one. Eleven. Five. Eight . . . My wrist began to ache.

"*M-a-k-e h-i-m c-a-b-i-n-e-t m-i-n,*" Mrs. Bite read out.

"Make him a cabinet minister?" King asked. "*Make him a cabinet minister?* You must be mad!"

"Rex! You're talking to your grandfather!"

"I don't care! It's the most ridiculous thing I've ever heard. Why? Why should I do such a thing? Tell me that, Mackenzie?"

"K-e-e-p u s-a-f-e a-n-d r-o-u-n-d," Mrs. Bite spelled out.

Damn. I must have gotten the taps wrong for the letter s. Luckily they got it anyway.

"To keep me safe and sound?" King asked. "But what exactly is Bandy threatening me with, Mackenzie? Is he working for my enemies?"

Just as he was saying this a shadow fell across the velvet curtain. Turning, I saw a gigantic wolf standing outside the french window.

No, it wasn't a wolf. It was worse.

I arose slowly and weightlessly, as if suddenly drained of all bodily fluids, organs, bone, and tissue. Mouth gaping, eyes gibbous, I stood there, busily aging.

My flesh crept, then folded, wrinkled, and sloughed. My hair stood on end, then turned white, and fell out. I ceased to breathe forever. Silent, dying shrieks echoed round my empty cavities, as I realized instantly that the séance had summoned up a creature from the spirit world, a succubus, incubus, or some specter's diabolical pet. A huge, slavering beast standing on its hind legs, looking in at me with red eyes, out there on the snow-sculptured patio, with matted fur and jaws agape almost as wide as mine; a phantom of the most ghastly and malevolent aspect.

Now it was lurching closer still, the moonlight illuminating a ring of ghastly fangs like a satanic Stonehenge. And it had staring, slime-streaming eyes.

Next, as if to demonstrate its intention to dematerialize, then integrate itself again inside the window and take me into an everlasting embrace of stench and agony, it pressed against the glass. Whereupon I noticed that it was not an astral body, familiar, booger, or cacodemon at all. It was George.

He was out there in the snow in his splendid coat, except that he had buttoned it up out of sequence so that one side hung lower than the other. And his Russian fur hat was askew, as askew as his face. It was quite lopsided, his face, even before he had cupped his hand on the window to see inside more efficiently, and suctioned his face to the glass.

He was drunk again.

He saw me. And rapped on the glass.

"*H*," read out Mrs. Bite. Then, as George rapped again, "*o-g*— or was it *k?*"

With my heart still banging away like a rotary with several defective cylinders, I gestured feebly for George to go away. He waved back, and tapped again.

"Did you get that?" Mrs. Patteson asked. "Was it an *m?*"

"It may have been. *H-o-k-m.* Hokum?"

"There you are, you see," King cried. "It was all hokum about Bandy! Make him a cabinet minister indeed. It was probably an unfriendly spirit who was talking—breaking in on Grandfather!"

In a mounting fury I gestured again at George, viciously trying to shoo him away. I started to kneel again to recoup the situation by tapping a more useful message on the parquet, but the bloody pest, George, just smiled stupidly, lurched, then took hold of the window handle. I only just managed to seize the inside handle in time before he started to rattle it.

Together, on both sides of the glass, we wrestled with the handle, our noses only millimeters apart through the glass—his mulberry with cold, mine rose madder with berserk fury.

"I see no point in going on with this," I heard Mackenzie King say, and a moment later there was a scraping of chairs and a mutter of discontented conversation. And now that it was too late, George finally got the message and, drawing himself up, gave me what was intended to be a dignified salute, which was spoiled slightly when he stuck his finger in his eye; and, with a wince of pain, turned and sprawled into the nearest snowbank.

After only a few seconds, though, he managed to struggle to his feet. Then, as he dusted himself down with floppy hands, he looked back at me with a lopsided smile and mouthed three words. It was quite easy to read them through the glass.

"Happy New Year," he said.

Wellington Street, Deep in Slush

Two months later, while I was trudging through the gray slush at the foot of Parliament Hill, after delivering a nasty speech at a club luncheon—it was on the usual subject, the Customs Department—I saw Mrs. Talbot driving alone in her big black limousine. And she was in her East Indian outfit again.

I watched as she stopped a hundred yards farther up Wellington Street and parked outside the main branch of the Molson's Bank, near the corner of Kent Street.

Of course it was none of my business what she was up to in her heavy disguise of silk, Bourneville chocolate, and fox fur coat; so as she billowed into the bank I darted across the street, narrowly avoiding a horse-drawn sleigh filled with junk and bad language, and nipped in after her.

She was filling out a pink slip when I entered, cuddling a canvas satchel under her furry armpit, the hem of her bright sari sodden with slush. I pretended to be busy at another counter until she was ready to join the lineup at a teller's window; then I strolled over and picked up the next pink slip in the pile, before joining her in the queue. I hid behind a bulky gent in a raccoon coat and fur cap.

It was obviously not the first time she had made a deposit in that guise, for the teller addressed her instantly as Mrs. Enerjee. He then went on to talk about the mild spell, and how it was sure to be followed by another fifty feet of snow before the disastrous spring arrived. As he talked he withdrew an extraordinary amount of cash from the satchel and counted it.

I was still trying to work out why she should be depositing money under an assumed name when she turned away. By the time I peered out of the main entrance of the bank she was already getting into her car.

I stood there uncertainly, turning up the collar of my China dog coat and wishing I'd brought the Pierce-Arrow, instead of taking advantage of the mild March air to walk to work, when a taxi drew up to discharge a fare. On an impulse I raced over and climbed into the back.

"Follow that car," I cried, pointing through the windscreen. Philippa's car was just driving past, its red taillights burning fuzzily through a vortex of exhaust.

The cabdriver, a large man with dewlaps and badly bitten nails, looked at me. "Eh?" he said.

"Follow that car," I cried, peering ahead anxiously.

"What car?"

"That one there! The big black one!"

"That car? That one there?" the driver asked, pointing with his ragged thumb.

"Yes!"

"It's a Packard," the driver said. "One of them big Packards."

"I know—hurry up, follow it! Look, it's driving off!"

"Yes, but what d'you mean, follow it?" the cabdriver asked.

I gritted my teeth. "Damn it, surely that's plain enough. 'Follow that car!' Go on, get going!" I stared frenziedly through the windscreen. The Packard was speeding away.

"I don't know. I ain't never heard that expression before."

"Well, you've heard it now—so follow it!"

"Nobody's never told me to follow a car before, though."

"Well, I'm telling you now!" I shrieked, bouncing up and down on the back seat.

The driver put the car into gear, drove ten feet, then stopped. "Well, I don't know," he said. "Nobody's never told me to follow a car before."

"Damn it, you'll be too late in a minute!"

"You got to understand my position," the driver said. "It's so unusual."

"Will you get going!" I shouted.

"But maybe it's illegal," the driver said, starting to nibble at his thumbnail, "following somebody."

"Oh, *merde*," I said, and slumped back on the seat. It was too late. The quarry was out of sight.

"You've got to see my side of it," the driver said.

I snarled incoherently.

"If I started following every car somebody told me to follow, I mean, where would I be?"

"I didn't ask you to follow every car, I just wanted you to follow that particular one," I said viciously.

"I know, but that's the thin edge of the wedge, you see," the cabdriver said. "I start following that car, and who knows where it would end up?"

"That's why I wanted you to follow it," I said exhaustedly. "To find out where it ended up."

"I know, but you got to see my side of it, you see," he said, carefully removing a shred of thumbnail from his tongue. "I could take you to the railway station, though."

"I don't want to go to the railway station," I whimpered, suddenly unutterably weary of the whole business. "Why would I want to go to the railway station, for crysake?"

"Well, that's a silly question if ever I heard one," the cabdriver said. "I mean, why does anyone want to go to the railway station?"

He looked back at me in an aggrieved fashion, but with just enough hurt inquiry in his face to compel me to answer.

"To catch a train," I said.

"Of course," he said, nodding until his dewlaps swung to and fro. "What time is it?"

I looked at my watch. "About two-thirty," I said hopelessly, and started to get out.

The driver pressed the accelerator and the taxi started off. "Two-thirty," he said. "We'll have to hurry."

I was just in time to close the door before it got wrenched off by a lamppost. "For God's sake," I said shrilly. "What the— Where are you going?"

"Why, to the railway station."

"But I don't want to go to the railway station," I shouted. "Why should I want to go to the railway station?"

The driver stopped at Constitution Square, looking unhappy again. "To catch the two-thirty, of course," he said, and edged the car into the stream of traffic. His tone was now filled with fatherly contempt, leavened with just enough long-suffering indulgence to take the sting out of the retort.

It silenced me completely. I just didn't know what to say.

We proceeded around Constitution Square in silence, the driver glancing anxiously at his watch every now and then.

Finally I snapped my fingers. "Oh, darn," I said, giving a strained laugh. "I've just remembered. I've forgotten my bag."

"Eh?"

"My bag," I said, giving another little laugh and shaking my head at my own forgetfulness. "It's at home."

"No, but I mean, we'll never make the two-thirty if we go back for your bag, now will we?" the cabdriver said, with somewhat less indulgence in his voice than heretofore.

"Well, I . . . I'm sure there'll be another train," I said. "Yes, I'm sure of it.

"At ten past three," I added, inspired.

The cabdriver continued on past the station, looking really irritable. "I mean, we might just as well forget the two-thirty," he said. "What's the address?"

"It's the, uh, Château McTavish farther along Rideau," I said, numbed.

"I mean, we might as well forget it entirely if we have to go all the way home for your bag."

I was utterly silent.

We arrived at the apartment building. The driver took me right to the Moorish entrance. I got out, then looked back at the meter. "How much do I owe you?" I asked.

"It's all right, I'll wait for you," the driver said.

"But—"

"Course you'll have to hurry now, even to catch the three-ten," the cabdriver said.

"But look here—"

But the cabdriver had already put his head on the seat and closed his eyes with a long-suffering sigh.

I let myself into the apartment and sat on my bed, digging my fingernails into my palms.

The taxi horn blared outside. Then it blared again.

"Oh, Jesus *Christ*," I said, and started to pack.

I didn't remember the pink slip until just before the division bell rang that evening in the Commons. I took it out and started to trace over it lightly, to see if the imprint from the preceding slip had gone through.

It was quite faint but legible enough. Mrs. Talbot had given the depositor's name as Enerjee all right, but the money had been credited to the account of one Yves Gassien. It didn't take long to look up Jacques Gassien's middle name and find that it was Yves.

Snowed Up

Though the pay was rotten, an M.P. did have a few perquisites, and among them was free train travel for his person and effects on all the railways of Canada. It was fortunate that I availed myself of the opportunity on the following weekend that March, for when I was halfway between the capital and Gallop a thoroughgoing blizzard smote the area and immediately blocked all the roads over a quarter million square miles. Had I been driving I should probably have been trapped in some hideous village for a week. As it was, it took the train four hours to travel the twenty miles or so to the railway station nearest to Gallop, which, naturally, had no passenger halt of its own.

On the Monday, as I trudged along Gallop's main street to the Queen's Hotel with a view to keeping in touch with my constituents, it occurred to me that this was my first full winter in Canada since 1916. I had forgotten what an ordeal it could be. Just as the sun had started to provide a few calories, and just as whiskers of sulphurous grass had begun to break the silver monotony, and the melted snow to gurgle in ditch and downspout, the storm had covered it all up again. And how. In places the wind had molded the snow into twelve-foot drifts.

It had taken hours just to dig my way *into* the Machin farm. To get into town today I'd had to beg a lift in a neighbor's cutter; trains, horse-drawn cutters, and sleds were the only moving transport for a thousand miles around. Even then I had to walk the last half mile. Queen Street was quite impassable. Many shopwindows were completely obscured by banks of snow, and the high winds, now mercifully spent, had created patterns like cirrus cloud high up the brick walls. The sky was still a rich, snow-pregnant gray, against which yellow-lighted windows burned, though it was supposed to be daylight. Only the vicious tips of the Presbyterian church railings were visible. A green lumber wagon stood abandoned in the middle of a side street, its freight of barbed wire fancily decorated with white lace, and the new post office looked like an iced cake in the shape of a neoclassical mausoleum.

The municipal force tasked with cleaning the streets comprised two men in wet plaid jackets, with shovels and hopeless expressions. It was like reliving the Moscow experience all over again.

As I floundered into the lobby of the hotel and paused to kick my snow boots into the corner, the proprietor, George Duckworth, nodded, exchanged comments about the weather—to cheer me up, he said that the road to Ottawa would not likely be open again until Ascension Day—then turned back to comb his mustache in the mirror behind him. Painted on the mirror was the legend, *Wiser's Canadian Rye Whisky—The Mingled Souls of Corn and Rye*. Somewhere in the dung-colored depths of the hotel somebody was playing a Caruso record on the Victrola.

Al, the waiter, still wearing a grubby white jacket, nodded gloomily as I peered into the tavern, or tearoom. He was busy at the windowsills with a hand brush, collecting last season's flies, then leaving them there in entomological pyramids. Not that there was much else for him to do, for the lunchtime crowd had not yet appeared. The place was empty, except for the resident bootlegger.

Toombs was seated in the far corner, sipping from a mug of coffee, his muscular frame seeming to take up three sides of the table. He did not look the least welcoming.

Draping my dog coat over a chair, I occupied the remaining side, wondering why he was in such a bad temper. It was the first time I had met him since my last meeting in town in which I had, among other rambling castigations, booted the switch-back operators. Assuming the scowl was meant for me, I immediately put myself at a disadvantage by apologizing for having attracted so much attention, lately, to his trade.

"What? Oh, that." He sipped from the enamel mug, clapping me in irons with his hard blue eyes. His voice, however, was mild enough. "I guess you didn't really mean it, eh?" he asked encouragingly, waiting for me to prove that I was even more of a hypocrite than he already suspected.

"Well, yes, I meant it, but . . ." I mumbled. Having lost yet another pipe, I snatched out a small bent cigarette and lit it, adding to the tavern's umber atmosphere of stale beer and mildew. "I still feel a bit guilty about attacking the business when I was in it myself."

"You sound like a politician, all right," he sneered. "Afraid you'll lose my vote, are you?" Then, his voice hardening: "If you thought it should be said, why shouldn't you say it, and the hell with what anyone thinks?"

He leaned back and took out a long cheroot, flamed a match with a flick of a hoe-sized fingernail, and blew smoke contemptuously across the table.

In reply, I took a puff of my cigarette, conscious that its insignificant length was placing me at a further disadvantage. He was gripping his long cheroot between his teeth like a Mississippi gambler. I was holding my little cigarette between my fingers like somebody at a Hipsey garden party.

"Politics is a business, after all," I said. "And obviously one has to stay in business."

"Oh, so *that's* what politics is," he said. "Gee whiz. We learn a little every day."

"And a business I'm proud to be in," I said, defiantly squashing out the cigarette and patting my pockets. Yes, I still had it—the cigar that the Governor General had given me. I whipped it out, lit it, and leaned back triumphantly. Now mine was bigger than his.

He didn't bother answering, but stared into his coffee mug as if it contained one of the Hippocratic humors, blood, yellow bile, black bile, or phlegm—or all four of them. Until he noticed my cigar; whereupon he stamped his cheroot into the floorboards and took out a Havana the size of a stonemason's chisel, bit off the end, and spat it forty feet down the brown tavern. Then, forming his lips into a big round O, he inserted the cigar, turning it lightly to moisten it before clamping it, lighting it, and sprawling back in his corner, his shoulders wide enough to jam him against both walls.

Overwhelmed, I laid my comparatively puny stogie in the ash-tray and stared moodily at the table top with its design of deli-cately interwoven ale-glass rings. "Anyway," I muttered, "I just popped in to find out what's going on in town these days."

"Oh yes? Well, I'll tell you what's going on," Toombs said from round the side of the cigar. "Mrs. Talbot has finally cut us off."

"Oh ar?"

"Since giving up the Montreal move she's about tripled the supply to the home market. There's trainloads of the stuff going to Toronto and points west. Naturally, of course, without the slightest interference from Chief Excise Officer Jewell."

"I wonder why."

His expression turned savage. "But hardly so much as a god-dam bottle top for Gallop," he said. I could see his teeth sinking deeper into the tobacco leaf.

Al, who had been loitering in the vicinity, vacantly flapping a filthy rag, put in, "Folks round here is gettun real desperate, Mr. Bandy. There'll be trouble soon, you mark my words."

"Shut up and bring us a couple of shots," Toombs ordered.

"Jeez, Fred, you know what the boss said. We gotta conserve our stocks," Al began, whining and hunching, until Toombs looked at him; whereupon he added hurriedly, "but seeing as it's you, Fred . . ."

"The bitch has had it in for Gallop for years, of course, ever since the Hipseys and that bunch snubbed her when she married Talbot," Toombs said, as two small whiskies arrived in chipped teacups. "And I guess all the insults when people thought she was pulling out didn't help. But, God damn it, to deprive people of their booze, that's going too far."

"McMulligan's seeing little green giraffes now," Al said, drift-ing up again. "Dr. McKay had to give him emergency treatment the other day. He knocked him out with a box of postmortem in-struments."

There was a thump outside as a ton of snow slid from a roof.

"Can't you reason with her?" I asked.

"How can you reason with somebody who acts reasonable?"

Toombs snarled. "She just says it's all a mistake, and she'll divert the hooch to us soon as she can. Then goes on hustling the rest of the market and bypassing us completely. The fact is she hates everybody in this town, and she's finally found a way to show it, the bitch."

"So she's concentrating on the home market, eh?" I said. "I guess that might explain why she's gone to the top, to do the switch-back act with the minimum of interference."

When he asked what I meant, I told him about the Molson's Bank incident. Then I leaned back, expecting him to be shocked to the core.

Instead, it was I who was shocked. Toombs was not the least surprised.

"Bribing the minister himself, is she?" he said, tapping white cigar ash into the ashtray. "Well, why not? She and the rest of the distillers seem to be paying off half his department, why should he be left out?"

As he went on to talk about the Customs Department's notorious chief preventive officer in Montreal, Joseph Bisaillon, who was said to be earning so much money from the booze racket that he was now a millionaire, I thought back over the past few months and was rather shaken by my own ruminations. I had been working myself into a muck sweat of righteous indignation about the smuggling business, sermonizing about the rips and tears in the moral fabric of the nation, popping up and down at question time like a tappet, pestering front-benchers at caucus meetings, moving motions, publicizing the facts and figures of the C.P.A. so persistently that even the yellow-press types now groaned rudely in unison whenever I brought up the subject. But until this moment I supposed that my real motive had sprung not so much from genuine concern for the public well-being as to strut in the limelight and make a name for myself in politics, just as any ambitious employee was expected to scratch and bite his way to the executive dining table.

But Fred Toombs's reaction to a piece of news that should have flung him over backward in his chair rather rudely peeled the film from my starry orbs. With the extension of the corruption into the very Cabinet, the situation was becoming positively fraught. Good heavens, the Governor General would be flogging knighthoods on Sparks Street next. If something wasn't done, the country would end up like a machete republic.

So as the days passed I fell to wondering how to squeal on Mrs. Talbot without irritating my conscience. Unfortunately I was thwarted by the deal I'd made with her last October. After forcing her to cancel the move to Montreal, I could hardly avoid keeping my side of the bargain: to keep silent about her illicit activities on the domestic front.

Nevertheless, over the next two or three weeks, until the crystal hills slowly melted in the April sunlight, I tried really hard to convince myself that our agreement could now be suspended. After all, had she not broken it herself by continuing to switch back liquor? But despite the most convincing arguments I remained intransigent. It was not that I was morally against the idea of betraying her. The reason was plain funk. I had gone back on my word once already, and look at the consequences: three years of turmoil with That Russian Woman, then nine months of living with George. No, I could not stab Mrs. Talbot in the backside, especially after I had forced her to cancel the move to Montreal in order to ensure my election. I owed her too much to declare moral bankruptcy.

By the middle of April I was feeling pretty frustrated. I had amassed some evidence of individual acts of corruption by lesser officials in the Customs Department, but nothing really significant; though it was obvious to anybody who knew anything about it that the improbity must reach at least as high as the port inspectors. The trouble was that, while the special investigation team that Jim Boyce was working for, for example, could legally collar bank statements and things, and compel witnesses to testify, I had no such clout. Nobody important would give me anything or talk to me, and even honest minor officials who were willing to snitch wouldn't allow themselves to be publicly identified. I couldn't even prove that Mrs. Talbot was Mrs. Enerjee, or vice versa, and without that evidence—which, in fact, I never did accumulate because that beast Anne Mackie refused to betray her boss—Jacques Gassien could, through his desperation for funds with which to distract his wife, continue to dishonor the government.

On top of those frustrations was a shortage of funds. Nearly all my colleagues had honest jobs to augment their pay, but I had no other income whatsoever. I couldn't even fly for a living. When the spring thaw finally arrived in April, the farm field remained a sea of muck and mire, and not even Father's prodigious kitchen fires could produce enough cinders for a firm runway. I seriously considered contacting my old father-in-law, Mr. Lewis, to request him to liquidate my entire assets in England—a motorcar, a painting, and a samovar. But knowing Mr. and Mrs. Lewis, they had probably used the painting to mend a hole in the roof, and had probably wrecked the car by accidentally driving it over the samovar.

It was in a typical springlike mood of mumbling dissatisfaction that I returned to the Ottawa apartment one mild but overcast Friday to pick up my valise for a weekend trip home. There I found Jim Boyce already in residence. He had finally persuaded his Belgian baroness to lease him her honor for the night, and as his own lodgings were unsuitable for the tryst, an adjoining apartment being occupied by another of his inamoratas, he had borrowed my quarters for the long-planned seduction.

The lady had not arrived by the time I got there. I found Boyce fluttering about in the kitchen, preparing a sumptuous repast—cooking and lechery were his principal hobbies—and fussing over half a dozen flower arrangements in the living room, dining room, and bedroom.

He had even brought his own cooking utensils. The scent of flowers and of bouillabaisse fought valiantly for ascendancy.

"M'm, that smells good," I said dolefully, sniffing. "George usually does our cooking, but the most I can expect from him is fish and chips from the corner store. I think I'll stay and have dinner with you."

Boyce panicked for a moment before seeing me dump my bag at the front door. "Look, clear off, will you, Bart?" he said, lighting the candles on the dining table. "She'll be embarrassed if she sees you."

"I'm going, I'm going," I said, leafing through a bound report. He had obviously been in the apartment all afternoon, for there were papers scattered over the coffee table. The report had the Treasury seal on the front cover.

"What's this?" I asked idly.

He snatched it out of my hands and stuffed it, and the rest of the papers, into his briefcase. "It's our draft report on the Customs Department," he said hurriedly.

"Corruption in?"

"H'm?" He looked over the dining table anxiously and moved a butter knife a quarter of an inch. "Yes, that's right. Well, off you go, Bart. And thanks again for the use of the . . ." He gestured around; then noticing that I had left the bedroom door open, exposing a vase of flowers, a bottle of wine beside the bed, and the turned-down covers, he rushed over to close it. It would never do to let his baroness see that he had already taken her for granted.

"I'll do the same for you someday," he said.

"How can you do the same for me? It's my apartment."

"I mean I'll do you a similar favor."

"Do me a favor now. Let me read that report."

"I can't, Bart. It's confidential."

"Well, at least tell me what's in it."

But he had already hurried into the kitchen to oversee his culinary seduction. Every gas burner on the stove was alight. Blue flames were flickering under his professional-looking pots and pans. I followed him and leaned against the doorway.

"Did I catch a glimpse of Gassien's name?" I asked. "In that report?"

"What? Yes, yes. Look, Bart, she'll be here any minute," he said agitatedly.

"Proving that Gassien is being paid off by a prominent distiller?" I asked.

He stared, a pot lid clutched between his fingers. Steam rose in clouds to the glossy yellow, flyspecked ceiling.

"What makes you say that?" he asked. "We don't have anything on that."

"I do, though."

"Christ. What we've got on him is bad enough," he said, slowly replacing the lid. But then: "Look, Bart, honestly—I can't say any more than that. That report is for the P.M. only. If it got out that you'd seen it I'd not only lose my job, I'd never get another in this town."

He watched me anxiously while I thought about it. "Which distiller has been paying him off anyway?" he asked reluctantly.

"Who do you think?"

"Tony Batt?"

I started to nod a complacent confirmation, but then adjusted the gesture rather spastically.

"Tony?" I said. "Course not. He's not a distiller. No, I meant Mrs. Talbot."

"She's been paying off Gassien?"

"Looks like it."

"And you can prove it?"

"No. But your team could, easily enough."

Boyce turned two of the gas burners lower and herded me back into the living room. "Look, let's talk about it later, okay? She'll be here in a minute."

"All right, all right," I said, and continued to the front door of the apartment, and picked up my bag. But then dropped it again and turned. "By the way," I asked, "why should you think it was Tony Batt?"

"Well, you mentioned a distillery owner, and he was the first I thought of."

"He owns a distillery now? Where?"

"In Montreal. Mrs. Talbot's new premises. She sold it to him last September."

He stared at me for a moment, then: "Oh no, you wouldn't know about that, would you? It's one of the things we've been investigating," he said, nodding toward his briefcase. Then, adopting a pompous stance, the effect rather spoiled by the frilly apron he was wearing, "She was forced into selling it, of course."

"Forced?"

"Well, you know what Batt's capable of. Come to think of it, I'm kind of surprised he hasn't bumped you off yet, for dragging his name through those speeches of yours."

As Boyce glanced agitatedly at his watch I sank slowly into the nearest chair.

"Do I understand you to say," I asked, "that Mrs. Talbot sold Batt the Montreal premises last September?"

"Yes. Why?"

I didn't answer. I was too busy realizing that Mrs. Talbot had not willingly canceled the move to Montreal after all but had had no choice in the matter; and that she had been perfectly well aware of it when she had pretended to give way to my subtle pressures. That she had fooled me good and proper.

Wet Through

The countryside was black with rain when, with George Garanine still acting as my chauffeur, I drove to the distillery on the following Monday morning.

Even with the headlights blazing, we could see little but black water. The rataplan on the canvas roof of the Pierce-Arrow was so fierce that the very noise of the engine was drowned out, as it labored and swashed from pothole to pothole. On our left, the Rideau seethed like boiling potatoes under the sinister deluge. For of course, now that the winter snowstorms had ended, the rain had taken over, sculpturing the remaining snowbanks with a million cold chisels, and polishing their gritty contours with its pluvial friction.

"This is incredible," I said, looking uneasily at the dark, saturated sky. "It's like the beginning of a biblical flood."

"But, as we say in English, April showers bring forth May flowers," George shouted elatedly as he drove around a tree that was floating down the road.

For the first time in months George seemed to be his old self again. I had begun to fear that his bouts of depression were delaying his recovery, so it was a relief when his physical wound, at least, had finally healed, leaving him with only a slight limp.

It wasn't *his* discomfort that had dismayed me, though; it was mine. The sight of his twinges had been a constant reminder of my own culpability.

I had even turned the hair at his temples gray, and it was no comfort when Anne irritably pointed out that it made him look more attractive than ever. This appeared to be true, judging by the melting looks he received from stenographers, politicians' wives, shop assistants, and chaps with wavy hair.

"It's stupid, blaming yourself for his condition," she said impatiently, "when all he needs is a good thump on the earhole. Can't you see he's living the life of Riley?"

"Or rather, the life of Oblomov," I said gloomily—and, as it turned out, presciently. I was referring to the famous work by Goncharov, about a character, Oblomov, who could rarely make up his mind, and preferred to remain in bed so as to avoid having to act when he finally did make it up. I'd often heard Russians using the term *Oblomovism* to describe the pre-Revolutionary Russian characteristics of indolence, irresolution, and indecision.

The concept of Garanine as a Son of Oblomov did not help in the least. To be the cause of a thirty-five-year-old artillery officer's hair turning gray was quite hard to bear. So I had decided to make another attempt to get rid of him.

Well, it wasn't just his miserable face; it was his erratic behavior. As well as that puzzling and rather disturbing occasion when he had crept so stealthily into my boudoir, there had been a couple of other incidents, like the one in the woods. We had stayed at the farm during the Christmas adjournment, which lasted until nearly March, and one afternoon, upon hearing faint shots, I trudged through the snow to investigate. I found George deep in the woods, practicing with my service automatic.

It was not just that he had taken it without permission and had been carrying it around with him. What disturbed me was that his target was an old election poster, the one reading BANDY TO WIN $\boxed{\times}$. He claimed to have been aiming at the boxed x, but it was the word BANDY that was peppered with bullet holes.

I had looked at him very queerly, hoping that it was the pistol's fault and not a subconscious error.

"George," I said, "you're not harboring any deep-seated resentments, are you, merely because I threatened your life, drove you from your beloved homeland, cursed you for months, worked you like a slave, got you shot, and finally ruined your health?"

"My dear Bartalamyeh," he said with a catch in his voice, and turned away, overcome with emotion—leaving me wondering whether the emotion was a decent one or whether he had turned away to hide the fact that it wasn't.

Which accelerated my determination to get him together again with Mrs. Talbot. But though I gave him plenty of opportunity to reestablish their former intimacy, he refused to cooperate. He was much more deeply offended by her rejection than I had thought. He merely smiled at Philippa, listened to her attentively, quoted a proverb or two, and kept an emotional distance.

"What the heck's wrong with him?" Philippa asked peevishly. "We ought to've been halfway to the guest bedroom by now."

However, today he finally seemed to have regained his former optimism and joy of living—inappropriately, as usual, as we were in danger of being washed into the river at any moment.

At last the tall distillery buildings appeared through the untoward murk. At eleven in the morning, every light in the complex was blazing, the sheets of rain sharply delineating the floodlight beams. At the main gate a uniformed guard in a shiny cape splashed over, glared, recognized us, and waved us through to the parking space next to the guardroom.

A few minutes later a raincoated and umbrellaed Anne arrived to sign us in.

"Mrs. Talbot is somewhere on the premises," she said. "She may be in the bottling plant—we'll try there first."

Being on duty, and aware that the guards were listening, she was behaving coolly, briskly, and in a businesslike fashion. Just like in the bedroom. Made me feel quite at home.

As we scuttled across the central square, past a few remaining rain-lashed hillocks of shiny, grimy snow, she glanced disapprovingly at George, obviously wondering why he had tagged on behind, instead of remaining with the car, like a proper chauffeur. I supposed he was coming along to watch the fun. Seeing no reason not to, I had told him about Philippa's trickery, though I did so in good parliamentary language in order to obscure the unpalatable truth. But the simpleton failed to understand. "You mean she made utter, blithering idiot of you?" he asked earnestly.

After some hesitation, and rather unhappy over my own deviousness, I had also told Anne, after warning her that what I had to say was confidential. But I had to know once and for all whether or not I could trust her. Actually I was already pretty sure by now that, while I had been trying to get her to spy on Philippa, Philippa had been getting Anne to spy on me and report on my every activity, except in bed—and I wasn't too sure that she and Philippa weren't having a good laugh about that as well.

Scattering explosions of black water underfoot, we skittered into the building on the far side of the square. Inside, the noise was enough to give one a thick ear. The air in the cavernous building jangled with the bellow of machinery and the clash of glassware. Bottles by the thousands were being loaded onto moving platforms, ranks of them being pushed and shoved along, then whirled around in dizzying circles. An apparatus like a boa constrictor with a headlock on a giant vacuum cleaner was hissing at the glassy march-past, presumably to suck out any grit, shards of glass, and dead mice, that had escaped the bottle-cleaning process; the bottles then clinking onward to a mechanical cow that was giving amber milk.

Then forward again, past the fatigued scrutiny of women in dust caps, the bottles now capped and labeled by other clever bits of machinery.

Everybody in the building looked white and exhausted, though the women who were snatching the bottles off the production line and ramming them into compartmented boxes seemed to be the only ones who were doing much physical work.

As George and I slowed to watch the vitreous drudgery, the lights blazing down onto the glass and metal scene suddenly flickered, brightened, then went out. But just as the machines began to die, the lights came on again and the clamor was resumed.

It was an eerie moment, as if the heartbeat of the world had faltered. I groped for the nearest female, a mobcapped chit with a lusty bust—an instinctive reaching out for human contact, you understand—but, as I said, the lights came on again too soon.

"Come along—she's not here," Anne said briskly, as if she were used to potential cataclysms, and led the way toward the far exit, dodging skillfully around humming motors, thumping along in her sensible shoes across bridges built over frenzied endless belts. I could have done with an endless belt myself, just looking and listening to it all.

As we emerged from the building the noise diminished to a dull roar, then dissolved to the pluvial pandemonium outside. I had never seen such rain. In a trice my trench coat was saturated black, and the water was sluicing over the brim of my fedora, as if I were walking under a waterfall.

Then I realized that I was walking under a waterfall—it was cascading from a broken gutter far overhead.

The next building we entered was not quite as clamorous as the bottling plant, though it was noisy enough. It was a high, dim place dominated by great copper vats with huge, hinged lids. And there, standing on a platform arrangement opposite the open lid of one of the vats, was Philippa Talbot. She was looking a bit dumpy in a black suit and green silk blouse, her auburn hair flaring under the overhead lights. She was busily berating a foreman.

The foreman, his face stiff as old porridge, turned away and Philippa descended the metal stairway alongside the vat, rolling up a sheaf of blueprints or drawings in a tight, businesslike way. However, when she saw us she uttered a cry of welcome and came forward to greet George as if there had been no hiatus in their relationship.

George merely smiled politely and looked around in naive curiosity. A couple of minutes straggled by before she turned in my direction. She offered her left hand, the other being wrapped around the roll of drawings. "How nice to see you again, Bartholomew," she said warmly. And, still holding my hand, walked off a few paces. "How's tricks, darling?"

"You should know, Philippa."

"H'm? How do you mean, Bartholomew?" she asked.

She knew, all right. I glanced damply across at Anne, but she wasn't looking at me either. She had drawn George aside and was talking to him in an unusually animated way.

"Maybe if you'd come clean about Tony Batt pressuring you to sell the Montreal plant," I said, removing my sodden fedora and wringing it out, "I might have been able to help."

"I don't know what you're talking about," she said, staring

down into a cardboard drum on the floor beside us. For a moment I thought it was my words that were making her look apprehensive, until I realized that I was wringing my hat into the contents of the drum, a bluish powder that was now hissing and bubbling in rather an alarming fashion.

"Anyway, why should I tell you anything?" she said suddenly. "You might have been in cahoots with Tony."

"I wasn't."

"I didn't know that then. They said you were on good terms with him once."

"What I don't get is why you felt you had to sell out to Tony, lock, stock, and barrel."

"In that case I'll tell you," she said coldly, taking a step back from the gurgling barrel. "He said he didn't want to threaten me and leave me wondering if he'd carry it out or not. So he said he'd give me an example. He named somebody in New York who wouldn't do what Tony wanted him to do and, would you believe it, by an amazing coincidence that same person was found in the East River a week later.

"Well, that was good enough for me, Bartholomew. Though, to give him his due, he did give me a good price. He's not mean, isn't our Tony."

She turned, as if not quite sure where she was going, and started to climb the metal stairs again. "Anyway, I don't see why you're fussing—it got you into Parliament, didn't it?"

"That's true," I said as I joined her on the high platform and looked around to admire the view of girders and copper kettles and things. "But why did you let me take the credit, when you could have done some good for yourself in the community by making the announcement yourself, that you were canceling the move?"

"To get back my good name, you mean?"

"Well, yes."

"You think," she asked with a smile, "I care what the provincial boobs here think of me?" Her pleasant, guarded face suddenly went all twisted, until it looked like my hat. "I'd as soon curry favor with dinges and dagos," she said venomously. "I hate this town and every man in it. Rubes who wouldn't even know how to make six cards do the work of five. They don't know a

thing about what's going on outside the highway on one side and
their stinking little river on the other, and, what's more, they
don't want to. They think their Rock Gardens are Times Square.
I hate this whole, smug, respectable, authority-loving province. I
couldn't do anything about that, except blow a raspberry at its
laws, but at least I could put the fritz on this burg—"

Realizing that she was starting to pop her buttons, she pulled
herself together, though the heat of pure malice still sizzled in
her eyes. "You want to know why I gave you a leg up the Hill?"
she asked, looking at me straightly for the first time. "I thought I
could use you. After I'd gotten the goods on you, by involving
you in the switch-back racket. I had you all lined up to join my
lobby."

"Really? What went wrong?"

"You were too goddam quick to admit you'd been in the
smuggling game, to establish yourself as the Frank Merrivale of
the Commons," she sneered, "all bright-eyed and bushy-assed,
and stuffed like a goose with righteous sage and onions."

"Ah. Well, now we know where we stand, Philippa."

"Right."

"So now I can snitch on you to my heart's content," I said.
"Beginning with your friend Jacques Gassien," I said, just as the
lights went out.

One moment we were teetering, feather-fluffing and puffing
and glowering up there in the glare from the dangling lights;
then abrupt, impenetrable darkness swept through the vast,
humming, gurgling, alcoholic space. As cries of alarm cut across
the dying whine of machinery, I reached hurriedly for the rail of
the platform. Instead I felt something wet and ribbed, like a
large dead bird of prey, or umbrella. And the next moment received a violent shove in the back.

I started falling, arms flailing for support. But the only contact
was against my legs. This further overbalanced me. And just as
somebody nearby started to scream, I pitched into the ultimate
wetness.

Encumbered as I was by a somewhat unconventional swim-
wear, it took me between thirty seconds and two hours to reach
the surface of the aboveground swimming pool. I clawed franti-

cally at the sides but encountered only a smooth surface. And
when I reached overhead there was more of the same.

I couldn't understand that. I should have felt only the air
through which I had just pitched. Instead there was a metal surface overhead. And worse, it was only inches above the surface
of the liquid.

Panic naturally ensued. There was so little space above, I
couldn't get my mouth out of the water. My fingernails were
scratching frantically at the encompassing smoothness. I had
swallowed several additional mouthfuls of what I was sure was
some deadly chemical, perhaps a solution of the bluish powder
that I had wrung my hat into, before it occurred to me to tilt my
head backward. Even then the liquid in the pool—tank—vat—yes,
the copper vat—kept swilling into my gasping, gaping cake-hole.

It appeared that the lid of the vat, which had been open while
I was talking to Philippa on the platform outside, had been
slammed down. Perhaps it was also locked in place, though it
hardly mattered whether it was or not. Even if unlocked it was
too heavy to lift, as I was suspended in liquid with nothing to
brace against.

I hadn't heard the lid clang shut. Presumably I had been
under the surface at the time. Though it wouldn't have clanged
anyway. It was spring-balanced. But whether it was locked or
not, I was trapped under it, with only about six inches of air between it and the surface of the liquid.

Nevertheless, with demented effort, I continued to press upward against the curved surface overhead. All this achieved was
to shoot me downward again through the oily medium. I was
bellowing every time I got to the top again, in gibbering animal
terror of the darkness and a distorting sense impression that was
rapidly convincing me that I was in a circular, totally enclosed
flask. As a boy I had once seen a neighbor trying to drown a cat
in a rain barrel. With head thrown back and eyes bulging like
stranded redfish, fingernails scrabbling at a maniacal frequency,
I knew how the beast must have felt. I tried to beat on the copper sides, but the resistance of the vat's contents reduced the impact to the most feeble thumps, made feebler yet by the absorp-
tion of further mouthfuls of liquid, which at least had the effect
of silencing the yowling sounds I was making. Even to me at

such a moment, they were beginning to sound pointless. Obviously nobody would be able to hear me in here. I was just wasting energy. It was going to be a race between the effect of the poison, or whatever was in the vat, and the diminishing air supply.

Funnily enough, though the situation was now confirmed as hopeless, I was beginning to feel quite tranquil. Presumably the effects of drowning. I knew about that, all right, having once parachuted into a water-filled quarry. Drowning also enabled me to use my head for something other than butting the lid of the vat. The lid seemed to be slightly concave. If so, there should be more air in the middle. Upon swimming a couple of strokes to the center, with head thrown back like a double-jointed birdwatcher, I found this to be the case. By treading water—at a decreasingly concerned pace—I found there was a good foot of space above the frothing surface.

Treading water at this peculiarly careless rate, however, almost drowned me a minute prematurely, for I was still wearing a trench coat, not to mention a stout pair of brogues, a suit—darn it, my best suit—and underwear. As I pushed off the shoes, then peeled off the coat, first off one shoulder, then the next, and then the final shoulder—strange, I never knew I had three shoulders—there was no need to remind myself to disrobe with a due regard for the saving of energy, so utterly relaxed was I. Presumably it was the relief from being able to keep my head above water. Oil. Chemicals. Whatever.

Surely somebody would open the lid of the copper vat sooner or later. Rephrase that. Surely they would open it in the next minute or two, which was all the time I had left. My head was spinning already. Shortage of air. But of course Philippa might have distracted them to give me more time to ferment. Fancy her doing a thing like this. Didn't someone say her husband had drowned in Long Island Sound? H'm.

I hiccuped. It was only then that I remembered Anne's lecture about the distillery operation. Let me see. They heated up the corn after it was chopped into teeny bits in the cresher pooker—pressure pooker, rather—then they popped in the yeast to make it go all boily and bubbly. Fermenting took from three to five days. Golly, I'd never lash that long. And what was the product called again? Oh yes, distiller's beer. Yes, that was what was in the vat. Distiller's beer. Before it was blended. Gad, that was a relief. It wasn't poison at all, but pure grain spirit. Thank goodness—I was drowning in alcohol.

Well, at least I was comfortable now. It was lovely and warm in here. All the same, what a waste of whisky. When they finally found me, they would have to pour out the entire contents of the vat, thousands and thousands of gallons of precious spirits, not to mention my socks, trench coat, and underpants. Or would Philippa insist on using the spirits regardless? She would probably maintain that it wasn't like finding a dead mouse in a bottle or anything— I would already have been emptied out.

I hiccuped again, then promptly sank. As I paddled feebly to the surface once more, I sputtered apathetically at the thought that even when I was dead people still wouldn't be rid of me. I'd live on in several thousand bottles of whisky. Interesting flavor, they'd say. Perhaps a trifle bellicose and with a strange color, even a little presumptuous. Good body, though.

Wouldn't be long now. My heart was going like a pile driver. Head spinning, eyes burning, limbs slowing. With a fading effort I managed to close a fist, and reach up, and rap on the lid with the knuckles. Then felt myself slipping under for the last time . . . which seemed only right . . . one was supposed to surface only three times before going under for the last time, but I must have come up at least a dozen times . . .

Then a hand was clutching at me and holding me against the side of the vat. I was breathing again. Waves of cold, glorious air, pouring out of the darkness. Then George Garanine was hauling me out, his muscles creaking audibly with the strain. I was doing nothing to help. Very shellfish of me. I was waterlogged to twice my normal weight. The process of hauling me out was painful, the edge of the vat scraping and grinding down my back, but I didn't mind in the least.

It was still dark in the outside world, though lanterns and flashlights were bobbing in the blackout. Next I guess I was lying face up on the metal platform. Then the lights flared on. The sudden brilliance caused a sensation like an engine-on outside inverted spin, and a gastric convulsion. There was a confusing babble of voices as if people were speaking from inside picnic hampers. Then George, almost as soaked as I was in distiller's beer, was cradling my head in his lap.

"Oh, Bartalamyeh," said he, his voice anguished, "I was in time to save you."

"No, you weren't," I mumbled. "'M, 'm hopelessly pickled."

About an hour later I reeled into the farm kitchen supported by George and enveloped in overalls, blankets, and fumes.

Mother was washing up after lunch. Father was holding a wet coat near the usual conflagration in the grate.

"Hello, Mommy and Daddy," I said, and sniggered.

"Bartholomew," Mother exclaimed.

"That's me," I said, and immediately lurched over and gave her a big, slobbering kiss.

"He fell into a wat of visky," George explained.

"No, no. Mean, mean wisk of vatsky, George old bean," I said. "Wisp of watsky. Wat of vodksy. W—oh, the hell with it."

"He fell into a what?"

"Not a wat, a vat," George said carefully, steadying me with one arm. "Great big vat, fifteen feet high."

"How the devil could he fall into a vat fifteen feet high? Where was he—swinging above it like Mr. Edgar Rice Burroughs' Tarzan?"

"It is true that it would not be easy," George said thoughtfully.

"Not be easy? It's all nonsense. You're protecting him, George. He's *intoxicated.*"

"Bartholomew!"

"He's dead drunk," Father thundered. "I knew it would come to this."

"I yam not," I said offendedly, and fell over the clothes horse.

"Go to your room this instant! This instant, do you hear?"

I went instantly to my room. So instantly that no time seemed to pass between getting up from the floor and lying down on the bed. But the moment I did so the bed was immediately hitched to a team of horses that drew the bed backward through space at an increasing velocity up to and including the speed of light. Entire planetary systems whizzed by. Worse, when I lurched upright I discovered that it was the room that was tumbling through space.

I lay down and continued the journey to the edge of the galaxy. Finally I slept.

It was dark when I awoke, with a mouthful of used cotton wool mixed with iron filings, ground eggshells, and fingernail parings. Back to the bathroom. Back to bed.

At midnight, fresh from a bath, scented and polished, George looked in, switching on a viciously bright lamp to see if I was awake. He was wearing the maroon dressing gown that Mother had bought for him. I learned later that he had been slaving in the barn all afternoon and evening, preparing the Gander for its first flight of the year.

Despite being crowned King of the Hangovers, I was glad to see him. I was anxious to discuss the vat-of-whisky episode.

"I really don't understand," I whispered, without preamble, "why she would want to kill me."

The smile on George's face faded. About to sit on the bed, he froze in a half-sitting posture, then straightened again. He turned away to the window, to gaze out at an interesting view of pitch-darkness.

"I think that woman must be mad, George," I said as softly as possible, "to think she could get away with it. If it was because I'd found out she was bribing Gassien, she knew I'd told others about it. . . . By the way, George—thank you."

"I don't suppose there is any whisky?" George asked, still staring into the darkness.

"There isn't a bottle available in the whole of Gallop, by now."

"I meant to get a case from Philippa, but in the excitement I forgot all about it," George said.

"Did you hear what I said? I said thank you."

"Yes, I heard," he said, examining his hands. In spite of his lengthy ablutions there was oily dirt under his usually impeccable fingernails. As he mooched away from the window he picked at the dirt with a thumbnail.

"You've done so much for me ever since we first met in the Evropeievskaya in Petrograd. And perhaps I haven't always been too appreciative."

"Please."

"No, listen. Good heavens, it's high time I showed some grati-
tude. I've been most surly with you, George. But you see, you're
so decent, I just couldn't stand it. But after this I'll try to be
more tolerant. This latest example really takes the cake."

For nearly a minute he continued to dig at his nails, his head
bowed. Then he sat on the bed, his mustache twisted into an
acute angle.

"Bartalamyeh?"

"Yes, George?"

"Do you remember a man called Sergei Ossipov?"

"Who?"

"Cheka agent in Petrograd?"

"Uh . . . Oh yes. Old Sergei. My official shadow in . . . Yes.
What about him?"

"Did you ever wonder what happened to him?"

"Can't say I did." I leaned back on the pillow, carefully supporting my head as I did so. I could feel my teeth beating and
vibrating.

"Round about the time you left Soviet Union, he was arrested,
interrogated by Commissar Stalin or General Secretary Stalin, as
he is now called."

"Stalin? I remember that name, too. That was Sergei's friend
Joseph. But, George, what on earth has that to do with anything?"

"Sergei confided in you, is that not right? I don't want to know
what he said, but—"

I started to answer but George put up a hand. "No, I don't
want to know," he said quickly. "But shortly after you escaped I
was called in by the General Secretary. I was told I was to be
shot for allowing you to escape."

"I thought you would be."

"But after leaving me to think about it in the cell for a few
days, he then said he would give me another chance. I would be
forgiven if I rectified the situation as far as you were concerned."

"But how could you do that? I'd already escaped."

In the silence that followed I thought about it, not too
efficiently, and finally spoke up. "My God, I never really connected Sergei's pal Joseph with the man who's been in all the

papers ever since Lenin died. They say he's likely to be the big Red cheese, now that Lenin's under glass. But, good Lord—" I sat up—a very unwise motion. It took two minutes before my head reassembled itself. "Sergei told me that Stalin used to be an agent-provocateur—"

"No, no, I don't want to hear," George cried.

"—in the tsarist police," I finished.

George stared at me, his face haggard. "I told you I didn't want to know," he said hopelessly. "Now you really have done me one in the eye."

"How?"

"Now I can't go back or forward."

He reached out and touched the bedside telephone for no particular reason. "So that's why he wanted to get rid of you," he said. "You are perhaps the only one left who knows. And now me," he added despairingly.

"I don't understand what you're getting at," I said uneasily.

"It's quite easy, Bartalamyeh. I pushed you into the vat of whisky."

I sank slowly back onto the pillows, holding my eyes in place with thumb and forefinger. "No, no, you've got it wrong, George," I said wearily. "I thought your English was better than that. No, George—you pulled me *out* of the vat of whisky."

"Only because I changed my mind, Bartalamyeh," he said. "When I heard you tap on the side of the vat. I could not go through with it, you see."

I closed my eyes. Crimson timpani were beating out an erratic Stravinsky rhythm.

"Like the other times," he explained earnestly. "Three times I have tried to kill you."

"I see. I see. M'm. M'm. And that was how you were to rectify the situation? So that there would be nobody left who knew about the General Secretary being a . . . So why didn't you, George?"

"I told you. I could not bring myself."

"Then why didn't you just forget it? You were safe here in Canada, surely?"

"My dear Bartalamyeh," he said with a wild, choked sort of laugh, "do you think he would let me leave country without taking out insurance? He said if I did not take care of you as he had already taken care of Ossipov it would be too bad for my relatives. They would all be arrested and sent to Siberia."

"Anna, Lisa, Natalie . . . that lot?"

"Yes."

He got up and stretched, wretchedly smiling. "Well," he said. "Now you know, Bartalamyeh."

"Yes . . ."

He sank, filleted, onto the bed again, the skin under his eyes sagging like a theater curtain, making him for a moment look captive rather than captivating. "What am I to do, Bartalamyeh?" he asked miserably. "What am I to do?" Then, listlessly: "You do not look as shocked as I expected."

"Shocked?" I said. "You think I'm not shocked? Not shocked after being very nearly drowned by one of the gentlest people in the western hemisphere? Not shocked to learn he'd been put up to it by a tsarist fink who may soon rule the party he was agent-provoking? Not shocked to learn that one of my most respected friends has been trying to decide for months whether to kill me or not? Of *course* I'm not shocked. I'm absolutely thrilled, I'm overwhelmed with relief."

I reached out and pumped his hand. "Don't you see?" I cried. "It proves I wasn't a barbarian persecuting a Christian, and there's hope for me yet. And hope for you, because you're not faultless, you're not perfect, you're—thank God—not a saint after all."

The Last of George Garanine

Fortunately none of these alarums and excursions affected my parliamentary progress. I continued to make a thorough pest of myself. While remaining silent for the time being about the ministerial malfeasance (apart from a few sly and, as one Liberal newspaper put it, dastardly insinuations), I brought up the smuggling issue in other ways. These included libelous remarks in constituency meetings, speeches and questions in rowdy caucuses, which were often shouted down, newspaper interviews, and even a radio address over the Toronto *Star* station, CFCA—though actually nobody heard that particular talk because the moment I spoke into the microphone the carbon granules fell out. It was obviously their equipment that was at fault, but the station manager said that microphones were not designed for voices like mine. He suggested that next time I should just stand on the roof and speak in all directions; he thought I would have no difficulty in being heard in Long Branch, or even Niagara Falls.

Naturally I also used the Commons as a forum, bringing up the subject in oral and written questions and through the moving of motions—which were invariably and noisily voted down—and even the occasional speech. Unfortunately for my reputation as a speaker, the debates rarely had anything to do with smuggling or the Customs Department, consequently my irrelevancies usually elicited groans from those of my colleagues who had not had time to flee behind the curtain.

In being called upon to speak on such occasions I was greatly

aided by the Whip, who for a while remained prejudiced in my
favor. Whenever I asked if he would write one of his little notes
to the Speaker—"Would Your Honor be kind enough to recognize the Honorable Member for William and Mary . . ."—he ac-
ceded, though with rapidly diminishing enthusiasm when he
heard what I had to say.

"You know, I really can't keep on encouraging you," he said
one day in the lobby, "when everything you say is either irrelevant or disloyal."

"But surely, sir, self-criticism is good for the party."

"With you, that's like saying the guillotine is good for head-
aches. Damn it, man, you're constantly supplying our enemies
with damaging material to use against us. And they are using it—
did you see Meighen's speech in the papers last weekend? Let
them dig up their own dirt. If you've anything to say, keep it for
the Wednesday meetings."

"But haven't I done that over and over again, with no result?
The Customs Department continues to—"

"Now that's enough, Bandy," he interrupted sternly. "I have
been very indulgent with you, not least because I felt a certain
amount of individualism should not be unwelcome in a party
overburdened with conformists. And it's increasingly obvious
that something should be done about the situation. But when
you repeatedly attack your own leaders and make improperly
substantiated allegations of government corruption, that's going
too far."

"You all hate me."

"We don't, Bandy. We—"

"You do. The Cabinet all hate me to a man."

"They do not. They—"

"They do, especially the P.M."

"Well, that's true enough. But—"

"And the other M.P.s hate me too, because I'm allowed to
speak more than them."

"Well, we can soon fix that," the Whip said, looking suddenly
fed up. "From now on, you'll take your chances with the
Speaker like everyone else. And I'm ordering you," he said, putting on his official face, "to cease these damaging public utter-

ances, or we shall be forced to take disciplinary action against
you." Then, pleasingly: "Will you do that, Bartholomew?"

"Won't."

"That's what I told them you'd say," he said resignedly. "Well,
don't say I didn't warn you."

"What they don't seem to realize," I said peevishly to Cyril
Hawkspat that same day, as we clattered along to the washroom
after a particularly long sitting, "is that I can't stop speaking out
now, even if I wanted to."

As we reached the washroom, the one with the tall porcelain
stalls, I explained that the more concern I showed over the clandestine trade the more eager were the people most affected by it,
the C.P.A. and the Canadian Manufacturers' Association, to feed
me with fresh gossip and scandal. "And I can't just ignore their
examples of corruption in the Customs Department, now can I?"

"I don't see why not. Everybody else does," Cyril said, moving
to the urinals. Each of the stalls had an interesting design built
into the porcelain at just below fly-button level: a representation
of a bumblebee, with a circle around it, to act as a target, or
aiming point. Cyril proceeded to douse his particular bee.
"Damn it, man," he went on irritably, "don't you realize there's a
general election coming up next year? You'll never get renomi-
nated at this rate."

"That's what they thought last time," I said smugly.

Even my desk mate in the House, Hormidas Talleyrand, felt
that I had still not grasped the idea that politics was just as
much a business as, say, the management of torts or contractual
right, or running a laundry. "And you don't get on in the world,
Bartolomieux," he said one day in the chamber, "by inserting
controversial clauses into contracts, or ruining your customers'
underwear. Especially if the customer is a minister of the
Crown."

"Gassien is ruining his own underwear," I retorted.

"So you say," Talley snapped. "But where is the proof?"

I hesitated, then started to tell him about the Molson's Bank
incident; until he suddenly nudged me and jerked his head toward the far end of the chamber.

Glancing in that direction, I saw that the Speaker had halted the proceedings and was glaring in our direction.

I must have been whining or booming even louder than usual, for: "Perhaps the Honorable Member for William and Mary would like us to postpone this debate so that he can continue his private conversation without distractions?" the Speaker asked icily.

I shrank halfway under the seat, coloring with mortification, and as soon as possible slunk out through the gold curtain.

I was followed a couple of minutes later by Talleyrand. He seemed to have something on his mind, so I was not too surprised when he suggested that we go out for a drink before dinner.

"Where are you living, by the way?" he asked as we emerged from the Centre Block.

"H'm?" I said. Then: "Oh, actually I have a suite in the Château."

"Let's go there for a drink and a chat, shall we?" he said, taking my arm.

As we crabbed across the fierce April crosswind toward the gates of Parliament Hill, I suddenly snapped my fingers and said, "Gee, I've just remembered. We can't go to my rooms there —the maid is making up the bed."

"It's six o'clock. Assuredly she'll have finished by now."

"Actually she's spring-cleaning."

"We'll ask her to clean some other season."

Halfway to the hotel's verdigrised towers, I clutched at my lower lip. "And then there's the redecorating," I said. "With ladders and paint sheets and everything. There'll be nowhere to sit."

"We'll sit on the ladders."

As we wended our way through the throng in the hotel lobby: "Gosh, I nearly forgot—there's nothing to drink up there," I exclaimed. "Though of course," I added cunningly, "I could offer you a nice glass of water—in a tooth mug?"

"That will be fine."

"But—but the water's all yellow and rusty, Talley. Personally, I never drink it myself."

As we stood there waiting for the elevator he merely hummed to himself, stroking his long chin and admiring the ceiling. But when the elevator arrived he asked the attendant for the tenth floor. "Well, in that case we'll go to my room," he said, giving me a bland smile.

The bugger must have known all along.

"The Molson's Bank incident you were telling me about," he said after we had settled down in his sitting room with its splendid view of the rubbish on the railway station roof. "What you saw is not exactly conclusive, is it? As evidence it sounds as flimsy as this Indian lady's sari."

"You don't believe me?"

"My dear Bandy, I wouldn't dream of doubting you," he said, gazing doubtfully into his glass of genuine French aperitif, which had presumably been smuggled from the French island of St. Pierre in the St. Lawrence estuary. "Especially as you have the copy of the deposit slip made out to this Yves Gassien. Yes?"

"Yes."

"But is it our Monsieur Gassien? There are other Gassiens, my friend."

"It's our man all right," I said, and was just about to explain that I had passed the deposit slip and the rest of my information, such as it was, to Jim Boyce's investigation team. The team was headed by an Inspector Duncan, who had quickly established that a Mrs. Enerjee had been depositing sums of cash to the minister's account every three months for nearly two years.

But then something stopped me. It may have been the cold look that Talleyrand was now directing toward me.

"And this Mrs. Enerjee—you can prove it was this distillery woman?"

"That's being investigated at the moment, Talley, but it's her, all right."

"But you haven't proved it?" he pounced.

"Do I really need to, anyway?"

"H'm." He got up and replaced the bottle of Dubonnet in an elaborately decorated Louis XV sécretaire. The room was furnished with his own antiques. "You've been trying to get an appointment to see the P.M.?" he asked suddenly.

"I've tried several times, but I haven't managed it yet."

"To inform him about Gassien?"

"Yes."

"I see."

Looking at Talleyrand's brooding face as he stood there pawing his secretary, it belatedly occurred to me that this was more
than a rag-chewing session before feeding time. And simultaneously I understood why our friendship had progressed only so
far over the past several months, before being brought up with a
thump against a wall of reserve. Good Lord, I thought, he's not
really on my side at all.

He was an establishment man through and through. For the
first time I believed the rumors that he would be in the next government if the Liberals won the 1925 general election. Actually I
had wondered more than once why Talleyrand occupied a background seat in the House when he was obviously on such good
terms with the foreground—including the Minister of Customs.
He ought really to have been in the third row, not the back
benches, and certainly not in the remotest corner. Perhaps he
fancied himself as a sort of assistant gray eminence.

His next question further alerted me that something was going
on, and I was glad I had not told him that I had been liaising
with Inspector Duncan's team. It was quite possible that if the
brass found out just how much dirt Boyce's outfit was digging up
they would do something to stop it. We Liberals had a habit of
suppressing unfavorable information.

"What exactly do you want, Bandy?" Talley asked mildly, but
regarding me fixedly with those heavy-lidded eyes.

"Want?"

"What are you aiming for? What do you hope to achieve by
these criticisms?"

"Well, nothing, really. Just doing my duty," I mumbled hypo-
critically.

"Of course. A reward of some kind, perhaps? A"—he gestured
gracefully—"a job?"

"I never thought of that."

He looked at me sharply, as if unsure of my meaning; which
was understandable enough. I wasn't sure what I meant either.

"Or perhaps this vendetta against Jacques, it's personal? You
don't like him?"

"Course I do. Course not."

"Pardon?"

"I mean, I'm quite sympathetic, really. His wife and all."

"So you're not hoping for, as you people say, 'a leg up'?"

"From Mr. Gassien? No. Matter of fact, I could help him," I said, trying to lighten the increasingly uncomfortable atmosphere.

"How?"

"Well, I understand his wife is continuing to betray him by refusing to take a lover. I know of somebody who could overcome her scruples, a friend of mine named James Boyce. For some reason Boyce is quite irresistible to women."

"Truly?"

"They invariably melt, the moment he applies a little heat."

"Interesting . . ." Talleyrand murmured, and promptly forgot what he had been talking about; or rather, what he had not been talking about. For I was now pretty sure that he was an emissary from Gassien; that he had been delegated to sound me out, to see how deeply I was committed to the facts, and whether I could be bought off with a favor or two.

Though I can't say I enjoyed being the recipient of snubs, fatherly advice, and various other sorts of hostility from my fellows, who seemed to think that facts and figures were subversive if they failed to endorse government policy or to enhance party unity, there was one compensation. I was becoming quite popular with the Opposition. Actually I was really impressed by how many decent chaps there were among the Conservatives. One day a member of their shadow cabinet, Mr. Pugsley, even treated me to a ham roll in the parliamentary dining room. "Congratulations, Bandy," he said, lowering his voice so as not to be heard several tables away. The curved ceiling of the dining room tended to bounce conversation a considerable distance. "You're really making your mark in Parliament."

"Some of my colleagues seem to think it's a black mark."

"Not at all, not at all, my dear fellow. You're doing just fine. We only wish we had somebody like you, with your inside knowledge and your amazing indifference to the fact that there's a general election coming up."

"You really appreciate my efforts, do you?"

"We certainly do."

"Maybe I should cross the floor and join your party, then."

"No, no, don't do that," Mr. Pugsley said hurriedly; then, patting my arm in a really friendly fashion: "No, you're much better off where you are, Bandy. So—keep up the good work, eh?"

Among the good work that I was keeping up were numerous attempts at a private interview with Mr. King. I felt sure that the Prime Minister would want to know that one of his ministers was accepting hefty favors from interested parties. With an election coming up in a few months, Mr. King would certainly be alarmed enough to take prompt action.

His inability to fit me into his busy schedule was particularly frustrating as I felt that he would surely be enormously grateful for my help in drawing his attention to a potential area of scandal. Unfortunately I never seemed to catch him at the right moment. If I moved toward him in the lobby, somehow a dense crowd would form around him, and by the time I had elbowed my way through he would have completely disappeared. And though I looked in the library every time I passed, he was never there, presumably having decided that he had no further use for reading and research.

Similarly, whenever I tried to make an appointment it was discovered at the last moment that he was abroad at some imperial conference, mending fences in Quebec, or visiting Tuktoyuktuk.

I even studied his habits, the better to nab him. He invariably rose at 10 A.M., read the Bible for half an hour, then dictated letters. He arrived for work promptly at noon. At one o'clock he dealt with cabinet business, then entered the House promptly at two-thirty, in time for prayers. *We pray for the King and the royal family,* and so forth. (Some malicious Tories claimed that he sometimes slurred his responses so as to omit the definite article before the word "King.") Accordingly I took to skulking around the private entrance to the west of the Peace Tower at twelve o'clock; but somehow that was always the day he used the main entrance. And when I hung around the main entrance he immediately went back to using the private entrance. But when I placed myself halfway between the two, it was always the day he decided to use the side entrance on the west side.

I just couldn't understand it. When I was there he wasn't, and when he was I wasn't. One morning I even hung around Rideau

Hall to try and catch him before he left, until two Mounties and three city cops closed in on me and nearly arrested me for loitering with intent to commit assassination or some similar nuisance.

However, Jacques Gassien proved willing enough to see me. On the day that the press reported my speech at a dinner dished up by the Manufacturers' Association, in which, among other topics, I had described in detail the luxurious life and sumptuous accommodation of Joseph Bisaillon, the Customs Department's chief preventive officer in Montreal (salary $3,850), one of my colleagues came up and said that the minister wished to see me in his office immediately.

"Oooh, now you're for it," he said.

Gassien kept me loitering without intent in the corridor for half an hour before calling me into his paneled office to ask why, despite many hints as to the government's displeasure, I was persisting in these allegations of "slackness" in his department.

"Well, you see, Minister," I said, shifting from one foot to another like Billy Bunter before the beak, "every time I run out of allegations, businessmen keep presenting me with fresh instances of irregularities among customs officials. So I have to keep talking, you see, to keep up with all the information."

He stared at me unblinkingly for nearly a minute, obviously attempting to discompose me; but today he had not the energy for the exercise. As it was a Monday, the poor devil was in a distinctly enervated state. He looked as drained as an embalmer's subject, with powerless grip and eyes like sunken ships. "Information?" he said at length, as forcefully as his shagged-out lungs would permit. "Is dat what you call dese disgraceful accusations dat are backed up wit' 'ardly an iota of proof?"

"It's—"

"Does it not trouble you dat you are slandering a department ooze only fault is dat it does not 'ave enough staff to enforce duh regulations—as I 'ave said repeatedly in duh Commons?"

"Trouble me? No, not really."

He studied me angrily for a moment before raising a feeble hand to gesture at the straight-backed chair opposite the desk. "Please. And 'as it not occurred to you dat dese business friends of yours—sit down, man, sit down—are making dese wild allegations against my department because of dere own inefficiency, because dey cannot stand duh competition from a few miserable smugglers? Dey are using you, Bandy, can't you see dat?"

"And here was I thinking I was using them, Minister."

"Does it give you pleasure to make dese vicious accusations against your own party?"

"No, sir."

"Why do you persist in doing so, den?" Gassien asked; then went on to employ the method that he had used effectively in the past, of following up a verbal trouncing with a gentle, regretful appeal, calculated to break down the most obdurate malcontent. "Listen, Bandy," he said softly, "don't you understand what damage you are doing to your own friends, by passing on dese mean slanders? Let me remind you of our recent 'istory, eh? After duh war, dis country was in a shambles, of 'atreds engendered by conscription and udder issues, including whedder we were to remain pawns and tools of duh imperial government, or whedder we were to strive to be an independent nation. Confederation seemed to be dissolving. The Maritimes were bitter and alienated, duh West was in revolt, my own province felt angry, isolated, and betrayed. Isn't dat so?"

"Wasn't my fault," I muttered defensively. "I was out of the country at the time."

"Five years later," he continued, "under a Liberal government, little of duh animosity is left. You agree, eh? We 'ave internal peace and quiet to pursue our affairs, dere is trust and friendship once more. Don't you t'ink dat in a situation dat should be encouraged, my friend, radder dan inflamed?"

"Yes, Minister."

"Of course. You see—you are a reasonable man after all," he cried, looking so touchingly grateful that I felt more caddish than ever. At which susceptible point he made the ultimate sacrifice. He rose to his feet. He forced himself erect with a shaky arm and tottered round the desk to put an almost weightless hand on my shoulder. "Now I personally," he said sorrowfully, "am not offended by dese wild insinuations concerning my department, for I know dey are completely unfounded. Dere are no more honest, conscientious, altruistic people in the entire government as my officials. I know dat for a fact."

"But—"

"Oh, dere is duh inevitable rotten apple in duh barrel, of course," he said with a regretful smile. "I would be duh first to admit dat. But is it fair to attack all duh apples because one or two of them have worms? Eh? As I say, Bandy, I am not personally offended. But dere is another 'oom you have caused much distress, and dat is Mr. King. Since we are elected 'e 'as striven to reunite duh country and 'as achieved it almost single-'andedly. Encouraged the people to unite once more and reestablished their self-confidence by making no upsetting decisions whatsoever, taking no action, overtly opposing no measure, speaking with no trace of dat forcefulness, originality, and logic with which duh leader of the Opposition repeatedly distresses duh country. Mackenzie King is a great leader, Bandy, and duh emotions you arouse with your letters and speeches and questions 'urt him very much. Why, only duh udder day when your name was mentioned in Cabinet, tears actually sprang to 'is eyes."

"Was only trying to help," I mumbled, drawing a circle on my kneecap with a forefinger.

"Of course you were, my dear Bandy," he murmured gently. "We all know your 'eart's in the right place. It's your brain that's mis— Anyway, honestly now, eh—does a man like dat not deserve at least a little loyalty, radder dan a constant barrage of lobbyings and pressures on be'alf of dese self-seeking commercial interests?"

By the time he had finished with me I felt such a disloyal swine that I very nearly promised there and then to behave less like a gritty Grit in future.

As if things were not difficult enough in Parliament, I also had George Garanine to contend with. A week after the wat of visky episode, he was still living in the Ottawa apartment and accompanying me every weekend to the farm, where we were readying the Gander for the moment the farm field was firm enough for a takeoff.

Actually he had offered to move out, "because you will be wondering if you are entirely safe with an assassin on the premises." But, "Nonsense," I cried, as we worked side by side outside the barn in the warm May sunlight. We were enjoying a brief hot spell that month, though as everybody agreed we would pay for it later. "Now that you've told me everything, I'm not the least worried," I said, adjusting the position of a short length of dead maple that I had picked up to tidy the farm field.

Nevertheless he was becoming more and more insistent on returning to Russia, to deliver himself up to the one man he truly feared. And one day, after completing the final engine test, he announced that he had made up his mind to do it.

"Do what?" I asked, picking up a wrench and idly twirling the knurled knob with an oily thumb.

"I must go back," he said, speaking down from the open cockpit of the Gander. He was leaning on the coaming, resting his face on his arms, the warm spring sunlight illuminating his unhappy mustache. "Even though that man will certainly find out that I know his secret, and will put a bullet in the back of my head, whether I have carried out his orders or not."

"Well, that settles it, surely. If he's going to bump you off, don't go."

"I cannot abandon my relatives, Bartalamyeh."

"If he's as ruthless as you say, will your going back save them anyway?"

"That is true. Perhaps it is already too late to save them," George said, brightening. "After all, it is over a month since I received final warning from Cheka."

A moment later he jumped down onto the grass behind me. I whirled, raising the wrench; then, noticing a nut, proceeded to tighten it.

But a few days later when I returned to the Rideau Street apartment from a late sitting, he was in an emotional uproar again, pleading with me to agree that it was his duty to go back, come what may.

"Don't you see?" he cried, twisting a brand-new necktie in his powerful hands—I knew it was brand new because it was mine. "I must at least try to save my relatives. All my life they have made such sacrifices for me. How can I not go back, if there is a chance to save them? Oh, my dear Anna—and poor Granny. And Lisa, Natalie, Grusha, Clava, and Dounatchka."

"And Irina and Olga," I said, feeling down the end of the living-room sofa for the butt of my automatic. It had slipped down there the previous evening.

The Victorian sofa so closely resembled a reclining woman that it was quite an exciting business, groping into its folds and crevices.

"Yes, of course," George said despairingly. "Irina and Olga."

"And Eugenie."

"Yes, yes. You understand, don't you, Bartalamyeh?" he cried. "I can't just abandon them to their fate." He clutched at his head. "Oh, God, why can I not make up my mind? What a weak, despicable creature I am."

He was so anguished, it was as if he were twisting his own heart between his desperate hands, rather than my necktie.

"Yes, you're right," I said somberly. "What else can you do?"

As he started toward me with the necktie I leaped over the furniture with one bound and sank my hand even deeper into the effeminate sofa.

"On the other hand," he said, halting uncertainly, "would Anna, Granny, Natalie . . . and all the others, wish me to sacrifice myself merely for their sake? I use the word 'merely,' of course, as they would use it, not in any demeaning sense."

He sat on the sofa, temporarily trapping my hand down the side. "Oh, Bartalamyeh," he said despairingly, "they love me, but how wrong they are to do so. I am not worthy. I am prodigal son returning not only with no talents in my purse—"

"Surely you have five hundred dollars in your bank account, the money from the smuggling trips. That should be enough to—"

"—but without even the enriching experience of dissipation," he concluded obliviously.

His eyes widened. He jumped up, fists clenched. "You see? My subconscious has already decided. I used the word 're-turning.'"

By then I was at the far end of the kitchen, pawing frantically through the knife drawer. He followed me in there, blocking the exit. "It is they," he cried desperately, "with their unselfish devotion, who are the worthy ones, not I. So I don't care what you say, Bartushka, I am returning. I am going back. It is my duty to go back. Do not try to stop me."

He started toward me. "Don't come any closer," I said, per-

haps a shade shrilly, as I snatched out a bread knife. Except that
when I held it aloft it turned out to be a tea strainer.

"You are making tea? Perhaps I also will have a glass. Possibly
the last glass of tea I shall ever drink," George said brokenly; but
instead made for his last bottle of Gold Bullion.

At midnight as I made ready for bed—sheet neatly turned
back, towel hanging on the radiator to dry, shoes polished and
lined up just so, sock filled with sand under my pillow—I heard
him lurching about in his own room, packing his few possessions,
arguing with himself and mumbling drunkenly; so I was careful
to slide the new bedroom bolt into place as quietly as possible so
as not to disturb his train of thought.

Naturally I didn't believe for a moment that he would return
to Russia and face the wrath of this Stalin fellow. He might be a
loving sort of person with his saintly tolerance and his affectionate behavior and his effortless charm, but he wasn't all bad.
He wasn't an idiot. I didn't think for a single moment that he
would actually leave and go back to his blighted homeland. And
he didn't. In the morning I found him sprawled face down at the
kitchen table, with a red stain spreading over his breast.

"George," I cried. "George. Oh, my God."

He looked up blearily. "What?" he asked.

"Haven't you been to bed all night?"

He looked around with bloodshot eyes to see whether he had
or not.

"So you didn't go after all," I said.

His face cleared, and for the first time in months he looked
just like the George of old, loving and serene.

"No," he said, smiling beatifically as he righted the ketchup
bottle. "I didn't go. I have made up my mind, dear Bartalamyeh."

And true enough, when I got back that evening he was gone,
leaving an empty whisky bottle, bedroom, and bankbook, and a
cotenant who did not know whether to feel delivered, soothed,
assuaged, or relieved.

But at midnight, just as I was emptying the sand out of my
sock, the doorbell rang. "I didn't think you'd be so ridiculously
honorable," I said scornfully as I hauled open the door.

"Me, honorable?" said Jim Boyce. He was holding onto the banisters outside in the corridor, his business suit stained and disheveled, his chin bristling with bristles. He was cockeyed, lit like the aurora, smellable from five feet. "If you mean women, last time I was honorable, it earned me a severe reprimand from 'Jolly' Roget, the port admiral at Plymouth," he slurred, "who was as ferocious as they come. I've been careful never to be honorable since. 'Cept, 'cept where it affects my self-respeck. Very 'portant, self-respeck, Bandy old man. 'M, 'm really quite an upright sort of person really, you know, 'cept in bed. 'N, 'n at this moment, of course."

"I thought it was George at the door. He's gone home."

"Gallop?"

"Moscow."

"My, my. But that's cause for celebration, surely."

"I guess. Come in."

He felt his way carefully into the living room, attempting to keep his balance by flapping his hands. He looked as if he were conducting a Mozart scherzo.

As he turned he lurched against the sofa. He lowered himself onto the cushions with great dignity. "A strange man, George," he said. "Christianity has always seemed to me a provincial playground for moral bullies, but I mush say George came close to the ideal. How else could he have put up with you all this time?"

"*Him* put up with *me?*"

"You're not the easiest person to get on with, you know. Fact, you're the most difficult I've ever 'countered. 'Cept Jolly Roget, of course.

"And that," he added, trying to aim his liquid brown eyes at me, "is the opinion of a friend, so 'magine what your enemies would say. I've been fired."

"That's ridiculous," I snorted. "I suppose you've got it the wrong way round because you're ossified. Good heavens, man, it's me who's the . . . he's the one who . . . You've what?"

"Been fired."

I stared at his bristly blue chin that had to be shaved twice a day to keep him looking unshaven, and at his otherwise nondescript features. "Fired? How? Why?"

"And not only me. The three of us on Inspector Duncan's staff who aren't pukka civil service have been axed. The three of us have been out all evening discussing the situation, as you can see."

I sank into the armchair opposite him, staring.

"And things were going so well, too," he went on, almost visibly sobering as the situation oppressed him again. "I was even invited to your Jacques Gassien's place, couple of days ago. 'Cept he had to leave early, to catch the night train to Toronto. But he insisted on me staying to keep his wife company."

"Oh?"

"Yeah. Trusting, wasn't he? Or was he? I thought it might be a trap—he'd come busting in at midnight, or something. So I didn't try anything.

"Funnily enough, it didn't have anything to do with my job, the investigation. He really did go to Toronto."

"Ah."

"He wasn't even aware there was a special investigation team. He just seemed to have heard about me from a friend of his called Clemenceau or somebody. No, Talleyrand. And wanted to look me over for some reason or other."

"M'm," I said, shaking my head to rearrange the carbon granules. "But to get back to you being fired. I thought your investigations were going well."

"'Zackly. Too well, I guess," Boyce said, as bitterly as his alcoholic depression would allow.

"And you don't think it was Gassien who got you fired?"

"I know it wasn't. He doesn't know anything about our report. Only one person apart from us has seen it, and that's the P.M."

"You think . . . ?"

"I don't think, I know. He's been sitting on it. Taking no action at all, even though the report proves conclusively that the customs is riddled with corruption, including his crony Gassien, of course. Until today. He finally did something about it today. He got the chairman of the Treasury Board to disband us."

"'Pon my word."

"So now the three of us are out of a job, and Inspector Duncan's going back to auditing shopkeepers' tax forms, or something equally vital. Got a drink?"

"There's none left. George drank it. . . ."

"Bashtard," Boyce said, but was apparently not referring to George. "He's been sitting on it. He isn't going to do anything about it, it's quite obvious. He'll do anything to avoid a scandal, with a general election coming up."

"Yes . . ."

"So," Boyce said, drawing a doubled-up, soft-cover copy from his breast pocket, "there it is. It's yours," he said, and laid the report carefully on the coffee table, then smoothed the cover with his hand, over and over, until at last it lay reasonably flat.

Gadzooks, it was good to be flying again, after a snowbound, cylinder-freezing, road-clogging, bone-marrow-harrowing winter, and not all the tribulations and trials, convictions and sentences of life could deduct one whit or tittle from the aeolian freedom. "Go up, young man," Horace whatsisname might have said. No laws or limits up here, no signpost clutter or irascible traffic, or farmers digging mud holes in the highway so they could charge the traveler to haul his auto from the gumbo. Even the most statebound bureaucrat had not yet thought of extending his spoilsport fiefdom into the air.

"Softly awakes my heart," I trilled as I danced the Gander over the vapor landscape. The clouds formed a dramatically broken terrain of plain and escarpment, mountain and valley, broken here and there with ragged, misty craters and deep, gray-green lakes of air, the bottoms of the lakes being the fields and hills eight thousand feet below.

A fleecy-edged field appeared ahead. It looked as flat as an anemic omelet. Just for fun I throttled back and landed on it; and shouted as the monoplane fell through, swooshing, stalling through the aeriform airdrome. For a moment there was the familiar sensation of guts strung from a kite, and a buffeting rush of wind; then we were into the sunlight again, below.

"Softly awakes my heart, tra-la-la-la-la-lalala." The compass was spinning, so I peered over the side of the open cockpit for orientation, to make sure we were still in the right country. Yes, there was the capital all right, roughening the horizon, hazily hatching the land with its straight street lines and the sun flashing Morse code from its wiggly river.

It was a gloriously warm day in May, or at least it was at ground level. After five months of ten-foot snowdrifts and ankle-snapping sidewalk ice, it was thrilling to see Mommy Nature brought back from the dead, the wan grass lighting up and the forests turning fuzzy green, and the lakes and rivers losing their shivery hues and changing to a merely frigid blue, or, in the case of the Ottawa River below, to a diarrheic umber. It was marvelous to feel warm again. No wonder Canadians went mad the moment the sun fed them a few decent calories—hordes of citizens rushing out of doors to hack at the flower beds and rick their backs, or hurtling up ladders to inspect the latest hole in the roof, or to throw off their winter clothing and sally forth in open necks or sleeveless dresses, exclaiming about the mildness—venturing ill clad into temperatures that, had they occurred in midsummer, would have set the populace to frenziedly stoking their potbellied stoves.

I was as appreciative as anyone at the sight of Mother Nature divested of her winter woollies. I felt quite carefree, in fact. After all, one couldn't always be preoccupied with such frustrating problems as how to approach an unapproachable Prime Minister, or to unrelievedly dedicate oneself to such vital national issues as compensation restraint, interim supply, or whether or not to chisel the bumblebees from the parliamentary urinals—a committee having been formed to deliberate on this issue, after it was learned that some Members had been competing to see who could hit the bumblebee target from the greatest distance, the champion so far being an Irish Progressive who, after celebrating St. Patrick's Day, had achieved a record of seven feet, eleven and a half inches.

As well as a revived joy of living inspired by the premature heat wave, I had an additional reason for celebrating. The restructuring of the Gander's tail appeared to have cured its rearing habit. After two whole years of aerodynamic posers, mostly caused by its amateur designer, the plump, high-winged monoplane with the comfy cabin and drafty pilot's cockpit was performing well. So well, in fact, that I intended making my first water landing this very afternoon.

So why, I asked myself now, was I wasting time joyriding in and out of the clouds, instead of getting on with it on this ideal Sunday? After all, though I had never put down on water before, I had accumulated a fair amount of information on the procedure from Jim Boyce. As a former R.N.A.S. flier, he had flown several types of seaplane, and he had assured me that it was far easier than land flying. For instance, in a seaplane you could almost always settle down and take off precisely into wind, and how often, he said, could you do that from an airdrome?

Boyce, who was once again staying with us on the farm, had gone over most of the pertinent points only this morning. "To begin with," he said, "for water operations you'll need three knots."

"That's pretty slow," I'd said. "Won't I stall into the drink?"

"You'll need to master three basic knots," he said patiently, having learned to ignore such responses. "The bowline, the square knot, and the double half hitch. To secure the floatplane, of course. I'll show you. Next you have to know how to control the machine in varying surface wind and current conditions. Have you ever handled a boat?"

"No."

"That's too bad. It'll behave like a boat, you know. Half the time you'll be pointing in one direction and going in another."

"That's all right—the Sopwith Camel did that all the time."

"Did it ever go backward?"

"Not while I was sober."

"Well, that's what's likely to happen with the Gander, when you're trying it out on almost any water surface. You could be moving upstream, for example, while headed downstream. And of course you've no brakes to stop you. Incidentally, I see you've no water rudders. How are you going to steer?"

"Gee, I never thought of adding those," I said, and listened more uneasily than ever as he described about a hundred problems connected with taxiing a plane through rough water, crosscurrents, brisk winds, and undertows.

I would also have to learn to work the floats onto the steps during takeoff, to estimate the wind direction from deceitful clues like choppy waves, to look straight ahead when landing and not glancing down and to the side as a land pilot did, and overcome the danger of bouncing back into the air if minimum speed was not maintained while landing in rough water. I would also face the difficult task of judging height in glassy water conditions—

"Great grief-stricken drumsticks, I thought you said it was easy," I shouted.

"'Tis, if you keep analyzing the situation every single second. Incidentally, are you sure those floats are properly stepped for unsticking? They don't look it."

"There's nothing wrong with them," I hoped loudly. "The man in the wrecking yard said they were off a U.S. Navy seaplane and had only been driven by a little old pilot on weekends."

"Did he mention how the floats came to be in the wrecking yard in the first place?"

"I'm beginning to detest you, Boyce."

"Well, they look awful shallow to me," Boyce said, kicking one of the floats. But then, making an effort to look optimistic: "Still, I don't suppose they'll dig in and cartwheel you into the riverbank if you're careful. After all, the rest of the airplane looks okay. Beautiful, in fact," he added, patting its sun-colored flanks.

"Tell you what, Boyce," I said, putting an arm round his shoulders. "For being so helpful, I'm going to give you the honor of doing the water trials yourself."

"What, in that horrible-looking craft? No, thanks," he said, hurriedly sliding out from under my arm. "You wouldn't catch me dead in any airplane you'd built."

"But you've already flown in it. From Long Island."

"Yes, you bastard, because you never mentioned that you were flying it for the first time, practically, and that you'd just built it from scrap."

"From scratch, you mean. Oh, come on, Boyce," I wheedled. "You've had hours of seaplane experience, I haven't had any. Look, if you'll fly it, I might even come with you," I said, giving him a really encouraging smile; which caused him to recoil a hundred yards back to the farmhouse for his prophylactics and another slice of Mother's pecan pie.

Darn him, I thought as I looked around for the Ottawa River eight thousand feet below, I should never have asked him for a

few tips, but simply gone ahead in blissful ignorance. After
learning how easy it was, I was now thoroughly apprehensive
about doing it.

However, there was no point in putting it off any longer—
especially as I'd used up half the four-hour supply of fuel—so I
hauled back on the throttle and began to glide down, imprisoned
behind the great bars of sunlight that were slanting from between the clouds.

Some minutes later the monoplane was droning along the Ottawa at a thousand feet, approaching the city from the west. I
had decided to try a river landing because I had been familiar
with the Ottawa since childhood and thought I knew it well. I
had a distinct memory of broad stretches of open water between
forested banks, or flat, cultivated fields, with hardly more than a
log here and there to break the monotony.

But now, as I goggled over the side, all the wider parts
seemed to be a sea of logs, corraled by vicious chains or great
sweeping booms. And where there were no logs there were rapids—frothing brown waters, swollen by the spring breakup, that
seemed to be traveling almost as fast as the Gander. The rapids
seemed to occur about every eight feet, a positive cascading cascara of hydrous material.

Parliament Hill came jutting up on the right. I could make out
a few tourists wandering about between the bulky shape of the
library and the steep cliff overlooking the swirling river. A group
of ladies in their Sunday best stared up, shielding their eyes from
the sun, as the Gander snored past.

By the time I'd reached the airdrome at Rockcliffe east of the
city, I'd confirmed that there wasn't a smooth stretch of water for
miles.

It was the same with the Gatineau River. As I turned north-
ward and flew alongside it, all I could see was boiling froth. So
obviously a river landing was out. Which meant that I would
have to try some lake or other. Well, that made sense. That was
why the Gander was an amphibian, after all: to take advantage
of the country's million lakes.

The village of Chelsea drifted by on the left, backlit by the in-
termittent sun. The afternoon train from Ottawa was just pulling
out of the station, two passenger coaches and freight cars loaded

with what looked like used mattresses. In a field on the outskirts of town, a farm machine was busily mauling the chocolate earth. On a dirt side road a jostle of urchins leaped and pointed as the plump yellow monoplane swept overhead.

After consulting the map, I turned due west into the Gatineau Hills, and by and by a lake showed up on the left: Pink Lake. But I didn't like the look of it, so I kept on, over the densely wooded terrain, civilized here and there by the posh houses of lumber barons and railway magnates, and finally a suitable lake appeared ahead and to the right.

After checking the instruments—the fuel gauge registered less than half full—I studied the flapping map again, located and measured the lake. It was eight hundred yards long, with an elevation of about the same number of feet. It looked very promising on the map, so I compared it with the reality as I flew alongside. The lake was surrounded by steep, wooded banks but otherwise looked very promising indeed. What was the name again? Kingsmere.

I'd never flown in this direction before, but the name sounded familiar. I tilted the stick and circled widely, nine hundred feet up, studying the shape of the lake and its approaches. It looked beautiful, a glittering, dark green body of water, roundedly rectangular in shape, with a little lake—Mulvihill—at one end, to the southeast. At the opposite end was a slope of grass. Otherwise the lake was completely surrounded by trees.

Kingsmere, Kingsmere . . . By the time I had completed the circuit I had remembered. Of course. The Prime Minister's beloved country estate.

He had purchased a cottage and a lot up here a few years previously and had been buying out his neighbors and adding to the property ever since. And here he spent every minute he could spare from his onerous duties. He would almost certainly be in residence, on a glorious day like this.

It occurred to me that I might be able to kill two birds with one stone: combine the water trials with a long-sought meeting with my leader. Accordingly, as I studied the sparkling waters for weeds, rocks, deadheads, and other hazards, I also kept an eye open for a plan view of Mr. King's distinctive pate. But though a wider sweep of the terrain disclosed his cottage

perched on a hill nearby—rather more than a cottage, actually: it
was a fine, symmetrical abode with a pair of dormers sleeping on
an expanse of green roof—there was no sign of its owner putter-
ing and pottering about the hilly retreat. Still, on a warm
insect- and floatplane-buzzing Sunday afternoon he was probably
having a nap, or communing with his mater. The only moving
creature in the vicinity was a deer in the front garden, busily nib-
bling the great man's peonies. It raised its head to stare at the
uncouth bird above before darting off toward the nearest sylvan
glade.

Satisfied that Kingsmere was as ideal a lake as I was ever
likely to find, I throttled back and circled to the west, then
banked around sharply. Five hundred yards ahead, the lake
slanted into view over the squat nose. The fuzzy forest unrolled
below, Mulvihill trickling past on the right.

I was having to make the final approach in a brisk crosswind—
so much for Boyce's assertion that one could invariably steer into
wind; he'd probably never put down in anything smaller than
the English Channel—but the wooded banks around the lakes
looked steep enough to shelter the airplane at the critical moment of touchdown, so I wasn't worried about that. I was aiming
the nose of the Gander about one third the way down the lake,
busily reviewing Boyce's other points and hoping they were
rather more helpful.

What was it he had said—concentrate on the point where you
expect to touch down? Throttle right back—you make a power
approach only when the surface is glassy and you can't judge the
height properly after rounding out. That was all right—the surface of the lake was scattered with broken glass.

The Puma engine was barely whispering as we passed over
the rocky ledge at the end of the lake. Two hundred feet up the
altimeter registered a thousand—this was a high-up lake, all
right. A quick glance at the air speed. Seventy—twenty above
stalling. Backward pressure on the stick, left wing down—the
wind was pushing the airplane toward the right bank. I could
feel warmer air gushing over my face. What else was there to
remember? If there was any difficulty about judging height
while holding off, I should pick a point ahead—a buoy, a boat, a
bank—and use that as a reference. Well, there was a rock about

halfway up the slope at the far end, but there was no need for it.
The dark green water, dappled with sunlight, looked as easy to
judge as the grass of the Machin farm.

The olive-green surface swept up. Quick glance at the air
speed. The only anxiety was the one planted by Boyce. Would
the long, shallow floats take kindly to the water? I really didn't
see why not—they were originally from a tried and tested seaplane—according to the supplier. I would find out in five seconds.

I leveled. Fortunately I was used to the not inconsiderable distance from the cockpit to the ground—my God, I hadn't cranked
the wheels down from sheer force of habit, had I? No, they were
up. But the thought hammered at my heart. The idea of landing
on water with wheels down—though maybe it wouldn't make
much difference. Cease these irrelevant thoughts, please. The
lake was flashing by underneath. The stick was properly inserted
into my belly button. We were down.

The sensation was quite unlike a grass-field landing. There
was no bump whatsoever, but a couple of seconds after the
touchdown the machine braked as if the tail had caught in a
purse seine. There was a loud hissing instead of a rumble, easily
audible over the whirring engine. Waves of white water lashed
back from the middle of the floats, and the machine continued to
slow at a rate quite amazing to a landlubber pilot.

But not slow enough to avoid running down the man who for
nearly a year I had been trying like mad to impress with my
dedication to the true principles of liberalism.

I don't know how on earth I'd missed the three of them. Perhaps they had been cavorting under the trees while I was scanning the surface. Even so, I had circled the lake three times to
assure myself that there were no obstructions. Of course, from
then on I had concentrated on getting down. Which was probably when the swimmers, a woman and two men, had entered the
water.

Thus much of it was their fault. They ought to have noticed
the floatplane when it lined up with the lake a third of a mile
away and approached with the faintly whirring blade and humming airfoil. But no. They had totally ignored the signs of an imminent landing and had splashed merrily into the path of the

Gander as if they had a perfect right to swim all over my aquatic
runway.

I didn't see one of the swimmers until I was almost upon him.
Then I became aware of a splashing ahead, and a circular face
with a rapidly widening hole in the middle of it. He was directly
in line with the rushing machine, which, though slowing markedly, was still shushing along at a rate of knots, spreading fat,
bubbly wakes from the two floats. But instead of thrashing off to
one side to get out of the way, the fool stopped swimming and
gaped, paralyzed, until his own inactivity caused him to sink
from sight.

A moment later he bobbed up like a cork, gasping and spluttering. At least the ducking had shocked him into action. Except
that, instead of behaving sensibly like diving under the surface
again until the airplane had passed overhead, he started swimming away from the aircraft as if he thought he could outdis-
tance a hefty six-seat cabin monoplane which had smacked into
his swimming hole at fifty miles an hour six or seven seconds
previously and which, despite the aforementioned braking effect,
still had a considerable momentum.

He realized his error only a second later and struck off to the
right—just as I trod on the right pedal. I had hoped to avoid him
by catching a dying breath of air with full rudder. Unfortunately
I managed it. The floatplane curved slightly to the right. Glancing wide-eyed over his shoulder as he thrashed along in a demented combination of the crawl, the sidestroke, dog paddle,
and backstroke, a method of propulsion suggesting that he was
being dragged under by a crocodile—it must have seemed to the
swimmer that the towering machine was deliberately trying to
intercept him. Which was nonsense, of course—except that it did.

Fortunately the nearest float didn't biff him on the boko but
merely scooped him onto its dorsal surface. The next thing he
knew he was dangling over the front of the float with his legs
trailing on one side and his baldish head swashing along on the
other, the dark green waters sluicing the wax out of his starboard
earhole.

A moment later the airplane, with silent engine—for I had
switched off in case the propeller finished the job by chopping
him into fatty mince—nosed into shore, the floats grounding with

a crunch, with Mr. King—for I now perceived that it was he—still draped limply over the float, like spaghetti.

For a ghastly moment I thought I had killed him. It was a great relief when I saw him struggle more or less to his feet in the shallows—except that his long, navy-blue bathing suit seemed to have snagged on the float's mooring ring.

Meanwhile his companions, recognizable, despite their natatorial dishabille, as Joan Patteson and her husband Godfroy, who had been bathing closer to shore, and who had long since beached themselves, seemed too shocked by the abrupt sequence of events to utter a word. So to break the tension I called down from the cockpit, "Well—finally caught up with you, eh, Mr. King. Or run you to earth, as it were," and laughed lightly, in the hope that he would join with me in not taking it too seriously.

Instead the sound of my voice caused him to start convulsively. Simultaneously he uttered a choking cry so violent that his teeth actually flew out.

As he was facing in my direction I was the only one to witness this development. I don't think even Mr. King was aware of it, despite the aquatic gnashing sound the teeth made as they plopped into the lake. I thought at first the ejaculation had blown his teeth out individually, but a moment's thought convinced me that they must have formed a complete unit to make a splashing noise like that. Individual teeth would surely have peppered the surface like buckshot. Yes, they must have formed a complete set.

I hadn't realized until then that he wore false teeth—presumably because he had never once smiled at me.

After that harassed, bridgework-propelling yoick, he seemed to become more feeble than ever, clawing rather pitifully at his costume which, as already mentioned, had caught on the mooring ring. I was just about to clamber down when Mrs. Patteson, pulling herself together and exclaiming incoherently, rushed down the bank to help him.

"Rex darling, are you all right?" she cried, and reached down to help disentangle him; until she saw that the mooring ring was caught in the southern sector of his bathing suit; whereupon she drew back in confusion, plainly unwilling to clutch, wrench, or paw in that region.

It was plainly a job for a man; so I looked across at Godfroy, but he was looking almost as disoriented as Mr. King. He was automatically collecting a variety of towels, bathrobes, and foot-gear from the bank—appropriately enough, I suppose, as he was a bank manager. Still, it was rather an unhelpful sort of activity.

However, Mr. King finally managed to free himself, rather fumblingly extricating the ringbolt from his long blue drawers—God knows how it had managed to work its way up his pants leg—whereupon he tottered to the bank and sank down, panting.

"Are you all right, Rex?" Mrs. Patteson repeated, bending over him and resting a solicitous hand on his twisted shoulder strap. Then straightened and glared up at the pilot, high up in his wooden hole behind the bulky engine.

"You fool," she cried. "You could have killed him."

There was a really angry expression on her motherly features, though after that first animadversion she fell silent, as if words were not competent enough to interpret her feelings about a fellow who would impale his own Prime Minister on a ten-foot float.

For a moment the silence continued, broken only by the click-ing of the cooling engine and the swash of wavelets on the shore. I looked away, perhaps a shade guiltily; then, whistling faintly but tunelessly, hung my leather flying helmet from the joystick and clambered down onto the float, and immediately began to feel around in the water for Mr. King's teeth, my hand swishing self-consciously through the green medium.

"Oh yes? And what are you up to now?" Mrs. Patteson man-aged at last. "Got your hands a bit dirty, have you, after nearly killing this poor man? Washing your hands of the whole affair, are you?"

"No, ma'am, just trying to find his, uh . . ." I mumbled.

"Any more help from you," Mrs. Patteson said bitterly, "and he's likely to expire completely. How could you? Whistling down without warning like that."

By then, Godfroy was also recovering from a sequence of events that, though quickly concluded, may possibly have been a bit harrowing while they were in progress. He started to join in

with a volley of recriminations, his face stiff with belated outrage; but stopped suddenly when a whimper issued from his
wife's best friend.

Mr. King appeared to be speaking. We all leaned forward to
listen.

"What do you exshpect?" he was mumbling, a bit indistinctly.
"I knew it wash him again. I knew it inshtinctively as shoon ash
I heard that tremendoush splash and shaw that huge machine
bearing down on me with itch rasher-edged propeller shlicing
away just a few inches from my—"

But then it was his turn to stop suddenly, as he realized for the
first time that his portcullis was missing. He clapped a shaking
hand to his mouth and emitted an odd sort of diminuendo plaint,
of a sort suggesting that he would have welcomed an earth-
quake, complete with fissure opening beneath his wet, wrinkled
bathing suit, to swallow him up.

I guessed he was covering his mouth to hide his fangless condition from the other two, who had apparently not noticed the
dental ejection.

I must confess I felt rather bad about the whole business, and
after removing my leather flying jacket, for it was decidedly
warm at ground level, I began to search the lake bottom more
determinedly than ever.

Honestly, I had never had the slightest intention of causing
him distress. The truth was I felt sorry for the old fellow, not
least because he was such an awful flop as a personality. If only
he had given people a chance to like him he would have gotten
on much better. After all, it wasn't as if he had no redeeming
qualities. Though I had not experienced any myself, I understood that he had quite an attractive side to his character. More
than one of his acquaintances—two, in fact, the journalist Bruce
Hutchison and somebody else—had told me that he could be
thoroughly charming when he wished. He was even said to have
a sense of humor, having made many an amusing remark about
his cabinet colleagues—behind their backs, to save them embarrassment, of course.

As for his dull demeanor, it was said to be a front, put up
purely for political reasons, a wooden facade designed to fool his
opponents into thinking there was no structure behind it but a

few rotten two-by-fours. And though he was mean to his officials
and servants, he was invariably humble in the presence of men of
stature, deferential to them, it was said, to the point of absurdity,
considering his not inconsiderable accomplishments, such as
reuniting the country after the conscription ruckus.

But even if he had been as awful as he seemed, I could hardly
have felt anything but sympathy for him now, seeing him huddled up there on the grassy knoll, hiding his bridgeless mandible
and moaning brokenly through the celery stalks of his fingers. So
on an impulse I emerged from the lake and hurried forward to
help him, as his friends, not understanding the situation, seemed
to be at a loss as to how to comfort him.

"Here, sir, let me give you a hand," I said.

Before I could even grasp his arm, he had shot to his feet with
an amazing renewal of energy and recoiled, warding me off with
his hands as if I were something from ten thousand fathoms.
"No, no, ish all right, I'll managsh—keep away," he cried, and
stumbled away up the slope toward his cottage. And he was
soon traveling so fast that the Pattesons actually had to canter to
catch up with the poor bloated figure in its wet, crinkled bathing
suit and matching mouth.

Obviously in a state of shock, I thought, resuming my search
of the lake and trying not to feel offended at the way he and the
Pattesons had left their guest to search for the teeth all by himself, without so much as a word of excuse or apology.

A couple of minutes later, to my surprise, I actually found
them. Holding them triumphantly aloft between thumb and
forefinger, I hurried after the others. But when I got to the cottage the door was firmly closed.

Assuming that they were dressing and being nothing if not a
considerate person, I sat on the wall at one end of the veranda
and hung around the front of the cottage for a good fifteen minutes, enjoying the warm May sunshine, before deciding I'd given
them enough time to dress. Whereupon I returned to the front
door and rapped on it once or twice, until I realized that I was
using Mr. King's teeth as a door knocker. As this was quite likely
to loosen the incisors I transferred the teeth to my other hand—
with my eyes averted: they were a bit slimy—and used my
knuckles instead.

However, I had obviously not given the three of them enough time to dress, for nobody answered the door for quite a while, and I finally had to go to the window and peer in, shading my eyes from the reflection, then tap gently on the glass, before Godfroy, his face flaming, finally came to the front door.

Before he could speak I said quickly, "Sorry to bother you, but you see I have Mr. King's bridgework."

His affronted expression collapsed like a mud slide.

"What?" he asked after a moment.

"His, well, teeth."

"What?"

I held up the dentures between thumb and forefinger. Like me, the teeth were wearing an apologetic smile.

Godfroy started.

I proffered them—but then took them back for a second to pluck a slimy leaf from between two of the molars, before tendering them again.

"What . . . what were you doing with his teeth?" Godfroy asked faintly.

"I'm not doing anything with them, apart from, you know, cleaning them."

"He gave you his teeth to clean?" Godfroy asked, looking as usual, quite out of his depth.

"No, no. They were resting on a sunken log. Under the water."

"A sunken log?"

"They were sort of partly embedded in the rotting wood—almost as if they were biting the log. Man bites log," I added, to lighten the atmosphere a bit. "It was just as well, or I would never have found them otherwise in the debris—the slimy leaves, forest detritus, et cetera."

"I don't—" he began; but then stopped and closed his eyes. "I see," he said at length.

"Here, he'll need them, I should think," I said. Then, when Godfroy finally accepted them: "And while you're at it, old man, I wonder if you'd mind telling him that we have something of considerable importance to discuss." And I added that I wasn't leaving until I had done so, proving it by leaning against a veranda pillar and folding my arms.

Mr. King emerged only a minute later, dressed in baggy black trousers and a large, shapeless pullover. He still looked a trifle shaken. His face was the color and shape of a mushroom, round and mushy and sort of ragged at the edges; but his eyes were lively enough. They were like the points of two-inch masonry drills.

"What do you want?" he asked, quite visibly holding himself in. But before I could answer: "I should warn you that I have telephoned for the police to have you thrown off this property and taken into custody. They should be here at any moment."

"Oh dear."

"They always said I should have a guard up here. I never thought it was necessary. Until now. I forgot about you, Bandy. You're just the kind of person who would invade somebody's privacy—in as lethal a manner as possible, of course. Well, I'm going to press charges of assault—and for once I don't care if there is a scandal, if it will help to get you out of my, out of my . . ."

He was clenching and unclenching his fists and actually panting, as if from the exertion of forcing out the words through his restored and, I hoped, thoroughly sterilized dentures. "You are the most awful person I have ever, ever come across in my life. The most conceited, arrogant, interfering, insensitive"—he paused again to pant, and scan his inhibited vocabulary for further choice synonyms—"revolting, jumped-up parvenu I have ever come across." In a gesture remarkably dramatic for him, he raised his fists a good three inches from his seams. "You seem to think that because you attained some notoriety during the war and some highly dubious fame after it in America—"

"Ah, you've been following my career, sir—"

"Shut up, shut up! I will not have you speak to me in that heedless whine, or look at me with that face of yours, as if I were providing you with an interesting précis of your accomplishments. . . ." And he raged on and on for a good three or four minutes, until he was actually bouncing up and down on the veranda in his fury, which didn't seem a terribly good idea to me, as the planks were a bit spongy in places; until finally he saw a cloud of dust in the distance and concluded, "And here they are now. Now you're going to pay for it at last."

A large black car appeared in the distance and approached

rapidly along the gravel road that led to the cottage, its engine roaring almost as loudly as Mr. King.

"Interestingly enough, it's careers I came to talk about, Prime Minister," I said. "It's about the Customs Department in general and its minister in particular—"

"Don't you dare go on about that again with those vile insinuations," he screamed.

"They're more than that now," I said. "I have a copy of the Duncan report."

The black car skidded to a halt at the front of the cottage where the gravel driveway petered out into the grass, and four scarlet-coated Mounties dismounted and marched toward us, led by a large sergeant with a chin like a backhoe.

The sergeant clumped noisily onto the veranda and halted a few feet away. "Is this the man, sir?" he asked, frisking me with his eyes, while the other Mounties moved casually behind me.

There was a hinge-squeaking sound as the Pattesons peered cautiously from the cottage doorway.

"What?" Mr. King said.

A hand appeared from behind and encircled my upper arm.

"The trespasser, sir?"

"What? Yes. No."

"Sir?"

"No, this is . . . We made a mistake."

"Sir?"

The sergeant waited for Mr. King to continue, but he was busily staring into the distance. The sergeant turned to me. "Your name, sir?"

I started to answer but was interrupted.

"I'm sorry, Sergeant. It was a mistake," King said with an effort. "This is one of my"—he swallowed—"colleagues. Mr. Bandy. He's a Member of Parliament."

The sergeant looked at us uncertainly, trying to interpret the Prime Minister's rigid stance. But as I was jacketless and apparently not threatening the P.M. in any way, he relaxed slightly.

So did the grip on my arm, and a voice behind said, "Yes, it's him all right, Sarge. The one who admitted he was a rum-runner."

"A former rumrunner, of course." I smirked at the sergeant. "Now, of course, completely respectable."

King looked at me. Then he stared into the distance again.

"I see. Then you don't need us, sir?" the sergeant asked.

"No. You can go," King said curtly.

The sergeant was still looking puzzled as he turned back to me. "You weren't in the force at one time, were you, sir?"

"No."

"Funny. Thought I recognized you."

"You're thinking of Blenkinsop, Sarge," said the knowledgeable voice at my elbow.

"Blenkinsop?"

"You know. In that movie. Where he was doing the musical ride on a moose?"

A light dawned in the sergeant's eye. "Oh yeah," he said grimly, and for a moment looked as if he were going to arrest me after all.

Mr. King was silent for quite a while after they had left. The Pattesons had also withdrawn, after a reassuring if somewhat strained smile from Rex.

Finally he said tiredly, "I'm not involved personally, of course."

"Never thought you were, Prime Minister."

"The trouble is, there is a great deal of money in that business, and not all civil servants are convinced that the honor of serving the country is sufficient recompense." His face sagged as he looked at me. "And you, Bandy. What do you want?"

"Me? Gee, I dunno," I said. I didn't know what else to say. It didn't seem the time for moralizing. Except: "But obviously it should be brought out into the open."

The P.M. winced. "That's what you want, is it?" he asked. "To destroy the Liberal Party? For that's what will happen. We'll never survive the next election."

"I don't suppose you will personally, sir, but I wouldn't worry," I said reassuringly. "There's lots of other jobs."

"Look here," he said. "You approached the Defence Department last year, I believe. About an order for some flying machine you had designed."

"Yes, that's right, sir."

"I've been thinking, Bandy. Conditions have changed over the last few months. There's a growing awareness in the Cabinet about the importance of defence." He hesitated, his mushroom-colored face darkening with bitterness. "Look here," he went on with an effort, "if you tried again, it's possible that we might look upon the application rather more favorably this time."

For a moment all sound ceased. A woodland buzz saw stopped buzzing, a distant blue jay stopped screeching, the rotten veranda planks underneath stopped groaning. Then there was a patting sound. It was me, patting myself agitatedly.

I snatched out my new pipe and pouch and began to stuff tobacco into the bowl.

"There is certainly no doubt," King went on tonelessly, "that the air force, for instance, needs new equipment. It would be a genuinely worthwhile investment for the country. Assuming, as I think we can, that the machine is as good as you claimed."

"It certainly is, sir," I said. "It's the one that just ran you down."

For a moment I thought I had gone too far, when his eyes went all filmy and he clenched his fists so tightly that the knuckles seemed to be bursting from their dermatological gloves.

However, after a moment he said through his nice clean teeth: "Yes, well, the point is, we couldn't afford it last year but, as I said, times have changed and . . . Possibly we might consider an order for, say, ten machines?"

"Ten?"

"Twenty," he said harshly. "That's the best I can do without going to Parliament for more money."

I looked at him, then, forgetting I had just filled it, rapped my pipe against a veranda pillar. A shower of shag rained onto the planks.

"In exchange for the Duncan report?" I asked.

He didn't answer.

After a moment I picked up my flying jacket and started down the steps.

"Do I understand you're turning it down?" he called out, sounding as if every word was being forced through a mangle.

"Yes, that's right," I said, and as I couldn't think of anything else to say, strode off down the slope, and fifteen minutes later was up in the air again, having taxied against various crosscurrents, breezes, and undertows, and worked the floats onto their steps and rocked them off the clinging surface of the lake without actually figuring out exactly how it ought to have been done.

Question time in the House was usually quite a stimulating affair. Some M.P.s' queries were innocuous enough, designed merely to obtain information from heads of departments, but many were polemical, aimed at exposing federal fumbling, or at scoring political points, or at infuriating a minister in the hope of driving him into an intemperate remark or commitment.

Particularly entertaining were the series of questions that were actually speeches in disguise, decorated with colorful interrogative marks. I had never tried this trick myself as to do it well required the skill of an Arthur Meighen. With his cold, flawless rhetoric, the Tory leader was particularly adept at this method of driving the Speaker to despair and his opponents into a cats' concert of frenzied frustration.

Naturally it was the Opposition who asked most of the controversial questions, in order to embarrass the government. We Liberals were expected to be supportive and to bolster the bigwigs. If we had any nasty questions to ask, we were expected to reserve them for the caucus meetings. Kicking one's own party in the shins in public was definitely not done. So it was with considerable apprehension, seasoned with vaunting ambition, that on the following Tuesday, May 13, I gave notice of my most damaging question yet, on the operations of the Customs Department.

Shaped like an iceberg, it would certainly scrape the barnacles off the government bottoms, all right. It had an innocent tip but a subterranean mass—the evidence accumulated by Inspector

Duncan through his seizure of books and records, and the signed statements of his exceedingly reluctant witnesses. My question read: *Would the Minister of Customs and Inland Revenue provide details about the seizure in Montreal last October 21, by his chief preventive officer, of thirty-two thousand gallons of duty-free spirits?*

When Jacques Gassien got up to answer, it would be like drinking from a spittoon—once started, he would have to keep going. He would be forced to progress from one damaging admission to another, starting with an explanation as to how the two bargeloads of confiscated liquor had subsequently disappeared from a bonded warehouse.

He would know that, if he didn't explain in full, the Duncan report would do so for him, outlining the story of how the barges had been seized in the St. Lawrence by a group of customs men; how their superior, Joseph Bisaillon, the chief preventive officer, had released the consignment to Tony Batt a week later, after bribing his underlings into silence and augmenting his own $3,850 salary with a deposit of $30,000.

That would be only the first of a long series of disclosures about corruption in the Department, involving, among others, nine of the twenty-four inspectors of ports and the minister himself. First there would be a spilling of individual beans in the form of supplementary questions, and then the complete plateful, in the speech that the Honorable Member for William and Mary would undoubtedly be called upon to make in the debate that was bound to follow.

Well, I had tried to bring the matter up in caucus, but my colleagues, perhaps under the impression that it was to be just another series of, as they saw it, vicious accusations, had shouted me down, and the party leader had made sure that I was given no further opportunity to speak. So I could see no alternative but to open the Duncan report for public inspection.

I have to admit, of course—well, I don't *have* to, but the occasional admission of some minor fault is useful for impressing people with your overall honesty, especially when you are being deceitful—I must admit that my bean-spilling motives were not entirely altruistic. I was not *exclusively* concerned with the public interest. I hoped I was also furthering my career. I felt sure that the disclosures would establish me so firmly as a national figure—the fellow who had put the national interest above party politics despite enticements and pressures that would have tempted or crushed an ordinary mortal—that not even the enmity of the party bosses could undo me.

Of course I was taking a risk. More than once, Hormidas Talleyrand reminded me that Liberals were always ready to reward their loyal supporters with the juiciest jobs going, but were likely to be lastingly hostile to those they considered to have been disloyal. But I didn't believe that for a moment. While they were in opposition, Liberals had repeatedly asserted that the people had a right to the truth. Mind you, they hadn't asserted it quite so forcefully since taking office themselves, but still—I was ready to take them up on it. Though aware that I would not be regarded benevolently by the bigwigs for a while, I was convinced that ultimately my determined stand would gain me respect and preference. Sooner or later they would realize that I had acted as a true Liberal in the best interests of the country.

So why was I gnawing my knuckles and sweating like an unlagged pipe? About ninety minutes after I had gingerly shoved the verbal iceberg into the executive sea lanes, I was lolling in my seat in the House, physically present at the Health debate, but feeling as if I were in the trenches again, waiting to go over the top. Mr. King would certainly have been informed of the question by now. Having read the Duncan report, he would know what was behind the barge affair. I wondered what he would do. I almost hoped it would occur to him to announce Gassien's resignation from the Cabinet before my question came up, and then reveal the contents of the report and take the credit for himself. But I didn't think he would dare. The contents were so scandalous that they would almost certainly bring down the government. At the very least they would scupper King's chances in next year's general election.

So why was I doing a Hercules act on the Grit pillars? A chill ran down my spine as it occurred to me, really for the first time, that I could very easily bring the party crashing down. The French-Canadian Members would be safe, of course—Quebeckers had a high tolerance for patronage, pocket-lining, jobbery, and other political peccadilloes, provided they were in on it, but

the Puritan indignation of the rest of the country would almost
certainly result in a Tory landslide.

God, what was I doing? Suddenly I felt so chilled that I actually shivered. The more I thought about it, the more craven I became. No, but honestly—was the public's right to the truth worth
the devastation, even if the party had brought it on itself with its
own arrogance and complacency? I suddenly recalled those vicious cogitations in the Vimy, as I flew home from that disaster
in the woods. God, I must have really meant them, those anar-
chic reflections; I was behaving like a Kropotkin in the name of
truth. But what is truth? asked the jesting pilot. Would the people be any better off for knowing that one out of eighteen honest
departments and portfolios was riddled with corruption? After
all, it was the public, through its representatives, who had demanded the prohibition that had inevitably led to the corruption.
It was the public's fault that the greedy and the dishonest were
now burrowing like termites into the administrative joists. So
what bloody right had the ordinary citizens to a volume of facts
that might not philosophically add up to the truth at all?

But I supposed I was starting to dissemble out of pure funk.
Maybe they did have a right, for the alternative was infinitely
worse than the temporary harm to a mere political party. If the
afflicted government went untreated, the country might end up
like Russia with its state cancers.

All the same, Christ, I wished now that I had never started it.
Why, why did I always have to clash so disastrously with authority? Why could I not have been born complacently middle-aged
like most Canadians? Help, help, I thought, get me out of this.

"What's going on?"

I started, jerked awake from a nightmare image of myself as
the sole occupant on the Opposition benches next year, facing
massed banks of triumphant Tories, hated and despised by the
entire Liberal community. I looked up haggardly. Cyril Hawkspat had wandered over during the debate and was kneeling
backward on the empty seat in front of me.

"Say, bo, what's up with duh big shots?" he asked out of the
corner of his mouth, trying to sound like a gangster and looking
like an aging school prefect. "Why dey all lookin' so punk, huh?"

I looked dismally across at the front bench and had to admit that there was an air of ministerial tension down there. None of them was listening to the current speaker on the far side of the clerk's table. Several cabinet ministers had moved into the seats around the Minister of Justice and were holding a whispered conference.

"How do you mean?" I asked evasively.

"Well, for one thing, look at Nervous Ned," he whispered, indicating the Minister of Defence. "He looks as if somebody's just tried to run him down with a tank. And what's happened to Gassien? There must be something behind all these furtive palavers and corridor conclaves. Three cabinet meetings in two days, the P.M. twitching like an electrocuted frog—and it's something to do with you. Have you got us into a war with the Turks or something?"

He looked more alert than ever as a page appeared at my elbow and handed me a note. I read it, then nodded at the lad.

"What is it?" Cyril asked.

"Oh, just the P.M.," I said, tucking the note carelessly into a waistcoat pocket—the one covering a suddenly thumping heart. "Wants to see me as soon as it's convenient."

"You *have* got us into trouble with the Turks," Cyril said mock accusingly, but still looking annoyed at not being taken into my confidence, and even more so when he saw half the front bench turning to watch as I slipped out through the curtains.

I had only a minute or so to wait in the big caucus room adjoining the P.M.'s office, so that I had hardly time to read the mottoes over the doorways—*Honour God,* and *Honour King*—or, no—Honour *the* King, was it? before I was admitted to the noble office with its carved woodwork, exquisite windows, and the frescoes that Mr. King had commissioned to illustrate the concepts of Moderation, Toleration, Botheration, etc.

And there I was struck all of a heap when I received a handshake for the first time, a comfortable chair for the first time, and a fill of tobacco from a humidor especially ordered from Public Works.

Unlike his cabinet colleagues, Mr. King appeared to be in a relaxed, even confident mood that afternoon. "I understand you smoke the occasional pipe," he said, pushing forward the humidor with hesitant fingertips, as if torn between repulsion over its contents and a desire to appear hospitable. "Please help yourself, Bandy. I hope they have selected a suitable brand of tobacco for you."

"It's very good of you, sir," I said, nervously snatching out my pipe. "But you shouldn't have, honest."

"We're ready to go to any lengths to see you settled, my dear Bandy," he replied, baring his teeth—then hastily covering them up again.

He leaned back and intertwined his fingers over his bulging waistcoat and said almost heartily, "Well, I gather you managed to fly off from the lake without too much difficulty the other day."

"Yes. I really am sorry about that, Prime Minister. But you see—"

"That's all right,' he said magnanimously. "No harm done. Perhaps I'll even be able to relate it as an amusing anecdote sometime in the distant future." Swiveling his eyes away, he riffled a thumbnail over the deckled edges of his desk diary. "However, that's not what I wanted to talk to you about. I've brought you in to offer you the post of P.M.C."

In the cynical silence that followed, he shifted about under my blank stare, hunching his shoulders, then snatching up a paper knife in the shape of a Toledo sword.

"Well? Would you be willing to take it over?"

"P.M.C., eh?" I said, stretching out my legs and crossing my ankles thoughtfully. "That's . . . fairly flattering, sir," I said—cautiously, in case it wasn't. I had no idea what a P.M.C. was.

"What made you decide to offer it to me?" I asked, hoping his reply would incorporate a clue.

"We've discussed it at length, Bandy, and we've decided that it might work out quite well."

Not much help there. P.M.C., P.M.C. Prime Minister's Companion? That didn't seem too likely. He already had Joan Patteson. Postmaster's Confederate? Puppet Maker's Collaborator? Pre-Marital Caretaker?

In the air force, P.M.C. had stood for President of the Mess Committee, who was responsible for collecting sixty francs a week and ordering tins of plum duff, but I didn't think that could be it, either.

I listened carefully as he went on. "After all, you have many of the qualifications, Bandy. You were a soldier, your awards and decorations should be able to fill up at least two lines in the *Almanac*, you . . ." He faltered, as if already running out of qualifications; but then rallied manfully. "And so forth," he said.

So the job was military, was it? Something in the Paymaster's office? I wondered, as I tamped down my baccy, sucked a flame into the bowl of the pipe, and blew out great clouds of burning vegetation.

My noncommittal expression seemed to unsettle the old man. Speaking anxiously through a fit of coughing, he went on, "There would be an urgh-urgh, considerable monetary increase, of course, urgh-urgh, urgh. Seven thousand a year with the usual urgh."

I stared, and whined slightly. That was beaucoup de berries. Even more than I had earned in half a dozen rumrunning trips. Being a P.M.C. was obviously no minor responsibility.

However, I thought it was high time I asserted the eternal verities, temporarily, at least. "You wouldn't be wanting me to withdraw a certain question, would you, Prime Minister?" I asked archly. "You know, as a sort of 'exchange is no robbery' arrangement?"

"There are no conditions whatsoever, Bandy," he said.

I stared rudely. "Really?"

"Absolutely none that I can think of at the moment. In fact I admire a man who asks questions. How else are we to learn, my dear fellow?" he said, and started to take a deep breath preparatory to continuing; but changed his mind and instead fanned a cirrus of gaseous nicotiana away from his head, with a kind of restrained frustration, as if he were an East Indian with a sacred cow standing on his foot. "Provided, of course, that the intent is not purely eristic. As for the particular question to which I assume you're referring, that will be dealt with in due course. But not by Mr. Gassien. He will no longer be with us by then."

"Oh? You're finally doing something about all the bribery, after sitting on the Duncan report for weeks?" I asked, regarding him through dangerous slitted eyes—the pipe smoke was making even my eyes water.

A muscle spasmed in his cheek, but after a while he continued in the same even, almost wheedling tones. "For the time being, suffice it to say that I have every intention of acting on the report, sooner or later, just as I have always acted, where absolutely necessary, for the good of the country, believing as I do with all my heart that its interests will not best be served by acrimony and conflict, or by purely sensational revelations that might give satisfaction to the yellow press and to our enemies, yours and mine, may I remind you, Bandy, and to the enemies of God and truth and the democratic system, rending the fabric of a society that, at a time of sadly declining morality that amounts almost to sensual and intellectual nihilism, must for its own safety and ultimate well-being maintain at least a modicum of trust in the principles of government for which so great a sacrifice has been made throughout the centuries from the signing of the Magna Carta, not least by brave young men such as yourself—"

"I didn't sign it," I said quickly. "I never sign anything unless it's absolutely—"

"I was referring to the sacrifices, not the signing of the Magna Carta."

"What you just said—you mean you're anxious to save the party, sir?"

"Yes," he said simply, and with such humility and sincerity that his eyes actually filled with tears. At least I think they did, behind all the smoke. "But we can discuss that later. At the moment we need a quick decision on the appointment of a new head of the Militia Council. Richardson has agreed to step down on account, as we have convinced him, of his health. And with a general election coming up shortly it seems an appropriate time for a cabinet shuffle." He flipped over several pages of his desk diary, then flipped them back again and waited.

He wasn't looking at me. I wasn't looking at him either. I was staring at the paneling behind him, with eyes like manhole covers. My mouth, which a moment ago had been clamped over my pipe, was hanging open.

President of the Militia Council. It was another title for the Defence Minister.

He was appointing me to the Cabinet.

As the singing in my ears subsided somewhat, I became aware that he was droning again.

"Sorry . . . what were you saying?" I asked, my voice pulsing as if somebody were rhythmically beating me on the back with a Wellington boot.

"I was reminding you that defence is another field in which you have shown some interest, isn't that so? I seem to remember some comments about the services being somewhat underbudgeted?"

"Yes . . . I seem to remember that too," I reverberated, already visualizing myself at the head of the entire armed forces of the Dominion of Canada: one seaworthy frigate, dozens and dozens of officers and even a few men, several aircraft—*warehousefuls* of faulty Ross rifles . . .

There was such a hot feeling in my loins that for a moment I thought I had become aroused at the prospect of joining the government; until I realized that it was only my pipe, which had fallen into my lap.

The astounding thing was that there were no conditions attached. God, what a selfless person Mackenzie King was, what a sublime leader, what a splendid altruistic person he was.

"Oh, I forgot, there is just one condition," he said.

I waited, picking dreamily at my charred flies, prepared to make the sacrifice if he asked me to hand over my mother.

"The condition is that, for reasons that will shortly become evident to you, we must have an immediate answer. So that we can make our dispositions accordingly."

"You mean, I have to decide right now?"

"And you must also give me your word not to discuss the appointment with anyone whatsoever until it has been formally announced and confirmed."

"But," I cried, rising and pacing like a caged mole, "I can't possibly decide without thinking, not this time."

"Don't worry, I myself have thought long and hard about it. Do me the courtesy of reciprocating, Bandy. You must make up your mind now. A great deal hangs on your decision."

"But, but . . ."

"I had to fight for this appointment," he said gravely. "My cabinet colleagues were unanimous in their opinion that it was

far too risky a course of action, and it was with much difficulty
that I overcame their objections and persuaded them that I knew
your potential as well as your limits, and that it would work out
satisfactorily in the end."

"But, but . . ."

"An entire department might be yours, Bandy. The Ministry
of Defence. Think of it."

"But what's made you change your mind about me, sir?"

"I assure you I have not changed my mind."

"But you cordially detested me—not all that cordially, either."

"I have to confess that I had certain reservations in the past
but, believe me, that is all behind us now. We must consider
only what is best for the party and for the country."

"Me . . . Minister of Defence . . ." I whispered, sinking back
into the best armchair.

"It is an offer that will not likely come your way again, Bandy.
I have fought for you. You're not going to let me down, are
you?"

"And there are no other conditions?"

"None whatsoever. Only your loyalty—Bartholomew," he said,
with a second ghastly smile in eleven months.

"Of course I could do remarkable things in that position—
Mackenzie," I faltered.

"I have not the slightest doubt about that."

"But, Rex—how can I be certain I'm doing the right thing?" I
cried, tortured.

"I know I am doing the right thing, and that is all that matters. I was never more certain in my life," he said, and actually
looked me straight in the eye.

An entire two minutes sidled by before I finally gave him my
answer.

Whereupon he sat back in his chair, holding the little Toledo
sword—which had somehow become badly bent—and looking as
if an immense burden had at long last been lifted from his shoulders.

I was really touched by the suppressed intensity of his relief.
He had obviously had much more confidence in my abilities than
I had ever suspected.

I was still feverish with excitement late the following day as I drove the Pierce-Arrow to Rockcliffe Airdrome and hastened over to the Avro, trailed all the way by photographers, who proceeded to take numerous pictures of me as I fired up with the aid of an air force mechanic—one of my men—and took off, gloating, into the gloaming.

With the arrival of warm weather and firm ground, it had occurred to me that I could now fly back and forth between Ottawa and Gallop in minutes, instead of making the tedious trip by road or rail. Accordingly I had dusted off the Avro and flown it to Rockcliffe on the Monday. Now, on Wednesday, May 14, a date with no historical significance whatsoever, the arrangement came in exceedingly useful, as I was more than a little anxious to give the folks in Gallop the good news as soon as possible.

As I flew over Parliament Hill on the way south, I smirked down at the real estate as proprietorially as if I had just taken an option on it. Twenty-six hours after that momentous interview with Mackenzie King I could still hardly believe it, even though it had been officially announced in the House that very afternoon. Me, Minister of Defence. After only six months on the back benches. It was not an unprecedented promotion in parliamentary history, but it was surely the most controversial. When the resignation of the incumbent had been announced and I stood up to confirm my appointment in a speech throbbing with promises, there had been a stricken silence from my Liberal colleagues, followed by such an uproar from the other side that the Speaker had finally given in and abandoned all formal procedure until the House had more or less pulled itself together.

Actually I was rather disappointed in the Opposition. They had encouraged me vociferously enough in the past when I ventured some apologetic criticisms, but now that I was in a position to rectify a few problems, they were not nearly so enthusiastic. Noting the vicious expression on the face of the former Minister of Defence, the mysterious disappearance of Jacques Gassien, and the stony attitude of the P.M. and his refusal to amplify his original remarks on the appointment or to be drawn into the subsequent discussion—if that was the right word to describe the storm of scorn and cynical laughter that had erupted—the Opposition seemed to suspect that some arrangement had been made

that was unworthy of the dignity of Parliament. Rising on a
point of order, which, as usual, wasn't, Mr. Meighen had remarked that there was something spurious about the promotion.
"The Prime Minister is like the Red Queen," he said with his
usual icy contempt for my friend Mackenzie, "who, in the trial
of Alice in Wonderland, called for the sentence first, then the
verdict. The House surely has the right to know first what the
verdict is. Is the Honorable Member for Alice—pardon me, for
William and Mary—perhaps guilty of disloyalty to the Liberal
tradition of the cover-up? Is he to be sentenced to the Cabinet to
conceal the details of the verdict?"

As for my fellow Liberals, they were first aghast, then outraged by the announcement. By the time they had seethed into
the lobby they were in a frothing fury.

I guess they had reason to be a trifle miffed. They had been
dutifully silent during all the revelations of the damage that was
being done to the country, and what was the result? The fellow
who had been savaging the party had been preferred and re-
warded. "It seems that rape has become respectable," spat Arnold Bulmer. And even Cyril Hawkspat said something to me
about resigning from Parliament, though I missed most of what
he said over the uproar.

The press, however, were delighted by the fuss and feathers.
They competed so aggressively to interview me that I could
hardly disentangle one question from another. Perhaps it was the
journalistic chaos in the corridors that prompted the parliamentary secretary to the former Defence Minister to cut the grilling
short and get me out of the building, with a haste that was almost as unseemly as the press scramble.

There was one series of questions, though, that neither of us
could avoid. It began with: Did I intend to keep up my attacks
on the government's handling of the smuggling issue?

"The Prime Minister," I replied, my face shining with political
zeal or nervous perspiration, "has assured me that action is to
be taken to rectify certain abuses in the customs service to which
I have perhaps done a little to draw his attention, er, to."

"Does that mean you're keeping quiet about it from now on?"

"Some people have accused me of being incapable of keeping
quiet about anything."

"A Conservative M.P. said this afternoon that you've been bought off dirt cheap—and you're worth every penny of it. Is that right?"

"Yes."

"You admit you've been bought off?"

"No, I was agreeing with you—that's what a Tory M.P. said."

"But is it true?"

My parliamentary secretary was tugging at my trousers, but I couldn't walk away from that one, so: "I do not regard a carefully considered transfer of interest from customs to defence matters as having such implications," I intoned, feeling rather pleased at how rapidly I was learning the art of parliamentary zigzagging. After that I allowed myself to be shepherded out to the parking lot by my deferential P.S. and helped into the Pierce-Arrow.

"Don't push," I said testily.

As I raced Gallopward in the Avro biplane, I felt almost as much relieved as elated at having achieved such rapid success in my new career. Now I wouldn't have to work for a living. I could probably manage quite well on a salary of seven thousand dollars, so there would be no need for me to root for some other occupational truffle.

This was just as well, for nobody else had ever offered me a job. Which still puzzled me. Every other airman who had done spectacularly well in the war had either been urged to stay on in the air force as commanding officers or had settled into prestigious civilian positions, but for some incomprehensible reason nobody had begged me to stay on, even as a corporal; nor had any civilian outfit ever vied for my services. It seemed that I was not the right shape to fit neatly into the commercial jigsaw, nor was I the possessor of credentials that would advantageously grace a company letterhead. So I was all the more thrilled at finally making it in a thoroughly worthwhile profession.

Now at last I could settle down and have a grand piano and a legitimate wife and legitimate children and everything, be fawned upon by parvenus, and get out of the country as often as possible on holidays cloaked as business trips. What a wonderful life it was going to be.

It took only fifteen minutes to reach Gallop, but even though a

tide of purple shadows was creeping over the earth, I was too
revved up to land right away. As if I were not feeling sufficiently
light-headed with glee, I was further glorying in the joys of
flight. How blessed were the sensations, the feel of the controls
and the pressure of the padded seat, the sight of the wings glowing pink in the last rays of the sun, and the smell of the castor-oil
lubricant, and above all the sensation of unity with the machine,
as if I had been integrated into its wood and canvas and hot
metal on the production line. I was so suffused with pride and
delight, I couldn't bear to come down to earth right away. So I
looped. Into a shallow dive, then a pull-up on full engine, thumb
on the engine button, cutting the rotary chatter as the biplane
tilted over the top. Back into a dive, rolling slowly as I did so, so
that the darkening earth revolved like a giant charcoal and purple disc.

Next, diving to within a few feet of the ground, feeling my
weight double momentarily as I leveled off over a plowed field,
then halving as I humped over a line of trees, then restored to
my normal one-fifty pounds as I sped across a field of chopped-
up cornstalks; lifting over a wood, then down into a ravine—darting out again in a hurry: it was deep in shadow. The engine
blatted noisily as the sound bounced back from the ragged
banks. Pulling up sharply to avoid a row of elms with their stark
arms upflung in surrender. And over a field ruled with spring
shoots.

Now I was lining up with a cinder track that gritted its way
across a field. A farm dog was trotting home along the track. It
was the McCloskey mongrel. It had a habit of chasing the Pierce-
Arrow every time I chugged past, barking and snapping at the
tires. I ruddered the brute into an imaginary ring sight and
blipped the engine just as I hurtled past, three feet overhead;
then made a climbing turn to watch, chortling, as McCloskey,
Jr., fled, flat-eared, to its squalid kennel.

But soon even the long evening shadows faded, so I thought I
had better get down while I could still find the field. It would
never do to crack up and hurt myself, now that I was of vital importance to the nation. So I veered home, climbing cautiously
into the velvety dark through which a few stellar moth holes

showed, and a minute later was lining up with the field from a mile out.

As we drifted down, engine hushed, wires humming, I caught a glimpse of two automobiles heading in the same direction, helpfully splashing the road with their headlights. Then I had to concentrate on the landing. Another minute and it would have been a night landing. By the time I had taxied to the barn and tied down next to the Gander, the darkness was complete.

Mother was washing up after dinner and Papa was reading the local paper by the fireside when I walked in through the back door. "Guess what," I said. "I've been made a cabinet minister."

"Nonsense," Father said.

"Go and wash your face, Bartholomew," Mother said. "You've got oil all over it."

A second later two automobiles squealed to a halt at the front of the house.

"That'll be the people to see you," Mother said. "I told them you'd be home by eight. Did you say a cabinetmaker? Oh, Bartholomew, you haven't changed jobs again, have you?"

"Mother, I'm a minister," I cried. "A minister."

"But you haven't been ordained."

"Oh, *Mother*," I began, but was interrupted by the rattling of the screen door.

When I opened the door, in trooped George Duckworth, proprietor of the Queen's Hotel; Fred Toombs, the bootlegger; Frank Lough, the police chief; McKay, the doctor; Miss Rawsthorne, the professional poet; Mr. Wattle, the minister; and Captain Karley, the builder.

They had obviously rushed along to be the first to congratulate me.

"How did you hear the news so soon?" I asked as they settled themselves in the front parlor. "It won't be in the papers until tomorrow."

"We know all about it," Duckworth said heavily. "We sure don't need to read about it."

"You heard it on the radio, maybe? There was somebody there from a radio station, I believe."

"Somebody where?"

"Parliament."

"You mean they're talking about it there, too?"

"Why, yes," I said, "funnily enough." And laughed, expecting them to quit teasing and crowd around me, and pound me on the back, and shower me with good wishes and requests to bear them in mind when it came time for me to start ordering unnecessary supplies and put up superfluous public buildings, and hire staff to fill them with.

"We've got up this deputation," Duckworth said, fiddling with the large watch that dangled from his waistcoat like a metallic sporran, "because we thought you could do something about that bitch. Parn me, Miss Rawsthorne."

"That's all right, Duckworth. I'm a poet, I've heard worse language than that."

"People is getting real desperate," Frank Lough said. "You got to do something, Mr. Bandy, or I can't be responsible."

"I take it you're talking about Mrs. Talbot, are you, Mr. Lough?" I asked, sitting in the only seat they'd left me, a nursing chair with three-inch legs.

"It's pronounced Lock, not Log," he answered irritably.

"Log sounds right to me," Fred Toombs said cuttingly. "We wouldn't be in this pickle if you hadn't lain there and let her and all the temperancers sit on you."

"I was obliged to enforce the law, wasn't I?" Lough said. "Anyways, I always give plenty of warning, didn't I, before a raid, and never interfered in your operations."

"You smell of castor oil," Dr. McKay said to me, sniffing severely.

"The Avro uses it."

"Aye, it's high time you took my advice and gave yourself a good cleaning out," McKay said.

"For God's sake, let's get on with the business," Fred Toombs said exasperatedly.

"With all that castor oil he's absorbed, he *has* got on with it," McKay said. "Or will very soon." And edged away from me.

Karley, who had been looking at me curiously from the moment he took the best armchair, spoke for the first time. "Did you have something to tell us, Bart?" he asked.

"Evidently it can wait," I said sulkily.

"Yes, well. As Duckworth said, this is a deputation. Being an M.P., you're out of touch, of course, so you won't know what's been going on. We have another crisis on our hands, Bart. Mrs. Talbot has cut off our supplies."

"I know that," I muttered, kicking the gateleg table.

"Perhaps you don't realize how totally we've been cut off. There's not a drop to be had for fifty miles around, except in Ottawa, and their bootleggers say they have none to spare. Though we suspect Mrs. Talbot's had a hand in that, too."

"That's too bad. But what's it got to do with me?"

"You're our representative," Toombs said loudly. "Represent us. Get us back our booze."

"You've got to help," Duckworth added indignantly. "I mean, what kind of prohibition is this, when we can't even get a drink?"

"You've proved that you have influence over her, Bart," Karley said in his phlegmatic voice. "Like getting her to cancel the move to Montreal. Everybody else has tried, but now we can't even get in to see her. We want you to try and persuade her to see reason. I mean, she's ruining Gallop all over again."

"Much as I have always disapproved of the habit of imbibing," Mr. Wattle murmured in his introspective way, "I must admit that the deprivation is proving to be even more harmful. The consequences have, in fact, begun to convert me from a belief in prohibition."

He looked around as if expecting us to celebrate his conversion by dancing the tarantella. When everyone sat there like a log, or lough, he sighed ruefully and went on to describe what had been happening in Gallop over the past few weeks: a distressing increase in domestic unarmed combat, dangerously inflamed feeling between topers and temperancers, numerous fistfights, including a fatality following an argument over a pint bottle of gin, a full-scale riot outside the Queen's Hotel, and a veritable epidemic of delirium tremens.

"Aye, and I have been swamped with patients demanding medicinal prescriptions," McKay grunted. "And the worst of it is, I have not been able to earn a single two-dollar fee lately, for even the pharmacies are going short."

"Old Ossie Barrow half wrecked Monk's Pharmacy last Friday," Lough said, "when he went in for his usual case of Trumbull's Virility Solvent and Tapeworm Remedy, which as you know is seventy percent alcohol, and all they could offer was cough drops."

"And young Dr. Hipsey suffered a split lip when some parched besom attacked him with a pair of delivery forceps," McKay said, cheering up slightly. "You've got to do something, Bandy," he added, "or my liver will never recover from the shock of sobriety, and, worse than that, without prescriptions my livelihood will be ruined."

"And mine," Toombs said.

"And mine," Duckworth said.

"Well, I'll see what I can do," I said. "But now let me tell you what happened in Parliament today. I—"

"Did you hear about McMulligan and his pal Kicker?" Duckworth asked the others, lowering his voice.

Toombs nodded grimly.

"What about them?" Chief Lough asked. "They didn't try and break into the distillery again, did they?"

"They sure did. On Sunday."

"They wasn't handed over to me."

"No. This time the guards said they had orders to teach that pair a lesson. They got beaten up pretty bad."

"They can't do that—that's my job," Lough protested.

"Jeez, I really think that woman's off her noddle," Duckworth quacked, turning pale. "Sure glad you told me. My brother was goan to try it. He even bought a pair of wire cutters."

There was a disturbed silence for a moment, then: "Well? You going to help or not?" Toombs asked.

Without a word I heaved myself off the three-inch chair and went up to the bedroom telephone. Five minutes later I returned. "She said she'll be delighted to see me this evening," I said curtly.

Half an hour later, after a wash and brush-up, I was on my way. As I had left the Pierce-Arrow at Rockcliffe, Karley offered the use of his Moon light six, if I would first drive him home. The rest of the deputation chugged off in Fred Toombs's vast tourer.

As we jounced along the washboard surface through the cool

night air, Karley shifted in his seat, yawned, and said, "So, how are things up the Hill?"

"All right."

"I hear the Governor General had you over for dinner, a few days ago."

"A select few. Me and about sixty others."

"I heard it was just you and some pals of his from the old country," Karley said, trying to sound deferential, to jolly me out of the sulks.

When I merely shrugged: "You know, I must admit you've made much more of a splash than I ever expected. Though I don't know how I could have doubted it, knowing you. The first time you arrived in the trenches as a horrible, blank-faced, priggish, moralizing teetotaler disguised as a second lieutenant, everyone said you'd go far—or too far, as old Spanner put it. Remember him?"

"Is he still around?"

"He made it through the war, then died of influenza. What is it you were going to tell us, Bart?"

"Oh, nothing."

"Look, I'm sorry if we were preoccupied with the alcoholic drought, but it's a pretty desperate situation, old man. I'm not drinking much these days, but even I'm getting the twitch. I had to send one of my men all the way to Kingston the other day, for the same stuff that's being made a mile away." He squinted at me in the dark. "They haven't made you Gentleman Usher of the Black Rod, or something, to get rid of you?"

"If you must know, I've been made a cabinet minister."

He jumped as if a spring had come loose and corkscrewed up a contiguous orifice.

"You've *what?*"

"Minister of Defence."

His reaction was so gratifying that I proceeded to tell him all about it with revived enthusiasm. I was even blushing with pleasure over his amazement, the first time I had blushed, I think, since I was a boy and hid in a space heater in the schoolhouse, and was caught looking up through the floor grill and the school-teacher's skirt.

"I can't believe it," he kept saying. "It can't be true. There must be something behind it, there must."

I glanced sideways and was further gratified to see, suspended in the semidarkness, a pair of eyes stretched wider than they had ever stretched before.

"Of course," I mumbled, "I've had to compromise a bit."

"You have to stop asking awkward questions."

"Well, yes."

"Good Lord, my dear old chappie, as the English say, that's nothing. That's what politics is all about."

"I mean, I can hardly go on lashing the government, now that I'm a part of it. That would be pure masochism."

"Course you can't."

"After all, one has to be realistic."

"Course you have," Karley shouted excitedly. He grabbed for support as I swerved into his driveway. "My dear Bart, you don't have to tell me that. I've been a Liberal for too long to have any principles left. Good Lord, though—Minister of Defence? It's incredible. There must be something behind it. It's unbelievable. There must be some—"

He stopped almost as abruptly as the Moon light six, as it skidded to a halt in the driveway of his house.

For a moment I thought he'd gone all quiet because I'd sprayed gravel into his new fountain, the one that his men had built with surplus cement from the post office project; but he wasn't even looking in that direction. He was sitting frozen, staring through the windscreen, making no effort to climb over the Moon.

While exclaiming over the news his voice had been quite untypically vibrant with excitement. Now it suddenly regained its usual matter-of-fact timbre.

"And you say it's been officially announced?" he asked.

"Yes. It'll be in all the papers tomorrow. So you don't think I was wrong to accept the post, in the circumstances?"

"H'm? No, course not," he murmured, sounding as if he weren't listening to himself. His plump cheeks were wobbling slightly as the car stood juddering opposite his front door.

I switched off. A cloud of silence swept over the starlit scene.

"They say I've been bought off, but that's not fair. I can do a lot of good for the services," I said, fiddling with the gear lever. "Not that I've promised in so many words, mind you. I mean, they have absolutely no guarantee that I won't follow through on the, you know, customs scandal. Or perhaps I shouldn't say scandal—that's too extreme a word. Customs *problem* is perhaps more appropriate. Besides, it's being dealt with anyway. Rex— that's Mackenzie King, you know—has assured me that he intends to deal with the situation as soon as possible. In fact he's already shuffled Gassien out of the Cabinet. I expect he'll be prosecuted. So there you are, you see—my job was finished anyway, really, even before I handed back the . . . So I mean there's no point in going on with—"

"And you've confirmed it, have you?"

"Eh?"

"The appointment has been officially announced, and you've confirmed it in the House?"

"Yes, of course."

"You've formally accepted?"

"I've just said so. You're not listening, my dear Karley."

"No . . . sorry . . ." He glanced at me, then looked away quickly. The windscreen of his car was beginning to cloud over as moist night air condensed on the glass. He leaned forward to draw a picture of a gallows, complete with dangling noose, in a preoccupied sort of way.

But then the lamp of his face was relit. "Well, golly, that's just dandy, Bandy," he exclaimed, snatching at the door handle, his tones sounding a bit false, presumably because he wasn't too familiar with current usage. "However, I better not keep you from your appointment with Mrs. Talbot, eh?" he said heartily, proffering a ghastly smile as he heaved his bulk out of the passenger seat. "At least she's willing to see you, that's more than she would do for us. That's a good sign, wouldn't you say?"

For a while there I had begun to feel quite miffed at the deputation's lack of interest in the outside world, where so many historic events were taking place, like the death of Lenin, the abolition of the Turkish Caliphate, the proclamation of Greece as a republic, the Sacco and Vanzetti case, my appointment as Minister of Defence, and so forth; but with Karley's delicious ejacu-

lations and looks of awed wonder still echoing in my ears and
dancing on my eyelids, I drove onward with my faith restored in
humanity, Gallop division. And halfway to Philippa's house, it
suddenly occurred to me that I could extract even more pleasure
from the occasion by making one more detour, to Anne's boardinghouse. She was bound to be at least as excited and impressed
as Karley.

I found myself terrifically eager to see her again, especially as
she had not visited the apartment for some time now. Perhaps I
was fonder of her than I'd admitted, despite our unsatisfactory
relationship, a tiny portion of the blame for which had to be
dabbed onto my plate. Lately I had become a bit irritated over
her resistance, which suggested that she was husbanding her
emotional reserves or saving them for a better prospect; which
was absurd, of course, as there could not possibly be a better
prospect than I. There was also that lack of suppleness in her
embraces, as if she were encased in whalebone and doubt.

But the warmth and trust would surely come, perhaps this
very evening when I gave her the good news . . . and proposed?
Why not? Why not? After all, I was thirty years old—oh, very
well, then, nearly thirty-one—and it was high time I followed the
conventions and took on a load of family responsibilities, debts,
clean socks, etc. Yes, maybe I would ask Anne to marry me,
now that we had obtained the divorce. She would probably
warm up as soon as she was licensed to copulate. Maybe that was
the reason she had cooled off recently, because she was unhappy
about living in sin by installments. But now I could offer her not
only a permanent bed but the considerable prestige of a cabinet
minister's household, and the chance to lord it over the common
herd. By golly, why not?

So it was with much disappointment that, after squealing to a
halt outside the boardinghouse and bounding, jittery with anticipation, to the front door, I learned that Mrs. Mackie had given
up her two rooms with bath privileges over a fortnight ago and
had left no forwarding address.

Now it was with a strange unease that I continued onward
through the unhappily lighted burg, shortcutting to the posh
part of town along Queen Street with its geometry of power and
telegraph lines elucidating the distillery-lighted sky; past the

parked Fords spoke-deep in spring mud, and Willoughby's department store with its windows full of seedy sateens, the boarded-up Monk's Pharmacy, a candy shop with its whining peanut roaster, which was owned by the town's only foreigner, a Dalmation who had been on his way to Manitoba until thrown off the train a few miles away with his bags and his chicken-poxed kids, a family still referred to by Dr. McKay as the Spotted Dalmatians.

Then down the side street with the inevitable corner stores jammed with tin boxes, and buckets, teething rings, toothbrushes, cotton blankets, glass buttons, canvas shoes, fretwork kits, iron stoves, and greasy wooden counters; past intervening liver-brown clapboard boxes with starched curtains and peevishly battered screens, and their inhabitants, belly-bulging distillery workers, jaundice-colored under porch lights as they watched the passing show—stray cats, late-playing underclad brats, cheeky girls in mole velvet tam o'shanters, snotty neighbors, cabinet ministers.

Finally into the northwest, past Mrs. Hipsey's mansion with its stupid bricks. The Talbot residence was said to be just round the corner in the next street, number 40, but the houses were all set so far back from the avenue of trees that it was impossible to read the numbers without a telescope. Assuming they displayed anything so vulgar as a number. Her house was said to have a flat-topped light gray roof with dormers set in the steep sides in the French style, but a fat lot of help that was in the semi-darkness. I'd been round the block three times before I confirmed that her house did indeed display a number, carved six inches deep in each of the stone driveway pillars.

Anne answered the door.

"Oh, hello," she said.

"Oh, hello. I just came from your boardinghouse."

"Come in."

"Thank you."

All I noticed about the hall was that it was circular. Or possibly hexagonal. Or rectangular, with alcoves filled with ruby glassware.

"Philippa will be down in a jiffy."

"Oh, good."

She was wearing a navy-blue skirt, plain white blouse, and athletic shoes. I noticed these details because I walked behind her for several miles, before reaching the reception room, which was all in yellow, except for the wax bananas.

"You've cut your hair even shorter," I observed.

"Yes."

"I'm thinking of cutting mine too, and parting it in the middle."

"Wouldn't that make you look like a show horse? You know, all gussied up for a parade?"

"I thought it would suit me. Though I did wonder if the parting might be a bit abbreviated. The hair's receding so much from my noble brow, I'd probably end up with the parting only at the back of my head, which I admit might look . . ."

"Would you care for a drink?"

"I would care for it as long as it lived."

We sat on yellow chaise longues, facing each other across a hundred-and-forty-foot-wide Baluchistan. Or I may be guilty of an inaccuracy there. It may have been a Khuzistan or Kurdistan rug, or possibly even a Baghdad.

"She'll be down in a minute."

"Fine. Are you the new maid?"

She looked away, running her hand over the yellow silk chaise longue. "She invited me to stay here."

"What's the rent, a thousand a month?"

"You saw my boardinghouse. Wouldn't you move here if you had the chance?"

"Me move in with Philippa? That's quite a thought."

Silence, broken by the tick-tock of an ormolu clock.

"I don't understand any of this," I said at length, and looked at her inquiringly; but she was still feeling the silk, like somebody following a symphony in braille. The flushed color of her face rather clashed with the furniture's citron hue.

"It's simple enough," she said with an effort. "She said she was tired of living in a big house like this all alone except for her personal maid, scullery maid, cook, gardener, chauffeur, handyman, and so on. She said she had plenty of spare rooms. So."

"But," I began; then started again. "But how are you to have a life of your own?"

"Perhaps I've found a life that suits me," she said, and looked up briefly and defiantly, her broad face a bit blotchy, as if freshly scrubbed with Lifebuoy.

Then Philippa was entering the long, narrow yellow room, walking in a carefully straight line. By contrast her face was like a cosmetics ad. She held an amber glass in one hand. The other plump arm was stretched in greeting out of a daring chemise of the most delicate black chiffon and lace, which did wonders for her flaming hair. "Darling," she said, trailing mists of cologne and rye. "We were wondering when we were going to hear from you again." And added many other words of effusive greeting, while repairing to the gilt drinks trolley for a refill for me and another for herself.

"Have an apple," she said, abruptly offering a bowl of waxed fruit, and laughed merrily when I took one absently.

"So once again you've come to save Gallop," she said at length, perching on the arm of the chaise longue beside Anne. "Our knight in shining Bakelite, eh, Annie?" she added, playfully fluffing the hair at the back of Anne's neck. "Well, honey, I might as well save you the embarrassment of pleading on their behalf, even though I do so enjoy listening to that marvelously bizarre delivery of yours. I have such a thirsty market in Toronto and other places, you see, that I simply haven't a drop, haven't a drop to spare for Gallop. And that's all there is to it, darling."

"But of course, even if you had a drop, you'd allow them to expire of thirst before you'd let them have so much as a jigger."

"Damn right," she said, waving her glass in the air as if toasting the elements.

"It must be very satisfying, Philippa."

"You can bet your *cojones* on it, *amigo*," she said with a leer.

"The satisfaction includes having people beaten up?"

"Oh, sure, I forgot about that. That's another message you can take back to the respectable citizens of Gallop—old bean, as you imitation Britishers say."

"I think they've got the message."

"Anything else you want to know—old bean?"

"Why you're really doing it."

"Uh-huh. Well, you remember I told you how Tony Batt persuaded me to sell?"

"Yes."

"Maybe somebody like you would have fought back. But I was a woman alone in the world. You wouldn't know about that, would you, big boy?"

Abruptly her face went all awry, threatening to shatter the cosmetic lacquer. "Being threatened—you can't imagine what that does to a person, can you? Anyway, what with that, and everything else that was happening round here, people throwing rocks at my car, and being snubbed by the Hipseys, and all the rest of it—because I was a lousy woman upstart who had muscled in on a local family business—right?"

She slid off the arm onto the chaise longue proper, slopping her drink. The jarring motion also disarranged her red hair. It fell over her face as she stared into her glass—the personification of the victimized woman.

So at first when Anne put an arm around her, and rocked her gently, comforting her with murmuring sounds, the gesture seemed appropriate enough. Except that it went on for too long.

I was even more confused when, a couple of minutes later, Philippa glanced across at me from under her hair, exposing a face that seemed to be suffused not so much with woe as with triumph.

The Farm Kitchen

There was only one more surprise that day. Jim Boyce, who had been out all evening, returned shortly before midnight and found me in the kitchen staring into the icebox. I was trying to decide whether to eat or not. Though I had missed dinner, somehow I wasn't all that hungry.

"Hello, Bart. What are you doing home on a Wednesday?" he asked.

"Oh . . ."

"Are you going to eat? Good, I'm starving. Here, I'll put the kettle on."

He sat in Father's favorite chair, swung the iron kettle on its hob over the dying embers. "I think I may have landed that job with Willoughby's," he said, poking the fire.

"Have you?"

"Some sort of manager. They seemed to be quite impressed with the way I ran your campaign last year."

"That's good. I'm glad."

He wiggled the poker in his hand for a while. Then: "Your folks say I'm welcome to stay here as long as I like," he said a trifle self-consciously. "How do you feel about that, Bart?"

"That's good, Jim. It's fine with me."

"What's up?"

"Oh, it's such a rotten life."

"How?"

"I've been made a cabinet minister."

"You what?"

"King has appointed me Minister of Defence."

"Minister of Defence."

"Yes."

"You're in the Cabinet."

"Yes."

"And I'm in a glass case in Moscow."

"It's true."

"And that's why you're looking like a withered camel."

"It'll be in all the papers tomorrow."

He sat up slowly. "It's really true?"

"Yes."

"You're not just practicing your usual Bandyish mayhem?"

"I don't know what you mean."

"You know—saying upsetting things—as an alternative to in-furiating people, interfering in their affairs, playing dirty tricks on them, driving people into an early grave—"

"Certainly not. My appointment has been officially an-nounced."

"You really have been made . . . ?"

"Minister."

"Of Defence?"

"Yes."

"Jesus Christ Almighty."

"Shhh, Father will hear you," I smirked wanly; but a smid-geon of pride revived, and with it a flicker of appetite. So as I told him all about it I set out a few odds and ends—cheese, ham, plain pickles, mustard pickles, corned beef, dinner rolls, carrot pudding, and just a few country recipes, Dutch hustle cake, babka, poffertjes, and batter buns, as I wasn't all that hungry.

Neither was Boyce, now. For some reason he seemed to have lost his appetite. As he moved about automatically, making tea, he kept staring and staring at me, and swearing feebly to himself in astonishment.

But it was not long before it occurred to him to ask what they were getting in return.

"How d'you mean?"

"They've announced, what have you renounced?"

"Well, naturally I can't go on savaging the government, now

can I, now that I'm a part of it? After all, Boyce, compromise is essential. One has to be realistic." Then, when he said nothing: "All right, all right, I know I've been detoured."

"Gagged?"

"Detoured," I insisted breathlessly, snatching up a pickle. "But don't you see, I can more than balance the books. I can do great things for the services. You know how badly they've been neglected."

"Well, far be it for somebody like me to talk ethics," Boyce said. "If you think you can be heard while speaking through a gag, who am I to regard you with disappointment, disillusionment, ridicule, and disgust?"

I crunched down on the pickle and chewed noisily.

"By the way, what are you going to do now with the Duncan report?"

"Ah. Well, actually, I've sort of handed it back."

In order to keep his eyes trained on me he felt behind him for a chair and slowly sank into it.

"You've handed it back."

"Well, well . . . it's achieved its purpose, er, Jim," I said. I think it was only the second time I'd ever addressed him by his Christian name. I'd just gotten into the habit of calling him Boyce. "Rex says he's—"

"Who?"

"Mackenzie. King. After all, he's gotten rid of Gassien, when he reshuffled the Cabinet."

"Oh yes? Going to give him an even better job, I guess."

"Don't be a sap. That's absurd. Mackenzie," I said haughtily, "would never do a thing like that."

"You'll wake your parents."

"You don't seem to realize," I hissed, spraying shreds of pickle, "what an opportunity this is for me."

"Oh, but I do, Bart, I do," he said, now sounding almost sympathetic.

In the long silence that followed I pushed several crumbs of bread around the breadboard.

"So he says he's getting rid of Gassien," Boyce said at length. "What about all the other crooks, Bart?"

I pushed the crumbs into a heap, then moistened a finger and dabbed at the crumbs to see how many would stick.

"It hasn't occurred to you," Boyce continued, looking away at long last—until then he'd hardly stopped staring at me since I first gave him the good news—"that they'll make sure you don't get back in?"

"Back in? Why would I need to get back in, if I'm already in?" I said, sounding really unfriendly to my best friend. "You're havering again, Boyce."

"Well, you've resigned, haven't you?"

"Resigned?" I chortled. "What nonsense you do talk. I've just told you I've been made Minister of—"

"You mean you don't know?"

"Know what?"

"No, of course you don't, otherwise even you couldn't fail to see the implications."

"Now look here—"

"They've put on the fritz, old man, and you've fallen for it. The moment you officially accepted the appointment, you resigned."

"Course I didn't. I—"

"The rule is to be changed soon, I believe, but at present it still calls for a cabinet appointee to resign immediately and give the electorate a chance to approve the appointment."

I stared, feeling the blood drain into my socks.

"Except that in your case," Boyce said gently, "you can guess what will happen, can't you?

"You're out of Parliament, Bart," he said. "The P.M. has jammed the rule book up your jacksy, old man."

It didn't take long to confirm that what Boyce had said was true, that a cabinet appointee was required to resign and rerun; but I just couldn't believe the rest of his analysis of the situation until I turned up at the main entrance to the Commons chamber the next day and made to go in, and the dignified, white-haired sergeant at arms got in the way. "Excuse me, sir," he said, "but where are you going?"

"To take my seat, of course."

"But you no longer have a seat, Mr. Bandy."

"Course I do. I haven't resigned—I haven't said a word about resigning."

"Your resignation," he said, not quite meeting my affronted eye, "is implicit in your acceptance of a cabinet post."

"I'll have something to say about that," I said, taking a step forward.

"Sorry, sir, but no stranger may enter the chamber while it's in session."

"Look, you must let me in. And that's an order," I added, inspired. "I was an officer, you're only a sergeant."

He smiled thinly, as if this were the kind of remark he had come to expect from this particular source. "You may, of course, sit in the gallery if you wish," he said.

"Among the common people? Certainly not."

"Well, you certainly can't come in here," he said, and gently but firmly closed the door in my face.

Later the P.M. announced that, though the Honorable Member for William and Mary Counties was no longer entitled to sit in the Commons, the cabinet position would be waiting for him as soon as he was re-elected. In this case, he went on, he would not, as was the usual procedure, take the Honorable Member into the Cabinet on an interim basis, but that did not mean that he, the Prime Minister, intended to deprive the Honorable Member of his just deserts, of the reward for his undoubtedly noteworthy contributions to the deliberations of this august chamber. Far from it. In fact, as there was no pressing departmental matter requiring the urgent attention of a minister, the country having no defence to speak of, he was prepared, as a further tribute to the indomitable manner in which the Honorable Member had conducted himself over the past few months, to keep the position vacant, as a symbol of the Honorable Member's loyalty to the party, until such time as he had abided by the procedures laid out in the Electoral Act under the general direction and supervision of the chief electoral officer, and presented himself with the requisite qualifications.

So I would have to run for election all over again. The only trouble was that yet another door was being quietly closed in my face. On the very next day, while I was preoccupied with other matters, principally the madness that was about to engulf Gallop, the local riding association executive under the chairmanship of Captain Karley elected a new slate of executives that somehow failed to include any of my supporters—Miss Rawsthorne, the Reverend Mr. Wattle, our token farmer, and others—and their very first decision was to save pots of money by postponing the election until the general election next year.

And on the day after that Jacques Gassien was appointed to the Senate.

It was only then that I fully comprehended the look that Mackenzie King gave me on the only occasion that I had the heart to view the proceedings from the gallery. After answering a number of questions on the deferring of my promotion, he twisted round from the front bench and treated me to a look that to a disinterested observer might have seemed deeply sympathetic and regretful, but which suggested to the recipient little but gloating satisfaction.

Which I matched a few months later when I heard that he had been defeated in the 1925 general election.

"You mark my words," I said when the news came through, "Mackenzie King is finished as far as politics is concerned. That's the last we'll ever hear of *him*."

It was nearly eight at night when I drove away from Parliament Hill for the last time, and it was after ten when I reached the river road north of Gallop.

A quarter mile short of the distillery was the intersection where I usually turned right to cut across country to the Machin farm, but as I approached the crossroads the headlights illuminated some sort of obstruction. At first I thought there had been an accident involving a lorry and an automobile, but then I saw that the vehicles had been placed in position deliberately, so as to block all four directions. It wasn't a collision, it was a roadblock. An ambush.

This was confirmed a moment later. As I braked to a halt, three men appeared. They were armed. Shotguns or rifles. Assassins.

Well, this was it. They had caught up with me at last. It was either Tony Batt and the underworld, or Joseph Stalin and the Cheka, or the G.P.U. as it was now officially called. Unless it was killers hired by Mackenzie King just in case I found a way to claim my seat at the cabinet table. Or possibly it was the American millionaire, Chaffington. Or perhaps my former brigadier in France . . . Actually I supposed it could be any one or a combination of hundreds of people who had developed varying degrees of enmity toward me.

Whoever it was, I was obviously about to be blasted into cat meat. But not without putting up a fight. I slammed the gears into reverse, hoping to hurtle backward into the damp gloom with only a few mortal wounds. Unfortunately I stalled the engine, and before I could start it again they were upon me.

But it was only Mr. Jewell, the chief excise officer, and a couple of his men.

Mr. Jewell approached the driver's side as warily as if the car contained cocktail mixers filled with T.N.T. The other two came up on the other side, rather more casually.

"Oh, it's you," Jewell said sharply, flicking a flashlight beam round the interior of the car before aiming it at my nose. "What are you doing here?"

"I'm not doing anything," I said, feeling the adrenaline swashing about in my veins. "What do you mean?"

"Where have you just come from?"

"Ottawa. What's going on?"

"I'll ask the questions. Where are you going? To the train, right? To join your thieving friends."

I looked at him. In a fury he rapped the flashlight on the side of the car so violently that the light flickered out. However, his puffy face was still plainly visible in the bleary glow from the nearby distillery and the lights of Gallop, as reflected from the low clouds that were drifting in from the northwest.

"You're on your way to join the other looters, aren't you?" he shouted, twisting the flashlight in his hands as if trying to wring its neck.

I climbed out of the car. Jewell fell over his feet as he backed away, and actually pointed his weapon. "You get back," he squealed. "I'm warning you, this gun is loaded."

"Rifle," I said automatically. "One never refers to a rifle as a gun. I only want to know what's going on."

"They attacked us. They're stealing, plundering everything they can get their hands on, the filth. And they shot at us. Shot at us." He stopped, gasping for breath as if his skittering retreat had winded him.

"It was the distillery guards they shot at," one of the uniformed men said. "You didn't get close enough to get shot at." He sounded aggrieved, as if he felt that Mr. Jewell ought to have been closer.

"I tell you they were shooting at us," Jewell screamed. "We'd have been killed if we went any closer."

While he was busily upbraiding his underlings, I thought I had better see what was going on, so I got back into the car and, by driving with two wheels in the ditch, managed to maneuver round the roadblock.

"You just wait—we'll have reinforcements from Ottawa any time now," Jewell shouted as I continued on toward the distillery.

Driving along the west side of the complex, I glanced repeatedly through the high perimeter fence, expecting to see a battle royal raging in there between the guards and McMulligan—for I assumed that it was he and his bruisers who were engaged in another attempt to break into the compound; but the brightly lighted plant seemed to be all quiet. Indeed, the areas of open ground visible from the road were quite deserted, which was strange, as there was supposed to be a full evening shift at work.

A quarter mile farther on, though, the scene was far from tranquil. A great train robbery was taking place.

The freight train, comprising about twenty cars, which had been on its way out of the south gate of the distillery, had been halted just before it cleared the crossing over Gallop's main thoroughfare. The caboose and the last car were blocking this, the east end of the street. The rest of the train was standing in the rail yard on the far side of Queen Street, amidst an untidy mess of switches, signals, sidings, cinder tracks, and deep grass—and about a thousand looters.

Seething along the entire length of the train, they were busily jimmying open the last few sliding doors and handing out and loading hundreds upon hundreds of boxes, the shrill cries of the men and the bellowing of the women rending the damp night air. They were loading the boxes into a startling variety of vehicles. Parked alongside the train two or even three deep, their transport included automobiles, lorries, horse-drawn carriages, wagons of half a dozen different shapes and sizes, trolleys, tractors, wheelbarrows, prams, and even toy carts. As I squeaked to a halt, goggling at the chaotic headlighted scene, still more vehicles were arriving every few seconds, approaching along the main street and bumping and lurching at greedy speed over the grass and cinders of the rail yard. When I gaped to the right, up Queen Street, the sight was even more goggleworthy. The traffic

along it was shuddering and grinding along from as far west as
the Rock Gardens a mile away. In their eagerness to get at the
plunder, some vehicles were approaching on the wrong side of
the street. Even as I watched, the entire shebang came shuddering to a halt, the oncoming wrong-side-of-the-street traffic having
met the cars and trucks and wagons that had already loaded up
and were attempting to get away. An uproar of honking and
hollering broke out, adding to the already frightful freight-yard
din of yells and bellows, neighing of nags and crack of parting
padlocks, splintering wood, and grinding gears.

It was like the great retreat from Amiens in 1918. Except that
here the mood was far from one of defeat.

I'd barely had time to climb out before two men approached,
one of them porting an old-model Enfield that looked as if it
hadn't been fired since the Fenian raids.

"Oh, hi, Mr. Bandy," he said, lowering the rusty weapon with
obvious relief. "We seen this car coming from the distillery. We
thought it was the guards."

"You aren't shooting at them, are you?"

"Jake Fuller pulled his trigger by mistake. That's the only shot
been fired so far, I think."

"How long has this been going on?" I asked, gesturing feebly
at the vehicular chaos.

"Couple of hours, I guess," he said, peering nervously down
the road behind me. "Say, did you see any of the guards when
you come this way, Mr. Bandy?"

"No. But the customs men have a roadblock back at the crossroads."

Looking worried, he muttered something to his pal, who immediately pelted off into the milling throng across the road.

There was a cracking sound as somebody up the line took a
sledgehammer to a freight car that had not yet been broken into.
A Model T Ford, so crammed with boxes that its fenders were
almost scoring the dirt, ground across the street and started up
the road to the distillery. The rifleman waved it down and
shouted, "You can't get up that way, Harry. Revenue men."

"But there's no other way out," shouted the driver, and looked
a bit annoyed when he tried to back up and found that other ve-

hicles had taken his place, blocking the way back to the main street.

Across the street, two hefty women, plainly visible in the town lights as reflected back from the low clouds, were thrashing about in the long grass beside the track, giggling uncontrollably as they tried to raise boxes of whisky onto a stack that was already seven feet high, their efforts weakened by their laughter. Nearby, a steam-driven tractor backed slowly into a posh limousine, rocking it on its springs, then tilting it onto two wheels, which caused an outbreak of strangely good-natured recrimination, adding to the ecstatic din.

Fred Toombs came striding along the track, followed by the rifleman's companion. Toombs's checked shirt was open to the waist, exposing his hairy chest. Looking every inch a former infantry C.O., he rapped out a series of questions, ending, "And Jewell says they're expecting reinforcements at any minute?"

"So he said."

"I can't see them reacting that fast. What do you think?"

"What I think is that this is madness," I exclaimed, gesturing around at the pother.

"You think so?"

"Good God, man, it's outrageous. It's looting on an unheard-of scale. You can get shot for this."

"I guess so," Toombs said indifferently, watching a couple of post office employees as they lurched past, hauling sacks of clinking merchandise. They disappeared through a crisscross of misty headlights. There was a smash of glass as somebody dropped an armful of bottles onto a steel rail. A lady in a hat like a Norman helmet, who was helping her husband to load a horse and buggy, paused to struggle into a raincoat. It was only then that I noticed it was raining.

"My God, half the population must be down here," I gasped.

"And the other half is on the way," Toombs said. "But don't worry, there's plenty to go round. I estimate there's about ten thousand cases of the stuff available."

"Ten thousand? *Ten thousand?* And where's the police, for heaven's sake?"

"They're tied up at the other end of the train."

"You've tied them up? You've attacked the police as well?"

"No, no, I mean they're busy at the far end, loading the police car and the lockup van."

"It's shocking," I cried, looking absolutely shocked. "It's appalling. It's the most outrageous . . ."

"Right. Are you with us or not?"

"With you?" I bellowed. "*With you?* You seriously expect me to defy the government of the country and join in the wholesale theft of ten thousand cases of whisky?"

"It's not all whisky. There's also rum, gin, and a bit of vodka, I think."

"Oh well, that's different. Why didn't you say so? I mean, that makes all the difference, doesn't it?"

"There's no need to be sarcastic, Bandy," Toombs snapped. "Just let us know—are you helping or not?"

I stared at the intent, expectant faces around us, then across at the seething mob in the freight yard. A few of the faces were alight with guilty greed, and one group of men in the distance had smashed a case and were sampling the contents, but most of the people seemed to be wearing expressions of almost hypnotized elation, of something almost approaching ecstasy, as if attending, not a sordid looting expedition, but a particularly efficacious revivalist meeting. There was extraordinarily little quarreling going on, as one would expect, or of acquisitive passion let loose. A spirit of cooperation seemed to prevail, as if the supplies they were unloading were for the survivors of some natural disaster, rather than for their own comfort.

Finally I looked up Queen Street, at the horse-drawn and motorized vehicles jamming the street on both sides for easily a mile. Until Toombs, not used to being kept waiting, demanded, "Well?"

"Oh, very well," I said haughtily, as if giving way to some inconsequential request rather than one that would mark the third great turning point in my reluctantly nomadic life. "If only to bring some sort of organization to this shocking chaos. Or they'll never get away with it."

Toombs took a deep breath and a grim smile tightened the folds of his fair face.

After a moment he drew me aside. "McMulligan started it all," he said, plucking at his wet shirt. "Him and a bunch of others halted the locomotive just the other side of the freight yard and drove off the crew, and broke into the first couple of cars. Since then it's spread like a brush fire.

"I think the town's just had enough. The whole lousy prohibition scene, and hearing how the government's been handling it— a lot of it's your doing, bo—and the way things are with Talbots, and all the rest of it. Even some temperancers have joined in."

He passed a palm over his ginger hair and shook off a handful of rain. "But that stupid bastard, McMulligan, fouled it up," he continued, gesturing toward the caboose. "He stopped the train too soon, as you can see. So we can't get past that way, and as for going west, well, just look at it. It'll take hours to sort out that traffic jam. And now you say the excise men are blocking the way north."

A husky fellow in patched overalls hastened up. "There's no other way out of the rail yard, Mr. Toombs," he gasped. "I checked. The ground's too marshy where you said to try." Then, after shifting about self-consciously for a moment: "Say, can I go now, Mr. Toombs? The wife should have finished loading the wagon by now."

"Damn it, you stay and help," Toombs shouted, "or nobody'll get away at all."

There was a crash as two cars collided. One of them was an expensive Buick, with an open chauffeur's compartment. The rear, enclosed cab was loaded to the roof with boxes.

"If we drove the train a few feet farther on, that would unblock the road," I suggested.

Toombs was conferring with a couple of his men. He turned to snap, "I told you, the crew's beat it."

"I can drive the train, if steam's up."

He looked at me.

"I drove an armored train in Russia, once."

Toombs shook his head wonderingly, then: "It shouldn't surprise me. But we can't risk it, man. I mean, look at them. There's hundreds of people, men, women, even kids, milling around the wheels."

"No, I guess not. . . . I see you've uncoupled the end car and the caboose. You couldn't push them out of the way, backward?"

"We tried it. We couldn't budge them an inch."

By then we had an increasingly anxious crowd around us: a handful of Toombs's men, a few drivers who had given up trying to get their vehicles unsnarled, even a group of distillery workers who seemed to be torn between a fear of losing their jobs and a desire to share in the bounty—and Jim Boyce under an umbrella.

"I had to walk all the way across town to get here," he said. "There's cars converging on Gallop from as far away as North Gower. You can't move in the Rock Gardens."

He looked in amazement at the shoving, elbowing, frantically laboring throng along the track. The noise was fearful. A tractor was bellowing in pain as it climbed out of the ditch on the far side of the street, losing part of its load in the process. A girl in a delicate shawl, with the face of a Bernadette of Lourdes, was calling on the driver of the tractor to get going before the fuggen revenooers arrived. A fat chap nearby started, and dropped a box on his foot.

There must have been over a thousand citizens milling about alongside the train, dodging about amidst growing stacks of cases, which were being offloaded faster than they could be transferred to car trunks and rumble seats, car tops and back seats, running boards, buckboards, wagon floors and buggy steps, and everybody seemed to be hollering useless advice, while at right angles to the crazed scene half a mile of traffic steamed and juddered in a higgledy-piggledy line all the way from the rail crossing to the Rock Gardens, illuminated by hazy, haloed street lamps. Two drivers who couldn't get past each other were starting to punch. Within seconds they were down in the dirt, enjoying a right old barney.

As I climbed onto the rear platform of the caboose, Toombs was arguing with several members of the crowd. At length he turned away in disgust. "If that's the way you want it, why the hell should I care if you get caught?" he shouted. "It's not going to do my business any good, is it, with thousands of bottles of booze floating round town? It'll be years before I'm needed again. Why the hell am I trying to cook my own goose anyway?"

"Fred?"

"*What?*"

He turned to find me up on the caboose, resting a hand on an iron wheel atop a thick steel rod.

"Yeah, what?"

"While you were trying to move the caboose and the last car," I called down, "I presume you took off the brakes?"

"What?"

"The trainman obviously locked them before fleeing. Force of habit, I guess. You released them, of course, before pushing?"

Toombs looked at one of his henchmen. The henchman looked back at Toombs.

"Ah. The brakes," Toombs said. "As a matter of fact, no."

"Ah, well, there you are, then," I said, hauling the wheel around, then jumping down beside the track and dusting my hands and trying not to smirk. After all, I was the one who usually forgot little details like that.

"And you said he was a useless prick," Toombs said scornfully to his henchman.

"I did not—it was you what said that," the other replied hotly.

"Well, let that be a lesson to you, not to jump to conclusions just because he looks like a candidate for the knacker's yard," Fred snarled, and immediately strode over to the nearest tractor driver, and by a mixture of threats and intimidation persuaded him to unhitch his booty and drag the end freight car and the caboose clear of the street. And within twenty minutes at least one escape route was open.

By 11 P.M. we had the traffic sorted out and moving quite smoothly. To the general relief, the distillery guards made no further attempt to interfere that night. Apparently they had decided that they were being paid to guard the distillery, not the railway company's rolling stock. Nor did the customs and excise reinforcements arrive in time; though Toombs was not surprised. As civil servants, he said, they were hardly likely to receive a summons to turn out in the middle of the night, or to heed the summons even if they received it. He didn't think they would appear until midmorning at the earliest.

Which was just as well, as it was nearly dawn before the last of the citizens staggered home, leaving a rail yard that might have been mistaken for the town dump: fractured freight cars and a faintly hissing locomotive, a devastation of splintered wood and soggy packing, shards of glass, churned-up grass and

whisky-scented mud, broken and abandoned vehicles, saturated
cardboard, and a few drunks who had decided to sample the
merchandise on the spot.

At around five in the morning Fred Toombs and I walked
along the length of the train for a final check, to make sure
nobody was nestling under an iron wheel or anything. It had
stopped raining by then, but we were both soaked to the skin
and lurching with fatigue. After the bedlam of the previous nine
hours the silence was eerie. Our unsteady feet crunched loudly
and arrhythmically on the cinder track. There was not a hint of
wind. A few stars winked between swabs of misty cloud.

"Boyce doesn't seem to have returned with my car," I croaked,
shivering and feeling as hollow as a side drum. Sometime during
the night Boyce had borrowed my car to help a few of the
poorer citizens who had no transport of their own.

"I'll give you a lift," Toombs said as we reached his lorry.

He was certainly not leaving empty-handed. The lorry was
stacked eight feet high with boxes. It gave one an idea of the
scale of the night's enterprise. His share alone amounted to a
hundred and fifty cases. One thousand eight hundred bottles of
Mrs. Talbot's choicest rye.

"I'll be leaving town as soon as things have quietened down,"
Toombs said hoarsely, reaching into the cab for a bottle of Gold
Bullion. He took a swig, then passed the bottle to me. "I've been
telling everybody to hide the stuff well. I hope they were listening. The bureaucracy isn't going to take this lying down. They
don't mind making a few million themselves, but let ordinary
people have a share and that's a different matter, eh? They'll
turn this town upside down to get the stuff back." He glanced at
me, paused to sneeze, cursed, then said, "You're the first person
they're going to think of, you know."

"Me? Why? I didn't start it."

"Didn't you?" Fred said with a crooked smile, and walked to
the front of the lorry to crank up.

Half an hour later the heavily loaded vehicle rocked to a stop
opposite the driveway to the Machin farm. We sat there steaming in the cab, illuminated by the dashboard light, jerking pal-
siedly in time with the engine.

"And what are you going to do, Bart?" Toombs asked. "I guess things haven't turned out too well for you."

"Oh, I don't know. I'm no worse off than I was a year ago."

"As I see it, they've screwed you right royally. I'd be feeling pretty goddam bitter and disillusioned."

"Oh no. I found politics quite inspiring."

"You found it what?"

"Quite inspiring."

"Inspiring."

"On the whole, politicians are worthy of admiration, Fred. Most of them are honest and upright. They work harder and much longer hours than most people, and less selfishly. In many ways they're quite altruistic; they genuinely want to help the country, while at the same time looking out for themselves, which is only natural. I'm sure that even King honestly felt he had the interests of the country at heart when he got rid of me. He was dreadfully misguided, of course, but . . ."

"Did somebody drop a box on your head tonight?"

"No, I don't think so," I said, guzzling contentedly.

"They must've. Bleeding ulcers, man, King's played the dirtiest trick on you since his company union days."

"It was just one jack-in-the-pulpit outmaneuvering another, Fred," I croaked reasonably. "I don't blame him. He just had more experience at it than me, that's all. I mean, even if he is a pious, cowardly, treacherous, scheming, hypocritical, flabby, power-skilled cipher, it's not his fault. He can't help being a Liberal."

"Ah, you see? Just listen to you—you're not feeling quite so Christian about it as you thought," Fred said, nudging me with his elbow.

We sat there talking and tippling for another half hour, guessing how the authorities might react to the quasi uprising, and trying to decide how we might respond, and getting more and more spifflicated in the process; until finally the rising sun was shining straight into our eyes. Thus reminded—of something or other—I fell out of the lorry, and Fred, laughing demoniacally, drove off at high speed.

Saturated inside and out, I staggered into the house. Papa was already up, lighting the kitchen fire. "Oh, my land," he cried as I reeled in through the back door, beaming and steaming. "You've fallen into the vat again. Oh, my boy." And helped me all the way up to bed.

As it turned out, the customs men did not appear until that afternoon. We had forgotten that outsiders would not be familiar enough with the Gallopian topography to use the river route and all the other shortcuts. It was two o'clock when Toombs telephoned to say that a convoy of about a dozen automobiles loaded with uniforms and plainclothes customs men had turned off the Ottawa–Prescott highway and were busily being detoured across country, through middens, pigsties, rock-strewn fields, and across swampland by sundry helpful farmers and housewives. In fact, it was evening by the time they reached the center of town in a distinctly damp, chilled, exhausted, and infuriated condition.

But in the process of getting there they had made a grave tactical error. Discovering a cache of whisky under the straw in the barn on the Parker property, they behaved so vindictively, menacing the family just short of physical abuse, and threatening it with penalties so dire as to reduce Mrs. Parker and the children to hysterics.

Before this incident became known, many of the citizens had begun to have second thoughts about their part in the events of the previous night. Even those who had stashed away enough hooch to last them to the end of the century could hardly believe that they had shared in the madness that had swept over the normally staid community. Regardless of the provocation—the resentment arising from the distilled hostility to Mrs. Talbot, a provincial government simultaneously arrogant, hypocritical, and shifty in its administration of prohibition, and a federal department that had allowed millions in liquor revenue to be diverted into felonious pockets—the result had been a demented looting on a shocking scale. The citizens were really disturbed to think that outsiders might even consider them to be criminals.

But the Parker incident overcame the apprehensions in the twinkling of a shot glass. The parochial xenophobia revived. Moreover, as further news of bureaucratic bullying spread through town, it warned the inhabitants far more effectively than Toombs's exhortations as to what they would face if their own

hidey-holes were discovered. There followed a resurgence of the
night's feverish activity, as the spirits were exorcised from domestic haunts and relocated in woods and woodlots, roadway
drainage conduits, riverbank cavities or in the river itself, in hollow trees or tree houses, down wells and even cesspools, or, in
the case of townspeople who had no pastoral concealments, in
the cellars of public buildings—everywhere but inside the houses
where the presence of several score bottles of Gold Bullion, Gold
Vault, or Superb Extra Special De Luxe Rye Whisky, or Jolly
Roger Rum, or Talbot's Best Thames Gin, or Ivan the Terrible
Vodka could not be satisfactorily explained.

A few families panicked when the reports came in of authoritarian rummagings through bedsteads and barns, chimneys and
chicken houses. They flung their loot into marshland and swamp,
and then promptly informed on their neighbors; but most citizens remained righteously indignant and held onto their booty.
Many of the urban dwellers even went so far as to cooperate
with their neighbors. Later there would be stubborn arguments
as to how many boxes were due each family, but in the emergency they sank their differences and their supplies into a common pool, and secreted hundreds of boxes in places that even
the most persistent exciseman was not likely to search, such as
the spare cells in the local jail, the new drains in the northwest
part of town, a vault in the Catholic cemetery, and even, surreptitiously, in the furnace room of the Presbyterian church.

Fortunately the citizenry had plenty of time to relocate their
supplies. It was late evening on the second day before the customs men had established the Queen's Hotel as their H.Q., and 8
A.M. on the third day before they emerged, to fan out across
town and pin onto every available flat surface printed notices announcing that anybody who returned certain merchandise removed from CNR Train No. 4248 on the night of May 15, 1924,
by leaving it outside their premises, would escape prosecution,
and that anybody who failed to do so would be subject to arrest
and imprisonment.

But by then the truculent methods of the officials had roused
such outrage and hostility that only a handful of householders
obliged, and in some instances even these offerings were not
recovered. Many cases of whisky dumped onto sidewalks were

promptly appropriated by thirsty citizens from out of town, who had not heard about the attack on the train in time to help sack it.

By then, thirty-six hours had whizzed by since McMulligan had driven off the train crew at shotgun point, giving approximately three thousand citizens the opportunity to conceal an estimated nine thousand cases of liquor—owing to an embarrassment of alcoholic riches, not all of the cargo had been lifted—over thirty square miles of town and countryside.

By midafternoon the officers had recovered barely two truckloads of booze, and at least one platoon of customs men were in an exceedingly bad mood by the time they reached the Machin farm on the western outskirts of town.

Once again I had been out much of the night, helping Toombs and other volunteers in the emergency relocation work, so I didn't rise until after lunch that third day.

When I came downstairs I found the ground floor packed with guiltily excited people, neighbors, friends, strangers, bootleggers, messengers, and other overnight criminals in gingham and lace, and serge and celluloid. The populace seemed to be gravitating to the Machin farm, almost as if they considered it to be some sort of command post, though it was Fred Toombs who was organizing most of the resistance from his mobile H.Q., the three-ton lorry.

"What do you think's going to happen, Mr. Bandy?" a shopkeeper asked, plucking nervously at my sleeve. "I hear they're bringing in the Mounted Police."

"They're already here," somebody else said, shaky with excitement and apprehension. "They've took over the police station."

"Somebody tipped off the customs men that there was a whole load of boxes under Mrs. Hipsey's gaze-bo. They say she was carrying on something shocking, saying she didn't know nothing about it—"

"Millie Prosser said they just barged into her house without even asking and started to feel her unmentionables."

"That's disgraceful."

"Yeah, they'd just been laundered, too. They were in a laundry hamper, and—"

"Old Mr. Thomas out at Punk Crick peppered one lot with buckshot. They was so scared they drove into his duckpond, so then he give them the other barrel for running over his duck eggs."

When the crowd had thinned somewhat, I joined Jim Boyce and my parents in the kitchen. As Boyce relayed the latest news —a cache of Extra Special had been recovered from the Temperance Hall, Magistrate Hipsey had remanded McMulligan and three others for trial, the entire police force (three constables and the chief) had been suspended, pending investigation—I noticed that Father and Mother were in an unusually subdued mood. The week's developments had obviously been too much for them; first a trickle of mournful visitors congratulating them on my promotion, then a return visit from the same friends eagerly commiserating with them on my downfall; next a passel of journalistic importunates; then the excitement of the train robbery, and another rush of newspapermen; and now this latest wave of jittery visitors, including some exceedingly doubtful characters, bootleggers, bootlickers, gold diggers, gravediggers, and defrocked cops—the gravediggers offering to bury booze in consecrated ground, the cops, aware that they had been a trifle derelict in their duty, anxious for the moral support of the community—no wonder the folks looked disoriented.

While Boyce continued to regale them with increasingly bizarre rumors and gossip, I was called to the telephone—a Fox newsreel representative in New York asking if I would fly a cameraman over the scene of the crime; they would pay fifty bucks and expenses—and when I came downstairs again I saw Mother looking so dazed and vulnerable that on an impulse I put an arm around her and whined, "I'm so sorry about all this pother and perturbation, Mother. It must be awful for you." Which seemed to upset her all the more. Emotion rouged her cheeks, and she sounded quite breathless when she replied, "But, Bartholomew, I'm enjoying every moment of it."

"Eh?"

She was actually pressing a shaky hand over mine and patting it in a rapid, nervous way. "I must say that when you came home last year it took an awful lot of getting used to. All the strangers appearing, and airplanes flying around, and noisy talk, and . . . In my whole life I've never met so many people as this last year, and it's been wonderful, even if some of them were really strange, and . . ."

She saw the Reverend Mr. Bandy staring at her. "Well, it's true," she said almost fiercely. "It's been wonderfully exciting. We've been alone so much all our married life, first because nobody could ever really talk to a minister, and then because of —the other thing—nobody but relatives with nothing to talk about but church gossip and mixed pickles. But look at all the marvelous people who've been coming here ever since Bartholomew came home, even if we didn't take to all of them. All getting so excited over planes and politics, and that marvelous fair that James organized, and so much laughing, and I don't know what else." She looked at me, her eyes shining with tears. "Me, fussed about all this commotion? It's made me feel like, like when I was a girl and had some of Papa's brandy."

"Martha!"

"Well, it does. And I really believe now everything that people have said about Bartholomew, and he really has done all those things they said." And overcome, she actually turned and embraced me so emotionally that when she finally released me I had to turn away and straighten a picture of some sheep.

"I'd like to give you a hug, too," Boyce said in a husky voice. So I turned back, all choked up; but it was Mother he was hugging.

"As for you, dear James, no wonder women are so fond of you," she said, her voice muffled against his chest. "You . . . I'm so grateful to you and George. Oh, I miss George so much . . ."

Now tears were polishing Boyce's eyes as well, as he held my thin, worn mother in his arms. Quite carried away by the communal emotion, I opened my arms and started toward Papa.

"Gerroff," he said.

Boyce came into the sitting room where I was staring out the window, jingling a couple of coins in my pocket. I had been watching him out there, talking to a group of newspapermen who were following up the story by obtaining the reactions of a few prominent citizens of Gallop to the sensational robbery.

Temporarily occupied on the telephone, I had asked him to act as my spokesman.

"You told them," Boyce said, "that you hoped everybody got away with it."

"Oh, did I? What else did I say?"

"You said the whole thing made you feel proud to be a Canadian."

"I hope I wasn't speaking out of turn. But I'm glad I said that. After all, it's true enough. Such splendid cooperation, such initiative, such courage, such spiritual independence. I almost wish I'd had a chance to join in properly and swipe some of the stuff myself."

"Actually you did. You know, when I borrowed the car. There's half a dozen cases of gin in your bedroom cupboard."

"There's what?"

"It's all right—they wouldn't dare search your house."

"Oh, my God," I said, looking out the window again.

"Well, I didn't think it was fair, you doing all the work and not getting any for yourself."

"And you brought it to the house?"

"I haven't had a chance to put it anywhere else."

"Thanks very, very much," I said, just as a passel of customs men drove up and charged onto the veranda, led by Philippa's tame chief excise officer.

Except that, after hours of abortive hunting and finding little but uncomprehending expressions and a few empty cases, he was far from being in a tame mood.

"Search the grounds, the outhouse, the barn, everywhere," Jewell shouted. "I want you to be particularly thorough in this case. I'll take the house. Roberts, you're in charge of that party. Ireland, you come with me."

As I stepped out onto the veranda there was a flash and a puff of smoke. However this was no diabolical effect. It was just one of the press photographers taking my picture.

"A little matter of a search warrant?" I inquired, somehow getting in the way.

"I have special authorization from the Deputy Minister of the Department of Justice to take whatever action is necessary to recover the goods you looted from the freight cars two nights ago. Now get out of my way."

"Where is it?"

"I have no doubt we'll find part of it in a very few minutes," Jewell said with grim satisfaction.

The bastard knew something. "I meant," I said, sorting through and discarding courses of action with the speed of a cardsharp, "where is this authorization you mentioned?"

"You may refer, if you wish—though I doubt if you will wish by the time we've finished with you—to the Assistant Commissioner of Customs, Mr. Taylor, at the Queen's Hotel, who is in overall charge of this operation. Now you let me past, Bandy, or it'll be the worse for you."

"I'm terribly sorry, Mr. Jewell, I can't do that unless you present this authorization."

"I told you—you can go and see Mr. Taylor," he said, his voice rising. "He'll tell you, soon enough."

"Tell me? You mean it's not a written authorization?"

"I'll give you one minute to get away from that door."

Quick, quick—what was the name of the deputy minister? Newcombe. That was it. "I bet it isn't a written authorization," I said; and, casting a fib in the hope that it would hook onto something: "I know Mr. Newcombe—he wouldn't put anything this controversial in writing, in case it rebounded."

Jewell's face reddened and he began to splutter. The hook had caught—but on a deadhead; for it was obvious that neither Jewell nor any of the sour, frustrated men behind him would be deterred by scribblatory niceties. Laying about them with threats and the use of important-sounding titles had gained them entry to scores of houses already, and they weren't going to be put off by the tenant of a peeling clapboard farmhouse with uncut crabgrass and squirrels in the eaves; a fellow, moreover, who for months had been pelting the department with slanderous filth in Parliament and in a number of speeches, including one or two in Gallop in which he had more than vaguely referred to the local use of palm oil.

There was no doubt about it. Jewell was going to enter the house, by force if necessary. And when he found seventy-two bottles of gin in my cupboard the first page of a criminal record would be inserted in my dossier—assuming the authorities had forgotten that occasion in 1901 when I was charged with stealing jelly babies from Allen's Candy Shop.

And what was particularly unfair about it was that I didn't even like gin.

Nor could I put the blame on anyone else. They wouldn't believe me for one second if I turned on Jim Boyce and blubbered that it was him what had done it. I was *caput, fini, mortveh,* reamed, and buggered.

Then Papa came out onto the veranda. And as if to emphasize the gravity of the occasion, he was wearing his black coat and clerical collar.

Only a short time ago he had been dressed in the old jacket that he usually wore to work in his library of ecclesiastical biographies, sermons, and exegeses on the nature of angels. He must have dashed upstairs to reoutfit himself within the last couple of minutes. He was certainly breathing hard from some exertion; though his crackling dyspnea might easily have been mistaken for passion, for his first words were uttered in the intolerant, bitter manner that he used to reserve for Sunday school. In a loud, arrogant voice he demanded to know what was going on. Glaring at Jewell with a righteous ferocity that seemed to lift his thatch of white hair clear from his scalp, he requested the chief excise officer to cease goggling and dribbling, man, and speak up, and explain what these crumpled officers were doing on his property.

As Jewell, with as much respect for the cloth as he could filter through his malevolence, explained, Father's face suffused with additional rage.

"You are accusing my son of stealing liquor from that train?" he roared. "How dare you, how dare you?"

"He was there, I tell you. I have witnesses—"

"I was once seen outside a theatrical boardinghouse, sir," Father thundered. "Does that make me a mummer?" And he actually took a threatening step toward the chief excise officer. "You slanderous government snoop," he bellowed, thrusting his beak forward in an effort to keep Jewell, who had scuttled behind another officer, in sight. "You come trespassing onto private property—without so much as a shred of written authority from what

I've just heard—as if an ill-fitting state uniform gives you the right to terrorize the countryside. I'll have you know I'm a retired minister of the Church, and my son would never have anything to do with theft, even from that disgraceful convoy of rolling stock. You petty, corrugated state minion, I have been hearing about your infamous conduct in bullying and threatening the local people and gaining entrance by force in a manner that will almost certainly be found to be illegal, when I and a few other right-thinking and prominent citizens sue you for this Prussian behavior. By God, I'll have all your names," he shouted, and advanced another step, glaring from an eye like the vortex of a plug-pulled, hiccuping, black-ringed bathtub.

Jewell's heels promptly slipped over the top step of the veranda. He had to grab for support to prevent himself from floundering down to the dirt. Whereupon, with Jewell taken care of, Father rounded on the other uniformed men, who were looking distinctly uneasy at the prospect of having their names taken, and went on to savage them with equal eloquence and fury, ending with an observation that had even me staring at him in amazement. "I have seen a great many trains similar to the one that was broken into the other night, emerging from that government-approved gin mill," he cried, his eyes blazing, "filled with merchandise destined, I have not the slightest doubt, for hosts of other seedy lawbreakers in other parts of the country, and I am not aware that you have ever halted those caravans of evil. But you act in this despotic fashion the moment the consignees are cheated of their profits—which certainly raises the question posed many times by my son, as to just who is sharing in those profits."

Drawing himself up, he pointed, approximately in the direction of neighbor McCloskey's yardful of rusty reapers, tooth harrows, horse rakes and hay tedders—a gesture preserved for posterity by the milling photographers, who had been hanging onto the harangue with gaping ecstasy—and thundered, "Now go; for if you persist in attempting a forced entry, you will have to wreak violence on my person to do so."

It was not until he had retreated to the end of the driveway that Jewell recovered enough to shout, "We have evidence that your precious son was one of the ringleaders. We'll be back, don't you worry. With a scrap of paper, all right—a warrant for his arrest."

His voice rose to a screech as he ended, "We'll be back, don't you worry."

"God, Father," I said a few minutes later, "you were simply magnificent."

"You must not take the Lord's name in vain, Bartholomew," he said. "Though if I were you I would certainly take the gin from your bedroom cupboard before they return."

After the gin had been disposed of, we sat around the kitchen for well over an hour, trying to assess the situation: Father, Mother, Jim Boyce, and I, trying to decide whether the customs men had a case against me or not.

Boyce thought that they had, even without the case of gin. "You spent six hours at the scene, helping to sort things out," he said. "They probably won't be able to prove you started it, but I'm quite sure they'll find something to pin on you. It's the opportunity they've been waiting for."

"What do you think will happen, James?" Mother asked.

"As usual, Bart has made an awful lot of enemies, Mrs. Bandy. I don't know if they'd go so far as to send him to jail, but it is a possibility."

There was a nasty silence. Looking rather limp after his outburst, Father leaned over to poke the fire.

"But you insist on staying?" Boyce asked at length.

"Certainly," I said, thinly but stoutly. "No Bandy has ever been known to leave a battlefield in flight."

"I think you should go, Bartholomew," Mother said sorrowfully. "Much as we hate to lose you, now that we've got to know you. But I just couldn't bear to think of you languishing in prison, with a ball and chain round your ankle, hitting rocks in a quarry all day, with nothing but bread and water and a thin blanket, with cockroaches and rats scuttling over your sleepless form all night."

I stared stupidly at the kitchen wallpaper. It had a design of leaves and poisonous berries entwining strands of barbed wire.

"Incidentally," Boyce said as we stood once again on the veranda, keeping watch on the road, "I may have given the impression that I thought you'd been corrupted in record time."

"Oh, that's all right," I said. "I know you didn't really mean it."

"Course I did."

"Eh?"

"Well, you did sell us out, didn't you? Agreeing to cover up the facts—exchanging a report for a portfolio. Well, you got just what you deserved."

"I know."

"But I also wanted to say . . . well, I think you made up for it a bit, down at the railway tracks. Admittedly, it really was all your fault, the consequence of your agitations—"

"Now lookee here—"

"But you could easily have backed away—disassociated yourself. But you didn't."

When I just shrugged and plumped myself wearily into the tatty veranda sofa, raising a cloud of dust in the process: "It must have occurred to you what the consequences would be, given your reputation, by aligning yourself with Toombs and the rest of the populace," he added.

I mumbled something.

"Pardon me?"

"I aligned myself," I mumbled, "nine months ago, five thousand feet over Lake Champlain."

Mother brought us out cups of tea and a plate of homemade cookies. Just for the hell of it I gave her another hug. After all, if she was right about the rock pile, I might not see her again for ages.

"You're determined to stay and brazen it out?" Boyce asked after Mother had left.

"Absolutely determined."

"You know," Boyce said after a moment, "in Canada we pride ourselves on our tolerant attitudes, and all the rest of it. But the country's history doesn't entirely bear it out. The authorities, as our true representatives, have a deep-seated hostility to the individualism they purport to defend; and there's an element of cowardice in their intolerance—pusillanimity when faced with organized opposition, and vindictiveness when confronted with the opposition of the individual. Now you may be a dreadful person, infuriating, prejudiced, loud, revolutionary, blind to your own faults, deaf to admonition, often unfeeling, thick-skinned, vengeful—"

"I sincerely hope there's a 'but' coming up."

"But there's no doubt you're distinct enough. I don't think you'll stand a chance, Bart."

"You missed out the word 'stubborn' from your rude catalog," I said snottily. "Nobody, whether in uniform or out, in power or out, authorized or otherwise, is going to grind me down," I said, just as Gallop's only taxi shuddered up to the front of the house and out came three scruffy suitcases, a battered hatbox, a fur coat on a hanger, two pairs of shoes lashed together by their laces, and a handsome, broad-shouldered chap with a pencil mustache, accompanied by a pretty girl with good cheekbones and bad teeth.

"You will never guess what happened," George Garanine cried after he had finished hugging and kissing and praising everybody in sight, including Father and Mother, who had rushed out to the veranda the moment they heard his voice. "As you know, dearest Bartalamyeh, I left here intending to return to Russia and give myself up, confess my failure to that man, and no doubt receive a bullet in the back of the head. They say that he is becoming a very powerful figure, now that Vladimir Ilyitch is out of the way. Naturally, as soon as I arrived in New York, I went straight to Tony Batt's splendid apartment, for, as you know, whatever his faults, Tony is wonderfully hospitable to Russian émigrés, perhaps for sentimental reasons, because he established his fortune in Archangel. And of course I had stayed there before, last year, until I found out where you were living. So after the reunion with all the other émigrés at Central Park Vest—endless talk around the big Russian stove that Tony had installed in the kitchen—you remember the beautiful tiled stove, Bartalamyeh? Of course you do. Then after a while I proceeded with heavy heart but willing spirit to arrange passage on a ship to Constantinople, where I would be able to travel onward to Russian Black Sea ports. The weather along the Black Sea coast is beautiful at this time of year, quite subtropical, you know. Then one afternoon, while I was trying to decide whether to get dressed and wondering if I had time to get to the shipping office before it closed, who should turn up at Little Russia, as they call Tony's very big apartment, but—you will never guess in a thousand years—Anna! You remember Anna in Moscow? Yes? And here she is, as always smiling so sweetly and shyly—ah, is she not adorable? How I love her. Take the bags into the house, will you, darling? And do you know what she told me, Bartalamyeh? That there was no need for me to go back. There is not one relative left in Moscow. Not one, Bartalamyeh Fyodorevitch, imagine that. Three of them have died, Granny and Dounatchka of old age, while poor dear Olga fell from the roof of a train. God rest their souls. As for Grusha, Natalie, and Lisa, a recruiting committee ordered them to volunteer for work far beyond the Urals, and, of course, as they were sent by one of the million committees that are running loose in Russia, there is no way that that man will ever find them again. Let me see, who is left? Oh yes—Irina and Clava went to join another relative in Tashkent when they heard that there was plenty of food there, and they have completely disappeared. And that leaves only dear Anna here who, believe it or not, came all the way to America to find me, God bless her. Ah, what a brave soul she is—and Eugenie, who set off with Anna but came to a terrible end, I'm afraid. She married a Bulgarian en route. Is it not amazing, Bartushka? And there is no way that that man will ever be able to find them, except for Grusha, Natalie, and Lisa, and even if he does, how will he be able to send them to Siberia if they are already there, eh? Ah, truly, Christ is risen. Life is so wonderful, my dearest friends. But I was forgetting, Bartalamyeh. Anna and I are married. Yes, it's true! Ah, look at her struggling with the bags there, isn't she a dear, sweet girl, smiling, breathless with excitement to be home at last? As we say in Russia, *A girl in love is like a tomato blushing on a window ledge*. And do you know, it was Tony who suggested we get married. Ekh, what a matchmaker he is, to be sure. We had only been living in his apartment for a few weeks when he said that Anna, being torpid—in the best sense of the word, of course—would make a perfect mate for me, and besides, much as he enjoyed my company and the way I was organizing religious services among the émigrés, and converting his gangster friends, he felt that the simple life of the north woods, as he calls Canada, would be much more fertile territory for me than New York, where even he found it just a little difficult to resist temptation. So here we are, dearest Bartalamyeh, we have come back to live with you—just for a little while, of course, until I find my foot."

"I don't care what you say," I shouted at Boyce, "I've made up my mind, and that's final. I'm off," I shouted, and barely one and a half hours later, establishing once and for all that a Bandy never fled a battlefield without good reason, I was off, the bulky Gander trundling down the long field with all the grace and spriteliness of a manure spreader, and then the tail skid inscribing an arc through the crabgrass, fescue, and clover, and the Puma engine bellowing, then purring as the switches clicked, then bellowing again as a pair of feet plonked themselves firmly on the rudder, and one hand clamped onto the stick, another clawing at the throttle pedestal, and the amphibian was rolling down the squelchy meadow, the pilot peering over the fat nose with all the poise and alertness of a Rossum's Universal Robot. Then the waddling airplane was wavering into the breezy air, the barn tilting off to one side, with a clench of people nearby, wanly waving. They were standing near the Avro. Did I realize I was leaving it behind, along with an expensive two-year-old auto? Not a terrible lot of material goods to show for thirty years of endeavor, but at least it made leaving that much easier, I thought. Except that I wasn't thinking, it was various muscles, fluids, and strands of nerve, that were doing all the thinking. I was leaving a set of newly discovered parents behind, too. Six hundred feet. The air was already turning chill. As the floatplane curved round the farmhouse, my copilot, a box of gin, slid against my leg. The rest of the booze was in the cabin. I might be able to barter it for a couple of tankfuls of fuel en route. En route where? God knows. Passport! Where was it? My heart jolted. It was all right. There it was. Breast pocket.

As I drew level with the barn again, Mother, Father, George Garanine and his missus, and Jim Boyce were still huddled down there, gazing silently aloft. A handkerchief fluttered. I waved back, the very picture of the intrepid birdman, helmeted, gog-

gled, silk scarf streaming—except that the scarf had snagged on a
harness buckle. Waiting for the compass to settle down, I lined
up with the concession road because it headed east, and was just
about to start climbing again when two automobiles appeared in
the distance, traveling at top speed, straight toward me, toward
the farm.

I dived back to a hundred feet and shoved up the goggles for
a better view. The cars were filled with customs men. I could
guess why they were in such a hurry. I had gotten away with
only five minutes to spare.

A thoroughly childish idea occurred to me, one quite unworthy of a gentleman. I went ahead anyway. I trimmed for level
flight, then reached down and seized four bottles by their necks,
two in each hand, and I returned the bottles, even though there
was no deposit on them. I pitched all four of them over the left
side, just far enough out from the side of the fuselage to clear
the floats. I had to hurry as we were closing head on at a com-
bined speed of 120 m.p.h. The first two bottles went wobbling
through the gray air just like Cooper bombs, but I had never
been much good at bombing, and they smacked down on the
rutted roadway a good fifty feet in front of the leading automobile, and burst in a twinkling shower of glass and gin; and the
second pair went awry as well. One of them vanished completely, probably into the roadside trees. But then to my surprise
the other reappeared under the nose and scored a direct hit. It
must have given them a start. It whacked down onto the hood of
the leading car and bounced, miraculously intact, high into the
air, before sailing off, still unbroken, into the ditch.

"Cheers," I shouted as I hurtled overhead and continued onward into the sweet by-and-by.